THE MIDNIGHT THRONE

AN HEIR OF TIME NOVEL
BOOK ONE

AUDRIANA CHRISTIAN

To my dad, whose unwavering love and support throughout my life pushed me to make this dream a reality.
Until we meet again.

If you are family, please text me before you go any further.
I promise you will want to know which pages to skip.

S he had seen every possible path; this was the one with the least deaths, destruction, and a world still standing at the end. She ran with everything she had, her bare feet sinking into the damp forest soil with every thundering step she took; the leaves and twigs tugged at her as if to get one more look as she passed by in a blur. She could hear behind her the roar of Night Creatures, the vicious bark of hounds chasing after her scent. The moonlight shone through the canopy of leaves above her. She prayed to the mother of moons to keep guiding her way. Looking down, she glimpsed the sleeping child in her arms, her soft and unknowing face looking innocent and peaceful. Her small chest lifted in equally tiny breaths as she dreamt of the sweet figs her father had picked for her. The vision was a gift from the Seer and as long-lasting as the deep, magic-induced slumber she would not awake from for some time.

A twig snapped to her right, startling her from the trance the child's sweet face had put on her. Turning her head, her dearest companion, a woodland nymph, had caught up with her just in time. They exchanged sad smiles and began running faster, letting their otherworldly speed take over their limbs, knowing that time was of the essence.

Before they knew it, they all but slammed into the invisible realm wall. Taking a step back, the Seer straightened herself and placed her hand on the cool realm border. The ancient magic hummed through her with every second that passed. She pushed her forehead against the invisible wall and whispered forgotten words that only the ancient magic would know; her hand slipped through, as did the rest of her body. The nymph followed suit, slipping unseen through the wall. They both sent up a silent thanks and a prayer to the Gods that the realm breach would go by steadily unnoticed. Stepping into the realm of Spellcasters, the Seer and nymph turned to each other and clasped hands, the small child still sleeping soundly between them. In a blink and a rush of crisp air, they were inside the Royal Courts of the High Wizard in a field yet to be touched by the hands of men and stone. The mother of moons shone brightly for them, almost proudly, casting silver shadows over the field of tiny purple and blue flowers swaying in the breeze.

Taking a deep breath, the Seer nodded to the nymph, motioning her to get into place. They had mapped out this plan for months; she knew it would work. It had to work. She looked down at the child in her arms and blinked the raging, hot tears from her eyes, willing her composure to hold just a moment longer. She squeezed the child tight and placed a final kiss on her forehead, the spot shining with magic and love. With that kiss, a blinding white light thundered across the land. The Seer knew the border watch would be close behind, following the hum of the ancient magic she had just unleashed. Hurriedly, she placed the child in the arms of her dearest friend. The magic unraveled itself, wrapping around the child and nymph in sparking ribbons that faded as soon as they appeared. In a blink, the nymph and the tiny child were nothing but a small green tree sprouting, swaying in the wind with the rest of the flowers, completely unnoticed. The Seer lingered a minute longer to get one more look; the little tree sprout waved to her, shooing her. She could hear the border watch storming through the forest. With a final bow of her head, she dissipated into the cool night breeze, fading away into sparkling dust.

Five hundred years would go by, the nymph and the child, slumbering peacefully, suspended in time. The tree, with its shimmering bark, never turned with the seasons. It grew and blossomed, and no matter how hard they tried to chop down the beautiful never-changing tree, they couldn't. The axes would bounce off, not even chipping the bark. The Spellcasters, seeing this as a sign from the Gods above, built their castle courtyards around her, worshiping her, picking the always-blooming shimmering flowers from her branches and making wishes on them, letting them float away in the wind.

One night, when the moon was nowhere to be seen, tucked behind black clouds and a starless sky, the wind even held its breath as it watched the tree begin to move, creaking and shuddering, its blossoms and leaves floating to the ground. The twists of the tree gave way, and from the heart of that tree, a tiny child arose. The tree set her down gently as the child yawned, blinking the sleep from her eyes. She stood, stretching her small arms, her little hands making fists. All was silent, all was still, and the little child, all but three, teetered down the stone path. The mother of winds stirred, giving her a light push in the right direction. Her tiny feet began pattering toward the only sound she heard. A man was pacing the courtyard, pipe in hand, to clear his mind of the day's worries, as he did every night. Hearing soft footsteps behind him, he turned, his velvet robes dragging on the courtyard stones, and took a step back in surprise. In front of him, the child stood. Her golden-brown hair blew silently, her bright starry eyes staring back into his. Slightly perplexed, he tilted his head to the side in silent question.

"What are you doing out here, little one?" he said. Crouching down, he reached out to the child, willing her to come to him. She obliged and walked into his arms, placing a small, warm hand on his face. With that touch, a surge of power struck him like he had never felt before. Suddenly, he was hit with a vision, pure power knocking the air out of him—a story with a thousand versions and a thousand secrets, the story of the child. He picked her up, letting her babble words to him.

He stared at the incredible little child in his hands and realized what he must do. He wrapped her up tight in his robes, looking around; he said a silent thanks to the moonless night as he ran towards his chambers unseen.

CHAPTER

TWO

I sat, staring out the open bedroom window. Resting my chin on my knees, I gazed up at the night sky and silently wished I was looking out my old bedroom window at my parent's house. The neighborhood stray cat, an orange tabby, had taken a liking to me and the flower box outside my second-story bedroom window. Most days, he perched himself there lazily, basking in the warm sunlight or waiting for a pet. Tonight, I obliged him, running my fingers gently along his back and listening to him purr.

It had been an excruciatingly long day, from moving in the rest of my furniture to applying for job positions, having birthday dinner with my parents, and finally getting home to add the final layer of paint to the bathroom walls. Today was my 23rd birthday. My parents, Merin, and Tanja Kissinger, who had adopted me as a small child, had been especially emotional tonight, much more so than usual. A lot of, "Oh honey, your life is just now beginning," and "Soren, sweetie, we can't wait to see what kind of woman you will transform into," and tears, surprisingly, many tears.

I always thought that by this time in my life, I'd have figured everything out, and apparently, so did my parents.

So much pressure had built on my shoulders since dinner with them, and a considerable headache thanks to it. Looking at what my parents accomplished, I understood why they expect so much from me. My father was a world-renowned inventor with a master's in chemistry. In his free time, he did extensive research into creature physiology and anatomy, taking a particular interest in Seers. I had spent many nights up late to look at my father's work and the notes he had scattered around his office. My mother, on the other hand, was the most talked about botanist in Norware, along with also having her own bestselling cookbook. I suppose that by average human standards, I was considered successful. I have a master's in ancient arts and restoration, I landed a job for the most successful art restoration museum in all of Norware. I left said job due to a wildly failed relationship with the museum's director, Willem, and I managed to move into a new home all on my own. However, I felt no closer to figuring out who I was than I had been in any other year of my life.

Falling back, I heave a sigh, the velvety, yellow armchair creaking beneath me. A light cool autumn breeze brushed across my face, pulling me from my thoughts and rustling the sheer curtains. The wind carried the smell of fresh rain and cloves, soothing me. Leaning into the breeze, I held onto the smell as long as it would let me. Letting out a short breath, I risk a look at the clock, surprised to see it's only midnight. I examine the space around me and take note of the work left to be done, *a lot*.

I settled on putting away boxes of clothes that won't be

needed for months now. Carrying a box of tank tops and bathing suits to my bedroom closet, I flip on the light and analyze the top shelf. As I reached to wipe away the dust, my bracelet sounded against something metal in the corner I had never noticed before. Getting on my tiptoes, I ran a hand along the side of the closet, stumbling along a tiny metal handle. Pulling on it, the tiny door gave a creak and, in a cloud of dust, plopped open. The house was old, a rickety two story. With more charm than dust, I thought it was worth it. These homes were known for their trap doors, moving bookcases and small rooms under the staircases, but I was truly puzzled on how I missed this hidden door. It did indeed look like I had painted over it in a crisp white paint job the night before.

Intrigued, I grabbed the vanity stool, and climbed on top to peer inside the tiny opening. Saying a prayer to the many Gods for no cobwebs or mice in waiting, I stuck my arm in and reached as far back as possible, feeling what seemed to be the outline of a canvas. As soon as my fingertips made contact, there was a strange pulse that went through me, like a jolt of electricity searing right into my bones. I jumped back, sucking on the injured finger and cursing whatever old wiring must be up there.

As I pull the mysterious object out of its hiding place, the wind through my bedroom window rushes in, sounding like it was letting out a long overdue gasp for breath. Looking down at it just then, you'd have never known it was a painting; it was coated in brown dust, and none of the painting beneath was visible. Hopping down from my stool, I walk toward the study down the hall.

Placing the canvas on top of my desk, I turn on my tiny

desk lamp to examine it better. Brushing away the dirt and dust, my breath caught as I finally got a good look at what was on the canvas. It was the most beautifully hand-painted piece of art I'd ever seen. The painting depicted a breathtakingly gorgeous woman, with long silver-blonde hair, wearing a crown of stars that seemed to glow through the painting. She was holding a tiny baby, wrapped in gauzy white cloth, who also wore a crown of stars. The woman was sitting atop a bed with red blankets draped across it. Sheer plum-colored curtains were blowing in from the open balcony and the moonlight shone through them. The room itself was fit for a king. Golden lamps hung from the ceiling, and red and gold rugs were strewn across the floor.

Behind them stood an extremely tall man, his golden skin glinting in the moonlight. By the look of this man's physique and adornment, he was a very accomplished warrior. His Fae ears, with their slight elegant point, stuck through his hair that was braided to one side. Across his chest and shoulders, were ancient black tattoos, and to his side his hand laid on the hilt of a massive Fae sword. But why would a Fae Male, and a Seer, be in such an intimate setting together? I suppose it could be possible that the Seer was captured, and made a servant, or it was possible she had captured the Fae man. But that didn't explain much. I had never read anywhere in father's journals that Fae men, or any Fae at all really, had served Seers.

I stare at the painting forever, feeling this strange sense of belonging within the painting. Examining the painting further, I realize this painting had to be at least 500 years old. Incredibly preserved, the pinks, reds, white and golds gleamed as if just painted. What kind of marvelous glaze had the artist used? The canvas was old, stretched and beaten animal hide, dyed white. It had the feel and texture of ones I'd examined while working at the art house last summer. No longer an employee with access to a restoration lab, I knew I would have to take it to my father's labs at the University. Taking one last look at the painting, I set it down gingerly on top of my desk. Tomorrow, I told myself, I could take it in and worry more about it then. In a single wave, it hit me how tired I actually am and I lazily made my way back to my bedroom. I scanned the still-open window for my new found companion.

"Come on in, little guy. At this rate, I'll have to name you." I smile at the cat as he wandered into the room and curls into a ball at the edge of my bed. Following his direction, I closed the window and crawled into bed, wrapping the soft sheets around myself, falling into a fitful sleep.

MY HEART WAS POUNDING through my chest, and all I could hear were explosions all around me. I was running as fast as I could, my feet hitting the floor in painful thuds. Taking in my surroundings, I realized I was running down a castle hall, the high stone walls crumbling around me. I heard a voice then, calling me from down the hall.

"Run faster my child", a deep male voice called. Through the sparkling ash and dust, I saw him, the outline of man, with the golden-brown skin native to The Sands, his giant hand reaching out for mine. "You will make it, my little brave one.I believe in you."

I was so close, I could see the sweat dripping from his

face. I could almost touch his fingertips with mine, the ground rumbling under my feet. Right then, a bright white explosion hit me, massive and ripping and burning and painful. Screaming out didn't help. And everything had gone white.

I WOKE WITH A START, slamming my body up into a sitting position, reeling from the vivid dream. I swear I can still smell the smoke and ashes from the explosions lingering all around me. My throat coarse from a scream and seemed as if it could be coated in that sparkling ash as well. I hadn't had nightmares like this since I was a child, when they would constantly plague me. For years I was waking up at least three times a week screaming and drenched in sweat. One constant was always the smell of ash. Merin and Tanja always ran to my room, frantic, checking under every bit of furniture, the windows and finally coming to my side, with soft words and tight hugs until I fell back asleep.

Groaning, I roll over and peek over at the clock on my bedside table. It was 6 am, an hour and a half earlier than my scheduled alarm clock. Needing a cold shower to rid myself from the panic, I groggily made my way to the bathroom to make use of my extra time. I peel off my oversized shirt, still damp from the nightmare-induced sweat, and climb into my clawfoot tub, welcoming the splash of the cold water on my face. I scrub myself clean of the ash and dread that still clung to me. The water turned warm, seeped into my weary bones and began to soothe me, letting my thoughts roam to other places, like my planner. It was perfect, filled with organized lists of things that needed to be completed, day by day, weeks in advance.

I let myself stand under the shower until the water turned cold, forcing my thoughts away from the plan for the day ahead. I reluctantly pull myself out and wrap myself in my thick cotton robe. I made my way to my dresser and sought comfort in my favorite cream-colored cashmere sweater. I paired the sweater with my most flattering pair of dark wash denim jeans. Tugging my jeans, I contemplate what shoes to wear, but quickly decide to save that task for later.

Pulling back my curtains and opening the window, I let the cool breeze rush in and fill my room with the smell of autumn. I idly brush my thick golden-brown wavy hair, starting with the ends near my waist and gently working out the tangles and stare out the window. The sun was beginning to peek over the horizon, and I watched as it painted the world different hues of magentas and orange. Ready to be downstairs, I force myself back to my vanity to quickly curl my lashes and dust my golden skin with a bit of sheer powder, so as not to cover my freckles. I run blush over my high cheekbones, dab on just a bit of lip balm, and declare my beauty routine sufficient for the day's activities. I linger in the mirror to take in my appearance, admiring my handy work and the way my jeans hugged my naturally curvy figure. With one last glance out the window I grab the first pair of shoes I see and make my way downstairs, my hair flowing behind me as if trying to catch up.

My morning routine consisted of a fresh pot of coffee, a quick look at the calendar clinging to my fridge, and then finding my way to the bay window with a steaming mug and the newspaper to settle in for what was truly my favorite part of each day. Unfurling the Realms Times newspaper, I checked my watch, tracking the second hand's movement along the face. As the hands arrange themselves to display 9:00, I eagerly look back to the newspaper stretched across my lap. In awe I watch the page before me shimmer and swirl, each letter rippling across the page leaving updated news, weather, and time in its wake. For as long as I can remember, this simple yet beautiful display of magic has always been my favorite. Seeing the articles change never failed to make me smile.

Opening the newspaper properly, my eyes landed on the first shining article, the headline reading "The Royal High Wizard Aaren Lochhart Has Finally Chosen A Wife!" A holographic picture of the lucky chosen one was next to the article. The beautiful woman had a huge smile plastered on her face, waving her hand in royal mannerism, all while her dark hair blew in the nonexistent wind. The High Wizard stood next to her, looking at the woman lovingly, if he did indeed actually love her. Who knew though, maybe he did, but most marriages in the creature realms that had to do with Royal creatures were no mistake. They were usually built to create strong border alliances or for financial purposes.

The look in Aaren's eyes though, always caught me as familiar, something about him always made me stare a little longer than I would have anyone else. Not merely because he was handsome, but he gave me a sense of déjà vu, that I never could put my finger on. Skimming the article, it said here the Mated couple, a young royal wizard, was named Reyka and was only 57 years old, while the Royal High

Wizard was 112, making it the biggest age gap in the Spell-caster Realm history. To be Mated in Creature culture was as normal as a human marriage, but it's said, *by tabloid of course*, that Aaren and Reyka are soul tied Mates, which is rare. As rare as true love for humans. To soul tie, it is without consent of either party, divinely written and forever lasting. Which can make things a bit sticky, especially if the soul tie is unwarranted. Not every creature has a soul tied Mate, which could honestly be a relief.

The Spellcasters could live much longer than humans and kept their youth longer also, although almost entirely human themselves. The oldest Wizard, former Royal High Wizard, hadn't been seen in over 20 years, and was said to be almost 300 years old by now. Being missing for that long though, left people to speculate if those 300 years had come to an end. Thankfully for the Royal Wizards courts, The Royal Wizard Emrin had a grown heir, and he took over with the same grace and peacefulness as his father. Scanning the rest of the article, I learned there was to be a massive wedding held, all creatures, although invitation only, were invited, and even some high-ranking humans. A slideshow of possible would-be invited human celebrities, politicians and inventors flashed to the side of the article.

Rolling my eyes at the article I had wasted 10 minutes of my life on, I flipped through the rest of the Spellcaster Realm news, then decided to skip it, flipping to the Fae section. They were always the most exciting news to read. They proclaimed themselves the most powerful creatures on earth, and I supposed that was true, although an incred-ibly arrogant statement. But what would the Royal Fae be, if they weren't incredibly arrogant? I suppose then, just unbelievably beautiful, tricky, and immortal. I also rolled my eyes at that thought. I had seen a few Royal Fae in person before, in passing on the streets, or at my father's manner as they waited to purchase one of his many fine inventions. The stories were true though, your breath did catch in your throat at their beauty, and no, you shouldn't look at them in their stunning eyes, for fear that you might subject yourself to the tricky Fae enchantments that they liked to place humans under, mostly for their sole amusement.

The story that had arranged itself on the front page of the Fae Section of the *Realms Times*, the most important of the day, was the only article I cared about. Today's headline read: "The Hundreds Year War Between the Royal Fae and the Wild Faeren Could Come to an End, Treaty included", The war was so long, the traditional reason for the fighting was lost to history and had changed many times. Some history books will tell you it was initially star-crossed lovers that started it, leading the Fae into hundreds of years of war. Others said it was simply the have versus the have nots of the Fae world. The poor Wild Faeren had truly been treated worse than humans, and for much longer. Many of the Royal Fae saw the Wild Faeren as their lesser. Their reasoning being that their powers were not strong enough to be "worthy", with them only being able to do very low elemental magic and mainly having control of the seasons and when certain things blossom here or there. Their looks were also a concern to some of the Royal Fae, who called them "unsightly" for some of their "Wild" characteristics.

The Wild Faeren were the nymphs, sprites, gnomes, pixies, and other creatures of the like who often had bark for skin, or leaves for hair, antlers, and wings. Only the most powerful Wild Fae could shift into a "Royal" form, and even then there was a caveat: they couldn't use their elemental powers at the same time. Too much of their power being willed on their appearance. There were some Royal Fae though, who saw the treatment of the Wild Faeren unfair and fought for their cause and their freedom with them. I had read that before, but the Realms Times never gave their identity, probably deeming that unimportant to human lives, and I supposed they were correct.

The Fae were the most populous of all the creature groups, humans gaining on them slightly. The Royal Fae were split into reigning sections of the expansive Fae realms. There was the Royal Fae of The Sands. The Royal Fae of The Seas, which included the rather reclusive underwater Fae. The Royal Fae of the Orient. Some of the oldest Fae Clans reigned from The Icelands, the northern nordic belt of mountains and icy oceans. The Royal Fae of the Galarian Cities, which was an expansive and progressive portion of the Fae realms, kind of a modern metropolitan hub for all Fae. The Fae of the Galarian cities were the most seen in the human realms, and also known to be the most social. The Royal Fae of the Highlands, included all Fae of the mountains and also tribal Fae-which did not really plead loyalty to any court even with being , *kind of*, included in The Highland Court. It is said that High Royal King Ruairi had agreed to look over the very independent tribes across all the Fae Realms, offering his aid, however in the 140 years of his reign it had yet to be needed. No other court would attempt to touch the Tribal Fae, seeing them almost as lesser than Wild Fae. So when King Ruairi stepped forward with a gentle hand, it was looked at as surely as a mistake. The tribal Fae have been heard saying he is a wise and trust-worthy man, so it was probably safe to say this relationship was a harmonious one.

On the last page of the Fae section, the High Royal Faeren Elect, who was elected every three years by the High Royal Faeren council, Niklas Bergström's picture perfect profile rippled into view. He was handsome in an aristo-cratic way, as only someone with a long line of royal lineage could be. Maybe it was his long straight nose and slight cleft in his chin that gave him away. His glossy white hair was slicked back, hard features forced into a smile, and his piercing blue eyes stared blankly into the camera. His looks were at odds with each other, his sharp nose and high fore-head, but his dimples and plump lips gave him a sensual air, one even a stoic politician's pictures couldn't even take away. Although he came off as stern in every picture seen of him, my father assured me he was actually quite a fair man. I assumed this to be true, as he's been re-elected three times now. I'm sure his extreme wealth also had a play with his returning vote in as the Council Elect. His wealth came from not only his family, but his lengthy life.

It seemed to me, there was always some war or battle going on across the sea. Being an ocean apart from the Fae realms, it was often hard for humans to get a real feel of the creatures' happenings. Creatures were allowed in the human realms after an intensive and usually needless, ill-wish check, and of course time sensitive passports. But humans, by no exception other than royal invitation and an escort, could not enter the creature realms. We were told, this was only to see to our protection against some creatures old enough to still believe that we should be enslaved, but

I'd always wondered if they simply didn't want us in their realms. It was impossible for a human to enter the creature's lands without invitation. The humans who have tried to enter the other realms uninvited, often seeking the fabled forests of diamonds, or the wish granting gnomes, often got lost in an endless forest maze or buried in a sandstorm and never returned.

The Human Realm, Midengart, was broken down into sections: Noreware, Ballenstrat and Vellven. It was guarded by an ancient charm. All to be sure that humans were protected from other creatures, as well as from themselves. The charm protects against attacks that creatures might want to make against us. It was said that human kings from the three sections signed a treaty, stating they would agree to only occupy the Human Realm, as long as no creature race could wage war against them or try to enslave them again.

Midengart bordered the Spellcaster Courts, and I was thankful it was them and not the Fae, honestly. The Spellcasters of the world are made up of Wizards and Warlocks. Wizards being those of white magics: healing, protection and selfless purpose. Warlocks were few and far between these days, but their existence still held importance. Warlocks were those spellcasters who practiced the dark arts: Hexes, necromancy,and selfish purposes. For magic and spells to be balanced, good and evil must also be present. Most humans, though, believe this to be a bedtime story in itself, to help small human children feel safe, amongst a world full of nightmare inducing creatures who held their lives in the palm of their hands. My favorite as a child, had been about The Cursed One, about a prince who had a pet dragon, and who died protecting his kingdom.

Humans had a bloody start, if you looked at the facts. It was full of war, bloodshed, and enslavement. In the old realms, human enslavement, whether business or pleasure, was accepted as normal. And truthfully, we humans had come a long way since winning our freedom, almost 400 years ago. We were now renowned for our incredible intelligence and ability to create technology that the other creature races couldn't. Couldn't being a strong term, of course; they just simply didn't need to, because, well, magical powers and all. My father's inventions were extremely popular with the other Royal creature races at the moment, making him one of the richest men in the Human Realm.

Flipping back through my newspaper, the news on battles and wars within the creature worlds were always the same. Sometimes, the Royal Fae attacked the Spellcaster, sometimes the warlocks attacked the Wild Fearen. But what was always prevalent was that the Seers were the most hated, loved, and sought-after creatures in all the realms. From father's journals, I had learned that Seers were the oldest living creature in all the realms, even older than the Fae themselves. Their blood was older than any element we could put under a microscope. And they were females by nature, a male Seer had never been found or seen. For hundreds of years, they were to be believed almost extinct, that is, until the Royal Seer Synnove made her never ending reign be known again.

She made a surprise appearance in an interview for the Interrealm Talk Show, shocking the entire world. During her interview, which to this day was the most watched piece of television in history, she told the world of how genocide and war had made her lock away her kingdom, her Seers, and herself, and how she was ready to be a world presence again amongst the World Realm Council. She said creatures and humans alike would hunt them, to enslave them and use their blood for immortal life like the Fae. I could only assume they were also used as a tool against their will, in the never-ending wars, because of their abilities to thread through time. But even that was said to be a myth, their powers widely unknown; and most books of them and their history had been burned. Seers were immortal and ethereal beauties, Goddesses of the unknown. No one knew why or how they came to be. Some thought that they were replicas of what the Gods saw as the perfect specimen and placed them on earth for that sole purpose. Some creatures and tribes were known to worship Seers, believing they truly were Gods living among men.

On the very last page of the newspaper, the Aunders section was blank as usual, thank the old gods. Any news of Aunder activity was usually unwanted, much like they themselves were. The Aunders were the ugliest of the dark creatures of the world: the kelpies, changelings, goblins and more. The unwanted and unloved dwelled there, the rejected and the exiled. No one dared to enter, making it a safe haven for the pirates and the siphoners, those who siphoned magic from other creatures through blood letting. Anyone kicked aside or on the run would seek out the Aunders realm. Those that entered disappeared, never to be seen again.

But what dwelled there was far from a reflection of what their queen looked like. A picture of the illusive and deathly beautiful Queen Isleen shimmered to life. Her slender, pale face was illuminated by the moonlight, her desolate kingdom sprawled out behind her, black and barren. Her midnight-colored hair spilled over her shoulders, leaving streaks on her marble skin like spilled ink. Dark arched eyebrows framed bright eyes and the moonlight only complimented her sharp cheekbones even more, like the edge of a shining knife. Her subtly full lips the color of fresh crimson blood, a deep red that could only be seen gushing out of a soon-to-be corpse. She was the self-proclaimed Queen of the Aunders, Queen of the land in between realms. Her name ignited fear in anyone who heard it. Anytime there was news to be read in the Aunders section of the paper, it was often nothing you wanted to read anyway.

I stared at her picture a moment longer, and suddenly, her shining eyes turned to mine. A shiver ran through me, and I shook my head trying to make sense of what I had just seen, averting my eyes away. Glancing back at the picture, it was back to normal, her eyes cast into the distance, the night wind rustling her long hair.

Folding the newspaper hastily, I stared into my empty coffee cup and decided it was time to get some stuff done. Checking my planner, I noticed I only had two things on my agenda today: the painting and lunch at one with Vana, with a perfect amount of time in between.

Sending a quick text to my mother, I learned my father was gone today, on a trip for work and wouldn't be back for a week. Once I got the OK to use his labs, I was off. Taking the old painting and securely tucked it away in my leather shoulder bag. Meeting me at the door, my fluffy orange friend meowed up at me, I motioned to go out the door, and he obliged, curling up on the cushioned bench outside my front door.

Smiling at him, "I'll be back in no time buddy", he gave me a knowing look, letting me know he was sad I was leaving him, and closed his eyes again.

THREE

O pening the door to my father's chemistry labs, I immediately felt at home. The slight smell of vinegar and teakwood embraced me. Even with my father gone, I was so happy to be here. Flipping the lights on, I flopped my jacket down on the first table I saw and got started gathering my supplies. Seeing as it was Sunday, I should have the entire lab and office to myself.

Setting up my station, I laid the painting down on the flat surface of the clean metal table. Pulling over the massive magnifying glass, I placed a paper mask over my mouth, leaned in close, and got to work. Nearly an hour later, I was more perplexed than I had been last night. There was no sign of aging on the painting whatsoever, no watermarks, no peeling paint, no discolored varnish. The white hues were still crisp and fresh, not turned yellow by age and air pollution. It was as if the paint had not even been laid out but mere weeks ago. The bright reds in the swirls of the canopy above the figures' heads still smelled of beets and plums, the materials many painters used to make red paints hundreds of years ago.

Completing the visual exam, I massage my temples trying to fend off the building headache. With an exasperated sigh, I look over my notes:

- *The canvas was made from animal hide, unsure what kind.*
- *The middle eastern décor tells me it could possibly be from that region, if the painter was indeed painting their surroundings.*
- *The canvas is nailed to the back of the frame with hand made nails.*
- *The paints were made from rudimentary elements, like berries, spices and flower petals, nothing like the paint of today.*
- *This painting is possibly romanticizing a Seer and a Royal Fae Male, I believe, which is unheard of.*

PERPLEXED, I stared at the painting again; I knew I had found something that no one had seen in hundreds of years. Was the Royal Fae King watching over the Seer and this.... Seer baby? Was he actually a servant, or was the Seer captured and enslaved for sexual or breeding purposes? To my knowledge, Seers did not birth children; they were simply made at the beginning of the realms. The Fae King in the painting was handsome, his strong features were angled down, staring lovingly at the mother and baby. The sword in his hand was simple, elegant and made for fighting. He looked to be from the sands, and the shade of green in his eyes was how I knew he was the part of the royal Fae family of The Sands. According to my father's Fae anatomy records, I knew that Royal Fae families inherited the same eye color of the Fae Male, no matter the color of the mothers. Only the Royal Fae of the sands had those piercing green eyes, there was no mistaking them.

Turning my attention to the Seer, I was still struck at how beautiful she was. Her long silver hair was draped over her shoulder in soft curling waves, her head turned just enough so it wasn't in true profile view. Her pointed chin turned down, her blue eyes gazed upon the small baby in her hands. Her pale skin seemed to invite the moonlight in the painting to bathe her, or it was simply delighted to be in her presence.

Shaking my head, as to get myself out of the painting's trance, I set it down and laughed to myself. This had to be a hoax. This could have been painted by the last tenants of my house; although it had been said to be empty for the past 20 years, which did not match up with the hoax idea But still, I had to know, I had to get answers. Setting the painting face down, I took my tweezers, and tiny scalpel, and very carefully cut a tiny piece of the canvas from the back of the framework. After doing that, I flipped the painting back over, and found a brush stroke, taken too far off the edge of the painting to matter or be seen, and used my scalpel to scrape off the misplaced paint. Taking my samples, I walked over to the analyst machine that my father had built, and put them both in the waiting sample tray, and shut the tiny little door, letting the vacuum seal get rid of any contaminants that might affect the process. After clicking a few buttons here and there, I had ordered the analysis machine to analyze these samples for the approximate age of the painting.

"Good evening Soren, this analysis will take some time, approximately 45 minute. Please sit and relax," the machine that my dad had nicknamed Lola said to me.

"Thank you, Lola," I said back, knowing she was waiting for my response, and found my way to my father's office.

Truthfully, I would need my father's help to do more examinations, but this would have to do for now. Opening the door, the lights flickered on. I smiled as the room seemed to recognize my presence and began brewing my favorite tea in the nook of the room for me. My father's labs and office were where I spent most of my off time growing up. If I wasn't in his office reading, drinking tea and eating cookies, I was watching him build new brilliant machines, or lecture his chemistry class. He was never shy with me and always let me watch and learn and help. He never treated me like some little child who knew nothing.

Looking around, my dad's office had been the same my whole life. The smell of pipe tobacco, leather, and teakwood hung in the air, like he had just left here. The large mahogany desk, sitting in the middle of the room, still shone in the low light as if it were brand new, and sat atop a beautiful red Persian rug.

Slowly making my way towards the tea that was still brewing, I gazed at the familiar pictures that hung on the wall. Awards and family photos were hung side by side, showing how much he treasured not only his accomplishments, but his family as well. I wouldn't be surprised if he was invited to the Royal Wizard Locchart's wedding, seeing as Aaren was especially fond of Fathers inventions, always coming to the manner to purchase more. Walking over to the tea pot that was now whistling, I watched as it hovered in mid-air, the steaming honey-colored liquid pouring into the cup. Picking up the cup, I went over and settled into my favorite corner of the leather couch, turning on the tv..

Forty-five minutes later, Lola pinged as if she were a microwave. Opening the little vacuum sealed door, the machine said, "A very fine specimen you gave me today, Soren, it was a pleasure working with you."

A small smile crept onto my face, and I thanked her. She had never complimented me on my samples before. Pushing the print button on the screen, I waited for my results to print out, not really wanting to look at them. I walked over to the metal table where my painting still sat and set my results face down. Taking a small breath and trying to not get too excited, I flipped the piece of paper over, revealing my answers. Stunned, I made an audible gasp and dropped the metal sample tray with a loud clang. I rubbed my eyes, trying to make sure I was looking at this correctly. I had been right; Lola had calculated that these samples she'd tested had been around 500 years old. I stared at the piece of paper for what felt like hours, with my mouth hanging open.

Finally getting a grip on myself, I knew exactly what I had to do. I immediately picked up my phone and called my Dad. He'd want to run more tests, research this painting's existence and if it'd ever been talked about in ancient writings.

Getting voicemail twice and leaving a brief, "This is urgent, call me back, I've found something extraordinary," message, I decided on a second plan of action. I was going to take this to the Restoration House. I could talk to Willem; he could help me find out how much this masterpiece was worth. If luck was with me, I could possibly talk him into keeping it in the safe that no one ever used, until my father was home and I could let him take over. He would be so thrilled! A new mystery to dissect, and involving Seers nonetheless! At the auction house, it would be safe and sound, under lock and key and many surveillance cameras. Also, the safe would keep it completely unpolluted from any moisture that could contaminate further samples we might need to take to help pinpoint the exact time period and place it could've been created. This wasn't just a painting that was possibly worth millions, no, this painting was priceless for the creatures' intimacy in the painting alone. One question that wouldn't stop nagging me though, was why was this found in my closet? Why wasn't this up in a museum for the sheer self-preservation and age alone. Or better yet, why wasn't this painting hung up in the Seer Realms?

For hundreds of years the Seers had been locked away. Every creature race had tried to find the answers to the most elusive creatures in the world. Sure, Seers were made of stardust, and their powers were said to be time related, but honestly, no one knew for certain. Did this depict that Seers could be born, and not just simply made from the stars, never to be reborn after they are gone, like so many believed? That they could replenish their race and flourish? These were answers that no one knew. No one except the painter, and the people in the painting. Where were the subjects in the painting now? Are they even real people?

Something in my bones told me this was real, a real portrait of real beings. So many thoughts ran across my mind.

My phone pinged, bringing me out of my deep thoughts. It was a reminder of my lunch with Vana in 30 minutes. "Shit" I said to myself. With traffic, the restaurant is basically 45 minutes away. I was going to be late, and I hated being late. I was perpetually early for everything. Locking my dad's office, I grabbed the painting, rewrapped it, shoved it in my shoulder bag, running out the door.

AS THE CAB pulled up to a screeching halt, I thanked the driver and rushed out of the car. Looking up, I saw Vana already sitting in our favorite spot, in the shady corner of the bistro patio. Even lazily sprawled across a patio chair, she looked elegant, a feat I was sure only she could obtain. Leaned back, her arms laying over the side of the chair, with her legs crossed and foot tapping to the music being played overhead. It was odd, being the one to show up late this time, something that I could honestly say had never happened in our 7-year friendship.

Vana and I, we were exact opposites. While I was extremely organized and precise, she was a "go with the flow" and "color outside the lines" type of person. And Vana was *always* fashionably late. Any time anyone confronted her about her never-ending tardiness, her reply was always the same, "Time is only a concept we subject ourselves to; the earth lives and dies and breathes on its own accord. Why shouldn't we?" *Always the poet.* She was late to our Sunday lunch dates almost every

Sunday, even though her florist shop, which doubled as her home, was only two blocks from here. Vana waved her mocha-colored arm, adorned with golden bangles that clinked together when she moved. Giving her a genuine smile back, I made my way towards our table. Even just seeing her across a restaurant, a sense of comfort washed over me.

"Wow, has the earth stopped spinning? Are we all dead? Is this a dream? Never have I ever seen you show up anywhere late; I was about to call the cops and send out a search party," she said, throwing back her head in laughter, her long black curls bounced back and forth, her gold hoops that were braided into her hair clinking together in unison.

Shooting a glare back at her, I replied, "I swear people can hear you laughing from a mile away Van, geez. I was just at my father's lab and got caught in traffic, is all," I said, waving my hand in dismissal.

Folding myself up into the chair, tucking my legs underneath me, I broke off a piece of bread stick out of the basket sitting in the middle of the table. Groaning as the buttery garlic hit my tastes buds. I could come here every day of my life, and never get used to how good the food was.

Vana stuffs some bread in her mouth as well. "What in the Human Realm could be so important that you've left your best friend waiting for three and a half whole minutes?" she said, smirking.

I waited a minute before responding, trying to figure out if I should let her in on my new mystery. Maybe I should wait, I thought, until I told my father.

"Honestly, nothing really. I went to my dad's lab to pick

up some more gloves for painting and lost track of time," I said with a shrug.

Eyeing me suspiciously, she was about to say something further when the waiter came over. We ordered our usual and two glasses of elderberry wine; the dark sweet wine was our favorite to have in the fall.

After our meal, we both sat back in our chairs, full and groaning about the amount of food we just ate in one sitting. We had been sitting there for two hours, laughing, drinking and eating to our hearts content, that I had almost forgotten about the painting in my bag. Sitting up right, I checked my watch. It was three o'clock, and I hadn't even called Willem yet to see if he had time to see me. Getting out my phone, I sent him a quick message.

> WHAT ARE YOU DOING IN AN HOUR? COULD I
> COME BY THE ART HOUSE?

I stared at the message for a minute, thinking about deleting it, but reluctantly pressed send. I wasn't sure if I should even expect a response, not after the way things had ended between us. Willem and I's relationship had always been rocky, even from the start. We had met in college, taking the same classes. From the minute I had met him, I had been swept away. His sandy blonde hair was always slightly wavy, and tousled in just the right direction. His straight brown eyebrows framed his brown eyes perfectly. We had been off and on for three years now.

Willem's emotions were always running too hot or too cold. One day he was all in, the next he didn't want to see me anymore; he never knew what he wanted. When we had first met, his shy smiles and sweet notes had captured my heart. He had been the most amazing person, so kind and gentle. He always promised to not be the one who hurt me next. We'd spend our nights watching movies and never leaving the bed, ordering in take out so we could stay naked and next to each other. It had been an obsession, one I let myself slide into the sweet oblivion. His words had taken me, and his actions had inevitably caused the fracturing of the honey and sugar bubble we had created for all those years.

He turned into something I had never seen, or expected from him. His layers ran so deep; I still felt like I had never really reached his core. In the end, the only thing that kept us coming back to each other was the sex. It was the only constant that kept us connected. One morning, after a night of fighting and some make up sex, I woke up and I had just had it. I was tired of being someone's maybe. I got up without waking him, grabbed my clothes and toothbrush from their designated spots, and tiptoed out the door. He called once, and when I didn't answer, he never tried again. That was six months ago.

My phone pinged and I looked down at it, to my surprise, it was Willem.

"MEET ME HERE AT 7"

Forgetting where I even was, I looked back up at Vana. She eyed me slightly. "Who're you over there messaging, you hermit?"

"Uhm... just Willem. He wants to meet up with me at 7 at the art house. He must still have some of my things." I couldn't tell you why I was lying, and I also couldn't tell you why I thought Vana knew I was lying. The painting wasn't even a big deal, probably, but for some reason, I wanted to keep it my secret for just a little while longer, even if it was just until 7. *Once Willem appraises it, then I'll tell her,* I thought. Maybe Lola, and my education, had gotten this painting all wrong. Or maybe, I knew if I told her about it, and told her I was going to Willem to have it appraised and using it as an excuse to go see Willem also, that she'd take it and hold it hostage from me.

Vana sighed. "Listen, just don't be stupid and hook up with him okay? It's 1,000 percent not worth it."

I couldn't blame her; she was right. I had "I need to hook up with someone" written all over me. I was wound up tight, and it wasn't helping my anxiety at all. And she hated Willem, hadn't liked him from the very beginning. But what are best friends for, if they don't hate the toxic people in your life? Hugging Vana bye, I promised to call her after I left the art house.

I PULLED up five minutes early, but it was already dark outside. The streetlamp flame flickered to life next to my car. Getting out, I smoothed my sweater for wrinkles, making sure my cleavage was just enough to catch some attention, but also still said "I don't care enough to show off to you anymore." Giving myself one last check in the side mirror of my car, I was ready to go inside.

Walking up, the art deco style building looked closed; the lights inside were so low, they almost didn't even look on. Walking in, soft music was playing over the speaker, and there was no one in sight. Looking around, I noticed Willem had done some remodeling to the front of the art house. The brick museum walls were now white washed and the natural red peaked through here and there. He had added more benches and less couches, and the black tile floor shone in the dim lights as if it had just been waxed. The silver Edison style light bulbs hung from the high ceiling, casting soft shadows over the room. He was clearly going for a minimalistic style here.

Setting my bag down on the table, I walked along the lit-up walls, admiring the new art pieces that hadn't been there six months ago. One in particular caught my eye, and I wandered over to it. It was a painting of the fabled Ostorous Mountains. They were famous for their soft pale pink glow and snow-covered caps. Gems of all kinds were said to be found in those mountains, anything you could dream of. It was said that Night Creatures and Aunders of all kinds crawled into those mountains, drawn to the mysterious magic that lingers there. In this painting, the sun and moon both hung low, setting shadows of orange and blue over them, almost fighting over who would win, who could swallow the heartbeat of those beautiful mountain caps first. Leaning closer to the painting, I noticed the brush strokes were distinct, familiar, like ones I had been analyzing all morning. Almost all magnificent painters had signature strokes with their brush, and most didn't even know it. Could this somehow be the same painter? I reached out to touch the painting, but before I could, I heard footsteps behind me.

"I see you're enjoying the new works we have," a low sensual male voice said behind me. Turning around, I found Willem standing there silently, a wine glass in one hand, as he ran his free hand through his hair, and gave me a small, almost sheepish smile as my gaze landed on him.

"Long time no see, Soren. What in the Human Realm do I have to be blessed by your presence tonight?" Willem continued, sauntering closer. He stopped inches away from me, and offered the glass of wine to me. I obliged, and took a long sip, letting the dark thick wine coat my throat and calm my nerves.

"I have this painting I'd like you to appraise for me and hold here in your safe until I can get it framed. It's a gift I've gotten for my father, and I wanted to make sure I wasn't scammed for the price." I was not willing to tell him I found this in my closet; I knew he'd laugh and turn me away immediately.

Willem's eyebrows raised, as if surprised this was a business, and not pleasure, call. I walked over to get my bag from the table and turned to look at him. At the same moment, my phone began to ring. Digging it out of my back pocket, I noticed it was my father.

Looking up at Willem, I held my finger up, "Hold on a second, I should really take this," I said and walked a few paces away, bag in hand.

"Hello?" I answered.

"Hey, honey, what was so urgent earlier? I'm sorry I'm just now getting back to you; I've been in meetings all day," My dad said, his service cutting out slightly.

Taking one more step away from Willem and lowering my voice, "Well, it wasn't super urgent, I, uhm, found this painting this morning, I ran some tests on some samples from it on LOLA, she said it could be over five hun-"

Before I could finish my sentence, my dad's voice

erupted over the phone. "Soren, you must go home now, and not your home, my home. Leave wherever you are, get in your car and come home. Now. It's an order. I'm booking my flight home as we speak," I could hear him furiously tapping on the phone and without saying anything further, his end of the line went dead.

Stunned, I stayed silent for a brief second. Never in my life had my father ever talked to me like that. Ever. Understanding the urgency in his voice, I knew I had to make an excuse to leave right then. I felt an electric current sting the air around me, a familiar one. Turning back around, I noticed Willem had taken the painting out of my bag and had a knuckle-white grip on it. I took a step closer to him, already uneasy. He hadn't looked away from the painting yet, but with a heavy sigh, he set it down as I got closer, his shoulders sinking, he was shaking slightly. I set the wine glass down on the table he now leaned on; we were inches apart.

Finally looking up at me, we locked eyes, our years together flashing in front of me. I could easily stand staring at him forever, getting lost in those eyes I knew I loved. My dad's voice rang through my head again, and I remembered how urgent it was that I leave.

Clearing my throat, I looked up at him, "Actually, something just came up. My parents want me to meet them at their house for dinner and I completely forgot. Sorry, Will, I'll....", He just stared at me for a moment, before resting his strong hands on my arms, as if bracing himself for me to leave.

He cut me off before I could finish my sentence. Taking a step to fill in the gap between us, he leaned his head down, his tousled hair falling forward in an unraveling manner, just like my emotions. His fingers found my chin, tilting my head up towards him. He paused for a moment, his eyes roaming my face, taking me all in. Then our lips met. His were warm and familiar, gentle and urgent all at once. My world swayed as our breath intermingled. The chemistry in the air seemed to buzz in my ears as the kiss deepened, his other hand brought to the back of my neck.

His tongue found mine then, hot and sugary, like I always remembered. He pulled me closer, the urgency of the kiss rushing in, his hands finding my hips, crushing me into him, and I could feel his need. Suddenly, he was picking me up, his lips never leaving mine. He sets me down on the table, his hands hot against my thighs, sliding up them, parting them. He placed himself between them and leaned forward, his hips colliding with mine as he wrapped his arms around my waist again, letting his hands slide up my body until they found themselves swimming in my hair. Our breathing was ragged as he finally looked at me, his hands finding my cheeks. His thumb lightly grazed my jaw, tracing it. His eyes hazy with lust, he let out a pained sigh, the emotion brushing across his face. His head fell forward then, as if defeated. His warm mouth grazed my ear, the heat of his breath wrapping around me. His tongue reached out, lazily licking that spot on my neck that he knew was my weakness, and kissed it.

It was getting too hot in here. I had forgotten how much I had missed that feeling of his tongue on my skin. He was always so good at making me forget my problems, especially with that maneuver. I let out a soft groan that I prayed he didn't hear. His body stilled at the sound of it, and slowly, he shook his head, his arms falling limp, the cool absence of them leaving an aching pang in my chest. He slowly looked up at me then, a stranger staring back at me. His hands found my arms again, but this time there was no loving caress. He slid me off the table back to standing, his eyes never leaving mine. Even the air changed around us, cold discomfort and unease finding me.

Letting out a low muffled laugh, he said, "Ya know Sor, you were never good at lying." And in an instant, the grip he had on my arms turned from gentle to searing pain as his strong fingers dug into my skin. Letting out a scream, I thrashed, trying to shake his hold. He laughed again, but this time it was different; it was cruel and as if he was enjoying me struggling. It was low, throaty, and wicked, sending chills up my spine. His body was pressed against mine. I could feel his strong muscles flexing against me, and it dawned on me that I had never realized how lethal this beautiful body could be. The same one I had lovingly ran my hands across at night in our bed as we fell asleep. Twisting my arms behind my back, he pushed me up against the art house wall, making it shudder under his strength. The Ostorous painting next to me shook. Hot pain shot up my arm, and I let out another scream. He was crushing me, and I could make little movement.

Leaning into my neck, his whisper came out in short breaths. "Ah ah ah, none of that, Soren, You could alert the innocent bystanders walking down the street; we wouldn't want that." I knew he could feel my heart thundering in my chest, my breath quick with panic.

"Will, why are you doing this?!" My voice came out strained and full of terror.

"I'm going to need you to let me do this peacefully," He said as I struggled against him. "It is funny, how your father wants you home awfully quickly, and all seconds after you told him about this painting that you *found.*" His snicker came out in short breaths.

He continued, "And to think, what I've been looking for this whole time, you conveniently brought right to me, like a parting gift, the gift of freedom. So daft, little Soren, thinking I couldn't hear what you were whispering over there."

He rolled his eyes and smirked. "*Humans* are so funny, always so oblivious to anything around them, always thinking this human bubble you live in is so safe," He huffed another laugh to himself. "I've spent so many years inspecting this painting and that painting, *any* painting that had just the right hum of magic, wishing and hoping it'd be hidden in plain sight, maybe even something like the Mona Lisa painted over it. Hunting down this or that person. And here it is, in the hands of the daughter of a *human* inventor." He paused, turning his head to look at the painting again, "Does she know it spills her secrets? Ah, well I suppose she at least suspects," he laughed again, his lips curling into a killers grin. "She knows *everything.*"

What they wanted with you. Hunting down this person or that. She. His words rang in my head. Repeating themselves as if trying to make me understand.

Staring at Willem for what felt like forever, I could muster nothing but confusion. I stared into his eyes, looking for some compassion, anything. I found nothing; they were hard and glassy, flashing black for the slightest second. No emotions in the depths. His eyebrows fixed in an angry fashion. I had been right all along; the painting *was* important. I had to get out of here, with the painting in one piece.

"Now, we can conduct our business and part ways, shall we?" A wicked smirk spread across his face. His words came out in an almost snake-like hiss.

I thrashed my arms again, not willing to give up, but he wasn't fazed. He twisted his grip on my wrists, setting my skin on fire, his smile getting wider. My hope in escaping began to unravel. But no words came from my mouth, not even a scream; it was like I couldn't speak. I had gone mute. My body began to shake uncontrollably. Every breath I took felt like it passed in slow motion. My lungs felt like they were going to collapse along with the sharp pain searing through my chest. *Really? A panic attack... right now?* My hands began to tingle, heat building in the tips. *No, no, no, no, I can't lock up; I have to get out of here.* My thoughts began to overwhelm me. The tingling sensation that always accompanied my panic attacks began to spread up my arms, my body heating up from the inside out.

Then it happened, my nightmares becoming real life. I *smelled* the smoke before I saw the look on Willem's face; the smell was familiar and in this moment, almost a relief. The same smoke that had always shoved itself up my nose along with the ash that always coated my throat in my nightmares. For the first time, I realized it wasn't all in my head; it wasn't just a dream. I felt like I was an outsider looking in on myself, I could feel myself brimming over. Willem hissed in pain and yanked back one of the hands he had wrapped around mine.

The burning in my hands had *hurt* him. He stared down at his palm, trying to figure out what had just happened, and honestly, I was pretty interested too. Peering down, I noticed the outline of my hand and knuckles were seared into the skin of his hand, lined with a silver ash residue that sparkled in the low light of the art house. Delicate swirls of silver smoke danced around us, as if taunting him. Slowly, he looked back up at me with his head cocked to the side, then returned his focus back on the injured hand, confusion etched on his face.

"What in the Human Realm...." His voice sounded just as confused as he looked. "How did you...? Oh gods, it's *you*. It wasn't the painting, it was *you*, all this *fucking time*."

Seeing the advantage in the confusion, I used my newly freed hand, and all the adrenaline I could muster, and aimed for his head. Trying with all my might, I tried to bring back the burning and tingling. But nothing rustled inside me. So, my tiny fist met the side of his head in an unsatisfying thud. To my disappointment though, he did not scream in agony or cripple to the ground like I had foolishly imagined. He hadn't even flinched, and now my hand was throbbing. Turning his head towards me, he narrowed his eyes, the confusion gone and anger replacing it. Within seconds, his hands were at my throat and I was being lifted off the ground. My legs began to thrash. His fingernails dug into the soft skin he had just minutes ago been brushing his lips across. I honed all my extra energy into trying to pry his hand off my throat, drawing blood with every go.

In aggravation, he slammed my body back into the wall, my head bouncing off of it. I choked on a cry of pain. Bits of brick came crumbling down on my shoulders, along with drops of my own blood. He was crushing my throat, and my vision began to darken. At that moment, I knew he would kill me. It was the painting, or death.

"...please...sto...stop ..." my voice barely came out as he strangled me. Choking, I couldn't get the rest out. I could feel myself losing consciousness. The blackness closing in on me, the outline of his beautiful face blurring.

Before I was completely out, he threw me across the room. I slammed into the metal table, my ribs singing in pain. My bag fell from the table to the ground with a thud next to me, and I gasped for breath. I let myself lie on the ground, not bothering to pick myself up, because why would I when movement meant pain? Peeking up at Willem, I saw he still stood across the room and began slowly walking towards me, he was fixing the cuffs of the gray cardigan he wore. Blood, my blood, decorated it now in abstract patterns.

Hot tears welled up in my eyes as I realized he wasn't done with me. Every inch of my body ached and was utterly exhausted. Willem stopped in front of me, the point of his shiny burgundy shoes inches away from my face. He crouched down then, and took my chin in his hand, turning my face towards his. The pain in my head throbbed, and my vision began fading again. His grip on my chin was tightening until I reluctantly looked at him. "This was incredibly more violent than I pictured. And for that, I am truly sorry." Taking his thumb, he wiped away a stray tear, blood smearing with it.

"I wish we could've had a glass of wine. I wish I could've asked you nicely." He let out a strained sigh, "I should've just knocked you out and left with the damn painting, but I was being selfish, as usual. I'm sure you'd agree." He took the blood-smeared thumb and stuck it in his mouth. He moaned, his eyes flashing, a black void taking them over. "Gods, you taste good. But I guess you always have." He stared at me a moment longer. His strange madman façade broke, and for just a slight second, something that looked like maybe regret flashed across his face.

Clicking his tongue he narrowed his eyes again, as if making himself get back on track. "I wasted a lot of time here, but orders are orders I suppose. You made it worth it, for a while. If only I had known what a truly interesting *human* you were." He drew out the word human, as if he was chewing on it, savoring it, pondering it.

"It's no wonder every other creature is out here trying to track your existence." He gave my chin one last squeeze before gently laying my head back on the ground. "But you were not directly my assignment, someone else can clean up this mess."

I could feel myself coming into and out of consciousness then. One second, he was right in front of me, the next he had the painting in his hand and was walking toward the glass doors. Then I heard a crash, glass falling to the ground. I heard shoes scuffing the ground, shattering bone. I heard two voices yelling and a thunderous crack. And then, silence. I could still feel the hot and sticky blood dripping down my face, pooling under me, growing colder with every second. Through the slits of my eyes, I saw massive boots walking towards me. I heard a language being whispered above me that I couldn't understand. I saw piercing gray eyes staring down at me, long black hair framing a strong clenched jaw.

The smell of fresh rain wrapped itself around me in the

form of two massive arms, and in that comfort I let myself be whisked away by the black abyss.

I let the abyss take me, my thoughts drifting to the gray cardigan that Willem was wearing. A present I had gotten him for Christmas last year, and if my new fluffy orange friend had eaten, since I hadn't been home much today.

It's funny, the mundane things you think about, when your body feels like it's on the brink of dying.

CHAPTER

FOUR

B efore I opened my eyes, I knew where I was. The smell of tea, earth and fresh cut flowers greeted me as I sat up; I had ended up at Vana's greenhouse somehow. *She is going to be so mad at me.* Sucking in a sharp breath, I brought a hand to my side, as if to ease the shooting pain I felt in my ribs. Letting my eyes adjust, I realized I was in Vana's bedroom. Through the windows I could see the dark, plum-colored sky, stars still twinkling as the first rays of sunlight peeked over the morning fog that clung to the grass. It cast small glints of sparkling light dancing across the room.

Looking to the side table, I noticed a teacup that still had steam dancing from its surface. I leaned over and grabbed it, inviting the hot cup to bite into my skin. I took a long sip, sighing with joy as the hot tea soothed my soul. I just wanted a moment, a single moment of silence, to collect myself, before I had to confront what had happened last night. I knew as soon as I left this bed, there was no way I was going to get that.

Vana's home was an old greenhouse, covered in sparkling glass windows from top to bottom and connected to the back of her flower shop. She had renovated it into a little studio apartment. It was truly just as beautiful as she was. Plants of all kinds snaked up the walls, hid in corners and on tables, and hung from the ceiling. Her bedroom was tucked away in the corner of the greenhouse, against the brick wall of the flower shop. Her bed was small, and almost never made, even if she wasn't in it. Pillows of every color were constantly strewn across it like a spilled jewelry box. I wrapped the peacock blue comforter around me tightly, feeling the chill of the autumn air seep into me.

Her bedroom was separated from the rest of the green house by a wall of hanging green vines that hung from the slats of the glittering glass ceiling. Standing up, then winced in pain, pulling up my shirt, I winced again at the sight of the purply black bruised splotches that ran up and down my side. I wanted to get to a mirror and see the damage that had been done by Willem. Just thinking about him, about the struggle from last night, I grow nauseous. Images slammed back into me. I grew more and more clammy with every step I took and every moment I remembered.

I sluggishly made my way through the room, passing the tiny kitchenette and the pot-belly fireplace, all the way to the bathroom, whose walls were also curtains of hanging vines. Reaching the pedestal sink, I couldn't look up in the mirror just yet. I knew my face was a mess; I could feel the bruises blooming on my skin. Waves of sickness rolled over me again, and I leaned down to press my forehead against the cool marble, willing myself to calm. Closing my eyes, I counted to one hundred.

You can do this, you are brave. You can face this.

Finally, I looked up. To my astonishment, I didn't look as bad as I felt. Someone, probably Vana, had changed me into a violet-colored camisole and matching sleep pants. My hair had been washed of the blood that I knew had dried in it and had been brushed. There was a gash on my forehead, near my temple, that looked like it had been stitched up and was healing rather fast like it had a week to heal.

My heart quickened at that thought, I didn't know how long I'd been out for. It could have been hours, but days? My neck had bruises in the shape of a hand, every finger purple and outlined in a sickening yellow. Gingerly, I reached for the back of my head, *owe*. There were some stitches back there too, and a raised bump. Flashbacks of hot sticky blood running down my face rush over me, being picked up, and long black hair draping over me. I closed my eyes and took another deep breath. I needed to get shit done. I needed to find Vana, and...

And the painting?! Oh god. The painting. Shit. Shit shit shit. Whirling around, I ignored the dizziness and began to head out the door. I made it three steps into the shop and Vana was in front of me, arms crossed and not looking happy. And with my father in tow. *Great.* It was both a flooding relief and just something else to worry about, seeing both of them in front of me. Looking at my father, I could see every minute he spent worrying about me etched into his face. His black-rimmed glasses sat on the edge of his nose, so he could look down properly and see me. His usually kept and combed salt and pepper hair was slightly disheveled like he had been napping, matching his slightly wrinkled argyle sweater vest.

"Dad..." My voice came out small and whispered. I wanted to say so much more but couldn't manage it. I wrapped my arms around him, letting myself sink into his big warm hug, and before I knew it, I was crying. We stood there for a while, him hugging me and patting my back, me crying.

Sometimes he'd say in a hushed voice, "It's okay, little girl". Finally, I pulled back, feeling slightly embarrassed.

"Ehh hemm," I heard Vana grumble, and I turned toward her. I reached out my hand, silently begging her to grab mine. This was always our, "Do you forgive me?", and if the other took the hand, all was forgiven.

"I'm so sorry, I wanted to tell you, but I thought it could be dangerous or really just a big to-do for a fake painting. I didn't want to ... I didn't want to put you in any danger..." My words came out in a rush.

She squeezed my hand back. "Don't apologize, please.... Just next time... let me in on your big plans?..."

I smile weakly back to her and nod my head.

"Let's go back to the house. I closed the shop for the day, we have more important things to attend to," she replied.

My dad nodded solemnly in return, and I knew this wasn't good. Looking out of the shop windows and back towards the greenhouse, I always startled at the charm that had been gifted to it. From the outside looking in, the greenhouse looks like an old abandoned one, with broken windows and weeds growing up to its broken rusted ceiling. Vana was always very serious about her privacy, and her home was no exception.

Vana, my father and I all made ourselves comfortable around the pot belly stove. The temperature had dropped five degrees since I had woken up. My mother walked through the door with a platter full of food. Bless her heart, she had made all my favorites. Looking up at her, her beauty was not marred by age, nor by the red rimmed eyes she had from crying. Seeing her like this, silent and timid, she was nothing like the free spirited and loud-mouthed mother I was used to. Guilt dug itself deeper into my gut; I must've worried them so much, for them to all look as they do. Leaning down to kiss me on the forehead, my mother set a giant plate in front of me, nudging it forward for me to grab a lemon-glazed muffin.

Sitting down on the love seat I took extra care of how I twisted and turned my sides. My father grabbed a blanket and draped it over my legs, while Vana handed me another steaming cup of tea.

"You know, you guys really shouldn't fuss so much about me. I still have two legs that work," I said, trying to lighten up the mood.

"Yes, and you're very lucky for that, Soren. You almost died." My fathers voice was stern, the soft murmurs from earlier gone. When his dark eyebrows were creased, you knew he meant business.

Straightening up in my seat, I replied, "I don't remember much...I remember he..., he..." I stopped myself, I couldn't make myself say the words without every second of it coming back to. "Then I remember being picked up. But maybe that was a dream...". Then it all spilled out. I told them everything, from the very moment I found the painting to the last thing I remembered. I knew I sounded crazy, saying the painting shocked me, that it changed something in me, that I felt *different*. I turned to Vana, she sat strangely upright in her hanging wicker chair, her usually relaxed and carefree posture gone. She looked at me pointedly and cleared her throat.

"You were brought here two nights ago. The back of your skull had been fractured, and three of your ribs were broken, along with internal damage and bleeding. Willem left you to die there. You were brought here because this is one of the only places he can't locate you. Not only has he never been here before, but this charm does not just hide prying eyes, it makes locating this place with a locator spell basically impossible, and scents are thrown off." Vana finished her sentence with a sharp nod. His name being said out loud brought bile to my throat, that I swallowed back down quickly with a bite of muffin.

"Who was it that found me?" I asked, still remembering the strong arms that picked me, and the long black hair.

"Little girl, we have many things to discuss," my father stood up, and moved closer to my mom, and reached out his hand, she took it, and stood with him, both stared at each other for a long moment before he said, "We need to show you something that's been waiting a very long time to be delivered."

My father stepped forward, and leaning down, he took a warm hand, humming with crackling magic, and placed it on my cheek. Before I managed to ask him how he was wielding magic, a familiar tingling rustled in me, greeting the hand at my cheek. Closing my eyes, I succumbed to the hum growing inside me. Then, I felt a rush of cool heavy wind brush my cheeks.

Opening my eyes, I quickly realized I was no longer in the greenhouse, but a great silver sparkling abyss, empty as far as the eye could see. The air around me held an all-knowing weight, as if every light particle floating by was a watching eye, knowing my every move before I did. Tiny threads of silver hung in the air, as I moved, they brushed past me like cobwebs. Out of the corner of my eye, I saw one thread glowing more intense than the others. Instinctively, I walked towards it, holding my hand out, and as soon as I made contact with it, it burst, sending blinding light cascading down around me. As my sight came back to me, I was greeted by a different world, time, and place.

A STORY with a thousand versions and a thousand secrets, the story of a child.

The story of a shattering world. The story of what is, what could be and what will be.

The story of a Seer and a golden Fae King. A story of love, of struggle, of hope.

The story of a High Wizard, and what he had to give up in order to protect me, to protect the worlds.

The truth of my life, of my existence. The truth of my family, my friends, my world that had been wrapped up tightly, held secret inside of me, suddenly burst in blinding lights of colors, stars shattering around me.

The story of a woman, running through the forest, carrying me in her arms.

And then she spoke to me, the silver-haired Seer, the one from the forest, and the one from the painting. Her name flooded my thoughts, given to me from the vision–

Asta. My biological mother. Her eyes were a blazing starry night against the smoke and threads of this world.

She was here, but she was not. As she moved, shifts in her form made her see through for split seconds, the cobweb threads clinging to her white satin dress and her long blonde silver hair.

"My dear child, it has been so long. It is alarming how much you've grown since I last saw you. Time here is transcendent; a year can feel like a day and vice versa."

She smiled, soft and sweet, and so sad it tugged on my heart. A smile I never realized I missed until now. From behind her, a tall golden man, with golden braids and jade eyes stepped forward, placing a strong hand on her shoulder, looking down at her lovingly. The Fae King of the Sands, Jahan Amari, my biological father. The small memories I had of them flutter up from somewhere ancient and hidden. Love, gratitude, and sadness burst inside me. Tears blurring my vision. I can see by the look on their faces, that they understand, they feel it too.

Jahan turned his attention to me. "My fig loving daughter," he began, his laugh deep and warm, and his smile even warmer. "It still seems like yesterday I was wiping the juice from your chin." I realized then, that I recognize his voice, as the one from my nightmares, the one always guiding me through them.

Looking down at my mother again, he gave her a smile, and she gripped his hand harder, trying to find strength in it.

"We are so glad you could finally join us, even if it has to be brief. Your mother was getting increasingly worried. Her calculations were about a hundred years off, but time has a way of making its own rules." He laughs again, and I was surprised at the comfort it brought me.

I nodded my head, giving them a small smile in return. "I suppose it does." I had no clue what to say, all the images, memories, memories that weren't even mine, things to come, what could be, the paths to be chosen. I was simply overwhelmed.

As if hearing my thoughts, Asta replied, "We know that this is a lot to take in, but we cannot stay long. We are only here in spirit, and spirits cannot join the realms for very long, even in this between."

Asta looked around, as if trying to find a horizon, anything permanent, and looked back to me with disappointment in her eyes. "This is your first time here I realize. Here, time, life, and fate are kept in unison. The Gap is the passage between gates. Gates from the living realms to the Rivers, to the Well of Urd. Time weaves infinitely, people's fate being threaded together. Seers cannot infiltrate the time itself, only see inside it. This is the only place we have where we can be together, for this short while," She catches a passing silver thread in her palm, and lays it out for me to see.

"In fairy tales and bedtime stories, it is said that in the beginning, Seers were composed of three sisters, and they held the delicate balance of all the worlds. Sister Present controlled the present time, Sister Fate controlled what could be and Sister Future controlled what is to be intended. They wove the Tapestry, the tapestry of time, of life. Lifting threads from the sacred well. From their well, they could choose fates, but they also nourished the great tree, Yggsdasil, using the waters of the well to nourish it.

From Yggsdasil, all of life exists, its roots and branches hold the worlds together, tethering them. All three sisters worked hand in hand. They wove peacefully for centuries, catching threads and endlessly weaving, endlessly ferrying the worthy across to the rivers, using threaded silver baskets. Until one fateful morning, the sky opened up, and the three sisters came tumbling out, shattering and scattering across the world like pearls, falling off a broken necklace chain. The shattered bits... that is where it's said the Seers come from."

She paused for a moment, and sighed softly, slowly shook her head. Then looking back down at her hand. "Each thread represents a life that has not ended yet. The frays, you see, are all the ways a life could end. Looking at these threads, a Seer can decide if life was worthy by seeing the most probable paths they will take. The worthy lives are blessed and sent to the rivers. The worthy take the journey to Valhǫll. Only the Three Sisters though, could tie fates,". She sent the thread back out into The Gap, and waved her slightly vanishing arm, as if showing me this world in all its splendor.

This was all new knowledge to me, and shocking knowledge at that. Seers didn't just hold the powers of time, but the power of who crossed the rivers. Shivers ran across my whole body.

"What happens to the unworthy?" I asked, my voice echoing in the stillness.

"They are sent down the rivers to the Goddess Heliene, who reigns in Hel, the land of the unforgiven." Clearing her throat, she looked back to me. "It is saddening that I will not be able to teach you everything you will need. Maybe one day I can share the full truth, but right now this is best. There is too much mystery and darkness that I can't push back, hiding all your paths. There is no telling who will be able to infiltrate you, steal your knowledge. But our message is urgent, and we are already being pulled back." Indeed, they were growing foggier as the minutes passed, shards of rainbow light shone through her silhouette now, the hard edges of their bodies beginning to blur.

"From the vision we have gifted you, and with some small memories only a child could have that have been given back to you, you know some of what I am about to tell you, but as fate has it, I cannot wield your destiny to you. There is a curse that looms over your destinies, which leaves only you to be able to pick up the clues and piece them together.

"You were the first and only of your kind born; you are considered a halfling. There is a prophecy of three children, each who has a destiny to lead, each who could lead our worlds in vastly different directions: A child born anew, a daughter of two worlds, and a child created. Of the three children, your destiny is the least costly and has many life threads indicating you will lead our worlds in the right direction, if you do not sway from your right path.

Few know of this prophecy, but those who do, are dangerous. Before you, no one thought it was possible." She looked at Jahan before continuing, "We kept you a secret. We knew you would be hunted, killed for what you were. An unknown, a threat to those who didn't understand, and didn't want to. Your existence is a legend, a fairy tale in the creature realms. Take advantage of that, of no one knowing who you are, of no one knowing you're real. Your abilities are unlike any creature in these realms, but you are not the only one who wanders the realms with unique abilities; remember, there are matches. Those who are your equal, and made to best you. Your powers are raw, unhinged and you need vigorous training. You must overcome your enemies, you must survive. Your survival is the key to the world as you know it, you must keep it from crumbling around you."

Floating by, a dark silver thread came into view. Her brows furrowed, and she reached out and delicately grabbed it. She began to read the thread, taking a slender finger and fanning the threads out. For a split second, she seemed a shell of a person, here in only physical form, and suddenly she was back.

Her mouth turned down into a frown, and all the sorrow I had ever felt was reflected to me in her eyes as she looked back at me. "A great war outlines this notch in time, in your time, unlike the ones you've seen. This war is a black smear across the light of your being. I have not seen a dark thread like this in a very long time, and it is a precursor that there are many more to come," She paused again and looked up at my father.

He silently brushed a few stray silver strands from her face, and urged her to go on, "We are quickly dissipating my love." She turned back to me, glittering tears rolling down her face.

"I will leave you with this, my sweet child. Not all wolves come as they are. Emrin, or as you know him, Merin, will explain the questions I know you have to the best of his knowledge. There is still much to learn. We will return as soon as we can."

Slight outlines of them was all that remained as I heard a unison whisper of I love you, and saw the outline of a moon-white outstretched hand, that I was reaching out to touch too.

IN A RUSH OF COOL WIND, my eyes fluttered open, my arm still reaching out, grasping nothing but empty air. It felt like a second and a lifetime all in one. I stared back up at the people in front of me, as if seeing them for the first time. To my relief, they were all as they were before, unchanged, as I left them. My Parents and Vana, all staring at me, waiting for me to say... anything. Do anything. I could feel the air around me holding its breath. I let out a sigh, and with that, the world seemed to sigh as well.

"So you've known this whole time what the world seeks to know? The truth of the Seers powers? That they are the keepers of the rivers, the overseers of time and fate?" I asked, my question pointed to my father.

"Well yes, I've known since the day I found you. However I believe that it is not time you have control of, but life itself, fate. I believe that you are not simply freezing time, but *life,* and I do not think that goes unscathed, consequences follow." He says, and looks up into the sky, his finger wagging, something he does as his wheels spin, while he's brainstorming.

My father got up then, and walked across the room, "Seers are a finite resource, Soren, and when I say finite, I mean they do not produce more, from what I have seen. Without Seers, the spirits can find no peace, the balance of life and death is undone. You see, Seers not only carry over the dead, but they also decipher whether the dead are worthy of eternal paradise, or if they must aimlessly wander through the realm of despair, buried deep under the earth, boiling near the core." He paused for a moment, seemingly thinking on what to say next.

"We believe that the Royal Seer, She is the one who decides the fates of the living and dead, and the Seers ferry them over across the Rivers, but this is not much more knowledge then the general public knows about them. There are rare ancient scrolls, which describe three sisters, who would weave the threads of fate for each soul's life, but even the texts seem to vanish as soon as they are found, or those who find them cannot open them because they are not Seers. Without knowing the origin of Seers, there is not much to be done, information is key."

A cool autumn breeze came through the open window, rustling my hair, and with it, the familiar smell of cloves and fresh rain. Alarms sounded in my head, and instantly I remembered the boots, the long black hair, and the strong arms that carried me. Turning towards the open window, I finally saw him– the only change in the room since I had come back from The Gap. I didn't dare look him in the face yet, but I knew what he was. A Royal Faeren, and by the look of him, a powerful one. He was leaning against the greenhouse wall, arms crossed. His 6'5 frame towered over the room, making it seem increasingly more cramped by his presence in it. His simple white long sleeve shirt hugged his broad muscular shoulders. The sleeves were shoved up, which gave you a peak at his left arm that looked like it was covered in intricate tattoos that weaved in and out of ancient

Fae words. I could tell the markings started on the left underside of his neck where the bottom of his chin met his neck. A clean crisp black line ran down the center of his neck, as if bordering off the tattoos from the other half of his unmarked body. The tattoos ran all the way down to his fingertips, wrapping around his entire hand, including his palm. His right arm bore no markings; only a simple leather watch adorned it. He wore dark wash, almost black jeans, and the same leather boots that showed no signs from the other night's events, my blood washed from them. His long black hair was pulled back into a low bun, pieces of hair falling loose, hiding the elegant slight point of his ears that I knew were there.

Finally, I dared to glimpse at his face, the Fae Male who had carried me to safety. He couldn't be all bad, right? To my relief, he was staring down at his nails, analyzing his cuticles, as if him being here was taking up the time he had set aside to get them done. The sharp angles of his face were softened by the warm peachy glow of morning light that shone in through the glass walls. His skin was like smooth marble; the only wrinkle was between his eyebrows, an indicator seemingly there to remind you of how displeased he was to be here. His dark eyebrows framed his slightly upturned eyes, his thick black lashes curling just the right amount.

His storm cloud eyes finally met mine then, as if he was waiting for mine to linger up to his, like he knew I'd oogle him before looking him in the eyes. *An arrogant Royal Fae if I've ever seen it*, I thought to myself, along with an inner eye roll. The bored expression on his face did not fade, but for a slight second, I saw something else flash in his eyes, like lightning across a darkening storm-ridden sky. As soon as the lightning flashed, it was gone.

A devilishly beautiful smile spread across his impossibly perfect features, "Hello, Soren, you're welcome. You might want to be a little more courteous next time while staring; Royal Fae have made people dance for twenty hours straight for less. We practice politeness vigorously, and that will obviously have to be one of your first lessons. I'm Rhone, by the way" He winked at me and turned back to examining his nails, whatever interest he had in me, seemingly lost.

I heard my father clear his throat, and turned to see him give Rhone a pointed look. "Soren, this is Rhone, a close friend who will work with you as a mentor and bodyguard of sorts as we work through this. He has seen many wars, infiltrated every court. There is almost no corner of this world he hasn't seen. He is a master with his power and fighting skills. Although this might not be conventional for anyone, he is the best money can buy."

My father smiled at Rhone, who nodded back and replied, "You didn't tell me I was getting paid for this." They both laughed, Rhone's grumpy demeanor slipping as he spoke with my father.

His voice sent a heat wave over me, embarrassment and slight anger bubbling up from the surface. The first real emotion I had felt all morning except for guilt. I had never been spoken to directly by a Royal Faeren before. The power he evoked was truly incredible and made my hands shake at an alarming level.

There was something about him, the realization in the power he held, that reminded me of the power I somehow had acquired. I looked down at my hands, the hands that burned silver blisters into Willems skin. The initial shock hit me then. The vision was real, The Gap was a real living breathing world of its own, and it was no longer creatures versus me, as a human. I had never even been human, I was a walking lie, half Royal Faeren, half Seer and I was going to be *hunted*. My life was crumbling around me, my dreams and ambitions taken from me, this new and unknown future replacing everything I had worked for. And now I had a *giant babysitter?!*

Just my mere existence held so many secrets. The secret so many had searched for hundreds of years. The tremor in my hands began to worsen, and I could feel the heat in me begin to rise. Like in my dreams, like in the art house, it was happening again. My breathing was tight, my head was swarming with a thousand thoughts, and images of Willem's attack slammed against me, taking over my vision. I was back there again, his breath in my ear, his hands on my throat, his lips on mine. I could feel myself cracking under the pressure. Muffled voices were all around me, coming from every direction. Saying my name, trying to bring me back down from this PTSD anxiety-induced attack.

I heard Rhone yell, "Everyone get *back* and put your shield *up,* Emrin," he warned.

Vaguely, I knew this wasn't real. I knew Willem's face in front of me wasn't real, I knew the smell of him was a wretched memory now, but that didn't matter when it was choking me, shoving itself down my throat like his tongue had been. But the raging heat in me still flowed and was on the rise. The tingling sensation ran down my arms at miraculous speed, and the fear of the power in me, the fear of myself, was my unraveling. My vision turned star speckled, and I felt a hard blow to my side, knocking me down and keeping me steady. A calming wind, cooled by the soft mist of fresh rain surrounded me. Then I felt the power leaving my body; it felt like a thousand splinters being pulled. A quick sting of pain, and then a rushing relief, the pressure gone. In a burst of glittering blinding light, the image of Willem began to fade, my breathing began to calm. My body temperature began dropping, the mist kissing my burning skin with a hiss. I could feel the destruction my power had left behind before I even opened my eyes. Fluttering down from the sky, stinging my skin, the familiar smell of that silver ash and smoke hung heavy.

Opening my eyes, I soon realized that it wasn't just glittering hot ash that stung me, but shards of glass. Reality came slamming back to me as I also looked up into the eyes of a lightning storm, Rhone's eyes. He held up his arm above me, trying to shield me from the broken glass raining down, the other behind my back holding me up. His long dark hair was barely tucked back in its bun now. All around us, the shimmering mist shone in the air, dancing with the silver ash that now haunted my everyday life.

As ash and shards of glass came down like snow above me, I turned to my family and my best friend, praying to the Gods I hadn't harmed them. They stared back at me, my parents huddled together with Vana, shock written all over their faces. But they were unharmed, and that was the important part. In one swift movement, Rhone had set me back on my feet, and now stood feet away from me, the slightly annoyed expression back on his face as he brushed wrinkles and debris from his shirt. Burn marks and cuts from the glass marred every inch of the exposed skin I could see on him. The arm that had been wrapped around my waist, had shimmering silver and black burns running up it. But as soon as I blinked, they vanished, healing quickly. I looked down at my own arms, cuts welting with blood adorned my arms like freckles, but as fast as they appeared, my skin began weaving itself back together. I gasped and brought a still-shaking hand to my mouth.

Rhone huffed a laugh, accompanied by an eye roll. He then dissipated into mist, carried away by the wind.

I blinked several times before I turned back to my parents and Vana. Vana saw the look of confusion on my face, and said in a whisper, "He is simply traveling from one place to another. His Fae Powers control storms; that's why it looks like mist. Every Fae can travel through their nature. It's called shadowing, because all you see is their shadow as they vanish. Instead of creating the mist or storm winds, he becomes them, folding into the spaces in nature to travel almost instantly from one place to another"

My father stepped forward, concern written all over his face. "Are you alright, little girl?" He reached out to touch my hand, as if to see if I was still real, and sighed in relief. I shook my head yes and swallowed hard, my throat still dry and aching. From the far distance, realm patrol sirens sounded.

"Do you guys hear that? The sirens?" I asked whoever would answer.

Vana's voice broke the beat of silence in answer, "The realm patrol is on their way. They felt the surge of power; this event likely set the radars off the charts. That much power...." she stopped for a moment, her eyes boring into me, shaking her head in disbelief, ".... Is not allowed to be wielded in the human realms, by any means."

Vana's ears twitched and she turned toward my father. "We have four minutes before they are here; our charms have been unraveled by Soren's... explosion."

My father searched the field around us, looking for patrol on foot, the green house that once stood, laid around us in shambles.

My mother rushed to my side, placing a cool hand on my wrist. "Emrin hurry, a dislocating charm. When they get close to what they are searching for, their thoughts will scramble, making them forget what they came for."

Father nodded his head, and he walked towards her, taking her free hand. They closed their eyes and began working swiftly, softly muttering words I couldn't understand, stringing them together in a lyrical fashion. I never knew Wizard charms could sound so beautiful. The language was both warm, smooth, and throaty, like rich merlot swirling in a glass. As the charm began to settle, their hands began to glow a light shade of blue, the air around us crackling. A snap sounded through the air and the charm was complete.

"The charm will only hold so long against their armor, but it does give us an extra ten minutes or so," my father explained, turning to Vana, his tone urgent. "Can you shadow us out? We need to be anywhere but here."

She nodded. "Yes, just give me one second."

Vana walked towards her plants, scattered around and half destroyed by the damage of what I had inflicted. Hurriedly she leaned over each one of them, cupped them in her hand, and whispered, the vibrant life leaving them. With each plant she walked to, every shade of green crawled up her dark golden skin in swirls, seeping in. Her nymph-like features began to overpower her human facade. Her cheekbones growing higher and sharper, her eyes became larger and tightly angled, the irises turning from brown to a glowing golden green. Her long black wild curls vanished, twisted roots and leafy vines taking their place, her golden trinkets still wrapped around them.

One by one, her plants gave their life to her, her power growing. She walked to the middle of the room, and throwing her hands out, great vines and tree buds burst from the concrete, making me jump. The plants quickly went to work, taking over the demolished greenhouse, breaking down everything around it until it was like the little house had never even been there. Plush new grass covered where the concrete had been and great trees with blossoms hung over us.

Vana turned to me, a smile brushed across her face as she beheld her achievement, her razor-sharp teeth gleaming in the sunlight. I couldn't blame her for boasting, what she had done was truly remarkable. Looking at Vana, it was like seeing her for the first time. She was beautiful in this wild form. Her golden skin gleaming in the sunlight as she moved, an emerald sheen dancing across it. Yellow and white blossoms wrapped themselves around her body. Her wild and curly hair, now thick vines running down her back, gold charms still dangling throughout. But my eyes kept wandering back to her teeth, a predator's teeth. I had always heard Wild Fae's features were unnatural, but I never knew to the extent. Childhood stories of woodland nymphs stealing away men and newborn babies from families in the dead of night, feasting on them, flashed in my mind. As soon as the thoughts came to me, I knew Vana could never do something like that. It was the slight tilt of her head that let me know she knew what I was thinking, as I had stared. It was like I couldn't tear myself away from her sharp gleaming fangs. She snapped her lips shut immediately, the joy from her face gone. With inhuman-like speed, she was next to us. Her human form was back as her blurred shape stopped in front of us.

"Grab hands, and do *not let go*. I haven't done this in a very long time, so brace yourself, this is about to be a very bumpy ride," Vana exclaimed, as she grabbed my hand.

The pungent smell of fresh soil filled the air around us, and it was my mother I saw dissipate first, her body slowly shadowing into dark rich soil and flower petals, floating away in the wind. It was then I heard the border patrol cars screech to a halt in the street, only a shop distance away. *They are going to find us.* The sirens stopped; their car doors slammed shut. I counted the sound of ten car engines. I could hear the bark of the hounds, and I could hear them sniffing out the magic.

Looking at Vana, the nervousness twisted itself in my stomach. With a slight arrogance, she winked at me, and I screwed my eyes shut, the fluttering feeling beginning in my feet. Then an eerie lightness took over my body. I opened my eyes then, thinking she wasn't going to be able to shadow us all out, and gasped. We were no longer in a field behind the flower shop, but in my father's library, the fire-place crackling next to me.

MY VISION WAS BLURRED at first, but it didn't take long for the hard edges of the floor to ceiling bookcases to come to me. The smell of the burning cedar, old books and pipe tobacco made me sigh; I was so happy to be home.

Turning, I saw Vana was already sprawled out on the leather chair, playing with her hair. "See, it wasn't so bad;

you didn't even notice you had traveled." She threw her head back and laughed, her feet kicking along in time with her giggling. I was too exhausted to taunt her back. I turned around and grabbed a pillow from the couch behind me, tossing it in her direction. We laughed for a moment together, the slight dizziness of shadowing still affecting me. Then the weight of the day hurdled into me, and flashes of Vana's destroyed home brought me back to reality.

"Vana... I'm so sorry about your home, I don't know how I let that hap—" Words rushed out of me, the shame of what I had done flooding my thoughts.

"It was a drafty old thing anyways. I like it here much better," she said, cutting me off before I could word vomit anymore. She stretched her long limbs and grabbed onto the pillow I had thrown at her, snuggling her face against it. She let out a sigh, and before I knew it, she was softly snoring, the conversation seemingly forgotten. I let myself fall onto the couch behind me. I fell asleep as soon as my head hit the cushion, pure exhaustion weighing me down. I dreamt of the vision of Asta's angelic face, Jahan's deep and genuine laugh. I dreamt of all the things the vision had given me. The truth of Emrin and Tanja. The truth of Asta and Jahan. The truth of Vana, how she had held me hidden for those hundreds of years, risked her life for me, how she was my mother's best friend, and now mine. The truth of myself. I dreamt of the other Seer from the vision, her face hidden in dark shadows, the dark match to my mother, her inky black soul bleeding through her silky moon-white dress.

I AWOKE to what felt like ages later, a certain understanding calming me. Soft voices from the other side of the study and the smell of pipe tobacco hit my senses. Opening my eyes, I noticed Vana still sleeping sprawled out on the armchair, one arm hanging off. Tiny green leaves and yellow flower petals pooled around her, like her magic thrived and grew while she slept, rejuvenating her. *Interesting.*

The voices carried on their conversation. "Willem got away with the painting. I went after him, I got his left shoulder as he was shifting, but he miraged, shifting into a bird of hunt before I could make a pursuit. I couldn't bring myself to kill him, Emrin. I know I made a grave mistake... but I... was him once. Twisted and confused from Her. The things she does...."

It was Rhone speaking I realized, regret lining his voice, but it was still warm, honey coated, and raspy like I remembered from the greenhouse. A strong contrast from his cold and bored demeanor.

I could hear my father scribbling down notes as he spoke, the pipe in the side of his mouth slurring around his speech. Smoking was what he liked to do when he needed to think; he said it helped him sit on his thoughts longer.

"Like I have always assumed, and from the vision Asta gifted me all those years ago, Soren's powers would awaken when the painting was found. From what Soren told me of the electric shock she got after first coming in contact with it, and from how she said that Willem reacted to it, I believe it could be charmed also. To me, the electric shock Soren felt when first touching the painting, sounds like what I have come across with studying other spellbound creatures. The magic does not react, simply fizzles away. This could be why people have been hunting after Soren all these years, not only is she the first of her kind, but they are lying in wait for the painting to pop up, somehow knowing she would be connected. She wants to destroy it before it can show the world the truth of her, of her nature, of her secret reign of destruction, and proof the prophecy is real."

After a brief pause, it was Rhone's turn to speak again. "And as for Soren, what-ever are we going to do with that dreadfully dangerous and clumsy thing? How long do we have to train her?"

My father huffed a laugh. "Rhone, we do not know that with her powers awake from slumber, that she won't grow a little." He continued to laugh a while longer, and from the sound of it, a genuine one. "With her powers seeming to be at a very full capacity, overflowing in fact, it seems as if she has reached maturity for your kind. Now, if we just knew what exactly her powers are, and what others may lie in her..." Carried by a moment of silence, he sucked on his pipe, the tobacco popping. He let out a soft blow, "Aaren has informed me the wedding will be in a months' time. She needs to be as fully equipped as possible if she is to make an appearance there."

Who is She? The same "She" that Willem spoke of? Are they speaking of the dark Seer from my dreams, whose face hides in the obsidian shadows? And why in the Human Realm were decisions about me being made without me there to have any input. *Men.* It was with these thoughts that I knew I had to give them my two cents.

Getting up, I realized there were no more aches and pains in my body. I lifted up my shirt and saw the purple and yellow bruises were gone. Taking note to ask about that later, I turned around, continuing to make my way towards the studies writing table and quickly noticed it was unoccupied. I stopped in my tracks, Confused. There was only one other room my mother allowed my father to smoke in, his den.

I heard one of them clear their throat and the two men hushed. It was one of his most sacred areas in the house; a charm held in place at the threshold assured no one my father didn't trust could be let in. He kept his most valuable items here, his expensive cigars and whiskey that was hundreds of years old. His findings on his creature research, and books of all different sizes and colors that were locked away behind glittering charmed cases, that only he could open. The den was where he went when he had very important guests, or when he was extremely troubled. I had only truly seen my father enter his den a handful of times, and three of them were with High Wizard Locchart. The astonishment that I could hear them talking rooms away, made my nerves stand on end, which I had learned in the past couple days, was not a good thing.

I let myself take a few deep breaths, letting my nerves ease themselves, and made my way up the winding staircase. All the way, I idly wondered what other assets I'd acquire as my powers awoke from their hundreds of years of slumber.

Soon, I found myself standing outside the mahogany door to my father's den, blankly staring at it. Years of being told his den was completely "off limits" made alarms go off in my head, telling me not to go in. I could hear their breathing, so I knew I had been right. Tiny noises echoed all around me. The rustling of the leaves outside. Vana softly snoring, my mother downstairs snipping away at her herbs, softly humming.

Shaking my head, I focused on the door in front of me, and swallowing a huge gulp of air, I walked into the den for the second time in my life. My heart was beating against my chest like tiny fists.

With every bit of grace I apparently owned, I stumbled into the den, tripping on my own two feet. As I looked up, I noticed my father and Rhone sitting across from each other on adjacent couches, the fire blazing between them, sending a caramel glow across the room. Each had bourbon in their crystal glasses. My father's pipe stuck out of the side of his mouth as I knew it would, and he gave me a gentle smile, motioning me to sit next to him.

Rhone turned towards me, a smirk playing at the corner of his mouth. I supposed that meant he was amused by my elegant entrance. He sat his glass on the side table next to him. Even sitting in a large high back leather chair with wide cushions, he still looked just a tad too big for it. His long legs jutted out from under the coffee table, but not out of rudeness, just out of sheer need to put them somewhere. He leaned back and put his hands behind his head. We were in much closer quarters than we had been earlier today; he seemed to suck all the oxygen out of the room. The golden glow of the fireplace gave his rather stormy features a romantic glow. I could see how his kind pulled people in and trapped them with a single glance. Singularly, I wondered if Fae kind was born tricky, if it was a habit learned, or if I would become just as arrogant and scheming.

"Courteous of you to join us, Soren. I was wondering just

how well your hearing was truthfully. Every Fae is a little different. Some have better hearing, others... better reflexes..." Rhone's tone was smug, but I could see a playfulness in his eyes that hadn't been there at the greenhouse, the lightning storm in his eyes was now calm clouds of rolling black and gray.

I stood there for a heartbeat, repeating what to say next in my head, stumbling over my own thoughts. My nerves fluttered to life inside me, Rhone's eyes boring into me. I opened my mouth, and then shut it again, battling what I wanted to say, a sorry I interrupted on my tongue before I snapped my mouth shut.

No, you are not a meek little girl caught listening in on your father's conversations. These are your conversations too.

Clearing my throat, I stepped forward and straightened my posture as I began to speak, willing it to give me the confidence I needed.

"No, actually, I'm not sorry. When decisions about me are being made, I demand to be present, instead of you two up here scheming, making plans without my input." I was surprised at my own courage that I could hear resonating from my own voice. "So yes Dad, I will sit next to you, and I will hear what *we* are planning."

Both men were staring at me, surprise lining their faces. I grabbed a crystal glass from the bar shelf and took my seat next to my father. I leaned forward, and, maybe too aggressively, took the crystal decanter off the coffee table, the amber-colored liquid sloshing around violently.

I poured myself a hearty glass and reclined back into the loveseat. Rhone and my father both still stared at me, their eyes darting from me to the glass in my hand.

"What??!" my voice came out shrill and every bit as agitated as I knew I was. "A woman who just found out she's not human, who has powers that no one really knows what to do with, and who must save the world as she knows it from collapse, can't have a large glass? I think I deserve this more than any of you today."

I gave them both a pointed glare and took a huge swig, sitting down with a huff. The liquid crawled down my throat, warming me from the inside out. The intense flavors overwhelmed my pallet like nothing ever had before. I could taste the vanilla and cinnamon notes that usually lingered so much farther down it was barely a hint. The barrel it had aged in had been oak from the eastern coast of the Spellcasters Realm 270 years ago. I could taste the zest of the blood orange peel that had been used, the warmth of the sun still clung to it. It was unlike anything I had ever tasted. Staring down into my glass, I looked for signs of tampering, a small enchantment by a certain tricky Fae. I heard my father and Rhone both chuckle simultaneously.

My father gave my knee a pat. The tobacco in his pipe crackled and popped, and a cloud of smoke plumed out as he spoke, "I believe you will have many new surprises in the weeks to come, which, with your consent, I would like to document. Not only for our help, but possibly future creatures like you, or ones lingering that we simply don't know about yet."

I smiled at my father, realizing my small victory here. "Yes, I think that's a good idea." I took another swig, the bourbon's intense flavors settling, the initial shock gone. Distantly, I wondered what other things would taste like. Would I still like the lemon cakes my mother made?

Rhone reached for the decanter in the middle of the table, filled his glass half full and took a long drink. A ping sounded, and my father dug his phone out of his pocket. Looking at his watch, he stood and put his pipe to the side.

"Your mother requested my help to finish up dinner. You two talk and get to know each other a bit; we can have a formal discussion after dinner. The official plans need to be set in motion no later than tomorrow morning. Tonight may be the last night we have to truly be together as a family for a while. Let's make it count." He leaned down and kissed me on the top of my head, then made his way out the door, shutting it behind him. Rhone and I sat silently for a moment, letting my father's words seep in. *Does Rhone have a family that he will miss during all this?*

The silence around me was no longer silent in the true sense as I used to know it. The silence was now expectant with life; it filled a void I never realized I had until now. The feeling of silence always made me feel alone but I never knew why; I was constantly filling it with music or tv shows. But now it was all I could do to listen to all the life that was around me. The wind blew through the trees, and the birds made their nest nearby. Vana was awake now; I could hear her tapping her fingers on the marble countertop in the kitchen to the beat of the music my mother was playing, talking to my mom about plants. It was then that the question came back to me, the one that had dragged me up to the study to begin with.

"Who is *She,* the woman I heard you two talking about but only referring to her as She and not by name" I asked Rhone.

My eyes wandered back to his face, I don't know if I'd

ever get used to looking at him, I had honestly never seen someone quite so pleasing to the eye. He wasn't like the other Royal Faeren I had seen through the years. Rhone didn't drape himself in jewels and silk suits like the other Royal Fae. He seemed so unworried about the frills of it all. It made him all the more curious. I could just never put my finger on him.

Turning my attention back to his face, he was like the sun, hard to look at directly. The dancing glow of the flames made the markings that ran down his neck look as if they were dancing along with the fire. I could've evaluated him forever.

Slowly, my eyes met his ever so slightly slanted eyes, and they were on me. I looked away quickly, the weight of his stare too heavy, making me instantly nervous. My eyes finally landed on his mouth. It was sensuous and full, and almost always looked like he was on the verge of doing something menacing. I found my thoughts sneaking some- where deep and lust driven. What his lips might taste or feel like.

The corner of his mouth crept into a devious smile and instantly, I knew he had caught me practically drooling over him. It had to be the bourbon because I could feel myself heating up, just at the slightest thought of him. I let my eyes find his, but they were already on mine, and lined with a mirroring darkness. They were no longer a calm storm; it was as if I could not only see but feel the lightning and thunder rolling in, the air in the room becoming heavy and damp. A hot blush spread across my face and neck, and I instantly crossed my legs and turned my body away from him, willing myself to snap out of it. I heard a pounding in the distance, and vaguely, I wondered who was knocking at the door, but my thoughts were so consumed with him, that I didn't care. It could've been the god of the damned himself, and I wouldn't have looked away. I sucked in a deep breath, trying to claw myself out of the dangerous trance I had found myself in. *Damn him, had he woven a trick on me? Or was I just that enthralled with him?* Truthfully, I had forgotten where I was, that I had even asked him a question, I desperately searched my memory. *Ah yes, who is She?*

"I asked you a question, Rhone." I said, trying to sound as breezy as I possibly could.

He cleared his throat slightly and bit the side of his lip. "That, we don't know exactly. We were saying She because all seers are seemingly female. The dark Seer that you and your father have been shown in your vision, we don't know who exactly that is, because as both of you have said, her face is hidden. It could be any of them. One of our many jobs will be to find her, and stop her." His eyes never left mine, even when he leaned forward to grab the decanter off the table.

He filled up his glass, again, then raised a brow to mine in silent question. I leaned forward, empty glass in hand. Before I could let go of the glass, he wrapped his hand around mine. His touch sent a hot bolt straight through me, a warm blossom of heat rising in me. Slowly, he filled my glass. The smell of sensual spices and fresh rain hung heavy in the still damp air, wrapping around me with a familiar ease. It was a scent so familiar, and that's when it hit me, it reminded me of the same rain lined breeze that would sweep into my windows on many occasions. I scanned his eyes, looking for an answer to my question I hadn't asked. I shoved the thought aside, letting more pressing matters, like the feel of his hand on mine consume my mind.

His black hair was falling forward, undone from his low bun from earlier and hanging loose in slightly waving curls, his jaw clenched. His brow was furrowed, and I swear I could feel the air around us hissing with steam, the grip he had around my hand relaxed as it slowly slid towards my wrist, his fingers finding my pulse that had to be pounding through my flesh. His hands were rough but his caress was velvet smooth.

The decanter was long put back on the table, my glass full. He leaned forward further. Then in one smooth movement he was inches from me, one hand still on my wrist, the other found itself on my hip. He was so close that loose strands of his hair brushed my face. Slowly, he released my wrist, and took my face in his hand, running a rough thumb along my lips, parting them slightly. For a second, I thought he might kiss me; the smoldering look in his eyes telling me he wanted to.

It was then that I heard the distant pounding return, growing faster with every passing second. It was everything I could do to stop myself from gasping, when I realized that there was no knock on any door. That was Rhone's heartbeat racing. My eyes snapped back up to his, the lightning storm in them a violent wave against their constructs. Suddenly, Rhone stood, walking in three strides to the window across the room, and slid it open. The emptiness I suddenly felt from the absence of him shocked me. Autumn air rushed in, cooling the sweltering desire that had radiated around the room. It had left my skin pulsing, and it had left Rhone's heart still pounding a thunderous rhythmic echo.

The window seal creaked under the weight of him, his strong hands gripping it. With a great inhale, he turned back around, his expression back to nonchalant. That menacing but distantly bored gaze met mine again. I blinked suddenly, wondering if everything that had just happened was a daydream.

Rhone spoke then, his voice hoarse, "High Wizard Aaren's wedding is where we will, quote unquote, debut you. The Royal Courts are tightly woven, but new faces aren't as rare as they once were. This time, it will be yours. We need to get you in. Once we get you in, it will be easier to find Willem. Willem has vanished from the Human Realm. And from the Human Realm, we can't try and track him. That kind of magic is banned here, and highly dangerous to use. It will also be easier to gain allies, and we desperately need those. I can feel this war coming, and it is not like the others. I have fought in nearly every war since I gained my full spectrum of powers. This war, it will be unlike any we have seen before."

He stepped forward, grabbing his glass from where he had hastily left it, and leaned on the fireplace, crossing his arms. He hadn't directly looked at me since he had gotten up to open the window, which he now gazed out of.

He cleared his throat before talking again, "Part of my power is being able to..." there was a brief pause, "It's like I can feel a storm brewing. I can feel the winds of change, I can sense a change in..." He paused, finally looking at me, and took a sip of his bourbon. "*Emotion*, so to say. If they are strong enough." He drew out the word emotion as he said it, relishing in it. He gave a shrug and crossed his arms. His eyes ran down the rest of my body.

Embarrassment bloomed across my cheeks. *He had known.* The tingling in my fingertips grew as my anxiety and discomfort did. *So, he basically had been able to feel my mood shift, he could feel what I was feeling. What a prick. He was toying with me, feeding my emotions back to me. Weaving a trick, within a trick. He wanted to humiliate me. With no one watching, just us. That's how easy this was for him.*

"Anyways, by the time the wedding is around the corner, you must be properly trained. I have trained hundreds of Fae warriors, some even less likely than you. We must train you to control that explosion roiling around inside you, daring to kill us all." He raised his eyebrows and reached over and grabbed a candied almond from the dish on the mantel, popping it in his mouth.

"We have to train you to not only control your power but learn what other powers you might have. The emotions you emanate are strong. And important to guard. Anyone around you could be able to sense them. You must be a blank slate. There are demons of all sorts prowling around, just like me. Who can persuade you with a single brush of the wind. Willing to beguile the gullible. You will need to learn to protect yourself. There are creatures out there, whose powers are much more dangerous than mine. You need to be one step ahead of the person next to you, at all times."

Fuming, I was completely fuming over what had happened. I couldn't think straight. Embarrassment and rage ran through me like tidal waves. The familiar tingle slowly crept up my arms, the smell of the hot ash shoving itself up my nose. *How could he do that, make me feel like he wanted me to? What a piece of shit.*

I shot up from the couch, the bourbon swishing violently in my cup, spilling over. I silently sent up a prayer to the Gods that I hadn't stained my father's rug. I guess I had had a lot to drink, I was just noticing how buzzed I was when I stood up, slightly dizzy.

"How dare you treat me like some stupid little child. Who do you think you are? Waltzing in here and behaving like you do. I will *not* train with you. From where I see it, I have no clue how *you* fit into all this." I slammed my glass down on the table, the crystal cracking and shattering under my force. I could feel shards of glass cut into me. The hot blood running down my fingers, the tingling in my hands intensifying, silver smoke pluming around me.

I was tired of glass already. I was tired of surprises, and I was tired of this Fae Male in front of me, the amusement on his face growing with every word. The lightning in his eyes flashed as the crystal had broken, and every minute since, the lightning storm grew. A storm brewing in him as well. *Good.*

"You don't get to choose who trains you, Princess of hissy fits. There is no one better to do it than myself. I am one of the most decorated creatures in any realm, and I owe your father my life. This is how I shall repay him. Turning *you* into something formidable, something able to protect instead of self-destruct." He turned away then, running a hand through his hair, his agitation in full force. Turning back to me, he gave me a sweltering glare, one laced with hate and maybe a tinge desire "I liked you much better when you were getting hot and bothered just by looking at me." He winked at me, his glare never diminishing.

The rage inside me snapped, the pressure mounting. *No,*

no, no, no. Damn it. Not again, not again. The panic made the power surge inside me. A weapon of my own self-annihilation. I didn't know how to stop it. I was going to shatter my childhood home, ruin the charms my parents had just placed to keep us safe for the night. I willed myself to stop, but the more I struggled against the raging power inside me, the more it pushed back. That wretched ash building inside me, the explosion inside me seared through me, blinding light beginning at my fingertips.

Suddenly, a violent wind lifted me off my feet, whirling around me like a hurricane. Mist hissed against my furiously hot skin. Fine mist danced itself up my nose, and as I gasped for air, it soothed my burning throat, cleansing it of the bitter taste of ash. After a moment, the wind died down and my feet met the ground once again. I found myself being held up by a massive hand on my back.

"Steady. Take a deep breath," Rhone was inches from me, his misted skin a strong contrast from the heat of my skin. He raised his tattooed hand and brushed the hair that clung to my damp face, a mixture of mist and sweat. He helped me stand up right, his hands resting on my shoulders. I rested my head on his large chest, regaining the strength I had left, his clove misted scent calming my heartbeat. He was too close for comfort, his breath mingling with mine, both of us giving small pants, the power taking something from both of us.

And for a moment, we just stood there. Finally, I took a step back and looked up at him. His storm cloud eyes searched my face. Concern furrowing his brow, but the moment it was there, it was also gone. A passing thought. His face went back to the slightly bored normal. He took a step back as well, staring at his feet, a wide smile flashing across his face.

"Well, princess, that was your first lesson. And not just a lesson for you, one for me as well." He strode back over to the mantel, retrieving his glass. I stared at him, my mouth gaping open, astonished. *Lesson one?!*

"Let me explain myself. I was curious to see how that explosive thing inside you gets worked up. We need to learn as much as we can about it, to tame it. We have to master it, before it masters you. There are other powers, mingling around in that body of yours. I can sense them. I have noticed a pattern in you; your panic and anxiety is directly linked to the power surge. The more you struggle against it, the more it will rage against you. You need to be in harmony with it."

He paused, looking back out the window, clearing his throat, and slowly made his way back towards me, pacing around me in a circle, his hands clasped behind his back. "I have tricked you, without a trick. I wove no enchantments on you. I overloaded your senses, distracted you, and in your embarrassment, you let yourself drown in it and your emotions took over. I had an idea that the outcome might be another burst of destruction. And I was right."

He stopped in front of me, his massive frame towering over me, his hands still behind his back. "As I said before, you must be trained on self-protection, you must be trained on becoming attuned to your newfound Fae hearing and other assets we are still discovering. Your senses are now heightened. Everything you felt as a "human", you feel tenfold more as half Fae. If someone were to break through that window, right here right now, they would be less forgiving than me, and you would be dead in seconds. But we can fix that. I will give you this though, you held on longer than I expected. I expected an instantaneous explosion, and you did not give me that. It shows me you are trying, you just don't know how. You are afraid of yourself." I stood there, shocked, taking in everything.

He turned from me in one motion, his back towards me and his hand on the door knob. He paused before he opened the door. "I am not afraid of you; that is how *I fit into this*." The last part of the sentence, he used a cheap whiney imitation of my voice, leaving a deafening silence in his wake. I let out an aggravated sigh before leaving the den myself, my stomach grumbling.

CHAPTER SIX

Dinner had left me full and sleepy. I had eaten my weight in roasted duck, garlic bread, rhubarb pie, and strawberry cakes. Bottles and bottles of champagne and elderberry wine had been consumed, and I was as happy as a peach. I had laughed so hard I could cry, Vana next to me, my parents across from me. Rhone was at the end, spinning tales with my father and laughing with him. I found myself getting lost staring at each one of them, my father's words from before ringing in my ears. How this could be the last time we could be able to have a meal like this together, for some time to come.

I didn't want this feeling of wholeness to leave me just yet. My father had instructed us to meet him in the parlor in 15 minutes, and I knew that as soon as I entered the parlor, my life would be intractably changed forever. I decided to make my way to my room. As I walked back to my room, wandering through this grand house I was lucky enough to call home, an incredible sadness hit me. It hung over me like a big black cloud, consuming my thoughts. The dangers that I had seen in the vision, this world being taken down by great and dark power, it just couldn't be. This house, my home, had always been a safe haven for me. As I walked, I ran my hand down the side of the wall, needing to feel connected to something, anything.

My parents had left my room exactly the way I had. The heavy oak door still creaked as I opened it. Stepping onto the plush cream-colored carpet, my room lit up in recognition, the candles on my nightstand sending a dancing glow across the walls. Behind me, the fireplace crackled to life. I sighed in relief. *Home, this is home.*

My four-poster bed was the grand jewel of the room, I had spent hours upon hours draping gauzy white sheets of fabric across the wooden posts to create a wistful canopy. As a child, I believed it would help me keep away the Night Creatures I heard in my dreams. Once in a blue moon, I would have dreams of what I now recognize as The Gap. The gauzy calm atmosphere had always soothed me and helped me slumber peacefully. Vaguely, I wondered if it would keep me safe tonight.

My room smelled of clean sheets, and I smiled, realizing my mother had done up my bed just for me. She had laid the lilac-colored sheets back and put a fresh bouquet of lavender and baby's breath on the dresser. I walked towards it and opened the top drawers, sighing at the fact I saw only a grade 7 camp shirt and a pair of plaid flannel pants. Groaning, I shut the drawer. I thought of my new house. Of all the unpacked boxes and projects I had waiting for me. What would happen to my house? Or the little orange cat I had befriended. The same sadness began to plague my thoughts again. Wandering over to my window, I opened it, letting the cold air rush in and soothe me as I took deep breaths.

A small meow came from down below in the yard. Looking down, I saw my little orange tabby cat friend. "Hey little guy," I called to him. He slinked away, seemingly over being back in my presence. From the other side of the room, I felt the faint snap of magic ripple through the room. Whirling around, I saw a suitcase sitting on my bed that hadn't been there a second before. Cautiously, I made my way towards it. My parents had said they had charmed the house, nothing that meant harm should be able to enter or shadow in. So, this little suitcase must've come from someone inside the house. It was still faintly glowing with the sparkling Fae enchantment as I reached for it. Unzipping it, tucked inside was neatly folded clothes and on top of that, was a note.

"TRY NOT TO INCINERATE THESE. VANA GIVES GREAT DIRECTION -R."

Looking down at the note, I couldn't help but smile. I set it aside and stared down into the suitcase. I was surprised to see all my favorite clothing. Sifting through it, I realized this was no human suitcase, this was an enchanted suitcase. As I sifted through the carefully folded clothes, I realized this suitcase could go on forever, my entire arm getting lost in the bottomless luggage. Every favorite pair of shoes, my hairbrush, even my favorite socks lingered in here. As I reached the last of the items, I blushed as I held up a very revealing nightgown, a corset, along with a pair of thigh highs, and a garter belt. My blush turned into annoyance, deciding to lecture Rhone about raiding my panty drawer later, also noting Vana had something to do with this.

"You shouldn't be leaving your window open, especially at a time like this."

Yelping, I jumped in surprise, the racy garments in my hands flying out of them, adrenaline sending hot chills through me. Immediately, I knew it was Rhone. I could hear the annoyance in his voice as he spoke to me. Turning around, I noticed he was sitting at my writing desk, chair turned towards me, his legs sprawled out as he leaned back, playing with the tiny knick-knacks that littered my desk. I huffed a shriek of frustration and slammed the suitcase shut.

"You could have used the door, and *knocked*, like the polite Fae Male you say you are," I said, annoyed being an understatement.

I glared daggers at him and let out another sigh, crossing my arms tightly.

"I never said I was polite, I said *my kind* practices politeness vigorously," he clarified.

He paused for a moment, staring at me. His eyes were mostly hidden by the dark shadows of the room, but I felt him assessing me. His rigidness from earlier was gone. I suppose the wine and wonderful dinner we had all had together, had eased him out of it.

"Truthfully, I was wondering if your powers might react to being surprised, or sense someone sneaking up on you." He sighed. "I see the only reaction I got was a tiny dangerous little thing shrieking at me. Very unpleasant, you might actually scare an Aunder away." He seemed to laugh at his own joke, a small smile creeping across his face.

In one fluid motion, he stood and locked the window tightly and then shadowed, putting himself in front of me. Staring up at him, he towered over me, his neck at a difficult angle so he could see me clearly. The straight, gracefully sharp plains of his face showed no emotion, and I couldn't help but stare at him, taking in the unnatural beauty and the storm cloud eyes that never settled. His ink-black hair was pulled back, and I found my thoughts lingering as to what it might be like to run my hands through it. *Stop it, you complete idiot. He's not interested, you're not interested. This is just the reaction anyone would get when close to such a massive enchantment. Because that's all he is, a walking enchantment and sparkly Fae tricks.*

"What do you want, Rhone?" I said, my voice coming out in an exasperated sigh.

"Your father is ready for the family meeting," he said with a smirk and shadowed out.

Wrapping my fuzzy robe around myself, I made my way down to the parlor. Vana met me outside the guest room she was staying in. Her long, dreaded curls were piled on top of her head, looking as equally as comfortable as I felt, in her own robe. She shuffled over to me, delighting in the silk slippers my mother had gifted her.

"Loving the slippers Van. They really suit you," I said to her, and we both snickered.

She linked her arm with mine, humming lightly as we slowly made our way down the long halls. I looked at her, my best friend, thinking of her nymph form. Her sparkling fangs flashed through my mind. I wanted so badly to ask her questions, like which form she preferred? Did it hurt phasing in and out? What else could she do with her nymph powers? But I let those questions settle, and simply leaned over and gave her a light kiss on the cheek, savoring this moment of holding her arm in mine, her petal and patchouli scent hugging me gently, as she was.

I couldn't help myself though, and leaned over to her, whispering, "So, do you like, always, sprout flower petals and vines when you sleep... or?"

She shot me a look that said to *go to hel* and then laughed. "Only when I am in need of replenishing, it's my power's way of giving me some much-needed TLC. When it starts to over produce itself, it sprouts up as flower petals and such. It's honestly slightly annoying, so much to clean up" With an eye roll, she waved her hand, her golden bracelets clinking together. "Today, I used a massive amount of my stored powers at one moment. I haven't used an arsenal of power like that in quite some time. In your lessons, you will learn more about all this. I've been keeping my powers finely tuned, but I have not exhausted power like that since the days of being in the wars, often beside Rhone." She shot me a look, a slight smirk on her face. I could tell she was assessing my reaction to his name. "One time, I exhausted so much of my power, I slept for three days, and when I woke up, I was lying in a field of poppies." Her bell-like laugh followed, bouncing off every surface around us, my ears ringing in reaction.

"You fought beside Rhone in *wars*?! Vana... I could never picture you hurting anything, let alone humans and creatures," I said. I was simply astonished; I knew my mouth was basically hanging open.

She looked at me, a sly look creeping across her face, "There are hundreds of years of *Vana* that you don't know, and a hundred versions I have been. I have loved this version of myself a lot, but I would be lying if I said my creature instincts didn't have me itching to break out in full on battle. Or to even spar with someone, to try and best them in a fight."

She laughed a little, looking into the distance, lost in a memory, of doing just that I assumed.

"Jahan was an excellent swordsman, you know. He would always go easy on me, even let me win a few times," she said, looking at me, taking some of my hair and playing with it. I lit up at the thought of Jahan. I had so many things I wanted, no *need* to know about him. About both of them.

Before I could flood Vana with questions, a misty breeze fluttered past us, and Rhone appeared several feet in front of us, his back towards us as he walked the rest of the way towards the parlor, vanishing around the corner into the darkness. At the sight of him, I grew fidgety. Playing with Vana's bracelets, looking anywhere but up. I could feel Vana watching me.

"Stop it, Van, I can *feel* your judgment," I said without looking up at her. I felt her body jiggle in silent laughter as she took a slender cool hand and placed it on mine, calming my fidgety fingers.

"How could I judge you? He's one of the finest specimens in all the realms, that's for sure. I mean, did you see *that butt*?" she said, and she let out a low whistle, only meant for us to hear. We laughed together.

"You know, in the long years I have known Rhone, I've never truly seen him exhaust his power. He's never needed replenishing, even after days of constant battle." She paused for a moment, the silence in the air expectant for a reply, like it was listening to, wanting to know the secret too, but Vana didn't give one.

She looked at me pointedly, and just as I thought she was about to reveal a deep hidden secret, she poked me in the side, right where she knew I was ticklish.

"He'd probably be insatiable in bed." She burst into laughter, while I smacked her hand away and laughed along with her.

As we entered the parlor, our lighthearted moods faded. The air in the room was tight and somber, and I knew it was time to get down to business. We all sat around the fireplace. My mother stood silently with her back to us, her slender figure outlined by the fires blaze. My father paced along the fireplace, hands clasped behind his back. His long blue robe dragging across the plush rug and the crackling of the fire were the only sounds in the room. We were all holding our breath, waiting for our fate as of now, to be handed to us, sealed and delivered. Beside me, Vana sat still as stone. My arm was still intertwined with hers, the blood pulsing through her veins was the only indication she was real. Rhone sat on the other side of me, his arm draped over the arm of the antique velvet couch, but even he sat up right for the most part, his gaze on my father imminent, his eyes promising a forecast of thunderous storms tonight.

"I shall make this as short and sweet as possible because we will all be needing a good night's rest," my father said, stopping next to my mother as she turned towards us, her eyes red and puffy with tears as she looked at me. He took her hand and gave it a little squeeze. She was never good with me leaving her, not even for a day's time. I gave her a little smile, to show her just how alive and well I still was.

"Tomorrow morning, Soren, Rhone and Vana will head for the Royal Fae Highland Courts. There, Rhone and Callum, the Royal Fae Highland Prince of Clan McMurry, will train Soren. The Highland Courts are home to a great library, one with ancient scripts on Seers that even I have not had permission to read, as only Seers may open them. Rhone and Callum are two of the most powerful and deftly trained combat warriors of any of the Royal Faeren Army, and highly trustworthy with Soren's safety. From there, Vana will follow. She will be there to not only protect Soren, but to also become more in touch with her powers again, and to gain as many wild Faeren allies as she can." My father paused for a moment, and then looked to me. "Soren, your mother and I will be heading to the Spellcasters Royal Courts. We will remain in our mirrored forms. At this point, I will never take back my position as High Wizard, not only is it dangerous for all of us involved, but the Spellcasters have a generous and fair High Wizard. Aaren will now find out the truth of you, and from there with his help, we will prepare as if we are preparing for war."

Whatever air was left in the room was suddenly gone. My lungs tightened, as the word *war* hung dangerously above all of our heads like a swinging gauntlet. My father had never mentioned a war before. But Asta had, in the vision, but it had felt so far away then. Now the mention of war so close to home made my nerves flare.

"How can you be so sure of a war?!" I said, the words blurting out of my mouth before I had time to even think about them.

I had not told them about the thread Asta had pulled, how it was darker in color than the rest. The thought came through vividly, as I remembered her reaching out for the dark silver thread, as she fingered it slightly and slipped into a time yet to come, seeing the war my father feared to come. I thought of the way Asta had said each thread had frays, and each fray was a possible ending. At this moment, I knew I needed to go back to The Gap and find that thread. But *how* to get back to The Gap, was the real question.

"Soren." My father's stern voice brought me out of my thought-invoked trance, and immediately, I realized my outburst was not only rude, but uncalled for. I nodded my head, and silently wished I could work these damn powers and redo the last 15 seconds of time. As I internally scolded myself, my father went on.

"I am so sure of a war because of my hundreds of years of life. Creatures are no stranger to following a pattern, and the last time something different, that could cause a threat to their normal course of life appeared, they were killed in droves and vanished to the lands between the realms. As they still are, unprotected, misunderstood, and ruled by a cruel queen who gives them nothing. Is that what you want? To be as the Aunders are, or worse? I am so sure of war because of the visions Asta gifted me, the hundreds of ways this could come to an end, most of them leaving this world desolate." Stories of the beautiful Queen Isleen, her long silken midnight hair dragging on the ground was the last thing you heard, before she stole you away in the dead of night, to feed to her Aunder court. I knew my father was right. Shivers ran up my spine. That story still bothered me, I noticed, as I looked over my shoulder just to make sure Queen Isleen hadn't crawled out of the newspaper to steal us all away.

My father must've realized his point had gotten across, so he continued again, with the mission back in the conversation, "As I was saying, we must gather as many allies as we can, as many in high and low places alike. Allies who will see you as you really are, Soren, despite being an unknown. The best outcome we can hope for is that we push for allies and don't need them for violent wars, but get to keep them as friends for this lifetime. In one month's time, we will all see each other again, at the High Wizard Aaren's wedding. This wedding is the event of the century. All creature courts will be in attendance, which is exactly what we need. The creature world is vast, it will be easy to cover your identity as some unknown tribal Royal Faeren lover that Rhone picked up on one of his battles. Your mother believes the Huran tribe of The Sands are reclusive enough. This is also handy because the Huran tribe is loosely included in the Highland Court; Prince Callum's partnership in this will help dissuade questions. They also match your coloring well. Rhone spent a short time with them years ago, and has passed through their settlement enough to be able to teach you things of the Huran that will make you seem legit." I looked to Rhone quickly, who made no reaction to this besides simply shaking his head in agreement.

My father continued, "You need to be seen, even if your identity is hidden for now. To be seen is to be believed."

He sighed heavily, letting his stoic and confident demeanor slip. For a moment, he let his shoulders slump, his eyes showing the hours of sleep he had lost in the past week. He brought a hand to his face, rubbing his eyes. I realized suddenly, it wasn't just a week of sleep he had lost, but the hundreds of years weighing on his shoulders. I found myself wondering how many of those he had gotten to have stress free, how many were happy years? I silently hoped the years of raising me, away from his beloved son, away from his beloved kingdom, were happy ones. Slowly, I got up and walked toward him. I placed my small hands on his shoulders, and brought myself to my tip toes, so I could hug him tight.

"Dad, we will make it through this, we will find strong alliances, I will train hard, and we will make it. I promise," I said.

He hugged me in return, and I felt my mothers' cool hand on my back, rubbing in a soothing rhythmic pattern. With that, my father took a seat, all his energy seemingly lost to tomorrow's troubles, big shoulders slumping over.

My mother stood next to me and took my hand. Her lyrical voice brightened the room as she began to speak, "Traveling will pose as somewhat of a nuisance, but I believe we have found our way around that. Everyone has new clearance passports. Your realm visas will now be able to never expire, given the fact that whatever dates you need to be on there, will magically appear." The pride on her face was evident. Her and father had perfected the intermingling of human inventions with Spellcasters magic seamlessly, like no one else ever had and probably ever would.

"On that note, I believe we can wait for goodbyes until the morning. You all know I hate them." She let out a small laugh, and I laughed too. She was not good with goodbyes at all, always crying her eyes out. My sweet mother. I gave her a firm hug, one I didn't want to release from, but I could feel the exhaustion of today finally seeping into my bones. I kissed her cheek and bent down to give my father a kiss on the forehead. Slowly, I made my way to my room, saying goodnight to no one else. It wasn't until I had collapsed into my bed, already half asleep, did I realize how eerily silent Rhone had been the entire meeting, and how nice it might be to hear his voice again before I fell asleep. My nightmares made for a fitful sleep.

MY HEART WAS POUNDING through my chest, and all I could hear was explosions all around me. I was running as fast as I could, my feet hitting the floor in painful thuds. Looking around me, I realized I was running down a castle hall, the high stone walls crumbling around me.

I heard a voice then, calling me from down the hall, "Run faster my child", a deep male voice called. Suddenly, I was no longer in a crumbling castle, I was running through a battlefield, my friends and family slain all around me.

"Keep running, sweet child," Although this time, it was not Jahan's voice, but a woman's. Her face out of focus, her features unrecognizable. She was standing in front of me, as the piles of bodies grew, their blood seeping into the soft soil around me, the soft soil that was covered in beautiful poppies, Vana's poppies. I choked back a cry of pain and sorrow as I saw Vana's body laid crippled in an impossible position, her petals decaying next to her equally decaying body. The woman grabbed me then, her long hair flashing from silver to black in the moonlight, "I will keep killing you. Every night. Until I can track you down by the reek of your anguish. I will find you, I will find your hiding places'

No one saved me in this dream.

No one was coming for me.

She took her slender ice-cold hand and gently cradled my face, staring into my eyes. She slid her hand down my face, cupping my jaw between her fingers. Her grip instantly became excruciatingly painful, and it was her long talon-like fingernails I felt next, piercing through my skin, blood quickly filling my mouth, rushing down my throat, choking me, flooding my lungs. She lifted her other hand, black glittering magic pulsing in her palm. Gently she laid her cool hand against my chest, her palm flat against my breast bone. And then, with too much ease, I felt as she thrust her palm forward, her talons slicing into my heart as she reached inside me. She ripped it from me, and I gargled out a gasp of pain.

I looked down and there was my still-beating heart, which faded from a crimson red, to a shimmering black. Silver threads weaving in and out of it. It was black as her magic. A single golden thread was tied around it, glowing brightly. The golden thread jutted off and disappeared into the abyss, swaying gently.

Her eyebrows shot up, "You never cease to be such a source of amazement." She clenched it again, the soft tissue of my heart caving under the pressure, its rhythmic beats stuttering.

"Soren.... Soren." Rhone's voice called from behind me, or maybe from all around me. I couldn't tell, the pain was too real, it was flooding my senses. I could feel his presence getting closer and closer. The woman's moon white face brightened at the sound of his voice. Black tendrils of her magic erupted from the ground, wrapping around me like vines trying to suffocate anything else in its garden.

"Soren, I'm coming." It was Rhone again, but his voice was farther away, almost a whisper. The haunting woman laughed, seeing the hope in my eyes as I saw his form shadow in behind her.

That was when she broke my neck.

The blackness of death tastes like copper and ash.

The crack felt like lightning.

IT WAS my own screams that woke me up then, flinging my body upward, gasping for breath. Coughing wracked through my body. My hands were blazing, and the smell of burning cloth wrapped itself around me. The air around me was heavy with thick clouds of glittering ash. I could still feel my sheets around me, but I didn't *feel* like I was in my room, in the real world. Maybe it was the ash clouds surrounding me, blinding me and confusing dreams from reality. I heard my door creak open then, and I silenced myself. Using my new Fae hearing, I heard no footsteps, no breathing, no heart beats. My own heartbeat began to race. Was it just the wind blowing my door open? But I swore I had shut it all the way.

The woman's blurred face appeared in front of me suddenly, her eyes glowing through the smoke. She laughed. "I told you, I'd track that wretched smell of fear." Then she reached out her long boney fingers, her black talons shining in the silver glow. I threw myself back, kicking my legs as hard as I could, screaming.

My foot hit something solid, and I heard a low grunt from the recipient. I flung myself off the bed, rolling onto the floor. The smoke was thinning, but I still couldn't see much of anything. I ran towards the window, but a hand caught my arm. I screamed out, but this time, not a scream of fear or pain, a scream of defiance. I would not be torn down again. I flung my hand up, willing it to open the window. To my surprise, it worked, but a little too much. The glass shattered, but cold night air surged in, the shimmering ash rushing out in waves.

"Soren... It's just me. I... just... heard your screams. I had to check on you." Rhone's voice cut through the dreamy haze I was finally seeming to wake up from. He grabbed my hand then, tugging me forward. One hand in his, the other hand gripped the window pain, the wood groaning and splintering under my new strength.

"It was just a nightmare. Everything is okay. It's okay." He came closer, his voice hushed and soothing as I let him gather me in his arms.

I let him because I was too busy panting. Too busy still thinking of my dream, of Queen Isleen's face. Of her eyes. Looking up at Rhone, I looked up into the same eyes, except his were kind. A calm storm, at the moment. He leaned down, and took my head in his hands, smoothing back my hair. He hid his head in my neck then. A gesture so swift and intimate, I had no idea what to do, I was simply surprised by his suddenly gentle demeanor. I let myself lean into it, somehow. Into his soft lips and his sickly sweet hot breath.

No, no, no, no, no. I know this taste, the honey sweet tongue. This is not Rhone.

I shoved him back with all my strength. He stumbled, but not enough. My eyes began adjusting as his form came into view, a form I knew too well. His soft waves flung forward, but in one stealth movement he was standing up right again, one hand smoothing his hair back.

Willem. Just seeing his face made me nauseous. My head spun with memories of our last encounter.

"You're getting stronger, Soren. I'm impressed." He took a step forward, reaching his hand out to me. It wasn't his devilish grin that stared back at me, but the face of the young man I had fallen in love with. He was in anguish; he was exhausted and looked confused. He had so many masks, and I stared at him a moment longer, trying to discern which one was real. I found myself getting lost in memories, the years of waking up next to that face. My years of looking across the car at that face as we laughed together, of holding those hands....

His voice was soft and hoarse as he began to talk, "I'm sorry I had to come find you here. But we really must go now. She's waiting, and wants you alive. She's extremely interested in your *abilities*. But she's getting immensely impatient. My control here is lost. I tried to wave this off as long as I could..." He took another step forward as I took another step back, ramming into my side table. The surprise of it snapped me out of my daydream of what used to be. I heard banging at my door, it was splintering with every thud.

Willem looked back at the door and shook his head. "Don't worry about them, my shield is much stronger than Rhone's."

Gods, I was tired of this. Tired of feeling useless, tired of this Willem who wasn't even real, a wild creation, he didn't even know who he was himself. It was written all over his face. Tired of this fear, tired of this pain. I just wanted it to end.

And that's when it happened. I willed my powers to build, and they did. I raised my hand, begging every ounce of power I had to meet me there. Bursting from my palm, blinding silver light shot at Willem, weaving in and out of his limbs, around his neck, forming silver ropes. Instinctively, I closed my hand into a fist, and yanked back. I watched in awe of myself as he lurched forward, falling to his knees and struggling as the ropes twisted and tightened. I truly was gaping at the power I had unleashed, power I didn't understand. At the silver glittering ropes of power, *my power* wrapped around his body, and I could hear the silent whisper of my power begging to slice through him. It was his strangled screams that brought me back. Instantly I realized what I had done. Could I kill him?

The silver ropes dissipated into the air around us. My concentration had wavered, and my power had buried itself back into my body. Willem grabbed at his throat, flying forward and gasping for air. Braided glittering welts snaked along his neck, shoulders and wrists. I could've done it, I could've killed him, I could've let those shimmering ropes dismember him. Getting to his feet, Willem stumbled forward, his strength building fast.

"You *BITCH,*" he said. Reaching behind his back, he grabbed his dagger.

In that moment, Willem had let down his shield long enough that Rhone slammed through the thin shield that still lingered. Dark storm clouds rushed in to engulf the room. The thunder was a deafening rumble that rattled me to my bones, the dark gray shrouded mist already threatening my vision. Rhone wasted no time; he shadowed in between Willem and I. Taking the advantage of surprise, Rhone instantly slammed his shoulder into Willem's face, bones cracking, thick crimson blood gushing down his face, leaving Willem stumbling backwards, grunting and cussing, trying to regain his footing. In one swift movement, Rhone's dagger was out, and I watched as Rhone debilitated Willem in a matter of seconds. In one fluid movement, Rhone slammed himself down on his knees, using his incredible force to slide behind Willem, using his dagger to slice through the back side of each of Willem's knees.

Willem didn't have a chance to regain control, his entire body crumpling to the ground in a sickening thud, an all too human groan of pain escaping him. The blood pooling around his limp body was the last thing I saw before Rhone's body collided with mine.

"Are you hurt?" He surveyed me quickly, accounting for each limb, and finally decided that was good enough for him. He didn't wait for me to answer before he grabbed my hand.

"Ya know, only his shield is better than mine," I heard him grumble before we dissipated into mist, shadowing away.

S hadowing felt different this time. I could feel bits of myself still lingering in my bedroom, bits of myself still hovering miles above the earth, trying to catch up. It left me feeling dizzy, disoriented, nauseous. I was still living outside my own body when Rhone had led me to a chair and sat me down. His voice was muffled as he asked me something I couldn't comprehend. Sluggishly, my lead-lined gaze finally met his.

"I made up this tonic for you, you need to drink it. It will help with the shadowlag," His voice sounded like it was in a tunnel.

"Soren, take ahold of the glass, please," he urged me. I felt his rough hands wrap around mine, trying to make me grip the cup. It was his physical touch that truly zapped me out of my lethargic state.

I took the cup from his hand and chugged the tonic. Grimacing at the awful taste, the bitter tang of lemon rind and definitely something rotten coated my throat.

"Eck, what is this shit?" I said, letting my disgust be known.

He merely side-eyed me. Tilting his head slightly as if trying to figure out where I get the nerve, he said, "It's a tonic, made of questionable things and a bit of Fae magic. It was created to help soldiers in the Hundreds Year War to get over their shadowlag, so they could be ready for battle at any moment."

Almost instantly, my vision became clear again, noises around me settling to a normal range, like my head was finally above water. Looking around, the sluggish motion of my mind and movement faded. I realized I was in someone's kitchen, sitting on a soft black leather bar stool.

"Where are we? Is this your home?" I asked. He only nodded his head yes. I could tell he wasn't going to elaborate on the subject of *home*. I continued to let my eyes wonder. The kitchen was small but sleek and expensive looking. Black marble counters that matched the black marble floors. They gleamed under the hanging orbs of light that floated low from the high ceilings. This was a state-of-the-art kitchen, but the appliances looked like they had never been used. They came alive, noticing our presence, and sent a blue glow across the room.

"Do my parents and Vana know where we have gone?" I asked, hoping my home was still standing, hoping my parents and Vana were okay.

"Not yet, but I'm sure your father has a good idea. I will try and make sure we get some sort of untracked contact with them within the next few days. For now we need to worry about lying low, there will be no leaving," He said, the finality in his words leaving me uneasy. I decidedly ignored him, not having the energy to argue the fact he was essentially holding me hostage. Although I'm not sure I would entirely mind being his captive.

I turned back to Rhone and frowned, changing the subject before I let myself get too worked up. "Why did the shadowlag happen this time? I didn't get it before," I asked, forgetting my manners and wiping my mouth with the back of my hand, setting the glass down.

Picking up the empty glass from my hand, he answered the question matter-of-factly, "In the Human Realm, we shadowed only about 10 miles. We just shadowed about 5,000 miles, cutting through many realm borders, which is highly dangerous. I don't recommend trying that alone, by the way. Also, your power was slightly depleted. When your power is running low, shadowing has harsher effects. A mixture of both affected you."

He looked at me for a second longer before he continued. "Which is precisely why we need to start your training soon, like yesterday, soon. So you can use your powers smarter, not harder." His eyes slid over me, looking displeased at everything he saw. I scowled at him in return, letting him know I was equally as displeased.

I knew what he saw before I looked down myself. I knew I was a mess, not just physically but I could feel the immense exhaustion slamming into me. I knew I had blood splattered on my clothes, Willem's blood this time, not mine. The weight of what we had just shadowed out of bogged down on me suddenly. I looked back up at Rhone. He was casually leaning back against a black marble countertop, his arms crossed, and the never changing look of disdain lingered on his face. Blood was smeared across his unnervingly handsome face, his stormy eyes seeming to glow in the dim room. He was in a tight black long sleeve shirt that was reinforced with Fae magic that glinted in the low light. It was tucked into black glinting pants, and those same leather boots.

I had heard of the Fae military armor, had even seen pictures in the Realms Time, but had never seen anything quite like this. It was so stealthy and sleek looking, and not for just any foot soldier. Strapped to his back with a leather sling were twin swords, forming an X across his back. That same dagger, that I had minutes ago watched slice through the back of Willem's knees, was strapped to his calf, the blood still shining. Crimson droplets splattered across his chest, and spray patterns adorned his arms. He looked as calm and calculated as anyone ever could with blood decorating their entire body. Like a painter who had just finished their masterpiece, the paint droplets a hazard of doing what they love.

We existed there silently for a moment; the only noise was him wiping Willem's blood off of his dagger. His tattooed fingers worked in slow rhythmic motions, polishing the expensive looking blade. I knew then that this empty moment was him letting me process what just happened. Process that I was now 5,000 miles away, process the blood that now adorned us. I could not simply exist anymore; that was what I processed while we stared silently at each other.

I stood suddenly– a motion I, myself, was startled at. With my back straight, I looked Rhone right in the eye. "I would like to start training now."

He stared at me a breath longer, his eyebrows raising slightly in surprise, the corner of his mouth quirking up in that mischievous way I was starting to get used to. *Shit, what have I just gotten myself into*. In a motion so quick my human eyes wouldn't have been able to register, his dagger was flying at me. I twisted my body out of the way, begging the dagger not to find its target, and it never did. The blade had halted in its tracks, hanging in midair. A substantial weight seemed to settle around us, thick in the air like the cobwebs from The Gap.

Glimmering threads began peeling from the blade, floating away into the frozen surroundings of the kitchen. Were my eyes playing tricks on me? Behind the knife, my vision focused on Rhone, who was stuck on the freeze-frame also, the same glimmering light catching threads peeling from his form like embers from a burning log. I backed up, noticing the particles in the air clung to me like static, crackling with my movement. *Oh shit, oh no. What the fu–*

And just like that, the blade clattered to the ground.

Rhone's body lurched forward ever so slightly, his hand catching the kitchen counter. He stared up at me stunned. He straightened, and let out a slow whistle. "Now *that* is something I have never witnessed in all my years of life."

I couldn't tear my eyes away from the dagger, and when I did, Rhone was staring at me, his storm cloud eyes boring into me. "No wonder you were so heavily spellbound."

I stared at him, completely breathless, what had I just done?

Wait a minute, are we going to totally ignore the fact he just threw a dagger *at me?!*

Throwing my hands up, I let out a frustrated sigh. "Uhm, I'm sorry, but what was your plan if I *hadn't* just done whatever it is I did?!" I shouted, my voice rising with every word, anger lining them. He didn't deign me with a response. He simply shrugged his shoulders, making my blood boil even more.

"I believe we can make note of this event. And also the fact that when you begin to question yourself, your power has a habit of reverting back into you." He paused, evaluating me for a moment. "There is not one thing boring about you Soren, I'll give you that." He smirked. "And you're seemingly pretty immortal now. I am sure you would've healed in a matter of hours," he said with a shrug.

Unfolding his arms, he sauntered towards me, and stopped, he bent down and picked up the knife, returning it to its rightful spot on his calf. In a flourish of his tattooed hand, *a too dramatic and conceited flourish if you ask me*, a perfectly spherical droplet of water appeared in front of me.

"Use that to wash your hands and face off," he said, "Dried blood doesn't suit you."

"Whatever, Grandpa," I said, shooting daggers at him, and came very close to sticking my tongue out for good measure.

"Follow me," he said, ignoring my comment about his age.

Doing as he said, and begrudgingly fascinated, I reached out for the water. Running it over my hands, neck and face, the water cleansing me. I watched as the droplets absorbed the blood, instead of smearing it and leaving streaks. As it fell to the ground, it transformed into fine mist particles, dissipating away. I was not sure when magic would ever stop being so entrancing to me. I raced to catch up with Rhone, his long stride carrying him much farther than my tiny legs could.

Walking through the dark house, I observed no family pictures on the walls, just marvelous paintings. Some were battle scenes, others were serene landscapes, but no humans or creatures to be seen. The design of the house was decidedly brutal, with an elegant flare, the entire east wall of the house was the organic mountainside. We passed a living room that looked hardly lived in. A simple black leather couch and matching chair sat atop a black shag rug, and gleaming dark stone floors. The fireplace lit up as we walked by, showing the rest of the room to me. Minimalist style, no TV adorned the walls, but a vintage record player sat in the corner, well taken care of. Tall bookcases were framed by gorgeous floor to ceiling windows. Through them I could see the sunrise beginning to dance through the fog with the early morning stars. The all too familiar scent of fresh rain and cloves danced around, making everything feel eerily familiar.

We continued through the house, passing a few closed doors through a long hallway, and finally walked into a large open room. It was basically empty, black leather padded mats lined the floor, and mahogany cabinets covered the only wall without windows. Leather and the slight smell of sweat hung in the air, a strangely intoxicating scent. The other two walls were lined with the same towering windows as the living room, and looking out of them, my breath caught. The early spills of sunrise shone across glittering pale pink mountain caps.

"The Ostorous Mountains," I breathed, my voice coming out in a whisper. Soft fog clung to the mountain tops, the mist shone in midair. The sun seemed to be showing off, setting the pink mountains aglow. The room around me turned hazy hues of pink and gold with the sunrise, painting the gray walls and black marble floor in a warm dewy glow. I walked towards the windows, unable to stop myself, overtaken by the beauty that sprawled before me, a beauty I never in a million years thought I would witness.

"If you're afraid of heights, do not look down," Rhone said, his rough voice reverberating off me, making me hyper aware of how alarmingly close he was standing to me, looking out the window as well. Instinctively, I let my gaze drop, and realized what he meant. This house was built into the side of a mountain, the room we stood in hanging over the edge, nothing but open air lay under us, the floor of the mountain forest miles below.

"When you asked me earlier if this was my home, I suppose it is. It's the closest thing to 'mine' I have ever had. When I built this, I wanted no one to know of it. It was my secret, my own sanctuary, somewhere to be safe and this room was the first room I built." I stood there for a second, in awe of not only the view, but also him. That was the closest to opening up he had come to since we had met. How could this Royal Faeren warrior, who towered over most, and whose training made him a walking deadly weapon, not feel safe? The hard planes of his face seemed to bask in the sunrise shining through the windows, softening just ever so slightly. His storm cloud eyes nothing but a calm foggy highland morning.

I desperately wanted to know more; he was like an ancient work of art himself. I was itching to get samples, to run tests, to know all the things he knew, to know all the places he'd been. But I knew now was not the time. He continued to pensively look out the window toward the mountains for a moment, seemingly lost in thought.

He turned away from me then, clearing his throat. "This is where we will train. Behind those cabinet doors is every kind of weapon you could imagine. You will train with all of them, until we find your niche. We will train hard, physically and mentally. Hours upon hours a day, until you can fight, until you can control that destructive power, and until you trust yourself."

He walked over to the wall of cabinets and pushed a button; the cabinet doors slowly opened with a soft click. Yellow back lights from the cabinets lit up, and sure enough knives of all sizes, colors, and shapes appeared. Swords and weapons I didn't even recognize. I gulped, the hair on my arms standing up. Those weapons, those very real and deadly weapons, were what I would be yielding. To protect myself and others I loved. I looked towards Rhone, unable to hide my nerves from him, my face an open book.

"Ah yes, I figured this would garner that kind of reaction from you. And truly, right now I welcome it." The cabinet doors clicked shut. "I have lost many hours of sleep over the past few days, and I'll need my patience tomorrow," he said, his face impassive, his tone bland. He brushed past me then, giving a head nod to follow him down the hallway.

Rhone stopped in front of a closed door, and with his back towards me, he said, "This is where you can sleep. You have a private bathroom and plenty of room for clothing." He opened the door and stepped aside, giving me room to pass. Walking into the room, the Fae orb lights flickered to life. It was a simple room, a king size bed with a black comforter and a navy-blue throw blanket at the bottom. An expensive black fur rug laid under my feet. It was so soft under my feet, I could've curled up in a ball right there and fallen fast asleep. The fireplace roared to life, and the curtains shut themselves, sensing my exhaustion I guessed. I turned around and watched Rhone already leaving the room, and stopped him.

"Rhone.." I said, I knew it came out like I was afraid to even speak his name.

"Yes, Soren." He paused in the doorway, obviously one specially made for him because he didn't have to duck in it.

"I think I know how Willem broke through the charm surrounding my parents house," I said, and Rhone's eyebrow flew up.

"And how do you figure, little terror?" he said, and I rolled my eyes at his newest nickname for me.

"When I was younger, I'd stay up all night reading my father's journals, his research he had done. One of the most formidable powers a Fae can have is being a Miragen, a self-illusionist. I have a theory that he slipped through the charm unnoticed because he was disguised as the orange stray cat that I had taken under my wing. I think he had been watching me and knew that was the only way he could trick the charm, by being a creature I had come to trust and care for." I paused for a moment, considering if I should give away this next tidbit of information. "Also, when I awoke from my nightmare, it was you I saw first to come to comfort me. Your face appeared first, and then you vanished and Willem's face appeared in its place."

Rhone nodded his head, his face growing dark. "Mira-gen's are rare, but this is a very good insight. I've been waiting for that brilliant mind to peak its head around all the anxiety and terrifying explosions."

The compliment floored me. Rarely was I complimented on my brains rather than my beauty; it was so refreshing that I almost forgave how roundabout the compliment actually was.

Rhone was about to turn and leave, but before he could, and before I lost my nerve, I asked, "Is Willem dead?" The words came out sudden and small, making me feel small in return.

There was silence in the room for a moment, the only sound the popping of the wood in the fireplace.

"Do you want him to be?" was his simple response. The question frightened me more than I thought the answer would've. I contemplated it for a moment, replaying memories in my head, memories that no longer made me feel warm and loved. They made me feel sick actually, like they were digging a rotten hole into my soul. Confusion tugged at me, for only a split second I could think about how I loved him, before those thoughts would splinter into this new disdain for him.

"Yes, I think I do," I replied, fidgeting with the hem of my night shirt that still had blood stains.

"It is your kill, Soren, not mine," he said, his voice flat and hard. His answer shocked me. *My kill?!* He could see the confusion on my face. "So no, unfortunately he is not, but I will tell you this, it was hard to hold myself back from doing just that."

He added, "In the world of creatures Soren, it is beautiful and magical... but also violent and brutal. A fate I would not wish on anyone. In the Fae culture, to take a kill like this one, how he hurt you... is highly disrespectful. It would label you, Soren, as a coward for letting someone take that from you. It is an old tradition, to look at it that way, but I am an old creature and sometimes traditions stick."

His gaze on me became more intense. "Do not ever mistake a high-ranking creature to be a gentle one. They got there from their cruel deeds, the lives they've taken, the hurt they've bore onto others. Humans are the only exception, along with some Wizards. You are neither," he said, his tone sharp and unforgiving.

"You were better off staying human; you were lucky for the time you were allowed to pretend," was the last thing he said before he shadowed out of the room.

I tried not to think about his words too much as I peeled off the stained nightgown and crawled into bed. I welcomed the cool sheets against my bare skin, too exhausted to care that I hadn't showered.

CHAPTER

EIGHT

T he entire next day was the most grueling of my life. Rhone had woken me up by storming into the room, the lights flickering on and throwing training gear on top of me.

"Get up, sunshine. We have a lot of work to do today," he said, his voice booming in effort to get me moving. Rolling over, I made sure to keep the sheets covering me, barely remembering in time I had slept naked last night. *Gods he literally must've been born with* no *manners.* Sleepily I sat up, and snatched the clothing up, glaring at him. He stared back at me for a moment, those gray eyes unwavering, his mood glooming up the room the longer he stood in it.

"Fine, okay, I'm up. Get out," I said, my voice sounding as groggy as I felt.

I shooed him and threw the clothes off the bed at him as he shadowed out of the room. I rolled out of bed, realizing not even the sun was up yet and was pleasantly surprised to see a piping hot mug of coffee on my bedside table, steam still rolling off the top of it. Staring down at my training clothes, I had no idea what to think. They were the same style as Rhone's, a matching set of black shimmering long sleeve shirt and pants. Picking them up, I held the shirt in front of me. It looked incredibly too small, and I silently wondered if my left boob would even fit in this thing. I gave it a yank, and it didn't give at any rate. I groaned internally, *It really is too early for this shit*, and began to tug it over my head. The shirt took on a life of its own, sliding down my body, the warm hum of magic shivering against my skin. I looked down amazed, the shirt formed to my body perfectly, the reinforced armor glimmering in the fire light. It was surprisingly comfortable too, breathable and felt as soft as my worn t-shirt I loved to sleep in. *and wow, did my boobs look* great *in this,* I thought to myself.

"I'm losing patience out here", Rhone's voice called from the hall, startling me.

I let out an aggravated sigh, my cheeks burning red, not sure if I should be embarrassed to be caught, or disturbed by how he might know what I was doing. Stomping into my pants, I yanked on the leather boots that could've been the much smaller twin to Rhone's pair. I quickly pulled my hair back into a sleek, tight and high ponytail, and swung open the door, a scowl sure to be on my face.

There he was, towering over me, arms crossed, hair back in a tight bun that hung low at the nape of his neck. He didn't wear the same leathers he had given me; he looked like any regular guy on his way to the gym. He wore a gray T-shirt with the sleeves cut off, showing off his muscular arms, along with sweat shorts and tennis shoes. To my surprise, I noticed that I had been correct; his entire left side of his body was covered in black tattoos, dividing his body into two stark contrasts with a clean black line. Black tattoos peaked out the left side of his cut off tank, and his left leg didn't have a single blank spot left. From the look of his attire, I could tell he was not expecting much from me today. His gray eyes glowed in the dim hallway, and his mood seemed foul.

"Wow. Someone woke up on the wrong side of the bed this morning," I said and shoved passed him, ready to get this nightmare over with. Rhone shadowed away, mist slamming into my back, letting me know he was ready to be done with this also.

Rhone was in the training room before I was, his back to the door, selecting several different daggers from the wall of death.

"You would be incredibly more efficient if you used all that attitude and fused it into something more important like gaining the ability to shadow," he snapped, his back still towards me. I just stared back at him, already mentally exhausted and it had only been 15 minutes.

Stepping forward, Rhone handed me two four-inch daggers. I grasped them in my tiny hands, staring at their dark black metal, unease creeping into me.

"First rule, do not fear the weapon you are holding. That is the only way you will hurt yourself with it," he said, a slight snicker in his voice.

He stepped closer. "There are two ways to hold a dagger, either down, with the blade pressing against your forearm, for downward strikes, or diagonally across your palm, allowing the blade to jut outward from your gripped hand. Like this." Gently, Rhone took each dagger and placed them in my hands like so, each one with a different style of holding.

"Learning to handle a dagger is an imperative skill in close range fighting. You always want to be the first and hardest to attack. Do not ever hesitate while yielding a dagger. You are too close to your competitor, and they will kill you if you hesitate, even for just a second. Do you understand? Hesitation equals death," he repeated, waiting for me to nod, before continuing. "While not in your hand, your dagger should be kept on your body, in close range to your hands, easily accessible."

"Follow my lead," he said, and placed his daggers, twins of mine, in their leather straps along his body, one on his calf, one along his hip. I did the same, immediately recognizing the point of this. I needed to know how it felt as they slid in and out of the leather straps, smoothly, no hitching. The intricate flow of motions like waves on an ocean bank, he twisted his body around, and suddenly his daggers were out and he was in a fighting stance, waiting to attack. He swayed back and forth, his body ready to lurch at any second. He stared at me, challenging me to do the same. I held my stance the same as he had, and focusing all my attention, I crouched down and flung out my daggers, letting my body sway like wheat in the wind like Rhone. I prayed to the Gods I didn't look like an idiot.

We did these several more times; each time my half-breed body caught on quicker, my movements swiftly becoming second nature. He quickly ran through the motions with me, how to punch with a dagger enclosed in your hand, several different ways to break a choke hold, how to disarm someone in one swift movement. We practiced these again and again, sweat dripping off every inch of my body, my breath growing tighter. We danced on the floor together, a warrior's dance.

"Okay, stand still for a moment, and sheath your weapons." Rhone instructed, and I did so immediately, the authority in his voice making me forget how much I usually urged to defy him. Putting his daggers back in their holsters, he quickly wiped the dripping sweat from his forehead with the hem of his T-shirt, showcasing his just as sweaty and muscular torso. *Mother of gods, fea men are not built like human men.* I tried to look away and found myself just looking even harder. I snapped my eyes to the blank wall behind him, reminding myself why I was here, and to stare at Rhone's body was not it.

"Eyes here, Soren" he said, sounding exasperated. "I need you to focus with me, stare into my eyes." Rhone came closer, placing his massive hands on my shoulders, adding pressure. "I need you to be here, be present and only present to this moment. Listen to your surroundings, throw your hearing across the world as far as it can go."

And I did. Letting his eyes be my focal point, I let my Fae ears tune into the world around me. I could hear the sound of the snow falling, birds chirping, a stream that ran off the side of the mountain trickling a mile away. Twigs breaking as a deer ran across the forest floor in a clearing nearby.

The lightning storm in his eyes was calm, a foggy morning. Not distracting in the way I assumed they would be, and have been before, but soothing, helpful in this task.

"Okay, now close your eyes, and reel it in. Try using your selective hearing; this is what you will need during combat. The ability to assess precisely how far your competitor is away from you, and what move he will make next, is extremely important. It is imperative that you harness this; you need to be listening for every bodily movement," he said, and I closed my eyes, sucking in a long deep breath, trying my hardest to *reel it in*, so to say.

I let my focus rest in this room, allowing my senses to cling onto the living breathing elements around me. Rhone's heartbeat came first, a pounding thud mimicking my own.

"Okay, now use that, and try and trigger your foresight. Think of it as your own version of echolocation used by bats and other animals." I let out a snort, and Rhone pinched the back of my neck.

"Focus," he snarled through his teeth, not wanting to put up with any of my shit. I rolled my eyes, but quickly gained back focus. And it was just like that, I realized I was using my foresight. As quickly as that thought slipped through my mind, Rhone left my side.

"About how far away am I from you?" he said, I threw out my foresight like a fishing net and it pinged off of him.

"About twenty feet," I said, truly astonished at this ability.

"Perfect, open your eyes," he said. As I did, I noticed he had changed into his fighting gear.

"Alright, enough kiddie pool time. I can see how much your body has changed just overnight; your Fae side is shining through. This shouldn't be too much of a workout for you," Rhone said.

That much he was right about; this morning my body *felt* different. I felt stronger, I looked leaner, and I could feel the strong muscles tensing and releasing effortlessly as I moved my body to and fro like a fighter in the ring, daggers drawn.

Without warning, Rhone charged at me, daggers enclosed in his closed fists. I sprang to the side, surprised by my speed and agility. My Fae reflexes sensed his next move, I slid back and blocked his blow to the side without a second thought.

And there it was, a millisecond between the upper hand and death, this is what he meant. My brain was scrambled, I had so many questions, too much to analyze. *What do I do next, where do I hit next, are his sides or his ankles weakest?* I could feel that second slipping by, the triumph of blocking his blow fading as I let my questions override instinct. Rhone took the advantage, rushing me, his right hand, dagger ready, rammed into my side, the hilt of his dagger sending vibrations through my ribcage, knocking the wind out of me. He stood there for a second, his strong, sweat-slicked arms wrapped around me, and I realized he was letting me catch my breath before his next assault.

No, I think not. My lungs still burning, ribs still singing, I took his kindness and turned it on him. Using all my strength, I broke free of his hold, then I backed up and threw my elbow into his jaw. His face lit up in shock, a tiny trickle of blood already forming across the side of his jaw. Taking advantage of the shock of that blow, I surprised him with another blow to the ribs, the twin of the one he had given me, but before the hilt could meet its mark, his strong hand caught my wrist.

"I didn't know you were ready for hand to hand combat Soren," he said, panting, blood running down his chin.

He threw my wrist away, shoving me back and tossed his

daggers to the side. I did the same, even though I knew I didn't stand a chance. We ran towards each other, our bodies slamming together. He swung at me, a low blow aimed for my side.

Must be his signature move, duly noted. And as soon as I thought I knew what he was up to, his right arm came around for a choke hold, and I had no idea what move to dig out next. He kicked his heel under my foot, and I came down with a hard thud. Before I knew it, he had me pinned to the mats on my back, his massive body straddling mine, a strong arm stretched across my rib cage, holding me in place. He looked down at me, his black hair curling slightly from the sweat that dripped off his face. It had literally been months since anyone had been so close to me, both of us panting, and I could tell my body wanted to answer the closeness of this encounter. I shoved the thought down, the thought of him on top of my panting for *different* reasons. I swore I could feel his body react to mine, the tightening and softening of all the *right* areas.

Rhone broke the silence first, "Never. Ever. Challenge a competitor to anything but what you have in your hands at the beginning of the fight. You never know what they will best you at, and at this very moment, most people best you in every form of combat. And the fact you didn't use your foresight, disappointing indeed. The entire objective of this training session was to get you to instinctively use your foresight, without even trying," he said, shaking his head, still sounding slightly winded from our training.

He ran his eyes across me then, from my eyes to my lips, settling on the swell of my breasts under my armor, which his arm still draped under the cups. Something just clicked in me then, *Who says this battle is over? Because he tackled me, because he said so? Ha, right.*

I lifted my head up, not taking my eyes off his, and leaned in as close as I could, letting my lips graze his ear, and I lingered for a moment. He let me, and that made me realize I *had* him. His body tensed up and his breathing hitched as my lips met his ear and grazed down the side of his jaw. I could feel his pulse quicken as my lips traveled down his sweat-slicked neck. His clenched fist softened, and he slowly began to roam my body. His hand found my breasts. It was my turn to quiver, letting out a shaky breath as his thumb grazed my hard peak. *Traitors, giving away our secret.* I scowled at my own body, enjoying this way too much.

"Who said I was done?" I whispered, lips brushing his neck before I sealed it with a kiss, sucking softly. I lifted my knee and served a death blow to his crotch, trying to ignore the considerably hard length I felt pressing against me. Every man has a weakness and I gave him his. Rhone rolled off of me, groaning and cursing like I would've never thought I could've ever managed. I stood up gingerly, letting him gaze at my perfect round ass as it swayed out of the training room. I was in desperate need of a hot bath. And for more reasons than one.

"I guess I don't have to have the power to create storms in order to' 'feel the winds of change'", I said, mimicking back his line from my fathers office.

Prick.

CHAPTER NINE

S tepping back into my room, I quickly shut the door. I
stood there for what felt like ages, my back to the
cool solid wood door, panting, my sweat-drenched
clothes growing cold. I knew he was going to get me back for
what I had just done. *How foolish, how damn foolish.* This was
no human man; this was a Fae Warrior. I didn't know him. I
had no idea what he was capable of, what kind of grudges
he might hold. As he said, *no high-ranking creature sits on
their throne, any throne got there from their cruel deeds.* But
truly, he did deserve it. It was simply tit for tat for what he
pulled in my fathers office. And not only that, but I am stuck
here with him, and only him.

I puffed out a stressed breath. I could already feel how
much this training session was going to make my body ache
tomorrow. Looking at the clock, my jaw dropped. It never
occurred to me how long we had been training. We were
there for *eight hours. Holy shit.* Two weeks ago I would've
collapsed at the two-hour mark, and here I am now, aching,
tired and winded, but still standing.

I pushed myself off the door and headed for the bathroom, in desperate need of a shower. It was as exquisite as
the rest of the house. Heated black marble floors, and the
same floor to ceiling windows lined the wall looking out
towards the Ostorous mountains, sunset gleaming golden
off their pink snow caps. Steam crept up the windows. The
bath had already been drawn and the smell of lilac and bath
salts hung in the air. Next to the bathtub, a small pedestal,
and on it, a glass of white wine. I smiled to myself, almost
becoming giddy. I loved long hot baths and now to have a
glass of wine, and the single most amazing view I had ever
seen?! I sighed a long sigh, peeling off the soaked clothing,
and sank into the tub. The water lapped over the sides in
lazy waves. I let out a soft groan, my muscles finally relaxing
and almost melting into the scorching hot water.

I knew I couldn't let my thoughts drift off too much, my
mind wanting to go to my parents, Vana, and Willem. To the
painting, to Asta and Jahan. I shook my head vigorously and
slowly lowered myself into the water, submerging myself
fully. Head under water, just how my life currently felt.

AFTER A VERY LONG soak and finishing my glass of wine, the
aches in my muscles thawed and my mind calmed thanks to
the soothing salt bath and oils. I towel dried my hair and
threw on a deep emerald colored turtleneck and black
leggings, throwing my still damp hair over my shoulder and
headed toward the kitchen.

I stopped in front of the vanity mirror before I left the
room, staring at my reflection. The same, but vastly different

simultaneously. I was slowly becoming aware of the power in my veins pulsing under my skin. Instead of seeing myself, I saw Asta's features, and Jahan's golden hair and skin. I noticed my ears had slowly been coming to a point, and I knew this meant I could no longer pass as a human in any capacity. A part of me ached for that loss, felt that sorrow over what a normal life I used to live. My skin seemed to shimmer slightly, nothing too noticeable, but with the turn of my head, the slight motion of my hand, it almost looked like I held the glow of candlelight under my skin. My eyes were brighter and clearer than I'd ever seen them. My eyelashes were thick and black, curling naturally, no mascara needed now, and I touched them in awe.

I brushed my fingers through my long golden-brown hair, staring at the strands of what could be mistaken as pure spun gold weaving in and out of my tousled locks. As I looked back at myself in the mirror, I couldn't quite let myself believe it was really my true self gazing back. I didn't know this version of myself. She was entirely me and entirely not all at once. She looked alluring and enchanting, like she could sing a siren song and lure some helpless soul to their death. It was eerie. I don't know if I'll ever get used to looking in the mirror anymore, I thought to myself as I left my room.

Surprisingly delicious scents met me in the hallway. The smell of cardamom, cilantro, coconut, and cumin fluttered from the kitchen. The hunger quickly grew more intense as soon as I realized I hadn't eaten anything all day, my stomach tossing and turning. Rhone stood with his back to the hall, a chef's apron on while he chopped pepper and onions, tossing them into the simmering pot on the stove.

"Wow, how domestic of you, Rhone the Almighty," I said, smiling silently to myself. He looked so out of place, his massive form hunched over a cutting board. He said nothing in return, and I sat myself on the bar stool, leaning over the island slightly so I could peek at the deep pot in front of him. Chicken, carrots, lentils, onion, and green and red peppers simmered in the deep, creamy, orange-colored broth.

"It smells amazing," I mused again, stomach growling louder than I appreciated. I could tell by his continued disgruntled silence that he was still mad about earlier in the training room. Truthfully, I *was* sorry *I guess*, and I did feel bad, *I guess*.

Rhone continued cooking, not bothering to look in my direction as he spoke, "I learned this recipe in my time I spent with the Ito tribe, a warrior tribe deep in these same mountains. It's been one of my favorite meals ever since. It's good for cold nights after a hard day of training." He trailed off as he continued cooking, leaning over the counter and tossing minced garlic into the pot. "Nami, the healer and mother of the tribe, always told me that food can heal in ways medicine can't. It can bring people together in ways that temples and Gods can't. That it can make the most inopportune moment intimate," he said, and I found myself wondering if this was his peace offering, an invitation to be friends even.

Freshly made naan bread sat next to the oven, the yeasty garlicky goodness wafting my direction. *Man, this guy can cook.*

I wanted to keep this light conversation going, because I'd be lying if I said I wasn't dying to know more about him. He truly was the most fascinating person I had ever met.

"Is the Ito your family tribe?" I felt it was a valid question, but I knew it was prying, and the Fae *hate* their privacy being invaded.

The slight elegant slant of his eyes and the jet black of his hair could lead anyone to believe he was at least somewhat of the elusive mountain warrior tribes of the east. These mountain warrior tribes were hardly ever seen and were made up of several different branches of tribes, who to my knowledge, lived somewhat harmoniously. I had never seen one out and about in the Human Realm, one had never visited my father's estate, and I had never seen any of them in the Realms Times. They were highly secretive, didn't involve themselves in conflicts outside their territory, and were the deadliest warriors in all the realms. Their stealth and killing abilities were things from bedtime stories and war movies. They could land a dagger to the heart of any target within 600 feet, their archery skills were unmatched, and they could disembowel you before you ever knew they were hunting you.

Without answering my question, he turned to me, bowls and plates lined up both of his arms, and nodded to me to follow him. We walked into the living room, which Rhone had shifted into a dining area. The wide coffee table I now realized, doubled as a low sitting dining table. Rhone had dragged two floor cushions and positioned them on either side of the table. Little tea lights sat in the middle. Rhone carefully sat down the platter of spiced rice, chicken curry, and naan bread. In a blink, two steaming tea mugs sat adjacent to our plates, the fresh smell of the mint tea rising to meet me. I groaned, my hunger and excitement over this meal overwhelming me.

Even with the hot bath, my muscles still screamed in annoyance as I placed myself on the other side of the table from Rhone. With a snap of his finger, the food plated itself, rice on one side, curry on the other, with a piece of naan on the edge of the plate. *How does he do that?* I peeked up to him before I dug in, not wanting to ruffle any weird Fae rules about manners at the dinner table.

Rhone rolled his eyes at me. "You do not need permission to eat from me, Soren," he said as he picked up his own fork.

I did the same, trying not to shovel food into my mouth like a starved animal. "How do you do that, where magic just does things for you, like the plating of food just now." I asked, swallowing bites in between words.

"I was wondering when you would ask," he mused. "It's called a whim, and is very simple. Every Fae can do this, even with little to no magic abilities. You just think of what you want, within reason of course, and your magic will do it for you." He paused for a moment to take a bite, tearing a piece of naan apart and scooping up the chicken curry. "I say within reason, because you cannot force anyone to do something against their will."

I nodded, understanding what he meant. I could, most of the time, appreciate the random and plentiful rules that came along with Fae magic.

"Why don't you try it?" he said, sipping his mint tea, his gray eyes gleaming, challenging me. Well then, the challenge was accepted.

Thinking to myself, I thought of what I could possibly

want right now. Everything I wanted was too complicated. I wanted my simple human life back, I wanted my room at my parents back and my house projects that were still waiting for me at my own home. I sighed to myself, *Not right now Soren,* and closed my eyes. Simple. Let's start with something simple. A glass of red wine, that'd be lovely right now.

I blinked, and in front of me sat two glasses of wine. Rhone smiled. "Ah, you were polite enough to whim a glass for me as well," he said. *Well, I hadn't exactly meant to do that...*

Rhone interrupted my train of thought, "Sometimes you have to be careful; whims can be tricksters and can get away from you at times. Remember, all Fae magic is made from mischief and chaos; it derives from the pulsing chaotic energy around us. For instance, by the look on your face I take it you did not intend for me to get a glass of wine, pity that really," he said, laughing slightly. "Whims have a way of giving you what you really want, rather than what you tell it. You must be very precise. But what this does mean, is that you secretly *did* want to have a glass of wine with me," he said, winking and picking up the glass, taking a big swig.

I rolled my eyes at him and picked up my own glass, but I could feel myself smiling as I took a sip. This was not your average human wine, I could tell. It had notes of cherries and blossoms, and a honey sweet nectar I didn't recognize and was oddly full bodied. It was strong, too. I took another long sip, delighting in this new wine I had discovered, that I was definitely be whiming up some for Vana and I. The wine was already sending a flush to my cheeks and warming my limbs.

"Do you have any hobbies besides being a huge ancient

killing machine who lives in a hole in the side of a mountain?" I said, taking another long sip. I looked around the room and added, "A very sophisticated hole in the wall."

Rhone huffed a laugh, his glass of wine already gone. In a blink, the table was cleared and the fireplace behind me came to life with a soft roar. With a nod of his head, both of our glasses were refilled, and he leaned back against the couch that was behind him. "Come, sit over here." He nodded his head to the side, motioning to the empty spot next to him, patting the floor with his hand. "Your back muscles are sure to be screaming, as mine are. There's no need to be hunched over," he said.

I obliged, gingerly plopping down next to him, feeling like a schoolgirl as my knee grazed his, and a brush of hands as I adjusted myself next to him, leaning back on the edge of the couch. The proximity of him sent a flurry of butterflies cascading over me, head to toe.

"So you want to know my hobbies, Soren? What are we, on a date or something?" he said, laughing and playfully shoulder bumping me. "I am not sure if creatures as old as myself have hobbies, honestly. I was an orphan as a child, but one that was allowed certain luxuries. I always enjoyed art class. My instructor for the arts was a sweet woman; she was the closest thing I had to a friend growing up, which even as a grown male I have not made many more," he said, smiling. He ran a hand through his hair and took it out of its low bun, letting it drape elegantly over his shoulder.

"I enjoy cooking also and reading—anything but history. I've lived that. Huh...I guess I haven't thought of things I actually enjoy doing in a while. During my time in the war camps, we would play card games, sometimes a good boxing match," he said, shrugging.

I sat there, looking at him, wondering what it must be like to not even know things you enjoy doing, not having hobbies that make you happy.

Rhone broke the silence, "I guess because you tried a whim for me earlier, I could answer your previous question, about the Ito Tribe. The tribe took me in, in my greatest time of need. I was with them for two decades, and they were the most peaceful beings, in their own right. They showed me love, dignity, and trained me to be a top warrior. They were the closest thing to a family I have ever had," he said, taking another long sip of his wine.

I tilted my head, staring into those strange storm cloud eyes. "You said 'were'. What happened to them?" I asked, holding my breath, not entirely sure I was ready for the answer.

He just stared at me for a moment, and I could tell he was assessing me, assessing what kind of threat I would be to him if he put his truth into the wrong hands. He took another long sip of wine, emptying his glass. "They were slaughtered," he said, the words clipped. "My former *employer* had a priceless prize on my head, dead or alive, which I was unaware of. I would've never stayed and left anyone in danger. A mole within the tribe had leaked this information to her, and when she showed up, she and her army murdered my family– every man, woman and child, even the mole. Simply because they had taken me in," he said, his words hard, through clenched teeth.

A storm was beginning to brew, not only behind his eyes, but outside the window as well. Snow flurries whipped around furiously, lightning glittering in the distance. "She knew that I would forfeit my life for them, so she killed them. She put me in a time loop, forcing me to re-watch their deaths over and over." *Suspended him in time...* He looked away from me then, taking in a much-needed deep breath. I knew he was replaying those scenes in his head. I reached out a hand to him, grabbing his that still lingered on his wine glass.

"Society will talk; they will say I pick no court because I can't be loyal. 'A Hitori, a child of no one, can't be loyal, they are not born to be loyal,' I've even heard them say. That's okay, though. In order to keep others safe, I wander the world alone, as I was brought into it," Rhone said.

I could see the lingering pain in his eyes, and I could understand his viewpoint, why he wanted to be alone in this vast home in the middle of a mountain.

I sat there silently for a long moment. He didn't pull his hand away from mine. We sat there with our fingers intertwined.

Finally, I broke the silence, "Who would do such a thing to you?" I asked. I wanted to be gentle, but this elusive *she*. Was it the same woman?

Thunder cracked outside, the lightning flashing across the room through the windows. He looked up at me then, his eyes glowing. The severity in his stare sent my heart racing.

"Synnove, the Royal Seer," he said, his hand leaving mine then.

A Seer?! The same creatures who were looked upon as angels in the realms, the serene Goddess's...How could she?

"Are you... *serious*?! How could she do such a thing, how

is she still in power? How is this—Was this not front head-line news?!" I said.

"Your father asked the same questions, and for the most part dismissed my accusation, saying maybe it was a Miragen in her form, but nonetheless said accusing her in the royal courts would be too dangerous. When someone is as powerful as Synnove, it's easy to erase things you've done, cover them up." He paused for a moment, seeming to gather his thoughts before he began again, "Emrin, he is a good man, but he is too worried about ruffling feathers. He doesn't truly see the dangers Synnove could be capable of, not yet at least. He is afraid to enrage the beasts, he is afraid of putting you in danger. He would rather hide out in the Human Realm forever. It was your father I came to after I ran from Synnove, looking for another safe haven. I knew how to find him, Synnove had me tracking him for years as she did many creatures for various reasons. I knew his disguises, and I had seen just what kind of man he truly was, a kind and generous one. I never understood why she had me keeping tabs on him. Not until you came along. You were the only thing he ever had worthy of covering up.

"Synnove... She is not the woman everyone believes her to be. She is up to big and dangerous things, things she's been planning for hundreds of years... She's been building an army, hoarding power. She never thought I paid atten-tion, only thought I was capable of fighting and killing. Losing me, it was only half a loss for her, but one she won't tolerate much longer. I... I could not tell the truth to the world yet, not yet. That much your father was right about. I'm waiting for the perfect timing, and I believe you can help me with that." Finished, he picked up his refilled glass of wine and took a swig, his eyes never leaving mine.

"Okay, how could I do such a thing? I'm a 23-year old halfling who just found out my true self. I've barely trained.. My abilities are shoddy at best, and I have a psychotic ex-boyfriend literally on a mission to kill me," I said.

He looked at me for a long minute, and shook his head, eyes cast to the ground. "You are more capable than what you give yourself credit for, Soren. I believe you forget who you are. You are the daughter of two of the most incredible creatures in all our history. Your powers are unique and raw and you proved today that you can over power Rhone the Almighty with one swift graze," he said, his eyes falling to my lips ever so slightly. "Also, I guess you forgot you're actually over 500 years old," he said, a small smirk on his face.

I stared at him blankly for a second. Rhone saw something in me, saw something more than this lost girl who had no idea what she was doing, or who she was. It was one thing to be an educated human woman, who's up and coming in her field, and an entire other to be swooped up into the creature realms with powers you don't understand. I chewed on this for a moment, taking in the realization that this massive Fae warrior needed my help.

"So what is it that I can do for you, Rhone?" I said, taking another sip of wine.

"She'd do anything to get her hands on her niece. She had sisters in another life, sisters who she betrayed, sisters who swore to bear her ending. She wants no threats to her throne, and certainly none that are potentially more powerful than she is. She killed her sister and her sister's husband, but she's never been able to find her niece, *"the prophecy"*. That was all she ever called her. This girl is the last piece that poses a threat to her plan of waging war across all the realms."

"Who is her niece? How are we going to find her, if she's been searching for her so long and even if *She* can't?" I asked, truly dumbfounded at this Fae man sitting next to me. *So what does he want me to do? I'm already being hunted myself, training to fight my own wars. What else cou*—I stopped mid thought. *It couldn't be...but Asta and Jahan's faces flashes through my mind, and what he said, it was too many coincidences.*

"We've already found her, Soren. It's you," he said. "And only a rightful heir to the Seer throne can find and unseal the realm gates." My mouth hung open. *I mean honestly, can I just get one moment of peace,* I thought to myself.

"Follow me," he said, not even giving me a moment to gather my thoughts. We stopped in front of his hallway that was lined with paintings. "Every one of these paintings unlocks a clue to where to find the gates. I believe you're just the person for it."

TEN

I stood in the hallway with him, staring at the paintings. He moved behind me, placing his hands on my shoulders, and guided me down the hallway. They were all exquisite. There were nine in total, each a different landscape, some of them were realms I recognized, like the landscape of The Sands. But others were eerie, a land of ice, and one of fire. Immediately, I noticed they were all the same style, and with my sharpened Fae sight, I didn't even need a lab to see the brush strokes were all familiar. The canvases were old, but the paint looked smooth, not cracked with age or riddled with pollutants. Before my Fae sight, I would've needed to use a magnifying glass to see these details. My new and improved vision was better than any magnifying technology I could've ever found in the human realms, in any science lab. I walked over to the paintings, and lifted each of them off the wall, each one of them evoking a hum of magic. But each painting *felt different.* The thrum of magic beating to a different rhythm then the next.

Turning them over and analyzing the backs of them I

noticed key features. Sure enough, the canvases were almost identical to the one I had found.

Each of them is a clue.

I repeated that back in my head as I studied them.

"Well, just from analyzing the brush strokes I can tell you they are the same artist who painted 'The Birth'. The brush strokes and style of brush used are very unique and the same with every painting, as is the type of paint used," I said.

"You named your painting of you and your parents, '*The Birth*?' Seems a bit disconnected, doesn't it?" Rhone said, his eyebrow cocked in question. I didn't return his gaze, and instead kept analyzing the paintings.

Finally, I turned back to Rhone, eyes narrowing on him. "Okay, so let's just say I could break this code and find the realm gates. We don't know anything about the Seer Realm, no one really does. If Synnove, my apparent Aunt, is as brutal as you say she is, we need a better plan. So we just open these realm gates and then what?! We could be sitting geese to a bunch of guards. We need to find someone who has some sort of knowledge, anything, an old map, literally just anything. Maybe my fathers research could give us some clues."

I had begun pacing without realizing it, walking up and down the hallway corridor, my mind racing. I suppose this would be one of those things Asta meant when she said she couldn't wield my destiny. She couldn't tell me things that would alter the possible paths in my life thread. *What was I even saying right now? My apparent Aunt?*

Ringing my hands together and worry knitting my brows together, I paced. So I'm not only being hunted for what I am, but hunted by my aunt, who just happens to be the Royal Seer. My slumbering magic could sense my panic, and I could feel it awakening, rushing to save me. I stopped immediately in my tracks, closing my eyes and taking in a deep breath. I focused on the world around me, the snow falling outside, the snap of branches on the forest floor, the steady beat of Rhone's heart. Opening my eyes, I looked up at him, leaning nonchalant against the dark hallway wall, arms crossed. He gave me a wicked smile, pushed off the wall, and sauntered towards me. He stopped mere inches away from me, his scent wrapping around me, and leaned down, his mouth alarmingly close to my ear.

"What if I told you we already had someone who knew the inside of that realm like the back of their hand, no map needed?" He said smoothly, sending a shiver down my entire body.

"How?! Who in the world would *you* know?" I asked.

He smirked. "An orphaned child, who was brought up under strange circumstances, and allotted certain luxuries," he said.

My eyes widened at him, taking in everything he just said. "No *way*," I said in a whisper, my hand flying up to my mouth in utter surprise.

It was his turn to begin pacing. "During the old times, it was believed by humans and creatures alike, that if your baby was lucky enough, a Seer would bless it. This blessing would give the baby new life, a rebirth. Some of these babies were given up because of simply not wanting it. Others because of birth defects, the inability to feed another little one or even stillbirths. Synnove told me she found me swaddled in burlap, nestled between some dead brush, atop the blessing hill, which every village had at the time'. Synnove claimed she instantly knew I was too special for a rebirth, and took me with her," he said matter-of-factly.

"The humans weren't wrong ya know. For a while, Seers did give these newborns rebirths. For a thousand years actually. Synnove once told me, these rebirths were exactly that, they were reborn to different lives, for better or worse, but reborn all the same. It's a kindness that these angels of life and death were able to grant. It was only after Synnove locked up her realms, that the blessings stopped."

He continued without prompting, "I grew up in the Seer Realms, and stayed there for many years after. My childhood was good enough. I had a huge comfortable warm bed, toys to play with, and the best teachers the realms could offer. I trained for battles before I knew what one was, and by age 8, I was known as the best archer in the realms. Synnove was whittling me into her own personal warrior, one unlike any the realms had seen. My powers were strong and had broad range, a range that made me in many ways indestructible. I hardly ever saw Synnove, and when I did, I was only to call her Royal Seer. Nothing more, nothing less, and certainly never her name. She was in no way motherly, but she made sure my instructors and maids were, I know that much." Rhone stopped and began walking to the couch, where I sat with him, intently waiting for him to go on.

"It wasn't until I had truly grown into my power, in my early twenties, that the assignments began. My powers are unlike any other in the Fae realm. I can manifest storms, manipulate water to my will, and I have also been able to undo enchantments cast by Spellcasters, and even cast small ones," he explained. "The Seers were never able to understand it, or figure out why I could have so many different fractions of abilities, especially of those not granted to the Fae. I am an anomaly, and you are now one of the only other creatures in the world to know. Synnove had said she knew I was special when she found me, and I have no idea how she could know I would harbor such powers as these, but it made me her ultimate weapon," he said as he leaned back into the lush leather couch, his long arms spreading across the back of it.

His rainstorm scent washed over me, his warmth radiated off of him, and I let myself lean into it, ever so slightly. His lightning storm eyes stared into the fire, flashing with every pop of the burning wood. He continued, "At first, they weren't anything crazy, walk the realm border, shoot anything that comes near, little assignments like that. They gradually became more and more complicated. From securing the realm borders, to torturing the creatures she brought back from her excursions. I was never to ask for information; she had already done all that. I was just a tool to harm, to wreck them enough so when she sent them back, scared, battered, and fucked up, that their Royals would know what would happen to them should they wrong the Royal Seer again.

"For years, that's what I did, bloodied and tortured the men and women whom Synnove saw fit to be mindbroken and destroyed. For a long time, I truly believed I was doing these things for the better of the Realm, for the better of the Seers who had raised me. I believed I was protecting them." He paused, and looked at me, his eyes searching my face. I knew he was looking for signs of disapproval and disgust in his past. I forced myself to keep my face neutral, even though my heart was crying out for this poor male. He ducked his head a bit, shifting ever so slightly closer to me.

"Please go on," I said gently. I wanted him to know that it was okay, that I wanted to know these things about him, that he was worth knowing about. I had a feeling he didn't believe he was worth knowing. I leaned into him, leaning against the back of the couch, resting my head lightly against his arm. In a soft brush of mist, our glasses of wine were refilled, and Rhone continued, a look of reluctance on his face.

"Synnove had just finished a meeting with the council of the realms, and had been in a sour mood ever since she emerged from the Citadel, the castle that sits in the middle of where the four realm borders meet. Every third full moon the four borders bridge to meet each other. She had barked orders at all her Seers on guard that day after that, and she told me to be ready. I had no idea what for. The first village we came to, was a village of the wild Fae, the forest Fae of The Wetlands to be exact. It was quaint, with small thatched hut roofs, about two dozen of them. We arrived in the dead of night, and she gave me one command, *'Drowned them, all of them.'* I stood there for a moment, assessing what she had just said to me, and thought surely she didn't mean it. That had been a mistake. She took notice of my second guessing and I felt her power crawling up my arms, and looking down, silver tendrils of her power slithered up them, her power consuming me. Her insidious wants and needs became mine, and I did as she asked. Most of these village peoples had runes across their doors, enchantments protecting from harm. It was like they didn't exist to me, and

I walked right through them. I wrung the earth out of every ounce of water I could from the soil, from the air around us, and I drowned them in their sleep, shoved mist and storm down their throats until they stopped breathing. I could feel them struggling, I could feel my power recoiling at the pain it was inflicting. Two hundred and fifty wild Fae, men, women, and children. And that was just the first village, there were hundreds more, thousands more wild Fae, Night Creatures, ancient things." He hung his head a little, his voice trailing off.

The air had grown chilled, a thundering storm raging outside. He downed his glass of wine, and so did I, the silence around us seeping in. He cleared his throat, his voice slightly hoarse, "To this day, I have no idea how she had the power to control me, and I can't let that happen again. Who knows what else she is capable of."

She had forced him to kill hundreds of Fae, innocent sleeping Fae, creatures of all kinds, and the look on his face told me he only blamed himself.

"Rhone, you cannot blame yourself for this. I can't explain her power, I barely understand my own... but there's no way you could have stopped her. I know this because I don't believe you would bow down like that without a fight. There's a universe of powers in the stars, a million secrets to uncover. She made you do those things with whatever power it is she has," I said, my voice gentle as I tried to console the raw deep sadness I felt radiating off of him. He stood then, his face becoming unreadable, and the ease and comfort I had felt from him seconds ago had vanished.

"It's incredibly late, and we have too much on our plate tomorrow to be up listening to ghost stories of mass murders," he said. The edge of his mouth curled a bit in amusement but his eyes told me another story. He vanished in a burst of storm, sending tiny specks of rain dancing across the side of my wine glass.

I sat there for a moment, staring at the mist on my glass, watching the dew drops sparkle in the glow of the fireplace until they slid away. Truthfully, I was trying to organize my thoughts. How Synnove was a much bigger problem than I had originally thought she would be, and my aunt at that.

I thought of Rhone's past, how he had opened up to me, and then immediately shut back down, leaving in a flurry of sleet and mist, his parting words calling himself a mass murder. I could almost see his memories, the shackles of her magic wrapped around him, forcing him to kill the inno-cent. Shackles of magic much like I had created to subdue Willem. I squeezed my eyes shut to that, feeling guilty at the twinge of fear I felt not only towards him, but myself.

When Rhone had said we had a lot on our plate the next day, he hadn't been wrong. The first part of the day had passed in a whirl— early rise, choking down toast and coffee, tugging on my training leathers and heading to the sparring room. We trained for hours, repetition of basic battle stances, importance laid onto balance, and perfecting my foresight. My head was aching from the hours spent throwing my hearing, focusing, balancing, and my body was sore from using new muscles that hadn't existed last week. Rhone had been quiet today, quiet during our quick break-fast and quiet during training. It wasn't an angry silence, more of a "too in his own head" silence. I didn't pry; I knew the revelations of last night had been costly to him emotionally.

Training ended in silence as well. Rhone left me with a, "Very good job today," and shadowed, leaving me in the training room alone. Instead of making my way back to my room immediately, I decided to do a cool down round of stretches. My muscles felt as tight and tense as did my mind. I did the movements Rhone had taught me, easing my muscles in and out of the stretches, lunges, and a series of standing yoga poses. After the last toe touch, I sat myself down on the floor crisscross style. I faced the window, letting the pink and gold glow that spilled in over the mountain tops soothe me. I watched the snow flurries as they sparkled in the sun's setting rays. There was something so magical about being in the presence of these magnificent mountains.

I closed my eyes and inhaled deeply, stretching each arm across my chest before resting my hands palm up on each knee. Breathing out softly and repeating this pattern, my thoughts and worries escaped me. The emptiness of just sitting and breathing was a great relief, breathing in through my nose again, letting as much air fill my lungs as I could, and blowing out through my mouth. A tickling at my nose brought all my thoughts tumbling back into me. Frustrated, I puffed out a disgruntled sigh and waved a hand in front of my nose, urging whatever floating fuzz that had disrupted my peace to get lost. I opened my eyes and stood up, shoving myself off the ground.

Oh shit. I thought to myself, my eyes adjusting to the hazy gray-white abyss, rainbow colored fragments of light coming and going. *I was in The Gap. And that fuzz was a life thread.* I looked around aimlessly, trying to see a way out. *Okay yeah, this is totally fine. I am totally in control of this situation,* I tried to tell myself, when I was very clearly not in control of this situation. *Think, Soren. Use your time wisely.* I chided myself, mad for getting myself into this situation but also frustrated with my complete lack of direction within this accidental opportunity.

As a life thread floated by, I reached out and gently grabbed the thread, watching it shimmer as I rested it in my palm. Recalling how Asta had handled the thread and closed her eyes, I did the same. Nothing came and I tried again. Still nothing. It was like this thread was blank...no life left in it..

Frowning, I let the thread go, watching it float away in the non-existent breeze. Lifting my hand with more intention this time, Vana's face popped up in my mind. A thread appeared in front of me, and I knew without hesitation that this was her life thread. Her essence poured from it, and her sweet blossom and patchouli scent filled the air. The moment was bittersweet. First, excitement filled me, I had done it! I had summoned a life thread with intention. And then the realization of what I could do next hit me. All I needed to do next was grab the thread, and peer into her life. So many consequences could come with that knowledge. Would I know how her life might end? How could I look into someone's life like that, life they hadn't even lived yet? I stared at the thread for some time before a familiar lilting voice echoed through The Gap, making me jerk my head up.

"My child," Asta's transparent voice became more solid.

Her long silver white hair cascaded over her shoulder, her white satin dress catching the slivers of rainbow-colored light shimmering through the fog of The Gap. "I sensed you were here; I could feel your worry."

Asta stepped forward, one hand cupping my elbow and the other she laid beneath my own hand which still held Vana's life thread. Looking down, she smiled then, realizing whose life thread I held.

"I would recognize that scent anywhere. Vana has not lost her love for roses I see," she said smiling, her eyes creasing in honest joy. After a second, she continued, "I can see your hesitation, and I understand it. You never know what you might find."

Gently, she raised my open palm higher. "But fear of the unknown is something you must overcome." She nodded her head in a silent nudge for me to try my hand at the life thread. I swallowed hard, my heart thundering in my chest. Seeing into Vana's life thread was such a heavy bearing... But I swallowed my fear the best I could. Bringing my pointer finger forward, a soft glow sparked between my finger and the life thread as they met, a humming zap of electricity zinging up my finger. Shimmering silver light enveloped me and blurred my vision heavily. I could feel the rush of the world shifting around me. Blurs of colors and flashes of smells blew past me, whipping my hair around wildly. The salt of the Crystal Oceans, the pine of the Eastern Mino's mountain range all rushing past before the world around me became perfectly still. Vana's heady scent was all that remained as the shimmering light that blurred my vision dissipated.

As my vision came back to me, I realized I stood alone in

a vibrantly green forest. Just as in The Gap, the edge of my vision shimmered here, reminding me that this realm was the Inbetween, the veil between life and death, thinning and stretching just for me. Shafts of sunlight came streaming down from the thick tree canopy above, scattering fractures of rainbow colors across the forest floor. A snap of a twig alerted my attention, and I turned towards it. A figure glided towards me, the outline of a green body finally coming into focus. Vana's face stared back at me. She was in her true form. Her gold dusted green tinted skin gleamed in the sunlight, her long vine-like hair gathered over one shoulder. She was dressed in a white silk gown with white and yellow flowers embroidered into the fabric. She stopped a couple feet in front of me, her bright golden Wild Fea eyes gleaming with happiness, her face breaking out into a smile.

"Welcome to my forest, my dearest friend," she said, her voice as light and cheerful as her smile. I stared back at her, unsure what to say or do. She looked so real, but was she? Or just a trick of The Gap? Vana's form shifted and vanished as she moved, the hard edges of her body blurring, much like Asta and Jahan's had. "Here, let me help you," she said, her laugh bouncing off the trees, making me smile as well. She reached forward and placed my hand in hers. In a matter of seconds, the blinding light was back not even Vana who stood right in front of me was visible. The world began to rush past me again, faster than last time. I held onto Vana's hand tighter, not wanting to lose her, needing to feel her comforting touch. Every fray of Vana's life flashed before me, and as the world slowed to a halt, Vana's grip on my hand dissipated as she gave one last gentle squeeze.

"You still need the last piece, Soren. It is your end," She

said, her voice muffled, dissipating as she did. I lurched forward then, slumping down to my knees. The life thread jump leaving me feeling discombobulated, but it wasn't only that. It was the loss of Vana's presence. It was the grief I now felt for the many ways my friend's life could and would end. Very few frays ended happily for Vana; most of her lives ended in bloodshed and a hero's death with a sword in her hand. A lump formed in my throat, tears swelling in my eyes. Asta appeared then, crouching in front of me, and laid a comforting hand across my back. At the instance of her touch, I let out a soft cry, unable to hold it back anymore.

She enveloped me then, her long and slender arms embracing me in a hug, and I could hear soft murmurs as she tried to console me. After a moment, she led me to stand with her. Taking her thumb, she brushed away the tears left streaming down my face. I stared into her celestial eyes, so like mine yet so foreign.

"The first time is always the hardest, the shock of being the harborer of so many fates. But trust, that it does get easier. Vana could have a happy ending yet," Asta said, her voice just above a whisper but still demanding attention as she spoke. I took in a deep breath, willing myself to calm, and shook my head in understanding.

"Was that really Vana or was that my own interpretation of her?" I asked, my voice still raw and fragile from crying.

Asta took a moment to respond, her gaze focused on something in the horizon. Slowly, her gaze returned to mine. "It was truly her, but an unconscious version. If anything, she could possibly feel a slight hint of deja vu next time she sees you." As she finished her sentence, she began to fade then.

"It is time for you to go darling. Remember not to linger here too long," Asta said hastily, her eyes darting back to the horizon again before dissipating. I stared into her eyes as long as I could, until she floated away in the breeze that didn't exist. Turning around I strained my eyes. I wanted to see what she saw. A hazy darkness gleamed in the distance, seeping into The Gap, which definitely was not there earlier. Closing my eyes, I urged my consciousness back to my body, back to the training room that smelled of leather and sweat.

ELEVEN

M y eyes flew open as fresh air flooded my lungs, the familiar smells of the training room bringing me into the real world again. Looking around, everything was unchanged. I still sat criss-cross, my water bottle still off to my right, and the sun still in the same position in the sky. I sucked in another long breath, needing to continue to center myself.

Oh. my. gods. I just figured out how to enter The Gap.

The visions of Vana's many endings floated back up into my memory, almost as if a dream. I shook them from my thoughts as fast as they appeared. I couldn't dwell on those now; I could only try and figure out how to avoid the worst of them. I would be lying if I didn't admit my accidental slip into The Gap didn't thrill me. This meant so much, not only was I beginning to understand my power more, but it also seemed like it was willing to accept me as well. Standing, I thought about this as I walked back to my room, ready for a shower.

After my shower, I grabbed the robe off the back of the

door, finding it already warmed. I wrapped it around myself and sighed at the luxury of it. Towel drying my hair, I walked over to the bed, noticing a black box was lying on top of it. Opening it, I realized it was a sleek dark gray phone, with a sticky note on it:

> *You might have noticed your phone got left behind. This is the safest way to connect to your parents. Take all the time you need, but dress warm. We are going on an adventure. -R*
>
> *P.S. Try not to waste too much time telling Vana about my rock-hard abs, or how I've been kicking your ass during training. She already knows both of those are true.*

GOING ON AN ADVENTURE? I turned and looked out the window, at the snowy mountain caps and the heavy flakes that whipped around in the night air. I dug through my drawers, trying to find something suitable for a cold adventure. I pulled out a thick wool turtleneck and fleece-lined jeans. I tugged on some long wool socks and my training boots. Finally finished dressing, I picked up my new phone, feeling oddly nervous about contacting my parents for the first time since our escape from Willem. I touched the screen, the blue light glaring back at me, and it opened to the call page. I had only three contacts: my parents, Vana and Rhone. Unsurprising, considering even before my life turned upside down, I didn't have much of a social life either. My finger hovered over my parents' contact for a moment, before hastily clicking the call button. My parents answered on the first ring. Their holographic faces popped up on the screen, smushed together and smiling like crazy.

"Oh darling! We are so happy to hear from you. How have you been? Are you okay? Were you injured? We've been worried sick," my mother exclaimed, her sweet voice calming my nerves. My dad shook his head in agreement, his smile reaching all the way to his eyes.

"Oh yes, Mom. Really I'm fine. No injuries, just shaken up when we shadowed in. Rhone and I are on schedule with training. I am starting to understand my powers more and more."

My father chirped in then, "Make sure you're documenting them. Anything extraordinary yet?" he asked, trying to conceal his excitement unsuccessfully.

I smiled at him knowingly, "Actually, yes... I entered The Gap today and looked into my first life thread. Other than that, just strengthening my basic Fae powers. And I'm actually incredibly strong. You'd be so impressed!" I said. I could see him vigorously jotting notes down in his notebook. Only then did I take notice of the background of their video call. It was an unfamiliar room. Dark rich wood paneling and deep blue velvet curtains could be seen, gold thread glittering in the firelight I could see in the corner.

"Where are you guys at?" I asked.

"We reached the Spellcaster Court swiftly, Vana shadowed away as well, we watched her go before we did. Although I am unsure exactly where. I can only assume she is also on schedule, finding Wild Fae to add to our alliance. We have yet to meet with Aaren. We are trying to make our visit as unassuming to the rest of High Wizard society as possible. We plan to meet with him the night after next," my father said.

My mind drifted to that night, the night where we had all scattered across the seas. I instantly thought of Willem. He had laid crumpled on the ground, blood flowing. I couldn't stop myself and the words came tumbling out of my mouth, "And what of Willem?" I spoke quietly, not really sure I wanted the answer, but knowing I needed to know.

My parents looked at each other then, and it was my mother who spoke first. "He was gathering his strength as we prepared to leave. His blood loss heavily affected his ability, but as we faded away, he was as well." And that was it, the answer I had dreaded and hoped for all in the same fleeting thought. So he lived, and he got away. A twinge of fear gripped me, knowing he was out there in the world, healed up and still searching for me. I shivered a little, the violent moments of our last encounters still raw. I shut my eyes and took a deep breath, willing the moment to pass.

Opening my eyes, my parents stared back at me, even their holographic faces comforting. I smiled at them, but I knew it was time to get off the phone. I knew the longer a phone call, the more time someone had to try and locate the signal.

"Alright Mom, Dad. Rhone told me we have more work to do after dinner. So I better go. I love you guys so much! I'll call you back soon."

After my parents said their goodbyes, I tucked my phone away. I pulled my hair back into a loose braid and shrugged on my coat. Walking into the hallway, Rhone stood in the entryway. He was leaning against the wall, holding two small backpacks. His hair was swept back in a tight bun.

"About time," he said smirking and began walking towards me. He tossed one of the small backpacks to me. Catching it, I realized it was pretty light, and I stared down at it in confusion. What would I need this for? As I went to open it, Rhone reached out, laying his fingers over mine to stop me.

"Ah-Ah. Don't ruin the surprise, Soren," he said, motioning for me to follow him as he walked towards the kitchen.

I rushed after him. "So, do I at least get to know where we are going?"

He stopped abruptly in front of me and turned around. He ducked his head down to get closer to me and whispered, "We are going into one of the many Ostorous forests for a nightly stroll." My eyes got wide, and he let out a soft laugh then, the mischievous laugh reaching his eyes. I had heard tales of the Ostorous Forests, and as it got darker, it also got more dangerous. The magic in the mountains was raw, unabiding magic, and what came with that was powerful unabiding Fae creatures and monsters. I bit my lip, my anxiety sending a flush to my cheeks.

"Oh, don't be such a scaredy cat. You are going to be by far the most explosive thing we will encounter on our stroll. I feel like that already gives us an advantage. Now, if we want to get our adventure started, you'll need to hold on tight," he said, opening his arms.

Of course, you must shadow in and out.

My heart skipped a tiny beat, and I scowled at it for betraying me, knowing his Fae ears caught that. I pulled the backpack on and walked over to him, wrapping my arms around his wide torso. He tensed and stilled in return, his muscles contracting under my fingertips. His thick black turtleneck was buttery soft to the touch as I grabbed on it and his rain dusted scent engulfed me. The air around us growing misty was the only warning as we were whisked away on the non-existent breeze.

Opening my eyes, I let them adjust for a moment, my head a little dizzy from the trip. I could hear rustling all around me. As I looked around, my mouth fell open in awe. With my arms still clasped around Rhone, I stood staring into the forest, the darkest of dark nights staring back at me. With that thought, a Fae orb of light appeared, moving fluidly with just the slightest of my movements. Trees jutted up into the sky a hundred feet, their thick roots sprawled across the forest floor, braiding across one another. Vibrant moss and tiny mushrooms ran up and down the tree trunks, a low glowing shimmer casting off of them. Looking up, the sky was covered by the tree canopy, their deep purple leaves shimmering against the sky, so high up one could also mistake them for stars. Leaving Rhone's side, I took a step forward, almost afraid it was a mirage. The forest burst to life at the sound of my footsteps. Vines of night jasmine blossoms that hung in troves from limbs and clung to trunks opened, their heady scent flooding the night air. Their petals were illuminating, sending cascading golden light across the darkness. The rustling came again, and this time the culprits showed themselves. Tiny forest sprites rustled from their hiding places under leaves and fallen rotting logs, fluttering up every direction. Dozens of them hung in the air like tiny orbs of light, their chatter sounding like the muffled tinkling of bells. The sprites flitted away instantly, hanging in the air at a fork in the forest, only visible by their light.

I turned around and looked towards Rhone, and he shrugged his head forward in acceptance. As I took another step in the sprites' direction, more of the forest came to life, as if we were the first visitors in centuries. More blossoms of every color opened up from hanging vines and trailing up tree trunks. The tinkling bells of the sprites' voices became more intense, the longer I hesitated. Their melodic voices entranced me a bit, their twinkling voices wrapping around me. I took a step back, unsure if following these strange creatures in an unknown enchanted forest was something I should be doing, and backed into Rhone's statue-like figure. He didn't move, and merely placed a hand on my shoulder. I turned around to look up at him again, needing reassurance. Strands of his long black hair fell forward as he looked down at me. His fierce eyes were soft, as if he knew how I felt seeing this for the first time.

"This is...I've never seen anything like this before. It's all so....captivating. They do not have forests like this in the Human Realm" I said in a whisper, as if my voice threatened to awaken more of the forest.

"It is, isn't it?" he said with a slight smile, then nudged me forward then. "I think the sprites are here to take us on the adventure we were looking for, don't you?" There was a question in his voice, and his eyes danced with mischievous temptation. I looked back at the sprites, and they still hung in the air, their chattering ceased as they awaited my answer. I nodded then and started forward, Rhone trailing lazily behind.

It was a short journey the sprites took us on. There were about twenty of them, all moving in unison as schools of fish do. Some of them glowing a mossy green, others a golden yellow. They gracefully ducked and weaved under fallen branches and hanging vines as we quietly moved through the forest. I tried, and failed, to ignore the sets of yellow glowing eyes staring at us from the deep dark edges of the forest as we made our way. A silent shiver went through me as I imagined what Fae creature could be stalking us.

The sprites stopped abruptly in front of a giant grey stone wall, wisteria vines trailing across its surface. At first, it looked like nothing more than the side of the mountain, but the surface of the stone was too refined to simply be there of nature's creation. In one sweeping motion, the sprites turned and looked at us, and with a collective nod of their tiny heads, they were gone. Dead leaves rustled from their slumber in their wake, sending them swirling into the air.

Rhone and I turned to look at each other then. He shrugged his broad shoulders and pulled a dagger from his side. In one swift movement, purple wisteria petals were flying through the air as Rhone's blade cut through their thick trunks. Rhone cleared the dust and straggling bits of debris away, and let out a low whistle. A large arched door was carved into the stone, swirling etchings laid across its surface, as intricate as lace. In the middle, was the symbol of a triple moon. A full moon in the middle and two outward-facing crescent moons on each side, and cradled between the crescent moons' points, was a single star.

"What do you think this is?" I asked, stepping forward.

"That symbol belongs to Máni, the Mother of Moons. She is one of the oldest Goddesses, she is the keeper of the Moons. She is still prayed to by the oldest of creatures, usually for fertility and guidance through the night, but mostly she is forgotten," Rhone responded, looking up into the night sky.

"Why do you think the sprites led us here?" I asked, not taking my eyes off the door, amazed by the impossibly intricate detail carved into the stone.

"Well, sprites do not lead fellow good willing Fea astray; it is not in their nature. They abide by honesty above all other virtues. That is one thing for you to add to your arsenal of new knowledge: the only creatures you can trust in an enchanted forest are the sprites. Not gnomes, or dryads, or willow wisps," Rhone said, turning back to look at me. His hair had fallen forward; tendrils of ink-black hair hung over his eyes. His breath came out in gentle puffs, reminding me of the chill in the air. I hugged my jacket a little tighter. "Another reason they might have brought us here, is because I asked them too." He shrugged the backpack off his shoulder. "I put plenty of little trinkets in our packs in hopes we would run into the sprites. The sprites are notorious for helping those who have good intentions *and* leave offerings."

He held his bag open for me, showing me the silver and golden trinkets that clinked together. Looking back to the door, he explained, "I have been looking for this place for at least a hundred years. I just had a hunch that maybe, the sprites would like you. This is the goddess of the moons after all. She would naturally be soft-hearted to a Seer, whose blood is lined with stardust. That hunch proved to be true; I didn't even have to leave any offerings." He turned to look at me with that smug look on his face that he was notorious for, I was finding out. I was also finding out that

Rhone, although more kind than to be expected, was also self-serving. Very Royal Faeren of him.

"That being said, there is probably no harm in checking it out. This could be fun, if you're willing to, that is." He shrugged, then added, "It is more than likely an empty and dilapidated stone temple anyways. Plus, if there was anything dangerous in there, I'd wager you could bring them to their knees with one of your ridiculous explosions."

I scowled at him then. "You know, you have a weird way of back-handedly complimenting someone. It's honestly infuriating," I said with a huff.

He stood there staring at me for a moment, his hair still obstructing the view of his eyes, but I could see the excitement in them even then. Which had been extremely rare since I had met him. Being alive for 500 years, and actually living them unlike myself, I bet there seldom came a time to experience new things.

I smiled up at him then, a small smile, as to not ruin the moment. "Well, go on then, what are you waiting for Big Strong Mighty Warrior Rhone? Open the big creepy stone door hidden in the middle of an enchanted forest," I said, crossing my arms. He was way too excited by this finding.

Rhone reached his tattooed hand out and put his palm to the middle of the door, over the triple moon symbol. As soon as he made contact, the door lit up, the intricate carved weavings shining bright. The door let out a soft click and began to shift, moving to the side and disappearing into the wall, plumes of dust filling the crisp night air. Rhone let out a low whistle, turning to me with his eyebrows raised. He was brimming with excitement now; I could see it all over his face.

He stood there silently for a breath, his pointed ears twitching with concentration. Still holding his dagger, he took a cautious step into the darkness beyond the door, his boot-heavy footsteps echoing.

"I don't hear any presence, but stay here for a moment. I'm going to make sure it's clear," he said with his back to me, fully stepping into the ruin.

Within seconds he was back, grinning ear to ear, "Your ruin awaits, my lady," he said with a flourish, bowing extravagantly.

Tentatively, I stepped forward into the ruin, the Fae orb following obediently behind us. As soon as we both stepped in, the door slid shut behind us, softly clicking into place, the entire room illuminating. Hundreds of Fae orbs hung in the air all around and above us, and I gasped at what I saw. The temple was formed of gleaming rose quartz, veins of fire opal and moonstone spread throughout. Everything from the walls to the pillars was the same magnificent rose quartz, moonstone, and opal combination. Looking up, beyond the hanging Fae orbs, I could see a domed glass ceiling, the stars and moonlight beaming through. In the center of the room was a large bathing pool, the sides plated in fire opal. Hundreds of little statues here and there were scattered amongst the temple, all woodland creatures.

I looked over to Rhone, who was wandering towards a large statue that stood across from the bathing chamber against the wall. The statue depicted a breathtaking woman with long flowing wavy hair, standing straight, her head poised up, looking into the night sky. She was hardly dressed, a long sheer tunic clung to her body, leaving nothing to the imagination and pooling around her bare feet. In one hand, held out down by her side, she was holding a gleaming full moon made of opal, palm up. In the other hand, she held a crescent moon, made of moonstone, pressed to her chest between her full and heavy breasts, one of the many symbols linked to extreme fertility. On her shoulder perched a great owl, its large eye sockets devoid of eyeballs, and by her feet lay a six-tailed fox.

"I assume this is Goddess Máni?" I said, looking at Rhone.

He nodded and replied, "Yes, it is. Her familiar was the owl. The fox at her feet was actually her lover, Akio. He was a Royal Faeren of the 9th sea clan. When the other Gods discovered Máni was having a forbidden love affair with a Fae, they cursed him and doomed their love. They confined him to a non-sea-bearing animal form. He could only have his Faeren form once every five years and was tied to Máni's fate. He would live as long as her, but he would also suffer in all ways she would and endure whatever ending she did. But the Gods could not leave the curse unbalanced. Máni was cursed as well, doomed to the confines of her temples, unable to roam through the night any longer. "

My eyebrows raised. "I mean, why does everything have to be such a tragedy?" I said, suppressing a laugh. I didn't want to scorn her in her own temple.

Rhone smiled sadly, still looking up at Máni, "I always liked her history the most; it was comforting for some reason. That is why I wanted to find her temple so severely. That was always my favorite part of the day as a child when the history lessons were read aloud to me. It was like an escape from Synnove's cruel love and endlessly brutal train-ing. This temple was said to be Máni's most prized of them all. It is also said that if you pray to her shrine, and she finds your soul worthy, she will fill her opal pools with the natural hot springs that lay beneath the surface that have been blessed by the moons. The stories say that by bathing in her healing moonbeam waters, you will not only be rejuvenated but will be marked with her blessing, which will be visible to all Fae creatures. To disregard her blessing would be to enrage Máni herself, and she would exact her revenge viscously, as Gods do."

Rhone turned from me then and knelt at her statue. He rested a hand on her bare foot. He began to mummer a prayer in ancient Fae, one I could not begin to understand even one word of. As Rhone's last word filled the silent air around us, the floor began to rumble. He stood suddenly, subtly sliding his towering body in between the shrine and myself, casually laying a palm on the hilt of his dagger. To a stranger, this could have looked almost accidental, but at this point, I knew nothing about Rhone was accidental.

The statue split up the middle with a deafening crack, from it floated the shimmering form of Máni. She blinked rapidly, as if adjusting her eyes to a world she hadn't seen in a hundred years. As the seconds passed, her form became less ghostly, all the colors of her coming into view. Her milky white skin shone in the moonlight beaming in from above, and her opal-like eyes gazed upon us intently. Her hair floated around her, black as night, seeming to reflect every star in the night sky.

Her gaze landed on mine for a split second, her eyes unblinking, before it slipped to Rhone. She tilted her head then, her galaxy hair spilling over her shoulder in the movement. She hummed a soft tune then, the Fae orbs reacting to the high-pitched tone, their flames shaking and dimming. Her humming continued; it was an ancient Fae tune. Her voice was as sweet as a nightingale, sending shivers up my spine. She held out her slender finger and reached out to touch Rhone's cheek, sliding her finger under his chin.

Her unearthly ancient voice, sweet as honey but holding an unmistakable edge, reverberated off the stone walls, "Rhonan Hitori, given the last name of orphans. Unborn. Son of no one. Rhone the Storm Bringer. Rhonan the Void Barer. Destroyer of Villages. Destroyer of Kingdoms. Rhonan of Tribe Ito. Rhone the Wanderer. Warrior of No Realm. Keeper of None. King of the Darkness. King of Nowhere. King of the Faceless and Fateless." She paused for a moment, letting her finger slip from his chin, her eyes sliding from Rhone's unwavering eyes to the hand on the hilt of his dagger. The corner of her mouth slid into a smile, her eyes meeting mine.

"Rhone the Seeker. Rhonan the Prisoner. Rhonan the Dark One. Rhone of Many Names," she said, her smile not quite reaching her eyes as they burned into mine. She began to circle us then.

Her hand reaching down and lingering over Rhone's dagger-ready hand, the dagger disappearing, leaving Rhone empty handed. This was her quiet warning. She may be a cursed god, but she was still a god, and not to be messed with. She glides up beside me, her hair flowing out behind her. And yes, those were definitely real galaxies within the depths of her strands, the slight tug of the gravitational pull sliding across my skin in her strands' wake. She paused next to me, turning to look at me. She was so close I could feel the chill that seemed to emanate off her snow-white skin, her opalescent eyes boring into mine.

She began humming again before she began speaking, "Soren Kissinger. Soren Amari. Soren the Twice-Born. Daughter of Two Worlds. Soren Barer of Sight. Soren the Light Bearer. Breaker of Realms. Soren of the Anew. Queen of Two Worlds. Queen of All Realms. Queen of Fates. Soren of Many Names," My heart raced as she spoke my name, names I had never heard, names I had no claim to. She stepped away from us then, her long legs making long strides.

She could see the question on my face, a light-hearted laugh escaping her delicate lips. "You two are quite the pair. Even the old Gods have heard whispers of the children of the prophecy, although you are missing one. The Cursed One." She clicked her tongue, "But you will do. The death bringers, the destroyers, that is gift enough. And here you are, in front of the cursed goddess herself, asking for her moon-soaked waters. Come, give me your hands, children." Her opal eyes glistened with mischief, leaving an air of whimsy and affection I did not expect to find in an ancient goddess. She held out her hand then and beckoned us forward. Before I could think, or blink for that matter, Rhone and I were placed in front of Máni, her magic's gravitational pull sucking us in closer. Our hands rested on top of one another in Máni's icy palm.

She placed her other hand on top of ours, a surge of her power gently pushing against my skin. "Yes, you two are truly children of the night. Children of the stars. Reckless and dangerous, I see chaos in your wake. But there is also a great feeling of relief here, a break in the universe, a gentle fracture that will shatter realms." A soft smile spread across her face; this pleased her.

"I grant your protection, my children," she said, her voice trailing off before she dissipated into the air, her statue becoming whole again. We stood there in silence for a moment, the sound of the bathing pool filling behind us, Máni's sudden absence a deafening void.

"Okay, you *did not* tell me that was going to happen," I said, turning to Rhone and breaking the silence. He was slow to respond. His eyes finally let go of the statue of Máni, which was once again pristine.

He let out a long sigh, "A God presenting themselves for any creature is almost unheard of; it was not even on my radar of possibilities. Usually, one would pray to the goddess, and then the god or goddess would answer silently. I just expected a silent answer, the pools to either fill or not fill," he said, shrugging his shoulders.

Still feeling the dizzying effects of her presence, the warm scents of vanilla and night jasmine began to fill the air as the bathing pool began to fill. I looked over in curiosity. The giant bathing pool had steam rising from it, and small bubbles floated atop the water from the vanilla and jasmine oils. I ached to slide down into the pool. If there was anything I loved more than a nice hot bath, it was a nice hot *giant* bath with luxurious oils.

Rhone brushed past me then, looking back over his shoulder with a grin. "Well, what are you waiting for? Our present for being chaotic and dangerous awaits." His hands reached for the edge of his sweater, and it was as he was yanking it over his head, his bare half-tattooed back flexing in response, did I realize I had nothing to change into. A hot blush flushed my cheeks, realizing I would have to either jump in fully clothed or strip down to my bra and panties.

Rhone was at the edge of the bathing pool now, sliding his leather boots off and pausing as his fingers reached his belt. I was embarrassed to say I couldn't look away; his body amazed me every time I caught a glimpse. My heartbeat deceived me, picking up as his jeans landed at his ankles, leaving only his black boxer briefs behind. *I mean, even his ass is tight with muscle,* I thought, rolling my eyes at his annoying amount of perfection. He kicked his pants away and stepped onto the bathing pool steps, lowering himself into the steamy water. He spun around, lowering himself deeper into the water, only his mouth up was visible.

"You know, scorning Goddess Máni's blessing and gift would offend her greatly." He gave me a pointed look which snapped to the statue of Máni, bringing me back to reality. He was right, I couldn't stand here all night, I couldn't let her think I was displeased. Watching Rhone undress had fogged up my mind, and I did not want to figure out which galaxy Máni would send me off to if I declined her gift of protection. *Okay, bra and panties it is then.*

I let out a nervous sigh. How was anyone supposed to undress in front of Rhone after he had put on such a show? Something ever so slight had changed since our long talk the other night. A tendril of affection linked me to him; I could feel it when he looked at me, the spark coming to life in his eyes. Affection I didn't want and didn't trust. Fae were tricky beings by nature. Charm and cunning came as natural as breathing to them. I had already fallen into the trap of one certain Fae trickster, a Miragen himself. And I didn't exactly feel confident enough in my abilities to pick another partner, of any kind, just yet. But I would be lying if I said I didn't think this chemistry Rhone and I had was authentic in some form, even if just feral desire.

I decided to try and distract myself, trick the nervousness out of my body, although I was genuinely curious, "Who was The Cursed One she talked about? She said "*Children of the Prophecy,*" does that mean anything to you?"

"I have never heard of this other prophecy, just yours," He answered.

Just as I was about to ask Rhone to turn around for more privacy, he huffed a laugh. "Don't worry, I am a gentleman above all else," he said as he submerged his head completely underwater. I silently thanked him, the bundle of nerves easing a little as I hurriedly yanked off my layers of clothing. I looked down at my body then, grumbling at myself for not shaving my legs earlier today but also grateful I had chosen a matching bra and panty set, white lace with delicate pink embroidered flowers. At the time I wasn't sure why I did it, but honestly, with everything Vana had packed for me, most things were dainty and see-through.

Quickly, I stepped into the pool, the moon-blessed water sending a low hum of tingling ancient magic through my body. The water shimmered and seemed to cling to my skin, leaving behind glints of what could only be described as moondust in its wake. Before I could get waist-deep, Rhone's head emerged. His storm cloud eyes opened and he rapidly blinked the water out of them.

"You know, even Fae can't hold their breath forever. One might think you were trying to kill me with how slow—" He stopped mid-sentence as his eyes landed on me. I became even more aware of just how *almost* naked I was before him.

Blushing, I looked down into the glimmering water. I could feel his eyes following my every move as I dipped myself further into the bathing pool. Steam filled the room, and I silently wondered to myself if that was truly just the water or his power rumbling to life.

"Maybe I was trying to kill you, I guess now we will never know," I said, bobbing closer to him, that tug I couldn't seem to resist, drawing me closer.

His eyes met mine, a dark thundering storm behind them, the same storm I had seen in my father's office. We were inches away now, his legs finding mine under the water. His ankle wrapped around mine, dragging me through the water until my breasts were flush against his chest. My heart thundered, his body this close to mine sent waves of desire flowing through me, a desire I couldn't deny even if I tried. Gently, he brushed away strands of hair that clung to my forehead, running his finger down my cheek and taking my chin in his hand.

Tilting my face up to his, his lightning storm eyes flashing as they bore into mine as he said, "I wouldn't put up a fight, as long as you promised to be just as dangerous and unpredictable as you usually are," he said, his eyes sliding down to roam every inch of my body. "Drowning is really letting me off easy, don't you think, little Bringer of Death?"

His arm wrapped around my waist, closing any gap that would have existed. I could feel every inch of his warrior-honed body. His desire for me was a match of mine for him, thick and pulsing with the rapid beat of his heart. I pressed myself closer to him, if that was even possible. He let out a small groan, his lips brushing mine before he finally kissed me. His velvet soft lips slid over mine, his tongue slipping into my mouth, and it was my turn to groan against his lips. I could feel him break loose then. His arms trembling around me, his kiss becoming deeper, more demanding. His hand slid to the back of my head, tangling itself in my hair. He gave my hair a slight tug, opening my mouth wider to his.

He needed more and more and more, and I was ready for him to take it. He lifted me up then, setting me on the side of the bathing pool and placing himself right at my center. I leaned back, and he followed, his lips finding my neck. Nothing but sheer white lace and black boxer briefs were between us. I could feel his hard pulsing desire through the thin fabric, and it was promising to be my undoing. I couldn't help but to move my body against his, a low moan escaping his lips, the lightning storm in his eyes rumbling to life outside the temple walls. In one swift movement, he wrapped his arm around me and we were shadowing. A haunting laugh trailed behind us as we left.

We shadowed into a dark room. A fireplace was crackling in the corner and giant windows showcased the Ostorous mountains, rain pouring and lightning flashing. Everything was still a thick haze, my desire for him engulfing every other thought I could have had.

With Rhone's arm still around me, he picked me up and laid me down on the edge of the bed, spreading my legs to him and settling his hips between them. His pulsing desire nestled back against mine. As he leaned down, he brushed hair out of my eyes again. I quickly looked away, not wanting him to catch me staring too long.

"No, don't. Look at me," he said, his voice low and hoarse. I looked up at him then, his towering form leaning over me. His smoldering stare quickened my heart beat even more, if that was even possible. It was the same stare I had seen in my father's office, the same storm brewing behind them.

He leaned forward, hooking his fingers at the clasp of my bra between my breasts and unhooking it. My bra fell to either side of me. He let out a soft groan, one I was maybe not supposed to hear, as he looked down at my breasts. They felt heavy with desire, as my whole body did. I pushed my chest up, basically begging for his touch. Rhone obliged, sliding a rough hand up my thigh, lingering at my waist and skidding up my sides as he finally reached my breast. His massive hand cupping them, catching my hardened nipple between his fingers. Clasping it hard between his knuckles, he leaned down, sucking it into his mouth. His teeth grazed it as his soft hot tongue flicked its peak. I sucked in a breath, the contact of his teeth against my soft subtle skin, the feeling of *him* was too much.

I rolled my hips against his, pushing my aching desire against him. He let out a moan, one I knew I was supposed to hear this time, as his hips met mine in a matching thrust. His still slick skin glistened with the remnants of the shimmering waters of the moon-blessed bath. I sat up to touch him, letting my fingers slide down over the tattooed side of his chest. My fingers stopped around his still damp waist band, my eyes reaching for his reassurance. His fingers meeting mine were the answer. He slid his hand over mine, taking both our hands to pull his boxers down. His impressive length fell heavy against my palm. Barely wrapping my hand around it, I gave it a long stroke, using his drips from his already wet tip to glide down his entire length. I savored the feel of the hot velvet skin against my palm.

Rhone's head fell back then, his chest heaving as I stroked it again. Slowly, he took his hands and placed them on each of my knees, pushing them open wider. My core ached for him, and I knew I was dripping as he looked up at me and locked my eyes with his. He ran his hand up my thigh before stopping at my core. Shoving my panties aside, he ran a finger up my wet entrance, dipping his fingers inside me, both of us panting in pleasure.

"Fuck," he softly growled as he thrust his fingers deeper inside me. His other hand rested on my shoulder where he leaned me back to rest on my elbows. He dipped his head down and sucked my nipple back in his mouth, catching it with his teeth. Simultaneously, he slid his fingers out of me, I couldn't help it then, I let out a cry of pleasure.

I ached to get him closer, ached to have more of him inside me, to wrap my mouth around him. I reached down and stroked him again, quicker this time, and he met me in rhythm, thrusting himself harder into my palm. Rhone's head landed on my shoulder. His lips found my throat, soft kisses turning into bites as they trailed down my shoulder.

I began to reposition myself but before I could, Rhone grabbed my hand. Pulling it away from his cock, he set it down on my thigh. He lifted his head from my neck, his breathing heavy, his hands back on my knees. He ran his hand up my body before landing in my hair, his thumb brushing back and forth across my cheek. He didn't move for a long second, his gaze never leaving mine. He dipped his head down, his soft lips colliding with mine. It was no longer as urgent, but the desire was still there. I could feel it in the way his tongue swept against mine. In the way his length was still hard and throbbing against my thigh.

"Soren..." he said breathlessly as he broke away. He leaned back then, putting distance between us, the farthest away we had been from each other in what felt like ages. The absence of his body against mine had an unwanted sobering effect, stifling the flames between us. I suddenly felt self-conscious. Suddenly very aware of the absence of heavy breathing and the distance between us. Confusion shifted inside me and I waited for Rhone's guidance.

I mean, are we still doing this? What has made him change his demeanor so quickly? Did I do something wrong?

He cleared his throat again as he looked at me, his eyes more alert but still laden with a haze of sexual desire. He swept his lingering gaze down my body again before turning around and reaching for a cashmere throw blanket that laid across the edge of the bed. He shook it out and draped it across my shoulders, and then grabbed his robe and shrugged it on. He looked so domestic here, his form towering still, but domestic all the same. Disheveled hair hung loose down his back, his terry cloth robe tied tightly across his waist. The glow of the fireplace softened the growing look of concern on his face, which increased the pit of twisting anxiety gnawing away at my stomach, which had quickly replaced my oncoming orgasm.

Rhone took a deep breath before beginning to speak, "Soren...I... I had to get us out of that temple. The moon-beam waters.... I believe Goddess Máni entranced them with not only her protection but a heavy spell of seduction as well. Enchantment from the Gods... they feel heavier than Fae enchantments because they are much stronger. I could sense there was more than one. Gods are tricky, trickier than Fae and I think she was trying to trap us. Her blessing was the protection, but to fall for the spell of seduction... She *wanted* us to have sex in that bathing pool. That would have damned us to her, just as she is damned. Cursed us as her servants until her demise. I had my suspicions about the woodland creature statues that were strewn about the temple, but I let myself disregard them too quickly. I think those could be the unlucky ones who didn't get away."

I turned away from him suddenly; I could no longer look him in the eyes. My face grew hot with embarrassment, the embarrassment of not only him seeing me in that form, but from believing it was real.

Embarrassment for the fact I still wanted it to be real, and embarrassment over the fact he clearly didn't. *But it felt so real, so magnetic and natural.* But Rhone had made it extremely clear all this was for him was the effects of a God's trick.

With that realization, my embarrassment turned to anger quickly, my hands balling into fists around the throw he had laid across my shoulders in an attempt to cover me. He took a step closer to me, and I stood up quickly, not even trying to hide the scowl on my face. I could tell he was trying to formulate what to say next.

I lifted my eyes back to his, my anger bubbling over, "Why did you let it go so far once we got here if you felt it wasn't even real? It felt incredibly real to me; you must have known that. *Your* reactions felt incredibly real," I said.

He shook his head, putting it down in defeat. "I... Soren, it's not that I didn't want... haven't wanted...I just thought once we shadowed here it would be easier to shake..." He shook his head again and I could tell his was looking for the right words to piece together next. "I just couldn't let this happen. We have too much at stake here, and so much coming from so many angles. We have your crazed ex-boyfriend lurking everywhere trying to kill you, Synnove hunting *both* of us, training and honing your powers, allies to align for an impending war that is sure to happen *and* a wedding extravaganza to attend. Making this whole lover ploy real...It could put us in such a dangerous spot with real feelings involved. This would... complicate things even more," he sighed heavily, running a hand through his hair. "If it made sense for Cal to take my spot here, I'd do it, but Callum only takes male lovers. The whole of the creature realms knows this. To pin you to me for even just one wedding... It isn't fair. To pin you to me like this for real..." He took another deep breath, his thoughts moving faster than his lips could.

"Listen, I'm sorry this happened. If I would've known the goddess had this up her sleeve... I would have got us out of there sooner, before the enchantment could take hold. We just don't have time for complicated things. And I'd be incredibly selfish to let myself take advantage of you like that. You deserve something real and someone who is entirely present, Soren. When I have you, I won't let go of control, I know that's not what you want. "

I SAT THERE for a long moment, digesting everything he had just said. He was right, I did deserve something real and someone who was present, both things he was clearly unwilling to give me. *Stupid, stupid, Soren. Always throwing yourself at the nearest emotionally unavailable man. Even worse this time, he didn't even want to use you sexually. We had gone through this before, in my father's office. He had made it clear twice now.*

Even though I knew he was right on multiple accounts, I didn't want to give him any more space to explain, any more air to breathe in the same room as me. I brushed past him, dropping the throw onto the floor in front of the door. But fairness? In what realm was he an unfair partner? I collected myself as much as I could.

"You're right, no complications," I said, my voice purposely clipped. I turned and left the room, shutting the door quickly behind me. I didn't let myself fully crumble until I got to my room and closed the door behind me.

I crawled into my bed, wrapped myself in the plush comforter, and stared out the window, trying to ignore the hollow tug of sadness I felt in my chest. I had been dumped by boyfriends of years, I had been beaten by Willem, but still, this fresh wound with sharp cuts of humiliation lingered in my chest, threatening to bring tears to my eyes.

TWELVE

I t had been two weeks since the encounter with Goddess Máni. Two weeks of early mornings, two weeks of training for eight hours, two weeks of trying to ignore how close his body got to mine during training, two weeks of short conversations and quick dinners. Two weeks of memorizing Huran Tribal traditions and cultural norms. Two weeks of learning everything that was written about the Huran Tribe, and things that Rhone knew that wasn't common knowledge. Two weeks practicing bits of pieces of the Huran language, as none of it was formally written down. Two weeks that had me feeling like I had blinked and here I was. Two weeks that had felt surreal. Three weeks since anyone had heard from Vana. I had tried to call her several times with no answer. I'd be lying if I said I wasn't getting nervous over her silence. One week until we had to meet at Royal High Wizard Aaren's wedding.

I laid on my bed, flipping through the news section, missing the comfort of the newspaper from the Human Realm. Nothing alarming had happened since we left the

Human Realm. No articles over the famous human Inventor Merin Kissinger's house being broken into or being partially destroyed. Nothing over a downtown floral shop explosion. Everything seemed so quiet... too quiet really. My parents truly had done a wonderful job covering everything up. I was getting bored in this house. This house, whose only form of communication consisted of a phone that never rang, got shoddy service because of these damn mountains, and harbored the only person in the realms I very certainly did not want to be talking to at the moment.

I rolled over onto my back, letting out a frustrated sigh. My muscles ached from the hours of training today, but every day the aches became less of a nuisance. I had come a long way with training in two weeks. Even Rhone, who generally avoided conversation with me as I avoided conversation with him, had mentioned how swiftly I was becoming a skilled fighter. My powers had also been coming along, but much slower than fighting techniques. I could now slip in and out of The Gap, but calling forth the correct life thread was still a bit tricky. I could, however, call forth the silver chains that I had with Willem. My father believed the substance I am bringing forward is the stardust that lingers in the realms and in me. He also believed I could be able to form all types of weapons and things to my advantage. I just hadn't quite gotten there yet.

I began aimlessly forming silver stardust chains in the air, letting them dissipate and building them back chain link by chain link. We had tried tirelessly to find the end of my power. Rhone had said everyone has an end, and it usually feels just like that. You're falling and falling and then you hit the stone floor of the bottom of your power. I had gotten used to the feel of my power as well. I imagined it as silver threads of stardust, pulling themselves from the layers of time and galaxies as I willed.

It was funny, all the things that your power could do. I had learned so much in such a short time. Raw power was the untamed, chaotic and unformed version of your power. The most dangerous to wield, Rhone had warned. It was always better to wield your power with thought behind it, give it a form and purpose. Things were way less likely to go awry that way. I felt my power rise to my palm, and let it pool there, waiting for instructions. It was really something, the specks of stardust beautiful and glistening every shade of the rainbow as the light hit it. A knock on the door broke me away from my thoughts, and my power eased itself back into me. *It must be 8 pm*, I thought. Dinner was always at eight and was always promising to be delicious. I rolled my eyes anyways.

"Who is it?" I shouted back, snorting at my own remark, continuing my chain link by link, knowing it could only be one person. The door opened silently, and without looking over I said, "Alright, alright, I'm coming," sitting up and throwing my legs over the edge of the bed.

"Well, things are getting off with the two of you just as well as could be expected," said an unfamiliar voice, thick with the accent of the highlands. I snapped my head up in surprise, jumping off the bed quickly. My eyes darted around the room for the dagger Rhone had given me from the armory a few days ago.

"Aye lass, don't fret, I heard you knew I was comin'. Rhone, the old bastard, told me to come get ya for dinner.

But he didna' warn me you'd react like a feral cat," he said, laughing.

He stood in the doorway, straight back and arms crossed, he was tall for human standards, but considered average height for a Fae Male. He was well dressed in a ribbed short sleeve dark green mock neck, which was tucked into plaid trousers and adorned with a sleek black leather belt and matching black leather loafers. Silver and gold rings adorned his fingers. His biceps threatened to rip the delicate seams of his shirt, his arms riddled with tattoos and freckles. Tattoos of the Human Realm, interesting enough.

The patchwork layout and old school designs told me he had been collecting these in the Human Realm for at least the past eighty years, the tattoos shifting with the decades. I wondered silently what had drawn him to such specific human tattoos and not the traditional swirling and intricate geometric shapes of the Fae. He stared back at me as I considered him. His buzzed red hair stood out to me as well, as Royal Fae Males were known to love their silky long locks. Fae Males with short hair was rare, and buzzed even more so. He had brilliant green-brown eyes that were true to the heritage of the Royal Highland Fae, golden brown around the pupil, with deep green skirting the edges.

"We can't sit here staring longingly at each other all night. Wine is waiting!" he said, sounding truly excited, and he shadowed away.

I stood there for a beat longer, scowling at myself and the fact that there was yet another new arrogant Fae Male I had to get to know. I *hated* meeting new people. And seriously, *Did he honestly call me a feral cat?!*

~

WE ALL SAT at the bar top tonight, Rhone setting down my plate in front of me first. It looked incredible as usual. Tonight's dinner consisted of pan seared salmon on a bed of steamed white rice and a side of kimchi. It was simple, but I knew Rhone had even made the kimchi himself a few days ago. I took a sip of my crisp white wine, pear and honey blossom notes lingering on my tongue as I drank it down.

"So, Callum, you have finally gifted us with your presence, a week late," Rhone said as he took a bite of salmon, his eyebrows raised, an edge to his voice. This encounter between them was odd. Not the formal conversations I was used to hearing Royal Fae have together. Royal Fae were known to be arrogant tricksters, but polite and courteous all at the same time. I gathered Callum's incredibly late arrival had offended Rhone greatly, but it could've worried him as well. My eyes darted between each of the men.

Callum smiled, nodding his head in agreeance as he swallowed his bit of food, his eyes sliding to mine. "Rhone only refers to me by my full name when he's angry with me." He turned his attention back to Rhone, "Ah yes, dear friend, I got held up at one of the Wild Fae outposts near here, giving them some much needed attention to help to patch up one of their armory buildings and a grain storage elevator. Some of their tribe had gone missing as well. The war still goes on, but it could be hard to know that all the way up here. There may have been my interests in a Fae Male involved as well, but that's neither here nor there," Callum said, shrugging his shoulders.

"You know, the original plan was for you two to meet me

at the Highland Palace, but Emrin has explained the change of plans. The libraries can wait until after the wedding. They will still be there...gods willing. I will say, though, on my way to the outpost, you two looked pretty busy, rummaging around in the enchanted forest and all. Ducking into purposely hidden temple ruins," Callum said, looking up from his plate and flashing yellow glowing eyes in my direction, a devilish grin appearing on his face.

Suddenly, I made the connection, the yellow eyes following us along the darkest edge of the Ostorous forest. Callum had been there, watching us.

Callum continued as Rhone sat silently, intently listening to Callum's explanation and also very intentionally sending warning signals to Callum to cease speaking. "I don't quite know what has gotten into you, Rhonan. The dangers of entering an ancient God's sleeping place, and not just any God but Goddess Máni, the most unhinged of them all? She could have struck you down upon entrance, as most Gods would have. Fae simply do not enter temples of the old Gods anymore, not after all the strife between us. But I am not telling you anything you don't know. You lived through those times; I did not." Callum clicked his tongue in discontent, lifting his glass and taking a long sip of wine.

As his glass left his lips, he raised it in my direction, "But enough with the unpleasantries. Soren, it is so nice to finally meet you. I have heard absolutely nothing about you, but you will certainly be the talk of the Fae realm soon enough! You are just exquisite really, all that golden-brown hair, caramel skin and those eyes, they could harbor all the galaxies." He let out a low whistle, "It's a shame I am incredibly inclined to be solely attracted to the usually atrocious male of any species." He rolled his eyes and gave me a wink, and with that, I couldn't help but laugh, feeling the tension in the room drop considerably. I blushed at his flattery all the same, looking down sheepishly into the bottom of my wine glass.

We spent the next hour talking over dinner, our glasses of wine refilling as we emptied them. I learned that Callum, whose friends call him Cal, was one of the funniest creatures you could ever meet. He was High Royal Prince of the Highland Fae, and also the self-proclaimed rebel son of five brothers. He rejected his role for the most part, preferring to roam the realms freely, cut his hair as he pleased, and collect tattoos as he went. He told me of his many war medals nonchalantly with a wave of his hand, calling them nothing but silly. But Rhone interjected him, assuring me he vigorously earned every one of them and held some of the greatest fire affinities in all the realms. He could apparently ignite entire cities without depleting his magic.

Joke after joke, my nerves eased. We talked about life, shared stories of our childhood all the way up to finding out my true parentage and powers. Callum asked me how I was dealing with the changes, and I answered honestly. He was easy to talk to, and if my father and Rhone trusted him to be a part of our innermost circle, then I did too. Rhone sat back for most of the dinner, quietly subdued, but still laughed with us and chimed in here and there.

It was a nice change to the usually silent dinners and yes/no conversations we had been having since our night together. It was also incredibly necessary, with the wedding coming up and with me set to be Rhone's date. The awkward silence between us would not convince anyone in the ballroom of our relationship. Rhone was my "in" with the Royal Fae society, he had connections I could never dream of having, connections like Cal. I even caught Rhone casually gazing at me from time to time, a soft look adorning his face, as I turned my head to laugh at yet another thing that came out of Callum's mouth or talked with my hands in excitement. I tried and failed to not let my thoughts linger on that.

On my fourth glass of wine, I excused myself, leaving the boys at the table to talk amongst themselves. The wine and good conversation left me feeling warm and cozy inside and ready for a deep sleep that the alcohol promised to give me. As I walked down the hallway, I caught a snippet of their lingering conversation.

Cal's voice dipping in volume, "I can see why you risked your life to get the old Goddesses' blessing of protection," followed by Rhones' dismissive voice in warning, even lower, "That's enough, Cal."

Cal's knowing laugh was the last thing I heard as I clicked the door shut, deciding to unhear that last exchange.

ALMOST A WEEK HAD PASSED with Callum in the house. Days of late night dinners and good conversation, and early mornings with slight hangovers and hours' worth of training. As I got to the training room, I stopped in my tracks at the open door. Rhone and Cal were sparring, power and blades crashing together, blow for blow. It was quite the scene, both Fae warriors living up to their accolades perfectly. Their shirtless muscled torsos twisted in precise movement like a dance. Rhone effortlessly dodged Callum's blow of red and purple flames, while Callum tossed aside Rhone's strike of lightning that shot forth from his palm. *Oh he is definitely showing off for Callum, I have* never *seen him do that before.* They were so well matched, that this spar could loop on forever.

As if suddenly noticing my presence, both men stopped, breathing heavily but hours away from down for the count. Grabbing his shirt from the ground, Rhone wiped the sweat off his face as he sauntered my direction. He handed me his sparring sword, the hilt warm from his grip.

"It's time for you to train against a fire wielder. Your technique is fantastic, but we need to make sure you can hold up against someone whose magic is different from mine," Rhone said. I nodded in agreement, walking towards the middle of the sparring mat, readying myself into a fighting stance.

"Don't worry, I wore him out a little bit for you," Rhone said, a smirk on his face as he sat down on the ground.

Callum barked a laugh in return. "Hardly, laddie, I'm just getting warmed up." That was all the warning I received as red and purple flames danced to life at Callum's fingertips and laced up the sword blade, setting it ablaze. *Now that is something.* I jumped back just in time to dodge Callum's first blow, flames licking at my fighting leathers. We danced like this for a few moments, me dodging while Cal threw around blows. I knew I needed to make direct contact at some point, but he was fast. Just as fast as Rhone. But I knew Rhone's patterns by this time, I knew nothing of Callum's. I focused, watching Callum's feet as he bounced back and forth effortlessly. He favored his right foot, and I knew that was my hit point, it was the only slight weakness I could see in him.

For weeks, Rhone had pushed me to look for weakness in battle. He had feigned weakness on every part of his body, external and internal, badgering me to spar until I could find the weakness and strike. If I got it wrong, we went until I got it right. I had yelled out in frustration more times than I could remember, cursing him and calling him every name in the book, but he never budged, not until I got it right. I was now grateful for these lessons, praying I was right.

I took the sword and met Callum's in the air. The flames reached out, getting closer to my fingertips as the seconds passed. I used all my might to press against Callum's weight, my arms trembling with the effort. He looked across the flames in my eyes, his glowing a bright yellow. This was it, my one second of distraction. As he thought I was focusing on my full brunt of force, I sucked in a deep breath. I willed my power to build, feeling its familiar and now comforting tingle come to life in my fingertips. Throwing my power out into the world, a long thick heavy silver chain pieced itself together. Quickly, I whipped the chain back, sliding it forward across the floor and letting it wrap about Callum's left ankle. In one swift yank, Callum, Prince of the Highlands, was falling backward and hit the ground with a thud, letting out an "Oof" of pain with the contact. His sword knocked out of his hand, I ran to retrieve it. Turning swiftly, I placed the blade at the edge of his throat.

I heard a slow clap erupt from behind us, Rhone's smile plastered across his face. He was proud, beaming practically.

"What Soren lacks in size and brute force, she makes up

for in her cunning," Rhone said, his voice just as smug as the smile on his face as he sauntered over to Callum to help him up.

Callum's ego was bruised, but he was a good sport. He held out his hand, ready to shake this opponent he lost to. I obliged, beaming at him.

"Very impressive, Soren, let's hope you never get into your head too much during battle. Without the cunning, not having the brute force will shake your chances," Cal said matter-of-factly, and I knew he was right.

"Now, who wants to cut training short this morning and go shopping? I'm dying to get out of this smelly training room and have a long-awaited sip of an iced coffee," Callum exclaimed. He looked me up and down, then adding, "And you simply can't go to your first Fae extravaganza dressed like this." He shook his head in disappointment.

Rhone snorted in retort. "She looks fine just like that. And no one is going shopping. Find a different alternative; she's being hunted, remember? Her life is not worth a ball gown."

Callum groaned, but quickly nodded in agreement. "Fine, but she's coming home with me. Barbette can tailor the most perfect gown for her. She's a world class seamstress; her Fae gift is that of glamouring. They are truly incredible glamours, no seams, no glitches, and the clothing always manifests in your closet as a physical set when you're done!" He leaned closer into me and whispered, "Thank the Gods Rhone does not have his shackles around me like he does you, or we'd never be able to get away from his incessant brooding."

Cal grabbed my hand, the faint smell of burning embers filling my nostrils as we shadowed away.

THIRTEEN

Cal had shadowed us into a sleek penthouse apartment on the top floor of a skyscraper building, overlooking a city I had never seen before. The city was sprawling, seeming to reach the edges of the world in every direction. I had seen pictures of the Galarian Cities before, but seeing them from this view was truly something unlike anything I could have ever imagined. The buildings were all carved out of a matching cream-colored stone, the traditional swirling designs carved into the buildings and intricate arched windows adorned them all as far as the eye could see. The Royal Fae had truly blended modern design with traditional Fae architecture beautifully. A river ran through the middle of the city, busy roads bridged over it, its turquoise waters glinting in the sunlight.

Callum came up next to me. "It's pretty incredible, don't you think?"

I couldn't look away from the view, wanting to know what every crevice of the city was. "Yes, it really is. I had no idea they made big cities this incredibly beautiful. It looks pristine from up here. I mean, have you *seen* Vellven City? I mean, sure its a sprawling metropolis full of dazzling city lights and skyscrapers but..." I said in return.

Cal laughed, tossing his head back, "Oh I've seen Vellven City all right, but that could be the beauty of humans. They are so honest in their living. This city is pretty pristine, but not without the help of Fae magic of course." That was the truth of it all really, human made inventions could only do so much and would never truly match up to Fae magic. Cal spent the next ten minutes pointing out landmarks around our view of the city. Everything from the Galarian Libraries to the Council Hall building.

"Alright, we have got to get this show on the road" He looked down at his gold watch. "We have less than 20 hours to get you prepared for this wedding, and honey this isn't just any wedding, it's the wedding of the century, okay?" He looked me up and down, a cringe twisting his face in an exaggerated expression and I couldn't help but laugh. Now I knew I wasn't *that* bad.

"But honestly, I cannot be expected to do my best work without iced coffee, Rhone knows this," Callum said, rolling his eyes. He started vigorously typing into his phone, and I assured him whatever he was having would be great. Within minutes, his phone pinged, and he said he would be right back, shadowing before I could even respond.

With Callum gone, I meandered around his spacious apartment. Every inch of the outer walls were lined with floor to ceiling arched windows, and a large velvet moss green sectional sat in the middle of the room in front of a giant white marble fireplace. An intricate rug, woven with burnt oranges and golden yellows, cozied up the white marble floors. Oddities lined the built-in shelves on either side of the fireplace. He had everything from tiny woodland creature skulls, a set of sprite wings, a gaggle of rusty human relics-many of which I did not even recognize because they were so old, a dagger in which the blade was entirely made out of glistening ruby and even a golden fang from the long extinct Hydras that used to dwell in the caves on the Ostorous mountains. The living room opened up to a large kitchen. Sleek emerald green tiles lined the walls, gold accents sprinkled across every appliance.

Cal shadowed back into the apartment in a burst of fiery embers, his arms full of iced coffee. Enough for 5 people. I laughed, helping him set down the coffee cups.

"You need that much coffee to turn me into Fae Royalty material?" I said, and we laughed together.

"Oh no, no, this is for Barbette and her crew of course. She will be here any minute! You will love her. She has been the head royal seamstress of the highland palace for over a hundred years."

I grabbed the coffee with my name scribbled on the side and took my first sip. My eyes grew wide in surprise. It was absolutely *delicious.*

"Okay, is there actual magic in this cup?! My taste buds have no idea what to do with all this." The coffee was the perfect mixture of creamy but not too overly sweet. Sugared lavender and brown sugar flavoring hit my tongue, transforming into a caramelly aftertaste. I was surely going to be addicted.

"I know, it's pretty great. I get one every morning basically," he said, beaming, happy with my delight.

Suddenly, three Fae were shadowing into the kitchen. A small middle-aged Royal Fae female stood in the middle. She had a sleek copper long bob, her pale blue eyes darting across the room trying to adjust. She was dressed in a fashionable crisp white crew neck T-shirt crop and high-waisted wide pant black trousers. She had a belt with all sorts of sewing nicknacks tacked on to it. This had to be Barbette. She was holding the hands of two younger Fae females, each resembling her at a striking amount, and both equally almost half a foot taller than her. One had wildly curly long red hair, while the other had hers cut into a short, structured pixie cut.

Cal rushed over to greet them warmly, taking time to hug them each. He shoved coffees into their hands as they talked amongst themselves for a short moment before he turned back to me.

"Ladies, this is Soren, of Tribe Huran. She is the very lucky date of Rhone Hitori, to the wedding of the century. She is new to society, so she must look the part and we have about 18 hours to train her up on proper Royal Fae etiquette," Callum exclaimed excitedly, talking quickly and waving his hands around wildly.

He leaned into me, trying and failing to whisper, "I mean, not to say you don't know how to act proper, but your... upbringing was different from the other high royals that will be gathered at this event."

He turned his attention back to the three women. "Soren, this is Barbette Twinnings and her daughters, Melina and Elspeth. They are incredible seamstresses, Melina is a magician with hair and Elspeth does wonders with makeup. They will also work with me in teaching you proper social etiquette," Callum said to me. Melina smiled at me, her excitement matching Cal's as she twisted her wild curls back into a bun. Elspeth however, did not share the same amusement, she dug through her make up box loudly as she sucked down the last bits of her iced coffee, making as much noise as possible. Barbette cleared her throat in a pointed notion towards Elspeth to act right.

Barbette stepped forward, her small frame commanding attention in ways I wished to some day.

"Let me look at you, lass," Barbette said. She stood a few inches shorter than me, but raised her hand to lift my chin with her small slender fingers anyways. She made a complete circle around me, looking me up and down with her arms crossed, murmuring words in such a thick accent I couldn't quite understand. Her girls were busy behind her, setting up a station equipped with a makeup station, a stand for taking my measurements and of course a mini salon and spinning chair.

"Hmmmm..." Barbette mused before saying, "You are as beautiful as Callum exclaimed. But beauty will not get you too far at high society events. Everyone is beautiful there. Your dress needs to be striking, as striking as the starlight in your eyes. It needs to compliment your golden skin." She moved around me in a circle again, her hand on her chin in contemplation. "We will focus on making your dress provocative without giving away too much; we must keep it classy, but sexy enough to garner attention."

I stared down at her as she spoke, unsure how I felt about having no control over dressing myself for this event. The next six hours went by in a blur, we talked about fabrics, colors for my gown that wouldn't clash with other high courts that would be attending, —and considering I didn't belong to any court yet, I needed to try to avoid that scandal all together—, makeup to match my dress. We tried three different hairstyles, drank way too much champagne and went over just the way to greet a High Royal and what ways to avoid, such as to keep your head. The last hour and half was dedicated to memorizing high royal lineages and who belonged to what family.

As we finished up, Barbette's quiet daughters packing everything back up, Barbette came over to me with Cal in tow. She held what looked like a tiny makeup compact in her hands.

"Now, when it is time for you to get ready tomorrow, you will simply take this and open it. The enchantment will recognize your touch. Right now, you only have one event look in que, so this should be incredibly easy for you, darling. His highness Callum expressed you are new to such modern extravagant Fae magics, so I tried to make this easy enough for you," she said, giving Callum a side glance. I could tell she was perplexed by my situation. I was sure Callum had fed her the story of my Huran heritage and how I was some poor tribal Fae. It also seemed she assumed Rhone had stolen me during his plunder and decided to bring me up like Cinderella. I could see the motherly instinct of hers kicking in as she wondered just how I got into this situation.

As Callum walked away, Barbette leaned closer into me and began to whisper, "And if you should need *anything* at all tomorrow night, just say my name into the mirror. It will work like a cellphone— a direct line to me. That Rhone can be a brute I've heard." She quickly walked away, gathering her things and shadowing her girls away with her.

By the time we shadowed back to Rhone's hole in the mountain, I was entirely too spent. I welcomed my bed immediately.

I woke up with no alarm, and no knock on the door. Only the soft early morning light cascading over the black sheets I was wrapped in. I tried to think back to the last time I had woken up with absolutely nothing on my morning agenda. It was certainly at least over a month ago. It was an oddly satisfying feeling, to have nowhere to rush to, no training to warm up for. I could simply, be. Lazily, I whimmed up a steaming cinnamon vanilla latte. It presented itself in a lavish swirl of silver dust on my nightstand.

I groaned in pure joy as I took my first sip, the simple sweetness of the vanilla and the comfort of the cinnamon making my eyes roll. *Man, I had missed these incredibly human simplicities of a morning.* I sat up and leaned back against the headboard, fully enjoying my latte.

I spent the rest of the day in my room indulging in another latte, doing a long yoga routine and then soaked in the bath, using the new oils left on the side of the tub. They filled the room with notes of honey and orange blossom.

As the bath water drained and I towel dried myself off, the nerves began to hit. The clock said 5 pm, leaving only an hour to get myself ready. I had spent the day relaxing, trying to stave off the inevitable flood of anxiety that was going to come. I wrapped myself in my robe, truly wishing I could just go back to the bathtub and drown myself. I stared out into the Ostorous Mountains, watching snow fall and the sun beginning to set. A knock came at the door, bringing me out of my deep thought.

"Come in," I said, knowing it was either Rhone or Cal reminding me of the time crunch we were about to be in.

The door slid open and Callum stepped in. He was already ready for the wedding, dressed in a fine silk green and black striped tux, a crisp white shirt and a black bowtie to match. His hair had been newly shaved, tight and clean shaved on the sides with a low buzz left on top, his mustache trimmed as well. The green and black colors of the highland court suited him well, but I could tell his modern tux was going to differ greatly from the rest of the highland royalty's traditional attire. *Always the rebel.* He wore fine pearl cufflinks and a matching pearl and emerald on his lapel. The pin had the insignia of the Highland Crest, an arrow and a sword making a cross, with a sea serpent hissing in front of them. His normal silver hoop earrings had been changed out for gleaming white pearls as well. His outfit was complete with black leather shoes, so polished I could probably use them as a mirror later on to touch up my makeup. He had a dashing grin on his face, and gave me an exaggerated twirl, striking a model pose.

"So, what do you think? I clean up nicely, don't I?" he exclaimed as he came over in my direction, pulling me in for a hug, his smoky cedar and lavender scent welcoming me.

"Come on now, time to get excited! We are seriously going to have so much fun! It's like a murder mystery party, except *you're* the mystery," he said, shaking my shoulders a little bit.

I couldn't help but laugh, my solemn mood and knot of anxiety in my stomach instantly melting away. That was what being around Callum did to someone though, you simply couldn't be unhappy in his presence. He was right though; we could make this as fun as we wanted to.

"Cal, you really do look good, though! How does anyone ever resist you?" I laughed, stepping back and looking him up and down.

He threw his head back in laughter in return. "They usually can't resist me, lass," he said with a wink. He looked down at his watch, clicking his tongue in response.

"Okay, okay, enough about me, Rhone will have a fit if we are late," he said, and turned around, snatching the enchanted mirror compact Barbette had fixed up for me off the dresser and shoving it in my hand. I flipped the smooth, cold, silver compact around in my hand, staring at the swirling floral etchings. The butterflies beat against my ribcage again as I stared down at this tiny object. Callum grabbed my hand then; it was warm and big and soothing. I sucked in a deep breath, breathing out slowly and willed the butterflies to calm.

Cal gave my hand a squeeze. "You can do this, Soren, and you will do great. You are so prepared," he said softly, his emerald and deep red brown eyes staring intently into mine. I nodded my head in agreement, a small nod. I took my hand out of his grasp and took two steps back, opening the compact and closing my eyes in anticipation.

I felt a soft brush of wind rush around me, and I heard it rustle the curtains behind me. I opened my eyes then, no longer too anxious to look as I felt the magic rush up my body, my hair gently blowing back. I turned to the dresser mirror, and watched the enchantment finish its job. The magic moved around me in calm motions, glistening swirls turning every hue of the rainbow, the enchantment tugging at my skin slightly as it worked. My jaw dropped as I watched myself change and the magic slide across my skin.

"Watching you experience your own kind's magic for the first time... is truly remarkable. It just might not ever get old. You're like a 500-year-old newborn babe," Callum said, laughter in his voice.

My hair swooped up, drying itself and came back down in a perfect blowout. My hair cascaded down my back in full bouncy curls, one side pinned back with a diamond clip. My make up was glamorous yet soft. A soft purple and taupe smokey eye, a nude-peach lipstick, and bronzer shaded my cheeks. My robe unraveled thread by thread, replacing itself with a deep purple satin dress, the color fading from a deep purple into every shade of the sunset—orange, pink, corals, and blues appearing as I shifted in the dress. The neckline was unlike any I had seen before, a one shoulder dress with a cut out revealing a tasteful swell of my breasts. The other strap was diamond studded and dropped off my shoulder. The bodice of the dress was a trumpet fit, the gown fitting like a glove and flowing out in waves mid hip. With the last swirl of the enchantment, diamond and amethyst teardrop earrings finished off the look, glittering in the glow of the fireplace.

Callum let out a low whistle, his eyebrows shooting up as he crossed his arms, one hand coming up to his cheek in astonishment. "Barbette really outdid herself with this one. Look at you, you are the evening star shining across the last of the sun's rays."

I looked back at myself in the mirror, and I knew he was right. I had maybe never felt more beautiful than I did right now, and truly it was the confidence boost I needed, my mood shifting. I looked to Callum, thankful for his fast friendship that had gotten me through these last couple of weeks.

I carefully gathered my skirts and walked towards him, taking his hand. "I've been waiting on you this whole time; we are going to be late!" I said, laughing, and hurried him out of the room towards the kitchen.

Rhone's towering form was the first thing I saw as we entered the room. Leaning against the island, one hand in his pocket, he stared down at his nails on the other. He wore a sleek, black silk, fitted suit, a crisp white button down shirt and a silk black tie. An intricately designed silver collar pin was the only flourish his outfit had, but it suited him well. It clipped on either side of his tie at the collar, silver filigree and a single lightning bolt as its design. His hair was pulled back into a low bun, pieces of his hair already falling forward, framing his beautifully stormy features. It would be a lie to call him anything else tonight, *or any night really.*

"It's about time you two made your grand appearance," Rhone said, finally looking up from his nails as we came to halt in front of him. He stilled as his eyes found me, running them up my body before landing on my eyes. Storm clouds came to life in them, the moment fleeting, but I caught it nonetheless. We had looked at each other seldomly the past few weeks, usually looking away from each other upon entering the same room. To have his eyes on me was... alarming. The thrill of his stare sent shivers across my body.

Tearing his eyes from mine, he cleared his throat and quickly looked to Callum.

"Everyone looks well suited for a grand wedding, I'd say," Rhone said as he adjusted his suit jacket. We all stood there for a beat, before Callum broke the silence.

He took my hand and led me to Rhone's side, placing my arm around his, and came around to stand in front of us. "Listen, you two are going to have to loosen up a little bit, ya ken? Whatever has you two in a tizzy, it cannot exist tonight. Tonight you are in love, tonight you are a happy couple. Nothing can be amiss, and no one can suspect anything." Cal's voice was tight and serious, a tone I had only heard once before, when he was giving Rhone lashings for our adventure to Goddess Máni's temple.

Rhone grabbed my hand then, the skin-to-skin contact bringing back the butterflies I had done such a good job of getting rid of earlier. His hand was just as rough and warm as my memory recollected.

He gave my hand a gentle squeeze before saying, "I think you all will find I can take on the part of lover boy quite naturally." His eyes flashed as he looked down at me, storm clouds engulfing us as we shadowed.

CHAPTER
FOURTEEN

We shadowed into a corner of the gardens, rose bushes hiding us from view, the High Wizard's palace looming over us. The palace was luminous, made of beige stone, with giant glossy blue diamond-paned windows lining the walls. Towers jutted into the sky, sunlight gleaming off the golden spires that topped each of them. A balcony with ornate blue glass doors sat to the side of the gardens. The glow of our impending next few hours could be seen through the doors, shadows of creatures milling back and forth. Everywhere I looked, there were new details to take in, but Callum was nowhere in sight.

"Where did Cal go?" I asked, leaning around each side of Rhone to find him.

"He shadowed a bit closer to the doors. I figured you might need a second to take it all in. There will be lots of people around us for the next few hours, and I know I certainly wanted another moment to myself before all that," he said looking uneasy, his eyes darting to the castle.

"Wow, is Rhone the Magnificent *nervous* about being around large crowds of people?" I said teasingly, poking him in the chest. As I gazed up at him, his grey eyes staring back into mine, I realized that yes, he must be. It made sense, a lone wolf like himself, loyal to no court. A "brute", as Barbette had called him. I had idly wondered when she said that if that was what others thought of him as well, and in this moment, I saw they must.

He huffed a laughed at my jest, catching my hand before it fell away from his chest. He pressed my hand against it, and I could feel his heart beating rapidly against his chest, the same as mine.

"Even I, Rhone the Magnificent, get nervous sometimes, darling, especially around a bunch of pompous high flyers. But, we are in this together, remember?" he said as he turned my hand over, facing it palm up. He leaned over, and pressed his lips to the pulse point on the inside of my wrist, gently kissing it. The touch of his velvet lips brushing my skin sent a flush to my cheeks. He inhaled deeply, looking up at me, his gaze darkening.

"Your scent, it's radiating off of you tonight, and it's delectable. Sugared figs and warm honey," he said as he inhaled again, pulling me closer, his arm wrapping around my waist. Bending down, he began to leave a trail of kisses across my bare shoulder. A rustling came from behind us. Rhone stilled and straightened, rolling his eyes, a groan of annoyance slipping through his lips. Callum appeared around the bushes, throwing his hands up in a mirrored annoyance.

"This stolen moment in clear view of the ballroom

balcony is genius and all, but the wedding begins *very* soon," Callum said before shadowing away in a burst of flames, clearly angry. *For someone known to be chronically late, he sure hates being made late on the account of others.*

Rhone turned to me, the sun beginning to set behind him, and put my arm in his. "Get ready, Act I, Scene 2 begins now."

I'm guessing all of that was just as he suggested, an act.

WE SHADOWED into a dark corner of the hall beyond the grand blue glass doors, creatures of all kinds roaming around. Barbette was right, everyone here *was* beautiful, extremely so. Spellcasters, Royal Fae and a few select humans were dressed extravagantly and dripping in jewels.

The ballroom was illuminated with hanging chandeliers and floating candlesticks. A grand crystal chandelier hung over the middle of the ballroom dance floor, wisteria vines and strings of pearls and diamonds hanging from it. Tables of food lined the walls, decorated with massive peony and white rose centerpieces that lusciously spilled off the tables and wound around the serving platters. The dance floor had been recently polished; the blush and navy marble mosaic floor gleamed under the low glow of candlelight and the afternoon sunlight streaming in through the grand arched windows. As I scanned the room, my eyes stopping on every person milling the room, waiting for my eyes to land on my parents or Vana.

"Where does the wedding happen?" I asked Rhone as I

gazed around the room, expecting to shadow into a room full of pews and a groom standing by an altar.

"Only humans have public ceremonies. Fae and Spell-casters alike are very private in their mating ceremonies, only an officiant and the couple, it is very intimate. The public portion of a creature wedding, like the one we are at presently, is only a reception after the private ceremony is over."

I nodded, realizing there would probably always be something new to learn about my own culture that I wasn't raised in. Rhone and I walked together for some time, and it was more comfortable than I imagined it would be. My arm was linked with his, and he leaned into me, his body heat soothing the chill from the nerves. Eyes followed us as we walked together, Rhone's meeting all of them as they quickly looked away. All but one, a set of steely blue eyes I recognized immediately from the newspapers, the High Fae Council Elect, Niklas Bergström. And it wasn't Rhone his eyes followed; it was me.

He was tall and muscular, as they all were, and admittedly devastatingly handsome. But tall as in, *why the fuck is this guy so tall,* kind of way. Taller than Rhone, and that was just absurd. His silver blonde hair was artfully slicked back, a few pieces falling forward. His navy tux had a slight sheen, and was quite modern for Fae standards. In person he seemed slightly different from the Realms Times pictures. He commanded attention, his back straight and his demeanor stoic. He had a darkness to him that the papers smudged out. Maybe it was the mischievous look in his eyes as they locked on me.

I'd be lying if I said I didn't like his gaze on me or the

way his eyes roamed my body as we continued walking, a slight smirk spreading across his face.

I was fully entranced by him, and when his eyes finally met mine, it was like the world stopped, making me shutter. There was a pang in my chest that echoed against all the hollow parts of my body, filling me with a painful ache that made my heart lurch. I took a deep breath, the painful tug in my chest easing into a warmth that spread throughout. I felt my power react to it, dance with it. I took another deep breath, but I couldn't look away from him, it was like he had some sort of pull over me, my eyes not wanting to leave his.

Right now is seriously not the time for some weird ass panic attack, I thought to myself. And I took in one last long breath, filling my lungs to the brim, the feeling finally began fading.

A low "ehh-hemm" was what finally broke my gaze with Niklas, thank the Gods. My face heated in embarrassment as I realized how inappropriate that had been, even if unwarranted, especially with a date on my arm. I turned to see who had come to my rescue, and Callum approached us to our left. I looked to Rhone, whose gaze was somewhere across the room, aloof and cold.

"Glad you two could finally make your entrance. The Mated couple will be announced any second," Callum said to no one in particular, a champagne glass hanging lazily in his hand to his side. He leaned down to me, in a whisper so low only I could hear, "Niklas is an incredible specimen, don't you think? Notorious in bed *and* a fair councilman. I mean, how well endowed... I mean rounded, can one get?" He giggled, taking a long sip of champagne. My blush deepened, hoping Rhone had been none the wiser.

A deep chime sounded across the ballroom, followed by a piano beginning to play on stage to the back of the room. The entire room stilled, everyone turning to the middle of the ballroom. The lights dimmed, all but the chandelier that hung in the middle of the ballroom dance floor. A man appeared on stage, a microphone in his hand.

The man was short and stout, with a long gray beard and a black and white tux. He waited for the crowd to completely quiet down before he began, "Ladies, Gentlemen and creatures alike, I am honored to introduce to you to the High Mates, Aaren and Reyka Lochhart!"

The crowd broke out in polite cheers, and in a puff of smoke, the happy couple appeared in the middle of the dance floor. High Wizard Aaren stood tall, his slender and fit figure outfitted in a regal dark blue and gold suit, his High Wizard crown glittering in the low light. He looked like what I assumed Emrin had looked like before his transformation charm. A part of me deflated a bit, thinking of everything my father had given up for me, like this son who looked like his old self that he would never get back.

I turned to look at Reyka who was truly a vision, her black hair was in an updo with pearl clips, face framing pieces left out to emphasize her heart-shaped face. Her tan skin was radiant against her cream and blush colored dress with a full skirt and straight neckline. Peonies were embroidered across the bottom of her dress, real petals falling from her train as she walked.

One by one the crowd began to drop to one knee, taking a bow for the new High Mates of the realm. Rhone dropped to his knee, pulling me down with him. As we stood again, the music changed tempo, still slow and soft but slightly more upbeat. Aaren and Reyka bowed to the crowd and took each other's hands, bowing to each other before swiftly moving into a gliding dance. We watched them for a moment before another chime sounded, and couples around us started to head for the dance floor. I had dreaded this part the most, dancing in front of a crowd *and* with Rhone. I internally groaned as I knew what was coming next.

"May I have this dance?" Rhone said, bowing slightly, holding out his hand.

"Only because it is proper," I replied teasingly, but in a way, I meant it. I wanted nothing more than to disappear into a corner and wait for a sighting of my parents or Vana, but I knew that was not how tonight worked. I slid my hand in his, allowing him to pull me into his embrace.

As we began to glide across the floor with other couples, I could feel the eyes on us again, but Rhone never faltered.

"You are a remarkable dancer," I said, honestly surprised. He smirked down at me.

"There are many things I am good at, Soren," he said as he dipped me and brought me back up, pressing his body into mine as we moved into a spin. He clasped a hand to my back, letting it linger low. Flashes of our brief night together passed through my mind, the closeness of him making it hard to breathe.

"Did I tell you how incredible you look tonight? You put the moon to shame," he said, leaning down to whisper in my ear, his lips brushing my cheek as he pulled away, as he sent me out into a spin.

His proximity, his touch, and his words, they made the rest of the room disappear, the dance and the wedding vanishing from my mind. I stared up into his stormy eyes, eyes that seemed only for me, his hand roaming back up, his fingers dancing up my spine. The music coming to a fading end is what finally made me come back to reality.

Callum and his dance partner, a handsome shorter blonde Fae Male, came to a halt beside us. The rest of the guests began mingling again. In the background, I heard Aaren thanking everyone for joining in on their first dance, and announcing the hors d'oeuvre and refreshments were now being served. I had purposely not looked the High Wizard directly in the eyes yet, wanting to stay out of his wake for as long as I could. It wasn't that he frightened me, it was that I wasn't sure how I was to react around him. Do we know each other, do we decidedly not?

Callum and his date approached, "Rhone, Soren, meet Tiberius of the Galarian Cities. He sits on the Galarian council, a right hand to Niklas Bergstrom." The Fae Male politely nodded his head to us, and we back. He stood a few inches shorter than Callum, and his sandy blonde hair was worn fashionably mid length, smoothed down and tucked behind his elegantly pointed ears. His lavender eyes darted back and forth between Rhone and I, and then out into the crowd, like he was surveying the room.

Tiberius and Rhone began to speak at the same time, but Rhone motioned for him to continue first as he wrapped his arm around me, pulling me into his side, his hand sliding down my hip.

Tiberius cleared his throat, the show of open affection by Rhone seeming to rattle him a little, and I internally snickered, knowing that Rhone was doing this purely for that reaction. *Act 1, Scene 2, indeed.* Rhone was making a show of this, a show none of the other couples were making, the side eyes multiplying. The Royal Faeren were known for their high regard for politeness, and public displays of affection at an event like this... was anything but that. I was conflicted by how I felt, torn between slight embarrassment and relishing in the attention from him.

"Prince Callum has told me so much about the two of you over our dinners together recently. It is lovely to meet you both. Soren, how are you acclimating to your new environment?" Tiberius said, his eyes catching on Rhone's hand sprawled out across my hip.

I took a second to collect myself, tampering down the flood of thoughts going through my mind. I began flipping through the endless amounts of information I had taken in about the Huran Tribe during my training. "I am enjoying my time away from my homelands, the change of scenery has opened my eyes greatly. I am hoping to make a home here, explore my options, as women of the Huran are granted only to become educated and not to use their education," I replied.

"Yes, Soren is incredibly intelligent. It was her quickness and unashamed wit that made her so interesting to me. It's one of my favorite things about her, besides her beauty of course," Rhone said, his hand giving my side a gentle squeeze before returning to its rightful place on my hip. I smiled at that; even if it was part of the act for tonight, I knew he meant it in some fashion. We stood there awhile, people skirting around Rhone but flocking to Prince Callum. I introduced myself more times than I could remember, circling the ballroom as we went. Cal was truly in his element, people around and drinks to be had, a beautiful male on his arm. But he never forgot about Rhone or I, forcing the others to notice and engage Rhone in conversation. The ones who ignored his prompts to make friends with us as well were swiftly dismissed.

I felt someone approach, my Fae senses on high alert thanks to the bundle of nerves in my stomach.

I felt a tap on my shoulder, and a voice behind me said, "Excuse me, may I have a moment," and I knew who it belonged to immediately, my heart jumping into my chest. I turned to see my father, dressed to the nines in a very classic yet fashion forward suit, a burgundy tie matching his silver and ruby pendant that hung on his lapel. The human inventors symbol, a hand holding a hammer. I felt that uneasy guilt again, for the fact he was here in his hidden form, a brilliant human inventor, instead of a brilliant Wizard at his own child's wedding. I took his hand in mine, and his eyes lit up. I excused myself from the group.

"You look radiant," he said, his smile reaching his eyes. He took my arm in his, "Let's go get a refreshment while we catch up." With a sneaky flick of his wrist, he placed a privacy charm around us, so we could speak freely. We walked over to the refreshment tables, and he asked me about my days. I told him, and he told me of his nights back in the Wizard Realms. He grabbed me a glass of pink champagne, and himself a glass of whiskey. We walked out to the balcony for more privacy. The sunset had turned into the night sky, the stars shining down on us and the moon full.

"Where is Mom?" I asked. I had been so excited to see him, I hadn't noticed her absence at first, I thought she'd pop up next to us at any second, but twenty minutes had passed and still no sign of her.

My father's face fell a little as he began to speak, "That is why we came out here, for more privacy. We tried to reach you but your phone has not been going through, which is something we need to fix immediately. We do need a secure line, but a secure line that doesn't get us through to you is unacceptable," He paused for a second, and then continued, "A few days ago Aaren had gotten word of an attack on a Wild Fae encampment near the edge of the Highland border; there were several of our court's healers among them. Only two bodies were found, one wild Fae Male and a male healer. Aaren and a team of his men went immediately, and your mother and I as well. During the search, Vana's bags were found, her belongings were strewn across her tent. It looked like there was a struggle, and... there was blood found in her tent as well." My father paused for a second, putting his head down. "There is... one other thing we noticed... It was not Fae magic that was used in this attack. There was silver ash residue found...and scorched burn marks."

My head was spinning as I tried to take in every word he had said. I thought back to all those calls that had gone unanswered from Vana, my stomach twisting with nausea. I had been so caught up in the trivial things going on in my bubble I hadn't even thought to push harder to get in contact with her.

"Your mother is beside herself about this. She loves Vana as a daughter. She decided she couldn't come to the wedding, not when she felt she should be on the search team, helping in any way she could." He reached for my hand then, clasping it in both of his, I crumpled.

A sob tore from my throat. I thought of my best friend,

hurt and trapped, or worse. The ash found at the encampment... eerily similar to the ash I knew ran through my veins, *stardust*. My power rumbled to life inside me, the intense tingling of my magic burning my fingertips, aching to get out. Sorrow and anguish battled inside of me. My father's voice echoed at a distance. I could feel my body and my powers wanting to take over, but I held onto the sound of him.

"Soren, now is not the time for revenge; although, the timing is incredibly terrible. Remember why we are here, to socialize, to be seen. We are nothing without numbers," He took a step closer, resting his hand on my shoulder. "Take a deep breath, little girl. Vana... she is out there somewhere, and we will stop at nothing to find her. But for tonight, you must be present, here in this moment," He was next to me again, soothing and calming me. The glittering lights from the ballroom caught my eye and I gazed inside, seeing the people laughing and dancing. I knew he was right. I knew I had to step back in there and do what I came to do.

"I just need a moment to myself. Will you send Rhone my way after a few minutes?" I said, my voice hoarse from the raw emotion, from trying to hold back the sobs. He simply nodded his head and slipped away quietly, leaving me on the balcony alone.

I stood there for a long moment, gripping the marble railing of the balcony, staring up at the starlit sky. I silently wondered to myself what the stars in the sky had that I didn't. Why they were allowed to exist so unbothered, while every second since my birthday I had been incessantly berated.

A chilly night breeze swept my hair to the side, and I

welcomed the soothing chill, the burning power in my veins calming. I titled my head back, letting the tension fall from my shoulders and letting the cool breeze envelop me. The smell of fresh snow and amber filled the air. Tiny snowflakes floated my way, and I stiffened, realizing I was no longer alone, and the breeze had been a shadowing.

FIFTEEN

I turned around suddenly, a tall figure leaned against the wall of the palace beneath the shadows, blazing blue eyes cutting through the darkness. I had only noticed one creature in the ballroom with eyes like that, and as if on cue, he stepped forward. Niklas Bergstrom's tall figure sauntered towards me, his hands stuffed nonchalantly in his pockets. He was even better looking up close. He wore a sapphire and canary diamond silver pin on his navy-blue lapel, the Galarian Cities flag in blue and yellow gleamed, a silver hand holding a lighted torch in the middle. He looked every bit the stoic politician, and every bit the devilishly sexy Casanova Callum had mentioned. He drug a hand through his silver blonde hair, slicking it back before strands inevitably fell across his blue eyes again. His full lips were inviting, and I caught myself staring just a second too long. His gaze darkening was indicator enough that I knew he caught me. I scowled at myself, unsure why this man lured me in so much.

"I see you needed a breath of fresh air as much as I did,"

Niklas said, his voice deep, smooth, and rich. His eyes never left mine as he spoke. He lifted his hand, a burst of snowflakes carrying itself on the breeze to me, caressing me as it flitted down my body. I gave a small shiver, unable to hold it back. He stopped mere inches from me, his body heat inviting against the frost-kissed air he had sent my way, his warm amber and woodsy scent wrapping around me.

"Big crowds are not my thing," I said, leaning myself back against the balcony railing, needing to breathe in air that didn't belong to him, trying to shake his trance.

"If I were the male on your arm, I don't believe I'd leave you alone on a balcony in a palace full of dangerous strangers," he said, his voice low. "And that interesting human inventor is not who I'm alluding to." He reached out, taking a lock of my curled hair in between his fingers. "Soren, of Tribe Huran," he said, with a question in his voice as he rested the lock of hair back on my shoulder, his fingers brushing my collar bone. His touch sent shivers across my body, and I was truly unsure if it was his icy touch or the unsolicited buzz of chemistry that lingered between us.

"Niklas Bergstrom, Council Elect," I said back to him cooly, crossing my arms.

Footsteps sounded behind us, and Rhone came into view, holding two champagne flutes, the flood of orchestra music rushing out to the balcony as the doors opened. Lightning flashed in his eyes, a rumble sounding in the night sky above us.

"Are they more dangerous than me, Niklas?" Rhone said. I had maybe never been more happy to see him.

"Ah, Rhonan the Savage," Niklas said, not bothering to fully look at Rhone. Rhone stilled, and thunder cracked above us, shaking the balcony. Niklas seemed unbothered, turning his attention back to me, a card materializing in his hand. His name and phone number appeared across it in a shimmery swirl of blue and white frost. He leaned down to me and said so low only I could hear, "If you should ever require more pleasant company, *Min stjärna*." His icy blue eyes looked me up and down. I repeated back his comment, *Min stjärna,* in my head, holding back the gasp and trying to remain neutral. I stared up at him a moment, his eyes drinking me in, the card in his hand waiting. There was something here, something so familiar and tangible. I considered him for a long moment, his facade cracked, and I saw the ancient years mirrored back in his eyes, if only for the briefest of moments. I brushed past him, the brief contact chilling.

Reaching Rhone's side, I took the champagne glass in my hand and turned back towards Niklas. "I think I'll be just fine," I said, that devilish grin still plastered across his face as we shadowed away, hand in hand.

We shadowed into a dim room, the fireplace crackling to life in our presence, offering amber-colored light to spill across the room. It was a large room, a glossy writing desk sat in the middle with a matching red velvet chair and red velvet curtains drawn. Bookshelves lined the walls, and a velvet chase sat in the corner, books and a plush throw strewn across it.

"Your father shouldn't have left you out there alone, he knows better," Rhone said, his head tipping back as he downed the glass of champagne.

"I told him I needed a moment, he gave me a moment." I paused a moment before beginning, "Did he tell you about

Vana?" I asked, hoping to the Gods he had because I simply did not have it in me to repeat it.

"Unfortunately, yes." His reply was clipped, and he sat down heavily on the chase lounge, his long legs jutting out in front of him. He looked exhausted.

He sighed, his hand running through his hair before he said, "You can leave with him if you want. I saw the way you looked at each other. He would make an excellent ally and has far more resources than I do. Resources that could quickly find Vana."

I could not believe him, and I snapped back my retort, throwing my hands in the air, "You just want me to leave with him, just like that? After all the weeks of effort we have built into... whatever this is? All the training. The friendship we have created, you want to throw it away?"

My anger was hot and I couldn't resist the embarrassment I felt, the embarrassment of not wanting to let go of *whatever this is,* while he was so unbothered. Even after all the times he had shown me this was not what he wanted.

His silence got the best of me, my patience breaking, "You know what, maybe I will leave with him. At least he doesn't have to *act* like he wants me; he clearly does. No confusion, no hesitation, no hiding it."

Rhone scoffed then, condescending in its nature as he stood and began pacing. "Soren, how can you be so incredibly intellectual yet so incredibly blind. You think the wanting you part is an act?! The *not* wanting you part is the act, the staying away from you is the act. I have wanted you since the day I saw you, four years ago. Since the day your father assigned me to you."

My whole body completely stilled, my mind reeling at

Rhone's revelations. He did want me and was *assigned to me FOUR YEARS AGO?* I shook my head in confusion. "I'm sorry, *assigned* to me?" I said, my voice barely above a whisper.

"I told him to tell you, I told him to tell you all of this at dinner the night before we all dispersed," Rhone said, shaking his head. "After I fled from Synnove, I was in hiding for years. One of her last assignments for me was to watch the comings and goings of High Wizard Emrin, see why he was in the human realm disguised as a human, of all things. You were never seen; they must have disguised you to creature eyes as they disguised themselves with charms. It was only Emrin and Tanja going about a seemingly normal and cozy unbothered human life. It is why I chose him to go to. He knew how to hide; he could live a content life. I wanted all those things. He promised to give me those things on one condition, and for a while he did. I was able to build my own home, I had never had anything of my own, not a house and definitely not any money.

"You were the condition, Soren. You were my post. Your father knew what was coming, but not when, and he wanted me in your corner. It was a quiet four years, until it wasn't. I know you like the back of my hand. I know how you take your coffee, the bath oils you buy from the store, your favorite wines, all of it. And it feels so wrong to know all these things about you and you know nothing about me. It feels like I've cheated somehow. The second I saw you I was struck, something inside of me changed. I've never, in all my years, felt this insatiable effect with anyone but you. No one else has held me captive like this, and I haven't even *had* you yet." He paused a moment, huffing out a condescending laugh before beginning again. "I've wanted you for so long, and suddenly you want me to? It's too good to be true; it's some sort of twisted Stockholm syndrome." He cringed as the words came out. He began pacing again, his arms crossed, his eyes flashing in unison with thunder rumbling in the distance. The look on his face, the hunch of his shoulders, I was watching Rhone experiencing an emotion I had never witnessed him have before: Fear.

"If all that is true, then why did you act that way the night we were... together?" I asked, remembering it like it was yesterday, the wound of his rejection still raw.

He stopped in front of the fireplace and leaned against the mantel. "I couldn't have you that way, I've already told you that. I already felt bad that I was harboring this secret, and then to also have Goddess Mánis' enchantment lingering." He paused, shaking his head before continuing, "I wanted you to be free of persuasion, I wanted to control the situation, not her. I have never stopped wanting you. Stopping myself that night was so incredibly hard, to let go of you...I am haunted every night by your touch." His eyes darkened, the rain beginning to pour outside the window.

"I am not capable of the kind of love you deserve, Soren, not anymore. I know that something like this is not in my cards. I'm okay with that. But I know you will never settle for just my touch. I see it in your face. But seeing you alone on that balcony with Niklas..." he said, his voice shaking with emotion, his eyes meeting mine, finally.

Before he could even finish the sentence I had crossed the room. I wasn't quite sure what my motive was. Did I want to kiss him or slap him?

My voice came out high pitched, my emotions laced in

them, "Why are you deciding this for me?" I said, throwing my hands up.

It was then that Rhone closed the space between us. He cupped my face in his hands, tilting my head up to look at him. The storm in his eyes beating against its constraints. I grabbed him by his suit jacket and pulled him down, his soft lips crashing into mine. Lightning lit up the sky, thunder threatening to shatter the windows. He wrapped his arms around me, his heated scent engulfing me, mist clinging to my skin.

Our touch unlocked the floodgates we had both walled up around each other. Our kiss deepened, becoming more urgent, and I knew he must've felt the barriers break as well. His tongue slid across mine, he tasted of my wildest dreams, the world felt as if it was spinning around us. I couldn't take it anymore, I needed him. We moved closer, his hands running up my body, his touch setting me aflame with desire. His hand slid up to my neck as he gently wrapped his hand around it, his thumb resting on my pulse point. The simple gesture turned me molten to the core, and I let out a small moan, my control already slipping.

Breaking away from the kiss, he looked into my eyes. A low growl escaped him, his hand tightening around my throat. I couldn't take it anymore, the ache in my core turning into a throb. I roll my hips into his, his pulsing desire hard against me. A dark smirk spreads across his face, his eyes glazing over with desire like they were the night at the temple.

Suddenly he swept me up, his sensual voice a whisper as he said, "Put your legs around me. We are short on time." In a brush of mist, I hear the door lock behind us.

I do as he says as he hauls me up to him, my dress hiking up above my waist. The decision to go pantyless tonight was based completely on practicality and panty lines against the delicate fabric of my dress, but now I could not have been more grateful. With one arm, he held me up, and with the other, he ripped his belt from his waist, threw it to the side, and shoved his pants down. I wrapped my arms around his neck, anchoring myself further. He took his free hand and ran it up under my bare thigh until he found my dripping core pressed against his hard stomach, surely soaking his nice button-up silk shirt. He immediately sunk two fingers into me, and we both let out a moan.

"*Fuck* Soren, you are so wet for me," he said breathlessly. I moved my hips against him as he took his thumb and gently circled my clit. Stars already lined my vision, just his touch ready to send me over the edge, my breath quickening. I had dreamed of this for so many nights.

Slowly he removed his fingers from me, moving both hands to my thighs and gripping them tight as he lifted me up higher and rested my entrance on the tip of his pulsing desire, teasing me. I wiggled my hips closer, needing him. I could hear him moan at just the graze of me against the tip of his cock. Slowly, he lowered me on top of him, his hard length slowly sliding inside me.

"*Fuuuucckkkkkk*," he breathed as he slid the rest of the way in. I couldn't help but gasp at the size of him. He thrusted slowly, letting me get used to him. Then his mouth claimed mine as he quickened his pace. I couldn't take it anymore. Needing him faster and deeper, I rolled my hips against him, matching him thrust for thrust. I felt him smirk against my mouth, and he broke away from the kiss.

"Is that what you want, Soren?" My message had been received, the look in his eyes completely feral. His fingers digging into my thighs, he began to drill his cock into me harder. He walked forward, pulling out of me as he set me down on the desk. He positioned me just right, grabbing onto my waist to pull me forward, shoving my skirt aside, spreading my legs further apart, and leaning me back on my elbows. He threw off his tuxedo jacket and rolled up his sleeves. His neatly pulled back hair was now disheveled, falling forward into his face. I drank him in as he adjusted, his shirt crumpled, his pants pulled down to mid-thigh, and his impressively heavy cock glistening in the firelight. He took his cock in his hand, his gaze intent on me, his chest heaving as he walked forward again.

He stopped inches in front of me, taking his other hand and resting his fingertips at my entrance, sliding a finger inside me, teasing me.

"Rhone, please..." I said, my voice shaking with desire.

A devilish grin spread across his face. "Please what, Soren?" he replied. He took a step closer, placing his head against me. Gently, he slid his tip against my wet center, teasing me. *The bastard is good at teasing.*

"Please, I need you inside me," I moaned.

At that, he let out a deep primal growl and grabbed onto my hips. He pulled me forward, shoving his long hard cock deep inside me. We let out matching cries of pleasure, our hips meeting in perfect rhythm. Leaning over me, he pulled the top of my dress down, my breasts falling out. He watched them for a second before leaning down and sucking a nipple into his mouth, grazing his teeth against it. He thrusted faster, both of us panting and moaning. I could live in this moment, consumed by him, filled by him, where nothing else in the realms mattered. Just Rhone, feasting upon me, his lips on mine and his hands roaming my body.

He lifted his head from my breast and claimed my mouth, consuming me. The taste of him as he dove deeper into me with every thrust, his fingers on my clit, it was too much. I shattered against him, my orgasm ripping through me as I screamed out his name. At the sound of his name coming out of my lips, he was undone as well. Lightning cracked in the distance, the rumble of the thunder rattling the windows as he came. My power surged through me, humming against my skin as the intensity of the orgasm claimed my body, our legs shaking together at our release.

Rhone slumped on top of me, nuzzling his head into the crook of my neck, both of us breathless and panting.

"That was.... My gods... is this just what creature sex is like?" I said into his hair, my voice hoarse and muffled.

I could feel Rhone's chest shake with a laugh as he rolled off of me and onto his back on the other side of the desk. Glistening with sweat, small threads of lightning dance across his slick skin. He turned his head towards me, a lazy smile plastered on his face.

"No, definitely not," he replied as he reached over and cupped my face, his thumb brushing my lip. I resisted the urge to suck his thumb into my mouth, wanting another round.

The beat of silence between us is sobering, something we very much needed, reality setting back in. Rhone stood and pulled his pants back up. I sat up on the desk, beginning to readjust my dress, fumbling with the zipper on the side that had slid down. My hands were shaking, the sudden shock of the moment being over rattling me, the orgasm settling. Vana's face flashed across my mind. I suddenly felt ashamed, ashamed I let myself get so carried away with Rhone in a stranger's study instead of working on our next move to find Vana, my best friend.

Rhone was suddenly next to me, his hand over mine, guiding my hand up to zip my dress. I glanced up at him, noticing he was already completely dressed, even his hair slicked back in its low bun, looking completely untouched. Not a wrinkle to be seen on his suit.

SIXTEEN

U pon shadowing back into the wedding, Rhone did not let go of my hand. He laced our fingers together, ever so gently tugging me into him. Callum and Tiberius had been in deep and pleasant-sounding conversation with two beautiful young women as we walked into their conversation circle. They were twin Spellcasters, Tesynia and Olea Mganga. Both were tall and slender, with the same deep ebony skin and gleaming tight curls that were swooped up into elegant up-dos. Their dresses were both gold but different in style. Tesynia's was long, form fitting, and had a high neckline with a cape like silk shift cascading down her shoulders, while Olea's was strapless with a plunging neckline, her gold body jewelry plunging with it and her skirts flowing out at her hips. Features wise, they were nearly identical. Both had big almond-shaped eyes, wide straight noses, and high cheek-bones that helped frame exquisitely plump lips. However, Olea's eyes were a gleaming bronze and Tesynia's were maroon, a rare color for any creature.

"Tesynia and Olea are actually Healers of the Galarian Cities. Their coven found shelter within the Cities years ago and decided to stay. They go from here to the Highland Courts often. Tesynia prefers the Galarian City, while Olea prefers... the Highland's charms," Callum said, giving Rhone and I pointed looks. To my pleasant surprise, the twins did not shrink away from Rhone, or look displeased to be in his presence.

Olea gave a small smile and nodded her head slightly to Rhone. "Rhone, it is good to see you again. It has been many months," she said, her eyes sliding away from him and landing on me. The tone of her voice told me there was something she was saying without saying, and I noted to add that to my long list of items to talk about later. Her eyes showed no disdain for me though, mainly just curiosity and a twinge of something else. Pity?

Seeing Callum's plea to continue polite conversation, Tesynia cut in and went on, her accent thick even after years away from her home lands, "Yes, King Ruairi heard my coven's plea during the Iron Civil War between the Spell-casters and took us in with the help of the Council Elect Bergström. If it were not for them, our coven of healers would have been bled out by the warlocks. We have been inhabiting both areas ever since. Have you visited the Highlands yet? It is like Rhone's second home," Tesynia asked, a genuine smile on her face.

"No, I have not visited yet, but I have heard great things about the kingdom from what Rhone has told me," I said, squeezing Rhone's hand. When he didn't squeeze back, I looked up at him and immediately noticed something was wrong.

He seemed to be trying to listen in on something, a conversation across the room. I followed his gaze across the crystal chandeliers and flowers, fixed at something else away from the mingling crowd of the wedding reception. A dark back corner of the expansive ballroom, away from candlelight and partially hidden by a curtain of hanging wisteria. Finally, I saw what Rhone saw, my gaze landing on my father, my Fae sight coming in handy. He looked frantic, sweating... very unlike himself. He was standing in front of High Wizard Aaren, my father's hands gripping Aaren's shoulders. They talked back and forth to each other furiously, no doubt a charm of silence cast around them for privacy. Aaren's concern was growing at an alarming rate, as was mine, and his eyes darted around the room, as if searching. Until they landed on me. The pleading in them was imminent. I knew that if he was trying to communicate directly with me, this was bad. Without even thinking, I let go of Rhone's hand and began moving, not even feigning an attempt to politely leave the conversation with the two perfectly pleasant women.

Rhone reached out, putting a hand on my shoulder. "Soren, something is not right. You shouldn't—"

I was gone before he could finish his sentence, shoving through the crowd of elegant gowns and silk tuxedos. I knew better than to run full out, even though my anxiety screamed at me too. I could see the panic on my father's face. A million possibilities were flying through my head. Maybe it was mother, maybe she was missing or worse as well. Fear flooded my system, my power prickling at my fingertips, but I shoved it back down. I knew Rhone was following me, his rushed footsteps gaining on me.

As I reached the High Wizard, his new wife was nowhere to be found. My father was still in front of him, his eyebrows knitting in concern, and sweat beaded across his brow. He looked disheveled, his suit rumpled and his glasses sitting crooked.

I stepped into the charm; it tugged at my skin upon entrance. The chatter and music from the wedding fell away as my father's voice filled my ears. They were still in the same stance I had seen, Aaren trying to talk sense into him, and my father hunched over, gripping Aaren's shoulder so hard his fingertips were turning white. As I arrived, Aaren turned his head towards me slightly, his eyes slowly leaving my father's face, like he was afraid what would happen if he looked away. He shook his head at me slowly, his eyes finally meeting mine.

"Have you seen her? Have you seen Soren? And what about her mother. I have been looking everywhere," my dad said, his voice shrill and hoarse like he had been yelling.

"Dad, she is right here. Did you not see her walk over? She's right here. No need to worry," Aaren said, the look on his face almost apologetic as he nodded his head towards me.

"Yes, I'm here. What is going on? What do you mean where is Mom? We already talked about Mom.... Did you have too many whiskey neats?" I said, confusion sure to be written all over my face. Something was very wrong with my dad, sweat falling from his face.

My father turned towards me then, his eyes never really landing on me but really to the general direction of my voice. He fell forward slightly, his head hanging, and I grabbed his shoulder, helping him stand the rest of the way back up.

How many drinks did this man have??

With Aaren grabbing his other shoulder, we got him standing back up right again. His head rolled back around, and he looked up at me. Thunder rumbled around us, the curtain of wisteria shuddering, veins of lightning crackled against the privacy charm. *What was Rhone doing?* Turning around, I saw Rhone, his panicked face fuzzy but readable through the charm. He seemed so far away, but he had been right behind me? In fact, the world around me seemed to be in slow motion. Black and dark gray threads floated around us, the air becoming thick with black glittering smoke.

"Don't worry, you're still here. You're just also *not*. It's not a privacy charm. He can't get to you here, Sor." The words fell from my father's mouth in pained words, his eyes slowly averting to Rhone. I looked back at him confused, turning to Aaren, who was no longer there. It was just me and my father.

"Where did Aaren go?" I said, my voice small, almost a whisper. I let go of his shoulder, backing up slowly, the unease growing. My mind started backtracking. *What did I miss?* My eyes darted around the room, unable to make out faces clearly but there was Rhone, his body moving in slow motion, lightning crawling up his arms as he released it from his body. Wedding guests were fleeing from him.

I backed all the way up to the charm's edge, able to go no farther, pressing my fingers against it. The magic thrummed against my fingertips, and it recognized me. It felt familiar and foreign all at once.

Turning back to face my father, he had fallen to his

knees, his hand clutching his stomach, and his head hung to the ground as he panted. I couldn't bear to see him struggling like this. I could hear Rhone's voice ringing through my head, telling me something was wrong, not to go, but I took a tentative step forward anyways.

"A trap...trap..everything." My father continued, muttering under his breath, shaking his his head.

"Dad, I don't understand. What's going on? Can you explain, so I can help. What do you mean a trap, are you trapped? Did Synnove do this to you?" I asked, and I was truly begging at this point, begging for answers.

He held up his shaking hand as he said, "Don't. Don't come any closer. Yes, it's a trap. We are all trapped while she has this much power." Slowly, he lifted his head to me. A black void had replaced his eyes, and in a wave of rippling black smoke, my father's face faded away and Willem's bled through the mirage.

I stumbled back, gasping.

"I don't have much time, both physically and mentally. And don't even bother screaming; no one can hear you outside of this," he said, and he reached into his jacket and pulled out a dagger with a gleaming onyx. He leaned forward then and placed the dagger in my hand. My power surged at the touch, bursting at the seams, sending silver sparks scattering across the floor and bouncing off the charm's boundaries.

"I need you to take this dagger, and I need you to plunge it into my heart. I need you to kill me," he said, his voice shaking. And suddenly, he wasn't this other Willem, the Willem who had tried to kill me, but I saw *him*. The Willem I had fallen for, the Willem who had held my hair back when I threw up from drinking too much, the Willem who played footsies with me as we were wrapped up together in bed.

"There isn't enough time to explain everything, but I am a conduit, her conduit. It has been a trap from the beginning, Sor. All of it. What she's hiding in her realm, that's why I have to do this. You have to kill me, and you have to do it now. I have been trapped, trapped by darkness, trapped by them. They have taken over my mind, taken over my body. I cannot hold control much longer. I only have blinks of clarity," he said, shoving the blade into my shaking hand. It was heavy and ice cold, the hilt was made out of a gleaming dark gray metal. The longer I stared at it, the heavier it became, realizing what it was I needed to do with this. I tried to remind myself of everything Willem had put me through, how he had tried to kill me not once but twice.

"Willem, I can help you, I can help you get out of this, whatever she has over you, whatever spell you're under... I... we can help you. Rhone can help you. I can convince the others; I know you have good in you. We can help each other. You don't have to die like this," I said. My voice was a traitor to me, shaking with the tears that dared to roll down my cheek.

"Soren, there is no other way. This time warp we are in, this is her magic, but harnessing her power, coming here like this, is draining me. She needs her dark creations. I can't help but to do her bidding." He trailed off, shaking his head for a second, frustration lining his features. I couldn't help but feel bad for him. What Synnove was doing to him, how broken he was, it was heartbreaking.

"If you don't kill me now, I will have to kill you, the thing inside me.... And killing you means she wins. There is no world if she wins, Soren. You have to understand that." He leaned forward, his sandy blonde hair falling into his face, his brown eyes searching my face for the answer he wanted to hear.

"But like I said, we do not have much time. My invasion of her magic, it's costing us all too much, more than could be worth it. We have mere minutes, or even seconds before she realizes I am here, before she can track me." Slowly, I knelt down in front of him. Reaching out, I brushed his hair out of his face, his forehead clammy to the touch.

His eyes fluttered at my touch, and my chest ached for him. "Willem, I...I'm so sorry," I began. His hand met mine, and for the first time in a long time, I was no longer afraid of him. He rested his hand over mine, the freezing hilt of the blade a strong contrast from his warm and clammy hand. He leaned in closer to me, resting his forehead on mine.

"There's a reason she wanted me. There's a reason she wanted Rhone. It's also the reason she needs you. You burn too bright." He closed his hand back around mine then, a flash of light beneath his palm momentarily blinding me. Opening my palm, I found a black life thread.

He shook his head, ignoring my question. "You'll need this; it's the only thing I can give you. Synnove... She has ways of locking away life threads. I'm assuming so you can't access them. When you're done with it, burn it, destroy it however you can. My life...it is not worthy. No matter what I do now, I will never be ferried across the Rivers. Synnove will leave me to rot and spend eternity waiting in my own special hell. And maybe I deserve that." He shook his head softly. He stood up, his body shaking slightly. I tucked the thread away, snapping it shut safely into my silver compact.

"This has to look like a fight, Sor. She needs to see this as a scuffle, one that you won." He reached out a clammy hand, caressing my cheek. My body was wracked with tremors, my power searing my fingertips. Gently, he took the blade from my hand, and began meticulously slicing deep cuts into himself, not even flinching as he did so. One across the abdomen, one across his cheek, and several on his arms. *Defense wounds—smart.* And I knew this was part of his plan, to rough himself up, make sure he lost enough blood, that even if I didn't serve the killing blow he wanted and needed, he would still die. His blood ran gunmetal silver, so dark it was basically black, welling up instantly with every slice of the blade. The sound of it dripping onto the marble floor echoed through our etched-out space in time.

He was quick then, grabbing me by the arm and pulling me up to him, sliding his hand to my wrist, his touch as light as a feather. His face inches from mine, I could see the pain in his eyes. He clung to me, wrapping a strong arm around my waist. Fear raced through me. I trusted him and didn't all in the same breath. Was this a ruse inside a ruse, to make it easier to kill me? Was everything he said true, and he was just trying to make this look like something it wasn't? Instinct told me to flee, but I resisted, the part of me who remembered Willem in a different life trusting him. I could feel his blood seeping into me, soaking my dress. His body sagged and wilted against mine, and I knew he didn't have time. The magic was wearing on him.

The time spell dropped around us like a curtain, the world around us slowly beginning again, Synnove's magic dissipating back to whatever hole in the universe it leaked out of. His grip on my wrist turned searing pain as he spun me around, pressing my back to his chest tightly. I stared blurry eyed out into the crowd that had gathered. My shoulder screamed in pain. Rhone's lightning crashed around us, sending shards of marble scattering as it hit the floor, cracks welting up across the ballroom. Wedding guests shrieked and began running in all different directions. Complete and utter rage lined Rhone's face, his eyes glowing silver, pulsing with the thunderous storm that raged outside.

Willem shifted against me, his mouth caressing my ear as he spoke so low that only I could hear. "She would never believe I didn't get any blows in. Don't take this personally." And then in one smooth movement, he plunged the blade into my side, just below my ribs. Pain shot through me and a strangled scream left my lips. He pulled the blade immediately out and placed it to my throat.

He released his grip on me and my training became second nature. I flung myself into a spin kick, praising my small frame and slipping from his grip, the blade nicking my neck ever so lightly. My foot landed on its target, kicking the blade from his hand. I caught it in mid-air, and lunged forward, the wound in my side barking at me with every movement. I could feel my blood trickling down my leg, and I knew the wound would kill me if we didn't get out of here in time. Willem stood firm, even if swaying slightly. I could still feel my power at the edge of my fingertips, and I willed it to be free, but to be gentle. It obliged, bursting forward, laying across the world like a blanket of stardust. I had been working hard on my control of how much of my power I set free at once. Hours of practice in the training room had paid off.

Time didn't stop, it slowed. Even Willem, who was riddled with Synnove's dark stardust, came to a stuttered pace. Without letting myself think of it further, I slid the blade up into his chest, right where I knew his heart would be. He grunted in pain, and fresh black blood rushed forward as my power lifted, the world speeding back up. I knew that even with this being a ruse, he would not go down without a fight, and truthfully, he deserved one. In a last-ditch effort, he grabbed me by the arms, power surging and sputtering at his fingertips, and threw me back, sending me flying into Rhone. Rhone's strong arms lifted me, holding me steady, his stormy eyes assessing my wound, and he cursed.

"Put pressure on it, *now*," Rhone barked, his anger making every word come out with a bite. Lightning danced across his arms, prickling me where our skin met. He knelt down, took a knife from his tux pocket, and ripped the hem from my dress. Quickly he wrapped it around my waist tightly.

His lips were a tight line as he said, "This should help, for the moment."

I took a millisecond to glance around the room, knowing utter chaos had been set into motion. Although most wedding guests had fled, a crowd had formed around us. To my left, I saw my father, High Wizard Lochhart, Niklas, Callum, Tiberius, and a woman and man with tan skin and matching teal eyes I had not met yet. All of them were in a fighting stance, ready for whatever came next. *Good allies, indeed.* Olea and Tisyna were the biggest surprise though.

Both healers were standing ready and waiting, their golden orbs of power hovering in their palms, sending a glow across the now dark room, the chandeliers broken and powerless thanks to Rhone's lightning. Faces I vaguely remembered stared out at us, some in disgust, some curiously, and others, like the twins, stood ready to fight, not even aware of the cause they were ready to risk their lives for.

I turned back to Willem, the beat of a second over. He was down on his knees, life leaking out of him at a steady pace, blood pooling around his feet. With every second that passed, black veins began crawling up his arms, spreading like spider webs across his now ashen skin. As he crumpled to the ground, he yanked the dagger from his chest and flung it in our direction. It was too high for me to be its target. He had aimed the dagger at Rhone. This was his last act, I could see it in his labored breathing, the way he was almost entirely consumed by those black veins. I flicked my wrist, and the blade came to a halt, much like it had in Rhone's kitchen. I was too focused on the dagger to pay attention as Willem lifted his other shaking hand. Too focused on saving Rhone to notice the rip in the universe that was forming behind Willem. It wasn't until I felt the tug of gravity that I noticed the black portal. A darkness that only black holes know, threatened to swallow us. A loud vibrating hum emitted from the void, deafening and unnerving. A collective shriek rang out. Rhone turned to the crowd.

"*Go.* Get to safety. Emrin, Lochhart, get these civilians *out of here.* Those of you who are prepared to fight, be ready,"

Rhone bellowed, his voice steady amongst the chaos, a true commander.

Black shadows seeped out of the tear in the world and not just any shadows, shadows made of black and gray shimmering threads, *life threads*. They wrapped around each other, their gravitational pull whipping my hair around. Suddenly, they broke apart, scattering across the room, each drift forming a faceless soldier. A dozen formed in a matter of seconds, their eight foot forms towering over us, making Rhone look like an average-sized male. They shrieked in unison, an ear piercing sound, one that nearly sent me to my knees. The shadow creatures took a step forward, and I threw out my power with all its force, but it did nothing to stop them, the black vortex behind them still spinning, law unto itself. My power only froze the allies around me. *Shit.* A snake-like chuckle rang out in unison from the shadow creatures. I released the hold on the world around me, and Rhone turned to me, a knowing look on his face, his eyes searching mine.

"I can't freeze them, Rhone," I said, panic rising in me, an overwhelming sense of dread creeping into my mind.

CHAPTER
SEVENTEEN

B lack shadows surged towards us, and Rhone's lightning met them halfway. They shrunk back, and moonlight that poured in through the windows shone through the damage Rhone did to their bodies. No blood poured forth; just black shadows formed with life threads dissipating into the air. Again, Rhone struck them, his lightning crackling down his arms and racing across the marble ballroom floor. His lightning branched off, striking three of the shadow creatures in unison. It stopped them in their place, their forms weakening and shriveling slightly, their shrieks filling the air, but it only stopped them for so long. All we could do was back up, the shuffle of feet behind us echoing in the room.

In a flash of light, a brave Spellcaster ran forward. I recognized him from a brief conversation earlier in the night. It was Commander Arington, of the High Palace Guard. In one hand, he held a sword, and in the palm of his other, violet-colored magic gathered while he chanted his spell. He turned his hand towards us, a shield forming as he ran up on the creature, his movements like a dance, perfected over years of training and battle. His battle cry pierced the air, his sword gleaming as it made contact with the shadow creature's neck, a fatal blow. Or what would have been, on any other creature. The creature's body warped itself around the blade, Arington falling forward as the impact of his blow never came. He didn't even have time to catch his footing before the shadows sucked themselves away from every dark corner of the room, swirling around him and taking him down, curling around every limb like vines. They held him down on his knees, a shadow yanking his head back and another shoving itself down his throat. His screams gargled as he spit up and choked on his own blood, his body violently convulsing. As the shadow consumed him, he began to stand, his blood running down his chin, staining his beautiful Wizard's robe. His eyes were swallowed by darkness, pools of black, and the blood that ran down his chin began to change color, becoming darker, turning metallic black, silver sheened.

Black like Willem's.

In a matter of seconds, Callum and Tiberius were next to us, flanking Rhone on each side.

"See, this is exactly why I stay in the city. Crazy shit like this is always happening out in bum-fuck nowhere. I was hoping they had the wrong universe to torment and would turn around," Callum said, shaking his head, annoyance lacing his movements as he tugged at his sleeves, rolling them up.

"I *just* got this waistcoat," I heard Callum muttering under his breath. "*And* it's Lueralian silk."

I had to give it to him, it was a beautiful tux, one he

looked dashing in even now. And Lueralian silk was hard to come by these days. There were not many silk weavers left in the Lueralian Alps; machines and inventions had taken over the practice.

The Spellcaster's head snapped back at an inhuman angle, bones crunching as he rolled his neck, his shoulders rolling in unison, as if warming up the new body. I had a sinking feeling then, and I knew that the Spellcaster was with us no longer. It was the shadow creature puppeteering that poor man's body. He put his nose to the air, his nostrils flaring, filling his chest. He turned his head in my direction, his black eyes gleaming, his eyes falling to the wound at my side. My hand was still clamped down on it, the adrenaline numbing the pain, but I could feel myself sway, the edges of my vision blurring. After a long sigh, he lifted his hand, pointing in my direction, and let out another blood curdling shriek.

"Her," he said, his voice Arington's but also, entirely *other*.

The others snapped their faceless heads in our direction as well, and turned back to the one that must be their leader, the one who had possessed the Spellcaster's body. They must've been communicating telepathically, one nodding to the other, but no words came from their shapeless mouths.

Shit. Shit. Shit.

Niklas stepped forward, the air around him emanating a slight chill. I welcomed it, the frosty air waking me up a bit. He glanced down at me, ever so slightly—a motion so small, I was sure he didn't want me to notice. A slight and gently cool breeze brushing my hair back. Even if he was insufferable, I was thankful, the frost-bitten air taking the edge off the pain. I looked down at my wound; blood had seeped all the way through my dress and the makeshift bandage. *Not good.*

Rhone turned to him then. "I have an idea, but we have to be quick. Something about my lightning injured them. If you can use that ice of yours to hold them in place, it would be 100 times more efficient."

Niklas nodded his head, any strife they had had earlier seemingly gone, both thinking with their military training and not their egos.

It was a gravitational pull that turned my head; the creatures were flying towards us, their feet hovering above the ground. *Great, and these fucks are basically soundless on approach???*

"Rhone, *NOW.* It needs to happen *NOW*," I said, and they immediately stepped into action before even turning to look. Niklas walked forward, his long legs carrying him farther than it would seem one would want to go towards these creatures. He lifted his hands and ice blue power shot from them. Giant razor sharp shards of ice came bursting from the floor, making beelines for the creatures. As soon as the creatures came close to Niklas's ice, he struck instantly. His ice wrapping around their ankles and pulled them down. Waves rushed forward, freezing upon contact, creating an impenetrable iceberg around their shadowy bodies. Niklas closed his fist, turning his arm over, holding his power in place. They screeched, trying to pull their bodies out of their prison. A slow smirk spread across Niklas's face as he watched them squirm, his eyes darkening as their shrieks rose.

"Callum, I need you flanking my left; get that deadly purple flame ready. We have no idea what these creatures react to," Rhone instructed. Callum's nod was terse, fire gleamed in his eyes, embers sparking from his fingertips. Tiberius stood by silently, but his demeanor told me he was ready. Violet light flashed, and five more Tiberiuses pop up. They weren't identical copies, but it was him nonetheless. *Ah, he is a Divionisist.* I was actually surprised by this; divisionists were rare. But not rare in quantity, rare because they usually wound up going mad, the duplicates of themselves becoming multiple personalities within them. I remembered reading an autobiography of a female divisionist, that she had written before she flung herself off a mountainside. She said her other selves were taking over, setting her insides on fire trying to get out. And that's where the surprise came from; he seemed so quiet, so well put together. There was no telling what he battled with internally.

It took seconds for Rhone's plan to set itself in motion. His power crackled, a flash of blinding light, and he unleashed his lightning on the creatures, their shrieks filling the air. They were fazed, in pain even, the ebb and flow of their forms coming and going, holes forming as Rhone's lightning took from them. I glanced back at Niklas. A slight sheen had broken out on his tan and muscled arms, shaking slightly as the force of Rhone's lightning reverberated off his ice and back to him. He in no way looked worn out and it was definitely working, killing them but slowly, too slowly.

Something inside me clicked then.

Something Willem had said earlier.

You burn too bright.

That's it. Maybe my power could unravel them quicker, or help speed up the process, to send them back to whatever hellish universe they belonged. Maybe it wasn't Rhone's electric force, but the light his power gave off. I shoved myself to the front, a slight limp as the wound in my side burned and I cursed under my breath. I was light-headed, which was unsurprising; losing so much blood will do that to someone.

Rhone's head snapped to me then, Niklas and Callum's following after.

"Soren, you're injured. I need you far away from here," Rhone said, but he couldn't look away from the creatures.

I promptly ignored him. If we were all going to make it out of here, I needed to see if my theory would work. Niklas and Rhone couldn't go on like this forever, and who knew how long before any other disastrous monsters crawled out of that rip in the world.

I sucked in a deep breath, willing my power to rise, to build. I felt the familiar thrum of my magic pricking my skin, every nerve reacting to it. I let it flow to my hands and I felt the rush of heat down my arms, my fingertips burning. I didn't bother pulling from it, or shaping it. No time to waste trying to find the perfect weapon, whatever that even was.

Rhone is literally going to kick my ass for this, especially using my raw power on a hunch.

I let power flow from both palms, raw and uninhibited. The release made my body shudder, the force of it making me stumbling forward. I sucked in a sharp breath between my teeth, the blazing pain inside multiplying, my vision doubling. My power singed my skin as it left my palms, the raw power taking from me as I took from it.

I heard gasps from around the room, and I knew I was no longer a secret. I knew doing this could have dire consequences, a few of them. I could feel Rhone's glare like daggers, but he said nothing. I shook off the thought. Rolling my shoulders, I tried to remind myself to breathe as my power heated me from the inside out, a sweat breaking out on my forehead. Power slammed into the creatures, the force of it seeming to knock the wind out of them, if they even could breath. Rhone's lightning was acting like a conduit, my power sliding across his with ease, reaching each of the creatures his lightning clung to.

The creatures' bodies convulsed as our magic hit them, turning into silver ash a few seconds after being exposed. Rhone upped his lightning, which sent my power into overdrive. Within minutes he had sent all but one of these back to whatever ashen hel they spawned from.

Only one was left, his black eyes staring into mine as he cocked Arington's head to the side, as if challenging me. In unison, Rhone and I diverted all our attention to the leader. Power slammed into him, but he didn't waver near as easily as the others. Arington's body held firm; the minute it took us to turn the others to ash, had come and gone. My power raged inside of me, no end in sight, but it was wearing me out quickly. Even without a profusely bleeding wound in my side, I would have only had minutes left. Every part of my body ached and burned. There wasn't an inch of my body that wasn't harrowing with pain as raw power bucked against it, wanting out, getting more greedy as the seconds passed. I gritted my teeth as sweat fell into my eyes, willing myself to keep going. But I had begun to sway, black encroaching my vision, head pounding.

The leader began to squirm, and he broke free of Niklas's ice, a curse breaking from Niklas's lips. Niklas quickly retaliated, but it was too late. Arington was muttering a charm, his other hand glowing with flames beneath the ice. The bastard had been quietly chipping away at the ice that encapsulated his body. But how....

Shades of purple magic sputtered to life in the palm of the creature's hand, Arington's magic turning into flames. It was weak, but not completely unwilling; magic is fed by chaos through and through. My eyes widened.

No way.

It was just a mere spark, but the fact he could *wield* his host body's magic, fucking hells how this changed everything. That thing with Arington's power, this was deadly.

I had to end this now.

I shoved the power I had been desperately holding onto forward, a flood of it rushing out of me. *Gods, I was going to roast alive*, the heat making me squeeze my eyes shut.

I could see myself barreling towards the glittering black end, the threads of my magic becoming thinner.

"Soren, let go. We can finish this," I heard Rhone yell over the roar of my power, over the roar of the portal's ominous hums. I could hear Callum and Tiberius's footfalls as they rushed forward towards the leader.

I let out a scream through my gritted teeth; I didn't know if I could. I stared down at my hands, my arms shaking. They were glistening, not only with beads of sweat but I was beginning to glow. Rainbow-colored light flowed underneath my skin like waves, pulsing in time to the beat of my pounding heart.

"*Soren, Let GO,*" Niklas's voice rang out, a command.

Worry lined his words, his voice straining. I slid my gaze to Rhone's, his eyes a blazing silver, my stardust dancing with his lightning. It ran up his arms, his hard muscles flexing, slick with sweat as he tried to manage both raging powers.

I couldn't. I *really, really* couldn't. My body had stopped responding to my brain; it yielded to the power's need for release, its need for chaos and violence in tandem.

I heard shouts above me as I finally let the darkness take me, my vision finally blinking out. Nothing but black surrounded me. The roaring of my power ceased, but not the roaring in my veins or the pounding in my head. It was the sensation of falling that kept my heart from stuttering to a stop. The feeling of impending death encircling me. Clipped segments of shouts came to me as I fell into the endless dazzling abyss, pain scorching through my body.

"She's burning alive."

"She needs Olea and Tesynia. They are her only hope."

A frosty breeze embraced me then, a blizzard finally pulling me under. Something tightened in my chest, a clamping around my heart, and a twinge of pain. Like my heart may literally be ripped from my body. Then the overwhelming sense of home panged through me. I latched onto it, begging it to not let me go.

I was being carried into oblivion. A flash of rainbow-colored light taking over the darkness behind my eyelids was the last thing my consciousness held on to.

CHAPTER
EIGHTEEN

I awoke to the sound of glass shattering, a soft voice cursing under their breath. My eyes opened slowly, both from the wariness of my unknown surroundings and because my body was trying so hard to function. My mind was frazzled, and I desperately searched the depths of my memory for what I could remember. My body tensed, sensing the panic of the unknown. I was in an unspecified location, with an unspecified stranger nearby. I tried and failed to throw out my foresight, my head throbbing in protest.

Bright morning sunlight assaulted my eyes, and it was my turn to curse, my vision blurring. I began to try to sit up, the soft bed bowing under my weight, my side aching in protest. I let out a hiss and looked down, grabbing my side and felt it was bandaged tightly by a medical wrap. I frowned in confusion. What in the hel was going on?

"Careful, you are still in delicate condition." I finally remembered there was someone else in the room. It was the same soft voice that had cursed under their breath when the glass had broken.

A soft ebony hand placed itself on my arm, and I looked up. She was the first thing I could see clearly. Her beauty was enthralling; her black curls were pulled back by a thin gold headband, the glow of the sunlight casting a halo around her. She looked so familiar, her heart-shaped lips forming a smile, her maroon eyes reflecting the empathetic smile.

Her eyes... Where have I seen....

And then it all came back to me. The wedding, meeting Tesynia, who now stood in front of me, her glamorous gown gone and replaced with a deep yellow tunic, a medical apron tied around her waist.

The wedding.

Willem. I squeezed my eyes shut then, shaking my head ever so slightly. Tears threatened to form, and I swallowed them back.

The black void that had ripped the world open, the shadow creatures who had crawled out.

I heaved out a long and heavy sigh, my side barking. I hissed again as the pain ebbed through me, but definitely not near as bad as it had been. Her kind eyes studied me thoroughly and I could feel her assessing me. She was calculating my breathing, my heart rate, her cool, gentle hand still resting on my arm, more for comfort than anything else.

Rhone. Where is Rhone?

And Callum.

Fear and panic seized me again, but I tried to let it flow over me. My power did not surface; there were no familiar painful pricks at my fingertips, which caused the panic to flood me even more.

I opened my mouth to speak, and my throat ached. My mouth was like a desert as I tried to speak, coming out as a croak.

"Where is Rhone? Where are the others?" My voice was hoarse and strained. Every word I pushed out of my mouth caused a wave of nausea to slam into me.

Before answering me, Tesynia turned, reaching for a glass that was on the small metal table next to her. An orange liquid sloshed around inside it.

"This is a healing tonic. It has been doing wonders for you and will numb some of that residual pain and that throbbing in your head," she said, placing it on my lips. I drank, but also sensed I had no choice, as she placed a gentle hand to my chin and tilted my head as she raised the glass, making me empty it all at once. I looked up at her quizzically. How did she know I had such a throbbing in my head?

She laughed softly. "You are easy to read, the human upbringing, I'm guessing. But that is part of the gift healers have. Humans have X-Ray machines; the creature realms have healers. I can even sense ailments before most even know they are ailed."

"To answer your prior question, now that you've had your tonic, they are all fine. Scrapes and bruises here and there, but you were the worst of them. I will leave you now; you have a visitor who's been waiting days to see you. He even slept in this chair over here for the first 40 hours before I made him leave," she said, moving the metal table off to the side as she hurried out of the room.

I sat up. The tonic had kicked in already, my side no longer leaving me writhing in pain, just a small twinge of tenderness. I was in a huge bed, wrapped up in a fluffy slate blue comforter and dark charcoal sheets. I had been dressed in a simple white cropped T-Shirt and matching cotton shorts. The two piece was a smart choice; it made it easier for the healer to change my bandage without having to undress me every time. My hair has been pulled back into a long thick braid that laid over my shoulder.

The room was clean, both in scent and surroundings. High ceilings with crown molding told me it wasn't just expansive, but expensive. It smelled of freshly laundered sheets and leather. It also had a masculine air to it, the mixture somewhat intoxicating. It was a spacious room, with a wide, a tan leather chair off to the side, a navy-blue throw folded neatly and laid across the back. A wooden side table was next to it, a coffee mug and book adorning it. Polished wooden mahogany floors gleamed, peeking out around a large deep blue rug. An ancient looking mahogany bookcase lined the far wall, all the book bindings worn and tattered from years of use. Pictures were hung up on the feather gray walls, old and new. The faces were blurry, my vision still trying to catch up. A bathroom door was open, and I could see a giant modern tub sat in the middle of the all-white, pristine bathroom.

A tapestry hung on the other side of the open door depicting a silver snow-covered tree. Ancient words in a language I didn't recognize were stitched into the fabric, here and there but strategic nonetheless. The tree had a green and blue snake-like dragon wrapped around it. A giant goddess flanked the right side, her white-blonde hair whipping in the non-existent wind, snowflakes hovering in the palm of her hand. On the other side stood a male god, a raven perched on his shoulder, shoulder-length golden-blonde hair and golden skin gleaming. I rolled my eyes. *All Royal Fae believe they are connected to the old Gods this way or that way.* A white marble fireplace with dark veins sat directly across from the massive bed I laid in, the embers cracking, the true fire long gone. I turned back to the windows finally, my eyes beginning to adjust, the sunlight not as offensive as before. Glittering skyscrapers met my gaze, an expansive balcony on the other side of the windows, and one of the windows was actually a door, comfy patio chairs right outside it.

The door creaked open, and I peeked over. His tall form filled the doorway before he even came all the way inside, his white-blonde hair falling forward. He wore a thick white waffle Henley shirt, the buttons left unused. A dark blue tattoo peeked out just below his collar bones, the blue scales of it seeming to move slightly. Light gray sweatpants hugged his thighs, leaving not a ton to the imagination. I averted my eyes quickly. His bare feet padded the ground softly as he strode in. He gave me a small, almost shy smile. His shoulders were hunched, as only the exuberantly tall do, his hands shoved into his pockets.

I was puzzled for a second at how this Fae Male could be *the* Council Elect. His attire and relaxed mannerisms were so much at odds with the man I had met at the wedding. Gone was the stiff back and stern face. He was even more attractive like this, my eyes not wanting to leave him as I forced myself to look out the window.

"She lied; it was only 32 hours," Niklas said, his mouth sliding comfortably into an honest smile, like he did it often.

I laughed, the comment unexpected, *like he cared what I thought.*

"The dedication that must have taken," I said, my voice barely above a whisper, a slight blush heating my face. I could feel a pang in my chest though; this was not the "*He*" I thought she meant. I tried to not let the disappointment show on my face. I had pictured Rhone sprawled out in the chair, sleeping soundly as I did, all the while his ears still alert to any movement.

Niklas stopped at the edge of the bed, leaning against it. He folded his arms, his tightly corded muscles flexing with the easy movement.

"You look comfortable enough. I told Tesynia we were absolutely not carting a hospital bed up here; she would just have to make do with mine," he said, and his soft smile darkened a little as he continued, "It looks like I got you in my bed despite the failed efforts from the wedding."

His tone was playful, but I could feel his gaze wandering over me, his Fae Male territorial side of him practically purring at me being wrapped up in his sheets, wounded or not.

"You brought me here? Why didn't you take me to the Highlands?" I asked, ignoring his lightly flirty banter.

He scoffed a little. "Soren, this is *my* realm, the Galarian Cities. We are protected here, my condo is under heavy wards and protection charms, it was the safest and quickest option we had. To travel to the Highlands, that would take days, with the border crossings, the Aunders to get through. In your condition, we didn't have that kind of time. I mean, you bled through my suit. That's three layers of clothing. And plus, Tesynia and Olea were already in the Galarian Cities; I only had to call for them."

It was my turn to look down; I had not known I was bleeding out so badly, my memory still foggy.

"I can't let go; her power is still intertwined with mine. Callum and I can finish him. Take her, get her to Olea and Tesynia, they are her only hope."

Rhone's voice rang through my head. He had told Niklas to take me, to get me somewhere safe where the twins could heal me. A sour note of sorrow hit me, illogical and unwanted as it was, that it was Niklas and not Rhone who had carried me away. That Rhone had let him, or any other man, take me to safety. I remembered what was at stake, the war he was waging with those shadow creatures. The way his arms shook trying to maintain all the power, and still I wished it had been him. I knew I was being selfish.

I turned my attention back to Niklas, his eyes still on me. "*Days*, you said? How many days have I been here?"

"Three days, today being the third. You're actually healing a little faster than most would," he said matter-of-factly, running a hand through his hair.

"When you funnel out almost all your power like that, most would die. Some have died for less. At this point, now that you're coherent and awake, it should be another day before your powers recuperate to full capacity. What do you feel, when you reach for it, your power?" he asked.

Reaching down into myself, my magic answered, but where there used to be a roaring endless abyss I could instantly reach, I had to dive deeper into myself before I found it. I gasped. My mind's eye saw the glittering black stone well that I imagined my power rested in, and it was almost empty.

Niklas's eyebrows shot up, and he let out a low whistle. "Barely hanging on, is it? The power you unleashed, it was... unlike anything I had ever seen. That much available raw power is not common."

"When a Seer burns out, it is as disastrous as a supernova. You could have died," he said. His voice was soft this time, almost tender. But his charmful demeanor came back swiftly.

He playfully rolled his eyes. "You can breathe. As soon as I could find your father's contact information, I got him here as fast as I could. He made sure you were safe, and when he realized what an ally I could make, he told me your truth. He left only because he had to, your missing friend and all."

"Have you ever seen a Seer burn out?" I asked, my curiosity peeking. How old *was* this guy?

He narrowed his eyes on me, but where mine held curiosity, his held amusement.

"Yes, I have. A very long time ago, *Min stjärna,*" he said, crossing his arms. And there he was, using that phrase as a pet name for me. It was my turn to roll my eyes.

"Ya know, I'm not sure where you get off with calling me that. My *name* is Soren," I said, all politeness gone from my tone.

Hastily, I whipped the covers back and hopped off the bed. The quick movement made me dizzy. My feet were unsteady, and the world tilted. Niklas caught me, his strong hands wrapping around my waist. His scent hit me, his touch sending my head reeling for a different reason.

That clamp around my heart gave a squeeze, and in that moment, I wanted everything from him.

I wanted more of his touch. I wanted to know what he tasted like. I wanted him to say my name, to whisper it against my skin, to moan it in the middle of the night, to say it lovingly across the dinner table. I would've caved right there to hear him *just say my name, to give me anything and I'll take it.* The chemistry between us was tangible; it burned his touch into me. Gods, he was handsome, the kind of handsome they talk about in fairy tales, the kind of hand-some that made women and men drop to their knees. I let my eyes fall to his lips, and my body went tight. There was an ancient longing deep inside me and he sang to it. I snapped my head up to him, his eyes locking onto mine and they widened as he sucked in a strangled breath. Shock and awe lined his face, his easy smile gone.

Could he feel that too?

Quickly, he let go of me, his arms dropping to his sides, hands flexing, stretching wide, and then he stuffed them in his pockets. Like he could feel the flame that had ignited between our touch. Every thought and feeling tumbled out of my head the moment his hands left me.

What the hel was that about?! I mentally shook it off, the absence of my power and the weakness of my body clearly making me off kilter in a number of ways.

"I'll let you get freshened up. The bathroom is through there," he said, and in a blink he shadowed away. Snow flur-ries were the only thing left behind to tell me he had actu-ally been there, and not just a fever dream.

◞

I HADN'T BEEN ALONE for more than two minutes before Olea and Tesynia shadowed into the bathroom. *So much for privacy,* I thought to myself as their hands, light as feathers, began fussing about me. Tesynia carefully removed my bandage, my wound stinging as the cold air brushed it. I looked down at the scar that was about three inches wide; bruises had blossomed around it, but the scar was healing remarkably fast.

Tesynia's gentle gaze followed mine. "If you hadn't almost depleted your magic, you would have already been healed," she said matter-of-factly. Although I heard her words more as a chide, I knew they weren't. She was too kind and genuine to be snarky, and I really enjoyed this about her, secretly hoping we could one day be friends.

Olea worked silently in the corner, crushing up herbs and making them into a paste. She still had not spoken to me since the wedding, since she had addressed Rhone and mentioned his absence, which had seemed to affect her.

If they had been intimate, I couldn't blame either of them really. They were both gorgeous creatures. Olea was striking, even in the harsh bright light of the bathroom, her dark ebony skin seemed to shine, her rosy cheeks reminding me of a lustful flush a lover might have in the midst of passion.

After their prodding, and I had dutifully downed the newest tonic, the twins had started my bath water and left as silently as they entered.

I gingerly lowered myself into the large white tub, the scalding hot water welcoming against the permanent chill that the absence of my power had seemed to leave me in. Reaching over the side of the tub, I grabbed my phone, thankful I had decided to stash it in my small handbag before the wedding.

Turning it on, I frowned as I saw no new messages or missed calls. I sent Rhone a text, and my parents one as well. I knew that the code of silence would probably not be broken, but I tried anyway. What was everyone else even doing while I was held up here, healing? I wanted to know about Vana; I wanted to be involved in the search for her. And not to mention what the *fuck* went on with Willem and the shadow creatures who possessed bodies and could wield their magic... I desperately needed to be at the Highland libraries diving into the ancient tomes that could help lead us towards some kind of answer, if there even was one. Even if it was just to feel like I was doing something.

My phone buzzed with a notification, breaking me from my onslaught of worries. An unknown number flashed across the screen.

"MEET ME ON THE BALCONY AT 8."

I groaned, tossing the phone onto the floor.
How did he even get my number?

Since the minute I had laid eyes on her, I knew that even the old Gods would have come to their knees for her. Her very presence in this godsforsaken ballroom had sucked all of the air out of it. A low grumble thrummed through my mind, and I rolled my eyes in annoyance. Of course Jörmungandr would have something to say.

"Need I remind you I am at a very public event right now? Get out of here," I said to Jörmungandr, our mental bond opening as he awoke.

"Your thoughts are so loud, you woke me from my slumber. I do not see how this is my fault," Jörmungandr replied, his deep rumbling voice reverberating against the edges of my mind.

He slithered against my skin, and I felt him slide up above my tux collar. His head lifted off my skin ever so gently.

"Ah, stjärnan. She is as old as the galaxies, but alas, born anew," he said, his voice coming out in a hiss.

"Jörmungandr, why must you speak in riddles half the time?

'As old as the galaxies'. *Look at her ears. She is High Fae, is she not?" I asked, honestly curious at this point.*

He slithered back down to my arm and coiled himself around it before he answered, *"Is that not what all of these Fae think of you? With your pointed ears. Not all Wolves come as they are, my child. You should know this full well,* Niklas.*"*

He laughed at my silence before continuing, *"She might be the one you have been after, The Daughter of Two Worlds. She is... not as the rest are,"* Jörmungandr replied. I could feel his nostrils flare against my skin. My back stiffened at his words; he had never alluded to anyone being The Daughter of Two Worlds. Ever.

And then as soon as he slipped into my mind, he was gone again, his ominous presence leaving. The light nudge of his body up against my skin dissipated as he fell back into slumber. Jörmungandr was back to being a motionless, unassuming beast marking.

The old words sprang to my memory as Jörmungandr repeated them. Millenia old words, words that had been given to me as my goddess mother, Skade, gave herself to the earth, her hold over winter given to her children.

"Go, find her, the one they seek. She is your end, Nika. You must find her before The Dark One does. You must find her, Sæmingr, promise me."

My mother's sweet voice echoed in my head; she only used my true name when I was in trouble. Sæmingr. I sensed in that moment, this was a different kind of trouble. *My end,* she had said. Her words had haunted my nightmares for years. For five hundred years I had searched for this meaning. I searched records, archives, everywhere for answers of the Daughter of Two Worlds. I hunted down fortune tellers, Warlocks, and Wizards alike, and no one could tell me how she would end me, how she would give me to the earth. Truthfully, there was no one more ancient to find, no one who knew the prophecy like the old Gods would. They had selfishly locked themselves away, unresponsive to my pleas.

It had been at least a century since I had even thought of those foreboding last words my mother had given me. Although my mother was a captivating Jötunn and Goddess, there were even some things she could not control. She ruled over winter and hunt, and even then, she still feared for me and my siblings, as all mothers do for their children. I was her only living son of Odin. My father, Odin, had sired many children, but my mother had been the most unlucky of all of Odin's wives.

Because she had borne a new type of child. The Elven. They were not Fae, and were not Gods, but possibly something stronger, something *more* than both.

My mother became desperate to protect me. She had run to the Well of the Urd, to the Three Sisters: Present, Fate and Future. As they were called then, before they fell from the sky and shattered, scattering into a thousand pieces. They all weaved, all shared the same powers, but each had their own specialties, as their names suggest.

My mother asked to hear my fate and pleaded with them to protect my life thread. The Sister Future rebuked this, wanted nothing to do with a god's affairs, with this new creature. Even the Gods were at will to the Three Sisters. But the other two sisters, Sister Fate and Sister Present, had out voted the third, Sister Future. The price of protection of her remaining children was steep, and it was her life that would be in debt, to please Sister Future.

This was not all the Sister of Future would take from my family.

I had been protected, as promised, by the two sisters. I had led my family, the Elven, to the first kingdom—the Kingdom of Álfheimr, what is now known as The Icelands. In Álfheimr, all creatures roamed peacefully, Elven, Fae, and Giants alike.

But the fates had made a mistake. Sister Future said that the two sisters who had granted my mother's wish to protect me, had diabolically messed up fate, not only mine but for all the realms. She claimed the future was now ruined because of this new child.

It was here, where I was cursed.

The Elven were not meant to exist, Sister Future said. The kingdom of Elves, it was not meant to exist. They were meant to die with my siblings and I, with my mother. A grave misstep had given way. The Elven didn't need to eat Iðunn's golden apples to have immortality, like the Gods. They were a threat. Elven immortality was not like the immortality of the Fae, either. You see, Fae were not as seemingly invincible as the Elven. The Fae could succumb to disease and natural death just as Humans and Spellcasters. They were more powerful, harder to kill, and even more annoying to try to control. They were bigger, faster, and stronger in every aspect. The Elven, however, were as invincible as the Gods.

This was why Sister Future said the Elven could not exist. She said we were insidious, an invasive species that would take over. They did not bend to her like the Gods, the Giants, and the Fae.

She also could not take my life, her sister's protections were too strong, and this infuriated her. So she burdened me thrice.

First, with the demon God and sea serpent, Jörmungandr, who bore the wings and head of a dragon. This was a two birds one stone situation. I would be tied to him forever. Forced to carry him with me, to do his bidding, to be his eternal prison and prison guard. He would never be able to be unbonded to me. He had wronged Sister Future, refused her tasks. He was the most demonic of all the children of Loftur, the God of Chaos. She thought Jörmungandr would break me, and truthfully, for the first few hundred years, he almost had. His incessant and constant dwelling in my mind had almost driven me completely mad.

Second, she slaughtered the rest of Odin's children, making sure no other of Odin's offspring could sire this race she deemed undesirable. The race she said would taint the world. Any creature that was not pure, would not be allowed to live. I was completely and utterly alone in the world.

Third, she sent her creation, The Dark One, to end my kingdom. He came in the night, faceless and cloaked in her darkness. His power mingled with hers, creating the perfect storm. It took minutes for them to burn my kingdom and its people to the ground, only ashes remaining. Any creature with an ounce of Elven blood died, even the children of my now dead siblings of Odin.

Everyone died, except for me.

And then she erased us from history, burying most of

the knowledge of the old Gods as well. The only thing that mattered to Sister Future was her version of the world.

There was only one mention of my mother and I throughout history, passed down by oral tradition, bedtime stories is what they were thought to be. I was always referred to as "The Cursed One" and she was always the "Winter Mother." They both died in the end, every time.

I hated being away from my brother, from the only true family I had left standing in this world. I hated that we were still hiding, but being far from the Icelands, in the sparkling Galarian Cities, kept eyes off Freyr. Keeping him and his family safe had always been priority number one.

Even after all these years, I had never stopped searching for The Dark One, the one who came cloaked in shadows.

I had lost myself in memory, and shook my head, turning my eyes back up to the crowd, in search of the entrancing young woman. Why was she so different? Why did her striking face snag my eyes not once but twice in the seconds she had stepped into the room? There were many beautiful creatures here, but I couldn't shake her.

Maybe it was the male on her arm, that insufferable bastard recluse, Rhone. Although he was known to have lovers, he was never known to do something like this. And maybe that was it; he had her, which made her even more interesting. Rhonan glowered around the room, tugging her along, splaying his hand across her ass like she was something to be put on exhibit. It was unbecoming for such an event, but her ass *was* exquisite, one I could understand might be hard to pull away from. One I could picture myself leaving a handprint on. I ground my teeth in frustration.

Yes, it has to be that. It has to be that Rhonan makes her seem more alluring.

Even with that thought, I kept staring. Her long golden-brown hair hung loose, one side swooped up with a sparkling hair pin, and swayed gently against her shoulder blades, her dress dipping low in the back. Her golden skin gleamed against the candlelight, and her high cheek bones framed almond-shaped eyes. And gods, her mouth was stunning, her lips full and pouty. But it was her smile that was the best, I realized. It was sultry and inviting and sensual.

Suddenly, she turned her head in my direction, her blue-green eyes finding mine across the crowded room for the first time.

And there it was, like the iron jaws of a Jörmungandr, a relentless crushing weight clamped down on my heart. A weight that threatened to take me down. The world around me shuttered and the breath left my body as I felt my life thread anchor to hers. A searing tug of pain raked through my body as our souls tied, its knot eternally binding.

Oh, you've got to be fucking *kidding me.*

Jörmungandr's hissing laugh echoed through my mind.

I KEPT my eye on her throughout the wedding, waiting for her to be alone, if even for just a moment. My Hird, my group of commanders and warriors I considered family, mingled around me. They talked about work, the next election, and the wedding. All of them but Tiberius, who had wandered off with his new lover. I didn't care about any of it, even the vapid blonde, Evette, I had brought with me had gotten bored with my silence and brooding for the night. She hadn't been pouting or alone for long. She was mindlessly flirting with my second in command, Alexi and my third in command, his sister, Amara. She was clearly trying to see which one would bite first. Unbeknownst to her, it would always be Alexi. Alexi was a rake, and truthfully, this girl stood no chance with Amara. Alexi leaned into Evette further, titling his head my way, and I nodded mine in approval. We rarely shared partners, but tonight's events had changed everything, especially my planned night of rough sex with the blonde in question.

Alexi had easily taken to Evette, as most males would, his head tilting back in semi genuine laughter at something she had said. Alexi's deeply tanned skin glowed in the low light of the ballroom. His dark brown, shoulder-length, ringlet hair bounced as his head bobbed with laughter. Alexi flew through women, but the blonde didn't seem to mind it. I knew she had heard of his antics, *because who in the Galarian Cities hadn't*. I blamed his ability to get away with such antics on his striking teal eyes. His sister Amara had the same teal eyes, tan skin, and dark curly hair, but it was long with face framing wispy bangs that added to her mysterious allure. Her voluptuously curvy body was adorned in a tight black satin dress, her neck and ears dripping with her signature ruby and diamond jewelry. Her ruby red lips were downturned, and it was clear to me even more that Evette was not her type. But I already knew this. Amara had always required intellectual attraction, the outside shell mattering not.

I thought back to this morning, when Evette had invited

herself into my shower. She had gotten down on her knees and wrapped her mouth around my cock, and I had no doubt she would wake up and give Alexi the same prize.

I cared not.

I had to speak with her, this mystery woman. I mean, I was only slightly offended she had hardly reacted to our soul tie, a momentous rare life occurrence that creatures wait millennia for, if they even have one at all. I had thought I wouldn't have one, not that I had ever searched for one like some creatures do, until now. I had honestly thought they were a work of fiction. Or just maybe that the Elven did not have such bonds.

Clearly, this woman was entangled with Rhone, and maybe she wasn't ready to give up on that tryst yet, maybe this was a cursed soul tie and she was repulsed by me. I chuckled to myself. *How the fates will not let go of me, giving me a cursed soul tie.* I ran a hand through my hair again, my thoughts bombarding me.

"*Only* slightly *offended, prince?*" Jörmungandr said, awaking from his nap. I felt him slither up my arm and lazily wrap himself around my shoulders like a scarf. During events like this, I told him he had to stay under my clothing; we couldn't be spooking the dainty realm elite.

"*I have not been a prince for hundreds of years, Jörmungandr,*" I replied, my annoyance with him turning to anger.

"*Apologies, My King,*" he hissed snarkily before going on, knowing the Gods bowed to no king, "*It has just been so long since you have adorned your throne, it's almost like you plan to never return.*"

I decidedly ignored him, knowing at some point he would become bored and spirit away again. He knew why this was best... why I was not even a king any longer. Why my half-brother Freyr watched over the kingdom in my stead. Freyr, whose father was a powerful Royal Fae King of the seas, was able to rule our once decimated kingdom, in our mother's honor. He went unseen by all, assumed to be Royal Fae, as I had. He was not Elven, like the children of Odin, but my mother's undeniable curse of bearing children that were slightly *other* still plagued him. My mother's Goddess and Jötunn blood was there, but luckily for him, his father's Fae blood had hidden my mother's as well. Although he did not reach the same height and largeness of a full Jötunn, he was still extremely large and off-putting to most creatures. Freyr was truly the only good thing that had come into my life since Sister Future's eradication of the Elven.

Our kingdom, which we now referred to as a realm, was home to thousands of Iceland Fae, one where Royal Faeren and Wild Fae alike could roam together in peace. In this day and age, the two Fae kind getting along as such was rare, and definitely something to protect. Also, Freyr was not the The Cursed One, but the one known for his reign of peace and prosperity, and truthfully, that is what those creatures deserved. I had named Freyr my heir in absence long ago. He had married a Royal Faeren woman, and she had given him Fae children. Only a drop of my mother's Goddess blood tainted theirs. This was a blessing, for they had nothing to hide.

I turned my attention back to the girl. She stood next to Rhone, his arm wrapped around her waist territorially. My blood heated just at the sight, the champagne in my hand freezing over as my power lashed out. I sucked in a long breath, forcing it back down. My eyes locked on my nephew, Tiberius, son of Freyr, who stood across from her. He had been shacking up with The Highland Prince, Callum.

As if feeling my gaze, his eyes found mine, and then saw the frozen champagne flute in my hand. His brows knit in worry for a split second before he returned to the conversation he was making with Rhone and the woman, not wanting to draw attention.

It was during my distraction with Tiberius that she had fluttered away. I caught her at the refreshment table with one of the only humans in the room. *Odd.*

But this was my chance, and I knew it was as I saw her go out to the balcony with the human. Rhone had also disappeared. The Male's motto throughout the hundreds of years of being acquaintances rang through my head, "*I am loyal to no realm.*" I had always brushed it off as him not wanting to get close to anyone. *And yet, here he was.*

Quickly, I rushed over to Tiberius.

"Tiberius, what is her name, the girl who is here with Rhone?" My voice came out rushed, barely above a whisper.

He looked at me curiously. "Soren, of tribe Huran." I shoved the champagne flute into his hand, leaving without another word.

"Niklas, what's going on?" he said, but I ignored him, shadowing away.

I shadowed onto the balcony, hiding myself in the darkness. She leaned against the balcony railing, her face flushed and a sob broke from her throat. Suddenly, she turned around, her hair whipping in the wind. A flush of nerves rushed through me as her star-studded eyes searched into the depths of my shadowy corner.

I stepped forward in a long stride, stuffing my shaking hands into my pockets, willing myself to be the deception of cool, calm, and collected. I could not remember a time I had ever been less of any of those. Nothing rattled me, but it seemed that she was the exception. Her eyes searched me, and I could feel her gaze drag itself up my body, her eyes catching on my lips. The bond tightened, her eyes dilating in arousal. *Ah, so definitely not cursed in* that *way.* I gave her a devilish smirk. Her eyes darted away quickly, and she scowled.

"I see you needed a breath of fresh air as much as I did," I said, willing my voice to be as velvety smooth as possible, begging the Gods to not to let my nerves shake my voice. I raised my hand, sending her a gentle snow-flecked breeze. She shivered slightly as it caressed her body, and again the bond went taught. I eternally groaned, knowing the shiver was from the attraction she felt towards me, and not merely the chill. I took two more steps forward, stopping when her heated sugared fig and honey blossom scent wrapped around me.

But all the words I had waited hours to speak did not come. I couldn't bring myself to mention the soul tie. The question in her eyes, the unassuming and direct way she stared at me... it was like she didn't even know, or didn't even care.

Maybe I had been wrong, maybe that wasn't a soul tie snapping into place. Maybe it was just a visceral attraction.

Maybe.

CHAPTER
TWENTY

Tesynia had stopped by while I napped, dropping off a folded pile of clothing that she had acquired while I lounged around. Opening the door to the balcony, the night air rushed at me. I was grateful for the loose-fitting sweater, leggings, and soft knit socks she had dropped off, the night air chilling me. I looked down the balcony to the other side and saw a small fire going. Niklas was sitting on a plush loveseat, looking out at the sparkling city lights. He had changed since I had seen him earlier; his light blue shirt was unbuttoned at the top, his sleeves rolled up. A dark blue tattoo peaked out from one of his sleeves. Shining dragon-like scales gleamed in the firelight, and I swear I saw it move, the scales sliding up his arm. I looked back up to his chest, where his shirt hung open slightly, confused. *I thought he had had a tattoo there, with those same blue scales.*

I mentally shook off the thought, remembering how incredibly out of it I had been when I had seen him this morning.

As I approached him, he didn't turn my way, just continued looking out into the night sky, seeming to be lost in thought. Gingerly, I sat down in a cushy patio chair across from him, my side stinging, but a fraction worth of the pain compared to this morning. I stared at him a moment, wondering what was going on in his head. What had made him sit by my bedside for *32 hours?* I silently wondered how many hours I had taken away from his duties as Council Elect.

What had made Rhone be so absent? I had chased that thought away all day, shoving it into the back of my mind each time it reared its head. I was trying to be understanding, trying to think of all the reasons he had to be gone. I even felt selfish, like me feeling like he was the one who should be sitting across from me made *me* the bad guy. I just couldn't ever see myself leaving his side, not when he had come so close to dying.

And maybe that was my problem, maybe I was reflecting what I thought he should do, because it's what I would have done.

Maybe.

The longer we sat there in silence, the more I felt myself relax, like I didn't have to be constantly on the defensive. I honestly couldn't remember the last time I was just able to sit in front of another creature and simply exist.

He turned to me then, seemingly brought back into this moment, his bright blue eyes shining like stars, his white hair tucked behind his ears.

"The night sky shining against the city lights often

entrances me; something about it reminds me of home. So much so, I find myself spending most of my nights out here," he says, breaking the silence and stretching his long arms across the back of the love seat.

"Where is home?" I asked, genuinely curious.

He was silent for a beat. "It has been gone for some time now," was all he said, before quickly changing the subject. "I thought you might need some fresh air and a nice view. You haven't come out of that room all day."

I smiled at him. He had been right about that, the change of scenery giving me a little bit more life, the night sky recharging me. I got up from the chair and walked over to the glass balcony railing, leaning into the wind, my hair blowing in the chilled night breeze. I turned back to him, leaning against the railing, resting my elbows on the edge.

He smiled back, his dimples showing. "How would you like to see the best view in all the Galarian Cities?"

I raised my eyebrows slightly, a little astonished that he didn't believe that *this* was the best view. I mean gods, he probably had THE nicest penthouse in the entire city, and that was saying a lot. "Is this not it? I can't imagine a better view, honestly," I said, throwing my arms up in the air a little.

"Oh, this is nothing compared to what I could show you," he said, a playful smirk sliding across his face.

I blushed slightly and I knew the innuendo was purposely placed. "Okay, and how do you propose to see this magnificent view? It's not like I can leave, anyways," I said, and I felt that ache for freedom as I said it, an ache I didn't realize was there.

He stared at me for a second, his brows knitting in

confusion, his blue eyes flashing with an emotion I could've sworn was rage. "Who said you couldn't leave, Soren?"

My face heated, and I knew he was right. No one had told me I couldn't leave. Not Tesynia, not Olea, and certainly not him.

"I... Uh... I just assumed I couldn't, I guess," I said, stumbling over my words. I inwardly cringed at myself, at how ridiculous and pitiful that had made me feel and sound.

He stood up then, his long legs making quick work of the distance between us. He stopped in front of me, the closeness of him sending an unsolicited thrill through me, his amber scent radiating off of him. He looked down at me with those ice blue eyes, searching mine.

He lifted his hand, brushing the hair that the wind had caught and tucked it behind my ear. His fingers brushing my cheek, and the urge to lean into it was almost unbearable. He brushed his hand back, tangling his fingers in my hair and wrapping his fingers around the back of my neck. He titled my head up to him.

"You are no caged bird, Soren. It would never suit you," he said, his voice soft.

"And neither am I," was all he said as a streak of blue light flashed and a burst of frosted wind rushed forward. Enormous wings appeared behind him, stretching wide to their full wingspan before tucking themselves back behind him. They glistened in the low light of the balcony. Shimmering ice blue and deep sapphire-colored scales gleamed, an iridescent sheen causing them to shift in color, turning shades of green for a split second.

I gasped, my mouth falling open in shock and awe.

"Holy *shit*," tumbled out of my mouth before I could stop

it. His smile grew at my astonishment. I laughed, unable to hold it back, my hand flying to my mouth, the shock and the boyishly giddy look on his face infectious.

He held out his arms, and his wings stretched reflexively as he did, expanding twice the length of his arms.

"This is the only way up," he said, and I internally groaned, knowing the proximity of him would make me dizzy in the head again, but it was better to go ahead and get this night over with.

I walked towards him and tucked myself into his side, his arm wrapping around my waist. I wrapped my arms around him, the hard muscles of his abdomen flexing against me.

"You'll want to hold on a little tighter than that," he said against my hair, before he lifted us up into the sky.

I yelped and screwed my eyes shut. I felt his chest shake with laughter. He wrapped his other arm around my waist, pressing my body into his, every hard plane of his body pressing into the soft contours of mine.

After a few seconds, the wind calmed.

"Open your eyes, Soren, and look up. You're missing the most coveted view," he said, his voice a whisper against my ear.

Opening my eyes, I looked up. The night sky was laid before me, depthless and sparkling, all-knowing and silent. Every star a perfect shining gem against the deep midnight blue.

I had never seen anything more beautiful.

"What do you think the stars think of you?" he asked me, his voice sounding far off, like the question wasn't just for me, but for him as well.

I thought for a long second, contemplating what he meant, and all I could think of was how I had been so desperately jealous of them lately.

"I've never thought of what they think of me, I guess. But I have been jealous of them. They are just there; they exist for themselves, so unbothered," I said, my voice coming out small. I couldn't believe I was admitting this to him.

I felt him nod his head as if to agree. "When I was a child, my mother would tell my siblings and I bedtime stories, like most mothers do. One of my favorites was the creation of the worlds. Before the creation, there was this giant void called the Ginnungagap. In the Ginnungagap, all the magic in the universe raged, unkempt. To the far north of the Ginnungagap was the land of Niflheim, a land of darkness and ice. To the south, the Muspelheim, a land of light and fire. On one of the endless nights, although time didn't exist yet, a drop of water from Niflheim and spark of fire from Muspelheim met."

He looked down at me to see if I was paying attention, and I rolled my eyes at him. He huffed a laugh. "I was just making sure I didn't put you to sleep, is all."

He cleared his throat before continuing, "From this meeting of fire and water, the elements created Ymir, the Father of All. He created the first race, the Jötunn, or Giants as they call them now. From these Giants, came the first Gods. After thousands of years, Ymir had grown too large and too evil, and the sons of his son, the first Gods: Odin, Vili, and Ve, realized that he had become a threat to everything that had been created, so they killed him. The blood that flowed from Ymir's wounds flooded the 9 worlds, almost killing off all of creation. Odin and his brothers then took Ymir's body to create the universe. Placing Ymir's body over the Ginnungagap, they began to mold Middangeard, later known as Middle-Earth and then shortened to Earth. Nothing went to waste. They used his flesh to create earth, and his remaining blood for the sea. His bones and teeth created the mountains and hills, his hair made up the trees, and his brains were used to create clouds. His skull, which was held up by four great dwarves, made up the heavens, or Valhǫll. Then, they scattered sparks from Muspelheim, creating the sun, moon, and stars." He paused for a moment, turning his attention back to me, his eyes shining. "Do you think they are so unburdened now?"

I held his stare; the way he spoke enthralled me. I could see why this one would have been his favorite; it was fantastical and adventurous. Gruesome, beautiful, and intriguing.

"I have never heard that one before," I said, feeling even smaller than when we had first lifted up into the night sky. All the stars around us seemed to gleam brighter, like their truth had finally been freed.

"What happened to the Giants?" I asked, still gazing up at the stars, or maybe even the sparks of Muspelheim.

"You say that like the story could've been real," he said, amusement in his tone. "It's said they still live, but that most of them choose to dwell with the Gods in Ásgarður. Some say they've seen Giants in the Aunders, that they recognize Isleen as their Queen."

Slowly, he started flying us back down, his wings contracting as we went. The soft night air blew my hair. He set me down gently on the tile patio, and honestly, I was sad to be on stable ground again. I had not felt a sense of freedom like that in some time.

"It's funny, the things that can be so easily lost to history," he said, a flash of sorrow in his eyes, his calm demeanor returning quickly.

I watched as his wings shifted in the moonlight, the scales shifting colors from blue to purple to green. They tucked themselves against his back and then vanished, like they didn't even exist. He returned to the couch, lazily leaning himself back against it, resting an ankle on his knee.

I couldn't shake his wings though, and my curiosity got the best of me. "How do you have those...wings? I thought only Wild Fae had such things."

He looked at me then, his piercing blue eyes staring into mine, and he gave me a funny look, like he was puzzled by *me*. "That lone wolf of yours must revel in keeping you in the dark. Surely this deeply guarded secret of mine would have been one he was aching to tell you about, if even just to warn you of whose company you were in," he said, cocking his head to the side gently.

"I am The Cursed One, darling, the one they sang about in the old ballads, the one they etched into the now crumbling temple ruins that are littered about all the realms. The cursed son of a god. The one cursed thrice by the Three Sisters of Fates," he said, cutting himself off, leaving me with the feeling there was more to tell, but I did not pry. Maybe I didn't want to know how deeply this curse went.

He could not think I was seriously so daft that I would believe he was a walking bedtime story of old. I narrowed my eyes at him. "Alright, so, how are you Council Elect if you are some cursed creature. Who in their right mind would want a cursed being to rule their city?" I asked. I was truly astonished, and I couldn't help the snarky tone that came with it. It was all so… *ridiculous*.

He smiled at me then, a true smile, with an edge of mischief in his eyes. "How're you gallivanting around like some damsel of the Huran tribe, halfling? And the old Gods are but fables, are they not?" He paused for a second, giving me a knowing look as he straightened his suit jacket.

"You think you are the only individual around who gets to be one of a kind, *Min stjärna?*"

I scoffed then, waving my hand. "Please, all Fae Males think they are the only of their kind. But this is new, the son of a *god*? I'm starting to believe you are all the same person."

"If you are referring to your *absent* partner, I can assure you he is special, but not *a 1,000 year old creature born before the Seers*, kind of special."

My eyebrows shot up. *One thousand years old? He can't be serious. There is no creature older than the Seers…Is there?*

"If there is anything I am not, it's a liar," he said as he stood, looking off into the horizon before sauntering towards me. He stood in front of me for a second, like he was contemplating his next move. He took my hand then, gently pulling it towards him, his lips lingering above it.

"Even The Cursed One must sleep," he said against my hand, his soft lips pressing into my skin, sending a thrill through me. He lowered his eyes, kissing my hand gently, and I knew I had stopped breathing. The ache in my chest tightened.

My mind lingered on that title, "*The Cursed One*," and I racked my brain trying to figure out where I remembered that from. It seemed the haze that fogged up my brain had not fully lifted.

He turned his head slightly back to me as his hand was on the door handle. "I received word from Rhonan that we will leave early in the morning for the Highlands," he said before he disappeared into the darkness of his apartment.

I tried to ignore the fact that *Rhonan* had failed to make any contact with me. How his attempt to only contact Niklas felt pointed, leaving me with the familiar pang of rejection.

TWENTY-ONE

J örmungandr made his presence known as soon as we were alone, his talons scraping against mind.

"I don't see how you can be upset with me right now. You're the one who said she was the Daughter of Two Worlds. It didn't seem fair, knowing her entire truth, and her knowing nothing of mine. All this time we searched for the one who would end me, kill me. Maybe it's a different kind of ending," I said, knowing why he had reared his head. *"Maybe that's what this all means. This soul tie was completely unexpected. Why not an unexpected ending?"*

"You should go visit that blonde again, or maybe the brunette even. I think you're doing too much thinking with your dick. She believes she loves him, you know, the lightning bearer. I smell him all over her. And as for your ending, she could be just what we have always thought. Don't let that pretty face sway you, Sæmingr, you have lots of pretty faces you could choose from," Jörmungandr hissed. Yep, he was mad. Digging deep cuts as he went, chiding me with my true, gods-given name. The

baring of him having my true name clung to me, its effects like a truth serum.

He continued before I could reply, *"She may have felt the bond, felt all the things you feel, but she doesn't understand, Sæmingr. Who says she will accept it when she finds out?"*

Her murmurs from the night I carried her lifeless body to my bed slammed into me, remembering the way she had clung to me, begging me not to leave her. Her blood seeping into my tux, droplets splashing on the wooden floor as I rushed her through the apartment. As I had laid her down and she had screamed in pain, a sweltering fever racking her body. Her massive loss of power had greatly affected her body's ability to heal, to fight off the fever.

It was Tesynia who had ordered me to lay next to her, to use my winter to cool her, lest the fever take her to the Rivers before they had time to heal her. I did as requested, sliding myself carefully onto the bed and tucking her into me. We laid like that for some time, all while Olea and Tesynia operated on her, stitching her back together piece by piece. Their golden powers worked their magic as they hovered their palms above her body, tendrils of shimmering magic dipping in and out of her body with immaculate precision, stitching her up from the inside out. Their foreheads beading with sweat as they worked diligently through the night. Once her fever broke, I stepped away, feeling hollow as the contours of her body left mine. It was her pleas for me to stay that held me captive, unable to leave for that godsforsaken 32 hours. I couldn't leave her, not when she begged, repeating my name in her dreamless sleep. Our bond tethered us together even in her deathlike slumber.

I knew she didn't remember it now. From the utter

confusion on her face as I had entered the room earlier in the morning, I knew she expected Rhone to walk through that door. And the pain I felt as I realized she wasn't ignoring the soul tie, she just simply had no idea. I knew for certain the second I caught her as she stumbled out of the bed, the soul tie feeding me fragments of what *could be*. My mind was flooded with thoughts of her, of her saying my name in the dark across our bed, of her moaning it in ecstasy, or her saying it lovingly as she walked next to me hand in hand.

Rhone. I hated even thinking of his name. The spineless prick hadn't even shown his face since the attack, his phone going unanswered, even by Olea, who had been his bedmate for years. He hadn't even *checked up on her*. Hadn't even told her parents of her state, how she was clinging to life. Made no contact until he demanded to see us this coming morning.

Jörmungandr's puff of annoyance brought me back, and I bristled at every word that had come out of his mouth, at the thought of Soren and Rhone together, at the thought of her loving him, at the thought of her rejecting our bond. It was jealousy and sadness rolled into one, all of it unwarranted, and I knew that's the reaction he wanted. He wanted me to come to reality, to see it for what it was, what it could be. Not for what I wanted it to be.

That was also the other problem of all of this, I would never force her to choose. Her own uncoerced decision would have to be enough for me. Jörmungandr knew me too well, knew I would never force her hand.

"I didn't give her the full truth, you ass. I actually gave her very little information. But maybe that is the point of all this.

Maybe we are supposed to come together, two creatures unlike any other. The prophecy states three children, and if we ever find The Dark One, maybe we have a chance," I snapped back.

"Yet. *You haven't given her the full truth,* yet, *is what you mean. You gave her enough to ask questions,"* was the last thing he said as he slithered away, departing from my mind.

I thought back to those shadow creatures as they crawled out of the portal. How they had ebbed and flowed out of the darkness, taking down Commander Arington, putting on his body like a new suit. Their shadows, the darkness they emanated. I hadn't seen creatures like that in centuries.

Not since the shadows had obeyed The Dark One, turning my kingdom and its people to ash.

I was getting closer. I wouldn't lose him again.

TWENTY-TWO

Coming back into the bedroom, I quickly changed into my silk nightgown and tried to sleep. But nothing had worked; I had laid awake in bed for hours with my eyes wide open. A million thoughts ran through my head. How did the paintings connect to the Seer realm? Where had Willem stashed the painting of my parents? Where had Vana disappeared to, and was she okay? The fact that the phrase, *The Cursed One,* kept ringing through my head, and I couldn't figure out why it seemed so urgent, but I simply couldn't grasp its importance. The thought slipped away any time I reached for it. The way Niklas's lips felt against my skin, that ancient song inside me reacting to his touch in a way I didn't understand. The fact Rhone had kept his distance since the attack. The look on Willem's face as he handed me his life thread, the thread stained black, much like his blood had been.

I got up then, a jolt of energy forcing me to stand. I knew what had to be done. Slipping on my robe, I walked to the dresser. I found myself staring at the beautifully intricate silver compact, and next to it was the onyx blade. The same blade I had shoved through Willem's chest. The cold, smooth weight against my palm, damning. I had to reach into Willem's life thread. Not only had he asked for it, but there had to be clues there.

The compact came open with a soft click. Willem's life thread laid there, its inky blackness seeming to emanate off of it. I knew what I had to do, and part of me didn't want to do it alone. To dive into Willem's truth, into his past. But it had to be done.

I sat myself on the ground, criss-cross style, and shoved the compact into the pocket of my robe. I drew in a long breath through my nose, closing my eyes and clearing my mind like I had in Rhone's training room. I thought of The Gap, and it was then that I felt the slight shift. The shift that tugged at my skin and rustled my hair. The shift that woke the sleeping stardust that ran through my veins. The shift that told me I had left my world, and now lay in another.

I opened my eyes, and the familiar hazy rainbow-colored light shifted through the fog of the endless abyss, the horizon glittering with far-off galaxies.

"Hello, Soren," a lyrical voice said from behind me, my mother's voice. Turning towards the sound of her, I sucked in a gasp as I took in the sight. There she was, her silver hair blowing in the gentle wind, her legs crossed. She wore a white jewel-embroidered dress, and a crown of stars laid on her head. She sat upon an enormous throne, the rainbow-colored light refracting off of it. It was made of glittering silver and blue stone; the high pointed arch back was made of glass, stars, and galaxies shining through. The frame was ash-colored wood with intricate swirling etchings and stars decorating the sides. It was a throne made for a queen of the cosmos. Tendrils of fog danced around her feet. In the distance behind her, enormous branches of a giant silver tree swayed, its white leaves rustling softly.

"What is all this? Why have you..." I let my voice trail off. I was truly astonished; the branches of the tree seemed to breathe almost, softly expanding and contracting. The tree was cut off by the fog mid trunk, the rest of it hidden. My mother lifted her hand, and a gust of wind came sweeping through The Gap. The fog lifted, revealing the roots of the tree spread out across the shimmering ground, stretching out as far as my eye could see.

"*Oh no*," I whispered, a hand flying up to my mouth.

The shift in fog revealed the true state of the tree. The roots were black and rotted, black vines snaking up the trunk of the tree. Far beneath the tree's roots, a well stood. It was grand; black stone pillars jutted into the air and had a circular domed ceiling with a star-shaped opening. A glittering waterfall of stardust fell from the galaxy-speckled sky and fed the well. Black stone steps led up to it. I peered down at it, and deja vu slammed into me. The sight of the well, the swirling threads and glowing waters within, looked like what I imagined my seemingly endless pit of magic looked like inside me. She then stood, her throne behind her vanishing, and she reached for my hand. I began to walk towards it instinctively, but a gentle weightless hand grabbed my arm, stopping me. I turned to look back at Asta, and when I turned back to the well, it had changed drastically. It laid in shambles, broken beyond its former grandeur. Its glittering black pillars were destroyed, crumbling across the ground, the mist of The Gap dancing in between the shattered pieces. The glowing waterfall fell across the broken well, its waters flooding the area with nowhere else to go. Buried in the ground, what remained of the well, iridescent silver threads swirled in the well's water. The magic that thrummed from the well made my power surface, the hum in my blood beating in rhythm with it.

My mother's eyes shifted down to her feet, and I saw her close her eyes softly. As if me seeing this hurts her, or maybe even embarrassed her.

Gently, she reached for my hand. Her slender fingers were cold against mine and light as air, reminding me that she was not of this world. The Gap seemed to bend to her every will as she pulled me with her. The fog broke away from the borders of The Gap, forming into winding stairs that led down past the rotting roots of the ancient tree, and to the collapsed well. Every step down the makeshift stairs made me nervous, the fog dissipating back into the corners of The Gap with every step I took.

Asta stopped us in front of the dilapidated well. What was left of its glittering black stone was smooth, forming a perfect circle. How could I have known what this well looked like before its demise, how could I have reimagined this in my mind's eye, before I am seeing it for the first time now?

My mother saw the confused look on my face, a sad smile appearing on hers. "You are human in all the way I expected and hoped you would be," she said as she let go of my hand, bending down to dip her hand in the well, letting the powerful water run through her fingers.

I looked to her, and then back at the well. "I have seen this before, in my mind. Rhone has always told me to look inside myself for my power. And this was what I have always seen."

She sighed then. "It is possible that because the well's magic is within you, it showed itself to you. The Well of Urd is a universal mystery."

"What happened to it?" I asked, turning back to look at it.

"Many, many years ago, The Sister of Future became angry. She felt her two sisters wanted to overthrow her, rule for themselves. Even though there were three thrones, there is but one kingdom for the fates. One kingdom, sectioned off into three parts: The Throne of Destiny, The Throne of Midnight, and The Throne of Hereafter. They had lived in harmony for as far back as time would go. But nothing good lasts, as it would seem. There was a Jötunn and Goddess, who ruled over winter, Skade. She married the God Odin, and they had children together. It was not a completely love-less marriage, but it was also not a happy one. From her children with Odin, a strange occurrence happened. She bore a new type of child, a child no one had seen before. Sister Future became obsessed with these new children, obsessed with controlling them, deciding their fates. Eventually the fact that she couldn't do any of those things dawned on her. She decided swiftly that they were undesirables, that their existence would obscure the delicate balance of the universe, so she hunted them. Killing them all, all but one, the son of the winter goddess. When Skade came to the Three Sisters, pleading for help, two of them agreed, the third did not. But the decision was not solely out of the goodness of their own hearts. Sister Fate knew Sister Present's destiny; she had seen that her sister would also bear a child that was unlike any other. Two children that were *other*, they would form a Prophecy that would change the worlds. It would be worlds that didn't need the Three Sisters. A world that had complete autonomy to itself. A world that would free the Three Sisters, and would allow all creatures to not have to be bound by them.

"Sister Present and Sister Fate kept this hidden for as long as they could, protecting Odin's children as long as possible. They yearned to be free. And for years they were successful. Even Sister Present held her secret too, that her child was to be *other*." Asta paused for a moment, and she turned her eyes towards me.

My mind was whirling. The children of Odin, the last remaining son, it was *Niklas*. It had to be, his Winter powers and his father being a god. But Sister Present, maybe her child was... my thoughts stopped dead in their tracks. *Sister Present...* My eyes slowly met my mother's.

She stood then and took my hand in hers, the glowing water dripping off of her hand. Her hand was ice cold, and with the contact, I felt my entire body jerk. Every fiber of my power surged forward to meet hers, to meet the power of the Well of Urd.

"Sister Present had met a handsome Fae Warrior. It was by mere chance. He had traveled down the Rivers, chasing some demon god who had escaped Hel and killed his father. Sister Present had been by the river bend, collecting herbs and daisies. It was there she witnessed the great warrior as he took down the giant beast, cutting off its head and throwing it into the freezing rivers that flowed to Niflheim. He was unlike anything she had ever seen. His skin was a rich tan, intricate markings ran up his strong arms, and his

long black hair was braided back. Even with his deep
bronze armor shining with the blue blood of the demon
demi-god, she fell in love immediately. The Sisters had
taken lovers before, Gods, Jötunn, and Fae alike. It wasn't
until she became pregnant with his child that everything
changed, and she knew the prophecy had begun. Sister
Present fled, she and her lover escaping to his kingdom. For
years they were able to fly under the radar of Sister Future.
It wasn't until she heard Sister Fate's plea from the Ginnungagap, that she stepped forward. Sister Present and her Mate
came to Sister Fate's rescue, hiding their child in a spell-
binding charm. But it was a trap, led by Sister Future and
her creation. A trap that ended in the death of Sister Present
and her Mate. A trap that led to the universe ripping open,
and the two sisters to fall through their world, and into the
next. As Sister Present fell, and a death blow ended her, she
scattered across the realms of Middangeard, creating the
Seers.

"While Sister Present and Fate had been scheming, so
had Sister Future. She had created the ultimate threat, the
Dreygur. A threat able to take down the children that were
other, a threat that could create an army of ruthless creatures. Sister Future tracked down three powerful creatures,
one of each race, using their beating hearts and life threads
to form the Dreygur. The Dreygur could house any power
from any of the life threads, bending them to his will. He
could swiftly transform in and out of the different bodies
the life threads were supposed to belong to, multiplying
himself threefold. He was created to take and use. Take lives,
take memories, use creatures to their will. That's how Sister
Future erased history so easily. It took mere minutes for the

Dreygur to reach his leeching magic into the well and take the memories from each life thread. Since her first creation, she has made many more, an army of them, but her first: he is their king. Their army, though, has not grown in numbers in some time. Something tells me that you are a part of their plan, in some twisted way."

My mother continued, "Sister Future and her Dreygur destroyed The Well, the threads no longer able to flow peacefully through the well to the Rivers where they might ascend to the Heavens or Hel. The tree you see before you, it is Yggsdasil, and it will die without the waters of the Well of Urd. All the worlds will die."

Asta closed her eyes then, tears falling down her cheeks. "This is so much bigger than any of us, and the fact you are just one person, who has to hold all of this on her shoulders.... Part of me desperately believes I shouldn't have been so selfish. I should've left well enough alone. Jahan would still be alive, you would have been blessed by another mother, the memories of all of Middangeard would have stayed intact. But even as I say all that, I know this would've played out a different way, to a different woman, to a different version of you, at a different time. Some fate, it cannot be untangled. I loved your father so much, as I love him now. *We* love you more than you could ever know, Soren."

The visions of the Well of Urd and Yggsdasil faded away, and we returned to the hollowness of The Gap. The fog around us was stained with darkness; tendrils of black smoke rushed forward. The same black smoke that had appeared at the wedding. The fog began swirling together, a black portal beginning to form. That familiar ominous roaring hum rang out from the portal. The stardust-speckled mist began swirling faster, and a deafening crack echoed throughout The Gap, the portal splitting open the world.

Asta's eyes flew to mine. "They are tracking you, Soren. I do not know how, but I knew they would track you here, I hoped they would. That insidious black life thread, it was meant to turn you Dreygur. Once a Dreygur is created, it can infiltrate a creature's life thread and body, but sometimes, the true creature is strong enough that they can co-occupy its mind with the Dreygur, but forever remain a prisoner. Listen to me, my child, once a Dreygur takes over a body, there is no life left for the creature without its new host. The removal of the Dreygur kills the creature. A Dreygur host... is certain death."

I thought of Willem, how real he had felt, and a sinking feeling hit me. The black blood that had spilled out of him, his empty eyes that had been swallowed by a black void. He was never *him; there was no him.* He was always the Dreygur, The King. And he was clearly far from dead. *I wonder how much of the true Willem was left, the creature that existed before the Dreygur had taken over. How much of his mind he was still in control of.* I shook my head, letting the intrusive thoughts go. I could not harp on what there was to save. If what my mother said was true, it didn't matter once the Host entered the body.

"It is my life's greatest work that I was able to be here to change this last bit of fate for you. And not only that, but I had to tell you the truth. It's what you deserve, what should have been done this entire time. Ending me forever, that will keep Synnove distracted, at least until you can find Sister

Fate. She is Queen of the Audners. Seek her out; she will know you immediately. Oh, and you also need one more thing," she said, reaching for me. She took my head in her hands, her eyes filling with tears. She tilted my head down and kissed me gently on the forehead, her lips feeling like a brush of cold wind. A brief blinding light flashed.

"It is all the stardust I still possess. You are the Heir to the Midnight Throne, Soren. The Heir of Time. The Daughter of Two Worlds. Keep your mental shields up at all times. The harder your mind is to infiltrate, the less damage the Dreygurs can do, the less memories they can take. Do not forget that and do not ever bow to anyone." She paused, turning to look at the portal, and quickly turned back to me, her words coming out faster, "The Cursed One, he is the answer, he is your end." She brushed her lips on my forehead one last time. They lingered for a beat, and I felt her chin quiver slightly. An inescapable sorrow slammed into me. The finality in her words was sobering. My eyes welled with tears. I had only just met her, and now I was going to indefinitely lose her, a second time. I wrapped my arms around her then, her ghostlike form bowing under the weight of my very alive body.

The portal behind us ripped open, the gravitational tug pulling me forward, and I dug my heels into the ground. Dreygurs spilled out, their shadowy bodies mingling with the silver fog of The Gap.

Gently, my mother pulled away from me, placing her hands on my arms and giving them a squeeze. "I love you, my daughter. You are all that has ever mattered."

That was the last thing she said to me before I saw a silver-haired woman step through the portal, her silver crown glinting in the fractured rainbow light of The Gap. She wore a long white jewel-embroidered dress, the bodice lined with diamonds, flowing sleeves draping gracefully off her shoulders, her train dragging behind her. She was ethereal, as beautiful as my mother, but different in all the ways that mattered. Where Asta was soft and gentle, she was sharp and cold like a razor's edge. It was the power she emanated though, dark and scathing, like her soul laid bare. The same type of darkness that had bled through the dark Seer in my dreams, the woman who had laid my family in piles, dead, in my dreams. *This was her.* The Dreygurs slipped into her shadow, hovering around her. They started to surge forward, but she held up a moon white hand, stopping them in their tracks.

The Royal Seer.

The Sister of Future.

"This one is mine. My dear sister." She pointed to my mother, and then her silver eyes slid to mine. My power recoiled as her gaze fell on me, begging me to flee.

"And this one is his, a prize he deserves. Her prophecy says she will be Queen. So she will be. She will be his." Willem's dead eyes flashed in front of me, the thought of being his bride nauseating.

Synnove's magic burst from her, and my mother countered. Asta turned sideways, both of her arms flying out, a weightless palm laying itself flat against my chest. Blinding magic flowed out of each of her palms. Her magic hit Synnove, and I heard her hiss in pain. It was then I felt my mother's power searing through my chest, the force of it throwing me backwards. I flew through the air, but instead of hitting the ground, I was falling, plummeting through the fog. I threw my arms out, trying to grasp at anything, and that's when I felt it, the hum of magic I instantly recognized as my fingers brushed the realm border. There was a buzz of electricity as my fingertips slipped away.

The Gap rapidly became just another cloud in the starlit sky as I fell, like I was falling through worlds.

TWENTY-THREE

I opened my eyes with a gasp, my vision slowly coming back to me, the edges blurry. I was still in Niklas's bedroom. I flung myself up to my feet, running out the bedroom door. Niklas was sitting on the couch, a newspaper in one hand and a coffee mug in the other. The deep golden glow of the sun rising to meet the indigo star speckled night sky told me it was the wee hours of the morning. I had been in The Gap for *hours*.

I closed my eyes, remembering the electric thrum of magic against my fingertips, the electric thrum that had begun all of this.

The same thrum I had felt as I had touched the paintings in Rhone's hallway, the same thrum from my painting of my parents. I could feel it in my bones that this was the key that we had been looking for. And that had to be where the Well of Urd laid in pieces, where the tree of the nine worlds was dying.

"You look like you've seen a ghost," he said, a playful grin on his face. When I didn't return his banter or smile, his face went straight. Olea walked out of the guest room she had been staying in, yawning, a coffee cup in her hand as well, and she leaned against the doorframe.

"What has happened," he said, standing quickly. Olea's figure straightening in my peripheral. Suddenly, he was next to me, his gentle touch running up the back of my arm. I closed my eyes to it, letting his cool touch and amber-lined scent soothe me. I counted backward from 20, willing the tears that threatened to fall to cease. I opened my eyes finally, and Niklas's icy blue eyes were on me intently.

Before I could open my mouth to speak, the air in the room shifted, and a mist-lined breeze swept through the room. And I knew immediately who it was. My body went on high alert, the butterflies in my stomach coming back to life.

Rhone.

"Yes, what *has* happened, my little terror?" he drawled, adjusting his leather jacket from the shadow in. He stood there, his long black hair pulled back into a low bun, a gray shirt tucked into black jeans, and his signature black leather boots adorned his feet. His gaze landed on Niklas, and then dropped to Niklas's hand on me.

I was suddenly unable to control the sob that was lodged in my throat. *Gods, I had missed him.*

I ran to him, jumping into his arms and burying my head in his neck as he picked me up.

"I missed you so much," I whispered into his neck and breathed in his spiced scent. He let out a low chuckle.

"You have no idea," he replied, gently placing me back onto my feet next to him, his arm wrapping around my waist. The smell of embers filled the room, and Callum appeared next to us.

"Aye Lass, did you think you got rid of us or something?" he said, a smile across his face as he leaned in to hug me.

I turned back to the rest of the room. Niklas had gone rigid, and Olea had sat down in a chair, reading the newspaper that Niklas had disregarded. Niklas quickly pulled his eyes away, turning back to his coffee, murmuring something to Olea and she nodded in return.

It was Olea's soft voice that broke the awkward silence, "Did you have something to tell us? You burst in here like Goddess Hel was after you," she said. Her eyes meet Rhone's and shift away quickly.

"AND ALL THIS happened in Niklas's bedroom?" Rhone said, looking at me, his eyebrows shooting up. We all sat around Niklas's enormous mahogany table that was on the second floor of his apartment in his council room. Tesynia, Tiberius, Niklas, and two people I didn't recognize sat on one side. Olea, Rhone, and I on the other, with Callum sitting at the head of the table. The new companions at the table weren't actually new. I had seen them at the wedding, and they had stood next to Niklas when those Dreygurs crawled out of some star speckled Hel. Seeing my interest in them, Niklas stood to introduce them.

"Soren, this is Alexi, my second in command," he said, his head nodding to the deeply tanned Fae Male with dazzling teal eyes, his dark curls pulled back into a top knot. He was dressed in a black sweater that hugged his muscled arms. Alexi smiled at me, and then Niklas turned to the woman. "And this is Amara. She is my third. They hail from The Seas Court." The female nodded her head to me, her eyes telling me she was not yet convinced of me. She was similarly dressed in black, a tight V-neck long sleeve shirt, her ample breasts spilling out. *Gods she is so alluringly gorgeous,* with long curly black hair, tan skin, and those same glittering teal eyes. Her lips were full and painted red, which matched her teardrop ruby earrings and necklace. I found it hard to look away from her.

"They are part of my Hird, and my Hird go where I go," Niklas said matter-of-factly, breaking me from the trance-like stare.

The council room was an enormous area, with stark white walls and large windows, meant for serious conversations and little distraction. Fae orb lights hugged the high ceiling. A deep blue rug covered most of the rich wooden floors, and sculptures of the old Gods adorned the corners of the vast space, their stone faces staring into the room, almost as if they were judging us.

"I say all that, and all you can be concerned with is whose bedroom it happened in?" I said, turning my attention back to Rhone, shock lining my voice. I crossed my arms, turning myself away from him.

Rhone was seated next to me, his anger emanating off of him, his gaze shooting daggers across the table to Niklas. Niklas was unfazed, leaning back in his spacious leather high-backed chair, a smirk on his face.

"Is there something bothering you, Rhonan?" Niklas said, his eyes narrowing.

Rhone did not reply, but his hand that lazily laid on my

thigh slid itself up and he grabbed on to it, pulling my leg towards him, spreading my legs apart. My pulse quickened as his touch began to roam. I thanked the old Gods that this wasn't a glass tabletop as he ran his fingers up my bare thigh until he found the hem of my short silk nightgown. Slowly, he lifted it, taking his knuckles and rolling them over the thin fabric of my lacy underwear. His touch sent warning signals ringing through my mind, signals I couldn't place, but signals I definitely ignored anyways. The feel of his hands on me unbelievably unholy, and unbelievably *good*.

The rest of our team continued to talk, working out the details of getting us to Queen Isleen. Rhone continued in the conversation, but I couldn't. My mind was completely blank as Rhone put me on edge. I sat motionless, unable to rock against him, while simultaneously unable to shove him away. My anger flared, and I couldn't believe him, putting me in this position, when we were all supposed to be planning our trek through the Aunders. And here I was, unable to concentrate on anything because of him. And for what? Because Niklas had offered me his bed?

I was stuck between embarrassment, anger, and pleasure. I felt the deep red blush spread across my face and down my neck. I saw the sudden movement of Niklas's head, and I jerked my head towards him instinctively. His eyes locked onto mine, the ache in my chest as his eyes met mine going taught, and it was as if I could feel his rage. His nostrils flared and anger flashed in his eyes. I couldn't take my eyes off of him, and in that moment, I had never wanted anything to stop more than I wanted this to, a wave of guilt hitting me. Niklas stood, his grip on the side of the wooden table turning his knuckles white. Rhone then turned it up a notch, hooking a finger around my underwear and pulling it to the side. I heard his breath hitch ever so slightly as he felt how wet I was. *Treacherous body*, I thought, annoyed with myself. My hand flew down to his, and I tugged lightly at his wrist, his hand unmoving. He stopped for a second, sliding a rough finger across my clit one more time before he slid his finger down my crease, and then slid it inside me fully. It took all I had to keep still and not shutter in pleasure as he slid another finger in.

I kicked Rhone under the table, not wanting to garner any more attention from the others in the room. I was thankful the table was so big and the chairs so spaced out that no one had sat directly next to us. I gripped the side of my chair as Rhone's fingers picked up their unrelenting pace. I tilted my head to the ceiling, screwing my eyes shut, secretly seething with anger and pleasure, all at once.

A burst of ice and snow signaled Niklas's departure. He had left the room without dismissing himself first.

"I guess that means we can all take a 15 minute break," Callum said, with an astonished expression at Niklas's unexpected exit. He hadn't even finished his sentence before Rhone grabbed my hand and forced me to stand, shadowing us out of the room, and onto the roof of the building. The sun was up fully now, a clear blue sky stretched across the horizon.

I ripped my hand away from his. "What do you think you are doing? Finger fucking me in a room full of people?"

"Did you not hear him, Soren? Did you not hear yourself? He put you in *his* bed. He was trying to claim you. I needed to show him who had *claim* to you," he said, his voice booming, and I flinched.

"Oh, you're fucking joking, right, Rhone? You *put your claim to me* by pleasuring me under a table in front of our friends, during a conversation like that. Where is your reserve? *Your claim?!* You know, as hot as that sounds, and no matter how my body responded, that was *wrong of you,*" I yelled. I was angry, so angry I could feel my powers violently shifting inside me, recoiling from Rhone in anger as well. I continued, "I could've just told him myself. In fact, I have told him myself. What if he was just being nice, giving the girl who almost died the nicest bed in the house so she could recover in a strange room *alone,* in comfort." I emphasized alone with all the hurt and anger I could muster. Because that's what Rhone had done, left me alone.

"You think I wanted to leave you, Soren? It was killing me, being away from you. We had so much damage control to do. And all yesterday we searched for Vana. I couldn't get my mind off of you, Soren. Is that what you think, that I willingly left you here with *him?*" he said, his voice coming out in angry puffs, pacing back and forth.

I paused for a moment, searching his face. "Why didn't you tell me about him. About his curse." He stopped dead in his tracks, his head slowly turning to mine.

"What does his curse matter to you, Soren?" he said, and he stalked towards me. He stopped in front of me and reached for me, his strong hand resting on my hip, then pulled me toward him. I shoved away from him, but his touch did something to me and I paused, my anger easing and my arms fell to my side. I had ached for his touch, and now I had the nerve to turn it away? I thought of how good his fingers had felt, sliding inside of me.

"And are you telling me that you didn't enjoy that at all?

Because I think you're lying, I felt you clench around my fingers, I heard your breathing change. I know how badly you wanted to buck against my hand, wanted me deeper," he said, leaning down to me, his voice barely above a whisper. I breathed him in as he pressed his body against mine. His hand trailed up my side and found itself nestled in my hair at the nape of my neck. He balled his hand into a fist and yanked my head back slightly, tilting my head up to his. I couldn't even remember why I was mad at him, my need for him taking over. His lips crashed into mine, his kiss urgent and breathless. His arms went around me then, lifting me up. Then a mist-lined wind brushed my back and rested me on the ground, a soft blanket underneath me. He got down on his knees, his body hovering above mine and peeled his jacket off. I could see his bulging need pressing against his pants.

How could I ever be worried about what Niklas thinks of me, when this is right here in front of me. When this feels so right. Who even cares about his curse?

"We are going to... up here?" I said, looking up to the sky.

"So you don't like it there, with people around, and you don't like it here, with only the birds to see?" he said, a smirk tugging the corner of his mouth. He had already begun undoing his belt. *Yes, the birds, I remember something... about a bird's... wings.*

Gleaming blue scales flashed across my memory, and as soon as it appeared, it was shoved away.

I leaned up off the blanket, yanking my night gown above my head, the breeze sending chills across my body. Rhone had stripped himself naked, his hard muscles flexing as he moved. His cock was hard, the veins pulsing as he looked at me. He rocked himself back onto his heels, a low groan escaping his lips as he looked me up and down.

"I am going to fuck you like I have dreamed about the last three nights," he said, and before I could blink, he was on top of me. His lips met mine with burning need as he settled his body between my legs. He shoved his arm between us, resting his fingers against me, moaning against my mouth as he sunk his fingers inside me again, before pulling them out and circling my clit. I bucked against him, heat pounding through me. He grabbed onto my hip and thrust me back down.

"No, you'll cum with my cock inside of you." He commanded and took his cock in his hand, resting it against me for less than a second before shoving it deep inside. I let out a cry, his matching mine as he pumped himself into me all the way. He leaned himself fully over me then, his head dipping low and his mouth finding my throat. His soft lips ran themselves up my neck, his tongue leaving traces of heat in its wake, his teeth crazing that spot right below my ear that I loved, and suddenly he bit down. Hard enough he could've drawn blood, and he moaned against my skin, his thrusts becoming quicker. I moaned in reaction, bucking my hips up to meet his, needing him deeper. I reached for him, needing to feel his hard body against my fingertips, but his hand caught mine, and he threw it back, pinning it against the blanket.

"No, I want to make sure you feel this when we are done. I want every move to be labored because of how good I fucked you. You are *mine*, and everyone will know," he growled, pressing into me further. His eyes were hooded with desire, and something else lingered in them, something primal. Black storm clouds flashed in his eyes, lightning cracking in the distance.

I was his. He had called me his *and that's all I had ever wanted him to say.*

"Gods, it's as good as my dreams," he said in a hiss.

He let go of my wrist, straightening his body above me, the hard muscles of his chest gleaming with sweat. His hand found my throat, wrapping itself around it. Pleasure and the thrill of fear pinged itself through my mind, mingling together, its effect intoxicating. Those warning sirens sounded again, and I pushed them away, thrusting my hips up to meet his, his moan echoing through my mind as I rolled my hips. I could feel my release building, the pressure rising. His fingers dug into the soft skin of my neck, sending shivers across my body, and it was his eyes that were my undoing. They were raging and wild with pleasure, his gaze sending me spiraling into my climax. He took his free hand and pinned my hips down then, ramming himself into me harder, moaning out a cry of release as well.

He collapsed on top of me, his cock still twitching inside me.

"I could do that every minute of every day and never have enough of you," he said, his face buried in my neck.

He rolled off of me then, his chest heaving. I sat up, the sudden dispatch of his body from mine leaving me wanting and chilled.

"No, not yet," he grumbled, and pulled me on top of him, tucking me into his side as I draped an arm over him. I breathed him in, his clove and rain misted scent warming me from the inside out.

"I could lay like this forever," I said, my voice low.

"Maybe someday you can. But I know today is not our day for forever," he said, something in his voice turning sharp. "This might be the last *simple* moment we have together for a while."

My chest heaved, and I suddenly felt leaden at his words.

"Promise me something, Soren," he said, and I looked up at him. He was gazing at the sky, his chest finally rising and falling in even motions. His hair was disheveled, the hair around his face slick with sweat. But even unkempt, he was gorgeous.

"Anything," I said, my voice shaking.

He was quiet for a moment, and he closed his eyes. "That you'll remember this moment, and know this was me loving you the only way that I can."

I squeezed my eyes shut as the words fell from his mouth.

I had known all along, knew what these feelings were for him, and I had never let myself say them out loud.

Love.

I loved him.

And I loved him even if he couldn't love me back.

I didn't respond, but I clung on to him tighter. Thinking just maybe, the longer and harder I held on, that he would love me back the way I loved him.

TWENTY-FOUR

I shadowed onto the balcony, my anger making my vision go red. Flashes of the pleasure on her face ran back through my mind, unrelenting. I began pacing, my hands balling into fists. Frost covered the balcony as my power lashed out of me, uncontrolled in my raging state. Her face kept flashing across my mind again, but this time it was her secondary emotions that shone through, the ones I noticed a second too late as I shadowed out, the ones I was praying I had mistaken: fierce shame, raging anger.

"He only did that to get to you, to show you who had control of her, and I would even say to show her who holds the power in their dynamic as well, even if it is just sexual dominance. It is clear he feels some sort of threat from you," Jörmungandr said, rumbling to life. Even he seemed to bristle as he said the words, human emotions something he rarely dabbled in.

"Do you think Rhonan knows? That he can tell we have tied?" I asked Jörmungandr.

"There is no telling what that mysterious creature is capable of. I have always said he smells off. No one listens to me," he responded, his teeth snapping together in annoyance. I felt him slither up my torso and coil tightly around my shoulder, the weight of his head resting in the crook of my elbow.

He nestled down, getting comfortable before continuing, *"This soul tie of yours... it is something to keep to yourself. This can endanger you, and her. Especially if Rhonan knows. He is capable of great violence, as his history shows. I smell secrets on him, and his possession of this girl... It is not good. He will try and kill you for her, Sæmingr, and I would wager it is not love that leads him, which makes him just that much more dangerous."*

"*Do not forget what* I am capable of, *Jörmungandr,*" I said, my anger snapping back at him.

"No one has forgotten what you are capable of. Go for a flight. This girl, she makes you not be able to think straight. Even when I am not present, I can feel your inner turmoil," was all Jörmungandr said before he flung his wings out, the weight of them against my back causing me to shift my stance, stand straighter.

It was Rhone's face who flashed through my mind this time, his demeanor all business as he sat there, making decisions, casually discussing the layout of the Aunders. His hand seemingly innocently lay in her lap, but the fraction of movement, and the sparks of pleasure I had felt down our thread and I instantly knew better. My anger boiled as I replayed her hand flying down to his, the anger that had emanated off of her. I knew what that meant now, as I let myself think and not just react. Her shame, anger, and guilt had been real.

Undiluted rage consumed me. I could end him in two seconds, ripping his hands from his body and feeding them to him.

I felt Jörmungandr sigh, the puff of his breath against my skin. "*Sæmingr, you know the implications of that. Killing a Royal Fae with that much ease? Questions will be asked. Not to mention what happened last time.*"

Memories of the first hundred years with him bound to me flashed through my mind. My life had spiraled out of control. The loss of my family had been so immense, I had almost drowned in it. I had torn through kingdoms and villages, ripping creatures apart in my hunt for The Dark One. At first, Jörmungandr had relished in it; his demon blood pulsed with the love of chaos and slaughter as mine had. I had ripped through the Fae with deftness, choking out their kingdoms with a brush of my winter. The world began to whisper, saying a new demon god had arisen, and it came bringing an unrelenting winter and made their rivers flow with blood. To my horror now, it had all been true.

I thought that part of me had died when I had found Freyr alive, my search for The Dark One leading to my brother, halting my onslaught. I thought I had moved on from that time in my life. Until now. That same rage had surfaced, the images from the conference room turning red in my vision.

"*Maybe it's time for questions to be asked,*" I replied.

"*Den stjärnan, she brings out emotions in you I have not seen in some time. Do not let them lead you,*" Jörmungandr said, his wings twitching against my back. For as brooding and downright demonic he could be, Jörmungandr had turned into a mentor for me, as insane as that sounds. And in a way, I think his advice came out of love.

I thought of what he said. Yes, these were emotions I

thought myself no longer capable of. Emotions I no longer acknowledged in myself. I had made myself better, for Freyr. Made myself become a blank slate. Yet here I was, feeling as human as I ever had. But I was not human, I was *other*. And being other meant I needed to go through this world alone, if only to keep others safe. Like I wish I could've done for my mother, for my family, for the Elven. I knew I had to begin to ignore this soul tie. I needed a clear mind going into this.

I thrusted myself upward, the wings taking on the frosted breeze I had brought my way, and I soared upwards. Thoughts of ripping out Rhone's heart raced through my mind.

The only thing I would allow myself to do, would be to end him if she ever gave me permission. One word from Soren and I would not hesitate. One glimpse of another even slightly unwanted touch, and his head would be fed to Jörmungandr. It had been some time since he had such a treat.

Soren's moans chased me as I hurtled myself through the clouds.

TWENTY-FIVE

"I think that was more like a lunch break, but hey, we all look rather refreshed," Callum said as he eyed us knowingly. Rhone and I were the last ones to walk back in. I started to follow Rhone back to our seats, with him tugging me along. My chest sank as Niklas's eyes did not meet mine; they stayed focused on Callum at the head of the table. I knew he knew; I knew that's what his outburst was about. I could see it in the coldness of his stare, his rigid posture he held as he faced away from me. I was truly puzzled by this closeness I felt to him, it didn't make sense, had no reason for existing, yet it did. And I knew I wasn't going to be able to shake this deep-seated guilt I felt about it. I would've given maybe anything for him to look at me, to show me he didn't hate me now.

But feelings and emotions had no place where we were going, I reminded myself. And something clicked then, my mother's words to me ringing crystal clear. Clearer than it had been all day.

You are the heir to The Midnight Throne, Soren. The Heir of

Time. The Daughter of Two Worlds. Do not forget that and do not ever bow to anyone.

I couldn't let all this distract me again, not when the balance of the worlds hung on my shoulders. No amount of men was worth the worlds. And I couldn't let their feelings get in my way; I couldn't let *my feelings* get in the way. Without even thinking about my next move, I decidedly turned around, letting go of Rhone's hand, and walked to the head of the table, standing next to Callum. I didn't look at either Niklas or Rhone, especially not Rhone. I could practically feel his astonishment emanating off him as I left his side. I looked squarely at Callum, his green eyes shining with pride, a genuine grin spreading across his striking face.

He leaned over to me then, his voice only for me to hear, "I swear to gods if I had to watch you sit yourself at the table one more time and act like you are our equal, I was going to freak *the fuck* out."

It was my turn to beam with a smile. My heart lightened just a fraction at how proud he sounded. A weight lifted off me, and I sucked in a long deep breath. Callum grabbed my hand, giving it a squeeze before taking a seat on the other side of me, letting me have the floor.

All eyes were on me, a look of shock and pride in most, but Rhone's were indifferent, like he was unsure what to think. My heart swelled, looking around the table of misfits, of allies who might have not come together if it wasn't for me. I thought of the empty chairs, but they were chairs I knew would fill, eventually, with my parents, Aaren, and Vana. I heard my mother's voice in my head, *It's about time.* The words repeated themselves in her voice as I stood there. I wasn't sure what turn of events led me to this final decision. The decision I needed to make the entire time, to be the leader of my own prophecy, to be the leader of my fate and the leader the people sitting around this table needed me to be.

"The events that took place in The Gap earlier, they change everything about what needs to be done here. This isn't just a search for Vana, or a journey for me, it never has been. This is about stopping a worlds ending war, one that has been in the making for hundreds of years. This is about stopping Sister Future in her path of destruction, and her creation. She has built an army that could and will take over. She wants to purge anything she sees unfit, and replace them with her Dreygurs. But that is not all, she wants to see all worlds decimated, so she can build them back up. She is like Ymir; she's grown too big and evil in her thousands of years of life and we need to be the Gods who take her down. Our problems have grown threefold, but as I look across this table, I see a room full of loyal and worthy allies. Allies who I could not do this without." I paused for a moment, looking each of them in the eye, quickly looking from one to the next.

I sucked in another deep breath, readying myself to reveal even more. "I believe the Seer Courts do not exist. I believe it is false history placed into our minds by Synnove's Dreygur King. I believe that it's not a realm we are looking for, but a world. And not just any world, but the Ginnunga-gap. You see, when I shift into the spaces in between to get to The Gap, where I can access and weave threads, it's like I'm leaving this world and going into another. I felt the shift, as I fell from The Gap and into this world. If this theory is correct, then we are in even more imminent danger than we originally thought. The Ginnungagap is where all the worlds were created, where magic runs rampant. It is where The Well of Urd exists, and the tree of life that holds all the worlds together in balance. I believe she wants to kill the tree and infiltrate all nine worlds, with her Dreygurs in tow to take over as she goes. Placing Dreygur Kings in every decimated kingdom."

I could hear uneasy shifting in seats. Faces who were originally gleaming with hope and pride for me, had gone slacken, this grave news weighing on them.

"The plan has changed, and I need you all to trust me. I say that because I'm going to ask you to go on this mission blindly with me. I cannot give away the full plan to *anyone*." I paused for a brief moment, and I knew that was how this had to go. Vana's face flashed in front of my eyes, the last time I had seen her, laughing and happy at the family dinner with my parents and Rhone. I knew that was how she was captured, or worse, dead. All because she knew our plan. I couldn't risk that again; I wouldn't risk any of them.

"Asta told me that the King of the Dreygurs can take memories. And if he gets a hold of any of us, he can take this one too. It is something I am not willing to risk the fate of the worlds for. If you have any issue with this, I ask you to please get up from this table and leave us to do what needs to be done. Go back to your lives, and hopefully you can live unbothered and unknowing like the rest of the worlds. There is no time to waste. No more lying in wait, action must begin *now*. We need to be on our mission to find Vana before nightfall, no exceptions." I paused and crossed my arms, giving anyone the moment they needed to leave, staring down at the table.

I heard a chair scoot back then, and my heart began thundering. I didn't want to know who was leaving, who didn't trust me. My newfound confidence faltered for a second, but I mentally shook it off. I was going to have to be stronger than that. *Bow to no one.*

It was the slow clap that made curiosity get the best of me, and my eyes shot up, more chairs scooting back and my friends and allies beginning to stand.

"You have become the queen I have always hoped you would be," Rhone said, his stormy eyes meeting mine, a look of surprise and awe twisting his face. His eyes though, were unreadable, storms raging.

It was Callum's embrace that broke me from my stare. "Yes, you are so queenly, my dear little friend. *Finally.* You have commanded the hearts of all of us, and I think I speak for the table when I say that I will fight by your side honorably and unwavering," he said as he backed out of the hug and fell into a dramatic bow, dipping low. His head turned up to me as he held his bow and winked.

He straightened again, fussing about his shirt, smoothing the wrinkles before he went on, "Okay, but seriously, why don't you go get yourself ready to leave. We will get everything arranged." I took that as my getaway free card, turning to neither Rhone nor Niklas as I walked out of the room.

I FOUND myself leaning against the balcony railing, staring up at the sky. After a brief call to my father, I learned that their team had found traces of Vana's scent in the northern trek of the Ostorous Mountains, no more than a day old. I had changed into my fighting leathers and pulled my hair back into a high ponytail. The northern reaches of the mountain range were treacherous, at best, and I needed to be dressed appropriately. My stomach twisted in excitement and angst. Maybe tonight would be the night we could bring Vana home.

But where was home anymore? I could not return to Norware, even if I wanted to, but I had no home outside of it.

Great, what kind of queen doesn't have a realm or a home?

I sighed in frustration. *A possibly useless queen, I guess.*

I felt the winds change suddenly, my whole body tensing, and I braced myself for Rhone's shadowing. I wasn't sure how he was going to feel about my sudden call to be a leader; as the word queen was thrown around he had seemed to go a bit stiff. His words had said one thing, but his sudden shadowing out after had been jarring. A complete contrast to his kind words and claps.

A snow-dusted amber breeze swept across the balcony, and my entire body heaved a sigh of release. I turned around, Niklas's eyes on me. He was also dressed in his fighting leathers. They hugged his body, moving as fluidly as he did, the breastplate and shoulders adorned with deep blue and silver scales. *Those scales...* They flashed across my mind again, a snippet of a memory, or maybe a dream, but as soon as they appeared, they vanished.

"Expecting someone else?" he said as he sauntered in my direction, placing his forearms on the railing next to me to look up into the sky as well.

I laughed then. "I feel like 'expect the unexpected' is my new life motto, honestly."

His laugh in return felt like a reward. He turned his head to me as he said, "You looked good up there, like you belonged. Asta must have done what she came to these worlds to do."

His words caught me off guard, and my heart skipped a beat, not only from his compliment, but his mention of Asta. Tears began to well up in my eyes. I looked away from him quickly, returning my gaze to the sky, which was turning to dusk. My heart thundered with emotion.

"Yes, I guess she did. I am just sorry it took all of her," I said, my voice shaking with sorrow and guilt. I wondered about Jahan, how he felt now that he would have to roam the afterlife alone.

He shifted, his shoulder brushing mine. "I don't think she would have changed anything. But I am sorry she is gone. It's clear she meant something to you, even if you didn't get much time with her," he said, his voice gentle. I couldn't look at him, not when I knew the tears would flow. I sucked in a shaking breath. Not when I didn't know if I could take how vulnerable and real I felt around him.

I thought about his words long after he had shadowed away, leaving me on the quiet balcony.

THE OSTOROUS MOUNTAINS looked almost like any other forest in the daytime, the night creatures and wild Fae mostly hidden. Rhone had shadowed us all into a lush valley, as he was the only one with the coordinates. We hadn't spoken much since he had fucked the life out of me on the roof. His roughness could still be felt on my skin and between my thighs. He had not been lying when he said he wanted my movements to be labored, and he delivered on that promise. The valley was beautiful, vibrant shamrock-colored grass blowing in the wind, cradled between twisting mountains with pink snow-covered caps. An air of familiar magic was caught on the wind, thrumming over my skin and clinging to it slightly before it slid away.

I walked along next to Callum and Tiberius. Rhone led the team, while Amara, Alexi, and Niklas flanked the back. The twins had returned to the Highlands, needing to repack their travel bags with ingredients and fast-acting potions, wanting to prepare for anything. The hike had just started to get grueling as the sun began to set, the golden rays melting into the indigo sky.

"Why can't we just shadow in where we want to be again?" I said, complaining and just a bit out of breath. The ache in my legs reminded me of just how inactive I had been the past two days, the twinge of pain in my side reminding me *why* I had been so inactive.

It was surprisingly Tiberius who answered, "The Ostorous forests are enchanted, unlike many other places we shadow these days. The magic that festers in these mountains can be tricky and dangerous. Wild magic has a way of leading you astray, or worse, sending you off to one of the other realms or even worlds if it pleases. So it is better to shadow minimally and only when absolutely needed," he said matter-of-factly.

It makes sense, I guess, I thought as I finally was able to breathe normally again, the pain in my side beginning to ease.

As the sun continued to set, and the sky above bled into a deep midnight blue, the enchanted forest began to come alive like I had seen it once before. By the time we had reached the site that my parents and their team had set up for the night, the moons hung bright in the sky.

"Thank the gods we are here. If I had to hike up one more mile, I think I might have died of exhaustion and no wine past 7 p.m," Callum said, Tiberius and I laughing in return.

As we approached the clearing, Fae orbs hung in the air amongst the sprawling fabric tents that were situated in a circle. A large fire stretched its flames into the air, embers floating into the dark sparkling sky. A few creatures were milling about in between the tents, all dressed in similar gear to us. I searched for my parents, my eyes darting back and forth, my pace picking up in excitement.

But as we got closer, I could tell something was wrong... something was off. The creatures all looked too similar. All males, same height, same build, their clothing the same, their bodies shifting in and out of focus. My vision blurred slightly as rainbow-colored light caught my eye from the corner, and a shimmering silver thread floated past my vision.

My heart stuttered to an immediate halt, rendering me suddenly motionless. I took no further steps forward. I held out my arms, both males knocking into me, their chattering dropping instantly.

I felt the tug in my chest tighten, and I turned around instinctively, my eyes finding Niklas's. Amara, Alexi, and

Niklas had all stopped dead in their tracks. Niklas's icy eyes were glowing with concern, his brow furrowed. After a long second his eyes left mine and began scanning the valley. I followed his eyes to the horizon, and that's when every atom in my body began to panic. *Fog.*

No. No. No.

Callum's voice was barely above a whisper, "What is it, Lass?"

I swallowed hard, my throat dry, my power scorching my fingertips, rushing to save me as it felt my panic rising.

"It's a trap. We have walked into a trap," I said, my voice unwavering.

We are in deep shit.

CHAPTER

TWENTY-SIX

M y eyes darted around the valley for Rhone. I had lost sight of him; the last time I had seen him he was stalking towards the men in view. The men who were now gone. I could feel my heart thundering in my chest, my power raging inside me.

Those men had taken him.

I didn't think, I just acted, breaking into a sprint toward the tents, towards where I had last seen Rhone.

It was the crack of lightning slamming into the ground next to me that stopped me, my heels skidding to a halt as I dug them into the ground, trying to dodge the bolt. Heat singed my skin as I barely avoided colliding with it. A lyrical laugh fluttered across the valley on the wind.

The tents and valley vanished, The Gap's mist and fog sweeping in and swallowing it all. A deafening crack rang out again, and the mist began swirling, a depthless chasm opening up, and shadows spilled out, seeping into the world like a sickness. Leeching onto anything that was near, creeping into the far corners of The Gap, laying in wait. From the shadows of the portal, Synnove emerged, her silver hair shining, her eyes gleaming with malice. She looked as breathtaking as I remembered her looking the first time, her sharp features seeming to cut through the fog as she stepped forward. Even her silver crown seemed sharper, like it was the one she chose to wear to battle. Her dress was stark white, but she wore a gleaming silver breastplate this time, her arms plated in silver as well.

A devilish smile spread across her face as she looked around The Gap. She lifted her hands, and with a flick of her wrist, The Gap folded, the ground shifting us and closing the distance between her, and us. Niklas and the others raced towards me, and I put my hands up, telling them to stay. This was my fight. I would not let them put themselves on the front line. This was between myself and Synnove. I was who she really wanted. I threw my hands up, my body sinking into a fighting stance that had become second nature.

They all listened, each about a foot behind me. All except Niklas, his arm brushing mine as he stepped closer to me, his body easing comfortably into a defensive position.

Synnove turned her head slightly towards the portal, the sinister hum from it growing louder by the second.

"Come forward," was all she said, her voice cold, the command stern.

The portal widened, turning itself into an arched doorway, with massive black ornate stone pillars. The Gap's silver mist was being sucked into its gravitational force field.

A massive figure stepped from the portal; shadows from

the chasm clung to him. He was tall and hooded, wearing black armor with intricate details swirling across it. Every inch of his body was covered in leather and black-plated armor. He came cloaked in darkness, his face completely shrouded in shadows. Wickedness seeped from him, a true evil incarnate, the mist from The Gap shrinking away from him as he stalked forward, his heavy booted footfalls echoing. He settled himself next to Synnove, his stance stiff and his back straight, clasping his hands in front of him.

I willed my power forward, letting it hover in my palms, waiting for my go ahead. The sound of Niklas's sword unsheathing next to me rang through The Gap, a subzero chill sweeping in as his powers flooded the area.

Synnove's laugh was shrill, her eyebrows shooting up. "Let's get this over with," was all Synnove said as her power lashed out of her in a blinding ray of light. Her power burst up from the ground in all different directions, blinding vines of magic dancing up out of the fog. I raised my magic to meet hers, my silver stardust wrapping itself around hers, choking it out, but some of her tendrils had already met their mark. I heard shouts behind me, bodies hitting the ground with grunts, and then freezing in time. All but Niklas's. He stood next to me, shifting his body with unease. Winter had come to The Gap, the ground pulsed with his gleaming blue ice, and I knew he was waiting, holding back until the very second he needed it.

I felt down into my power, letting more through, the force of it pushing my body forward slightly.

"This is between You and I, *Aunt* Synnove. Leave them out of it," I said, willing my voice to be calm, smooth, to not let the fear for them that racked my body bleed through. I turned my head a fraction; her power was wrapped around them and had brought them to their knees. Her blinding vines turned themselves into rope, binding their feet together, their hands behind their back, and a swath of magic around their mouths. I knew her power burned into them where it touched their bare skin, welts blistering up by the second.

"Oh, dear girl. If only it were that simple. But I do need you, unfortunately," she said, clicking her tongue, annoyance spreading across her face. "I do enjoy a party though, but I see we are missing a couple." Her eyes darted across all of us in a playfully sinister manner.

She crossed her arms, and the shadows rushed forward, swirling into a human form at my feet. A form that was crouched into a squat, head against its knees and hands behind its back, much like the others behind me. The darkness slipped away from it, seeping back into the corners of The Gap, revealing a woman, her usually mocha-colored skin blanched, her hair matted with blood. Her clothing was tattered, and gashes marred her body.

I sucked in a sharp breath.

Vana.

I threw myself forward and grabbed her by the arm, yanking her up. Her eyes met mine briefly. They were hollow, the joy that usually shone through absent, her face littered with cuts and bruises. I couldn't look at her any longer, lest I forget what was at stake here. I shoved her behind me, throwing a shield around her.

My anger ripped through me, my stardust lashing against its constraints, itching to get out, itching to end whoever was responsible. Except I already knew who was: Synnove and her Dark One. *Willem.*

I shot daggers at him, searching the shadows of his hooded face for a glimpse of his eyes.

I threw my palm up and my power came pouring out. A wave of stardust skidded across Niklas's ice. A wave I sent to crash into both of them, to swallow them whole, to flood their lungs, choking the life out of them slowly.

Soundlessly, The Dark One stepped forward and in front of Synnove, throwing up an arm. A glittering black shield formed. My wave crashed against it. I pushed harder, the shield cracking, fissures forming across it. I reached down into my magic, its heated rage pulsing against my skin.

I heard Niklas, his voice sounding far away, fighting against the loud hum of the void, against the roar of my magic.

"You will not survive this if you keep going." It was a plea, a heart aching plea that came tumbling from his mouth. That ache in my chest swelled, my nerve wavering. He was right. I had to stay alive; Vana had to stay alive. We all had to make it out of here for the nine worlds to keep turning, to keep existing.

My arms fell to my side, aching and burning, my chest heaving at the toll it had taken. Even though the power had been given purpose, it was still so much. Too much pouring out of me at once. My confidence wavered as I thought about how much I still needed to do, to know, to train. I shifted my eyes to floor, away from The Dark One, away from Synnove.

"There she is, that timid girl. So much like her mother," Synnove said.

"Where is Rhone? What have you done with him?" Instantly a vision flooded my mind. It was Rhone, his dark hair matted against his face, blood spilling from his mouth. Threads of black magic held him down, glittering black galaxies swirling in the distance. Shadowy Dreygurs leaned over his body, tying him to a metal table. His bare chest heaved, slick with sweat and blood.

Rage threatened to blind me as the vision dissipated. "What makes a person who they really are, *niece*. Is it their soul? Their morality? Their connection to their physical body?" she said, her voice coming out in a hiss. Tears threatened to come, but I shoved them back.

"Oh.... Maybe it *is* love," she said, a mocking frown on her face. "Well that just makes this all even more delectable." She showed me him again, the King Dreygur shoving its hand into his chest. Rhone's body convulsed, and the shadowy hand emerged, dripping in blood, a long silver life thread being tugged from him.

I let out a scream, my composure finally cracking.

Black glittering vines of magic burst from the ground around me. I had hesitated; I had let myself get distracted. *Hesitation equals death.* The black vines leeched onto me, wrapping themselves around me, holding me in place. I felt Niklas shift next to me, his ice chasing the darkness, he wrapped his winter around it, momentarily halting it, until Synnove's clashed into him, sinking him into the ground in one swoop, rendering him as motionless as the others.

No. No. No.

My chest lurched, my panic rising as I watched Niklas

struggle, his beautiful face twisting in pain as her power burned itself into his skin. I thought of how the shadows had leached onto Commander Arrington, shoving themselves down his throat. I reached towards that tug in my chest, begging my anxiety to ease. I needed a clear head.

I will save you. I will save you. I will not lose you, I thought to him, wishing and praying he could hear me. That ancient song inside me called out to him, aching to free him, aching to ease his pain.

I struggled against the darkness that continued to envelop me. It had wrapped itself around my wrists, pinning my hands behind my back. Thick shadows ran themselves up my thigh, traveling towards my breasts, cupping them gently before snaking around my neck, constricting it lightly. Fear flooded me. I turned to Niklas, his eyes only on me. They were gleaming a hot white; rage lined his features as he thrashed against Synnove's power.

She couldn't kill him, but who knew what else she was capable of doing to him, what other loophole she had found.

She can't kill him, I repeated this mantra to myself.

Heavy footsteps echoed all around us, and I tore my gaze from Niklas. The Dark One was instantly in front of me, his wickedness seeping off of him in waves. He brought a gloved hand to my face, catching my chin between his pointer finger and his thumb. I jerked my face away from him, and he yanked it back to face him, his shadows holding the back of my head in place. With his other hand, he pulled back his hood, brown hair falling forward, Willem's face appearing, but it wasn't the face I remembered in my head. His skin was ashen, black veins scattered across his face in webs, his eyes glazed over and empty staring back at me. Oh gods, this was his dead form, his body as it was now. Bile threatened to come up my throat, and I shoved it back down. Then suddenly, his unseeing eyes blinked at me, glowing silver, wholly swallowed by the luminescence.

In a flicker of smoke, his face transformed, his true Dreygur form replacing Willem's. His face was different from the others. While the others were features-less, his held shape, thick brows across a high forehead, with sharp cheekbones and firm full lips. His skin was knitted together with shimmering black threads that glinted in the rays of light.

His lips were pursed in a straight line, his black brows creasing in frustration.

"Say that again, Soren. I don't think anyone else could hear you... Did you say, *I will save you. I will save you. I will not lose you.*" His tongue clicked against his teeth, and his eyes casted down, roaming my body. I felt his shadows pressing up my body again, forming into hands, caressing my breasts again.

"Surely, you were talking about someone else and not that winter *fuck* next to you," he said, his voice shifting from Willem's to something completely *other*, doubling up on itself in an unearthly echo. Jealousy lined his words, and he cocked his head to the side. His nostrils flared, and he leaned down to me, his nose brushing my neck. I struggled against him, and a shadow shoved itself between my thighs, a phantom hand cupping my core. I heard him groan, warning bells sounding inside my head.

A groan I had heard time and time again. A groan I had ached to hear.

A mist-lined breeze swept itself up my body.

My eyes went wide as Rhone's face rippled into view, his storm cloud irises taking form.

"Even in my true form I arouse you, and it is still just as sweet. *My little terror*," he said, and it was wholly Rhone's voice who spoke, the words falling from his mouth in a purr.

CHAPTER

TWENTY-SEVEN

I shoved against his touch, aching to get away, every bit of my composure lost. Deception sliced through me, my heart feeling like it was breaking into a thousand pieces. I tried to speak, but his shadows wrapped themselves around my neck tighter.

"Oh, don't look so forlorn, Sor. Some of it was real. In fact, *most* of it was real. You see, when I take a life thread, the creature is still there. Still alive and well, still has feelings, still cohabitating. But if at any time they do as I see unfit, I take over. Willem though, he was stronger than Rhone. Rhone is malleable. He's also just inherently more menacing, especially so when I slaughtered his dear Ito tribe. I believe that was when he finally realized who was in control here.

He continued, "That vision of Rhone's life thread being plucked from him, it *was real,* many moons ago. But Willem... his life thread was stubborn. His want to do good was too strong, too hard to snuff out. We will not make a mistake like him again. But his Miragen powers were too delectable to pass up. I had not seen one in so long," he said, his voice taking on an amused tone. I looked up at him, searching his face for traces of the Rhone that I knew. He wasn't there, and never really had been.

He sighed. "Those eyes, Soren, don't look at me with those eyes. Like I've wounded you irrevocably. Ya know, the whole tracking part wasn't even me. That fallen goddess in the rubble she calls a temple, Synnove bribed her too easily really. Letting her fox friend become human again. And as for Willem and Rhone, it's not their fault, what they feel. He's here, you know, beating on the wall that has been built up in our head. But unfortunately, your mother was right. There is no Rhone, without me. We are one. I'm insidious, you see. My power weaves itself into the very fibers of the life thread, and trying to remove me... well, it just shreds the life thread. We've tried, for various unremarkable reasons." He said nonchalantly, his shoulders rising in a shrug.

He slid his thumb up my chin, brushing it against my lips softly, before he pried my lips apart and shoved his gloved thumb into my mouth. The pungent earthy taste of the leather coated my tongue.

"Wrap your pretty little mouth around it, darling," he said, his voice low. I did as he said, all while clamping my teeth down on his thumb, ripping through the leather the best I could. He let out a hiss, but his eyes constricted with pleasure, a deep moan slipping out from the back of his throat.

"Fuck Soren, I didn't even have to ask you to do that. If you keep it up, I'll have to fuck you right here," he said, his mouth curving into a dark smirk, his storm cloud eyes flashing.

"Mmmm, yes. Your memory of my cock buried deep inside your pussy earlier as you clenched around it. Truly exquisite," he paused for a second, looking up into The Gap's endless sky. "But this one, of you losing your virginity to Willem, your innocent doe eyes widening as *I* entered you," he bit his lip. Next to me, Niklas shoved against Synnove's power again, and it flared, shoving him back down harder. Niklas's muscles in his neck strained as he used all his force to buck himself forward.

Rhone let out a laugh. "So this is still going on, is it?" He looked at Niklas to me, and then back again. "Should I give you a taste of her, so you can at least know how sweet she tastes when she cums before I pop that head right off your shoulders?" he said to Niklas.

He ripped his thumb from my mouth, my head jerking with the movement.

He sauntered over to Niklas, and crouched down in front of him, his leathers softly creaking at his swift movement.

He gazed at him for a long moment, before standing again and walking back to me. "Do you think you would have fucked him like you fucked Willem, or how you fuck Rhone?" He cocked his head as he spoke, clasping his hands behind his back, teetering back on his heels a little.

He took a step closer to me, again, his shadows rubbing against me, and I shoved back at them, the motion useless but I couldn't help it. His face was inches from mine, his breath brushing my cheek. "Do you think he would make you cum as hard as I do?"

It was Synnove's voice I heard next. "Enough theatrics," she snapped, her voice laced with agitation and boredom, rolling her eyes.

At her words, the shadows that had buried themselves in the corners of The Gap shifted. Rhone threw his hand out, his palm stretching wide, black stardust collecting in it. Piece by piece it began to form an onyx blade. Glittering dark threads stitched together, melting into a twin of the blade much like the one I had left in Niklas's room. He looked down at me again, a smirk spreading across his face.

Taking his other hand, he held it in front of my mouth. "Soren, darling, won't you help me with this?" he said, and he shoved a fingertip back in my mouth.

"Bite," he demanded, his voice hard. I did as he said, his shadows yanking my head back as we repeated the same motion with all his fingers until his last one, where he pulled his hand from his leather glove.

"You obey so well," was all he said before he held his palm out, spread it wide, and pushed the blade into it. Inky blood spilled forward as he sliced through his flesh, the drips hitting the ground with an echo. He sheathed the dagger to his thigh and closed the gap between us, his hand pressing into my lower back and pushing my body against his. My body reacted to his touch as it always had, and I cursed to myself, his rain and clove dusted scent shoving itself up my nose. The shadows ran themselves up the back of my neck, burying themselves in my hair and yanking my head back forcefully, my scalp screaming as hair was ripped from my head. My mouth was forced open at the angle, and I struggled against him.

Panic rose as he shifted his arm, the blood still flowing from his palm. My power surged, burning my fingertips, lighting me up from the inside out. I could see the glow emanating from me bouncing off his armor.

Synnove sucked in a sharp breath, and my eyes darted to her. Her eyes went wide as she stumbled backwards, they flickered from my eyes to forehead. She whispered something to the shadows that hovered around her, and then she spoke to Rhone in a language I had never heard before. He curtly nodded his head, and sighed angrily. And then she disappeared into the depthless portal, galaxies swallowing her, the portal slamming itself shut, leaving The Gap soundless again, my ears ringing with the sudden shift of change.

Rhone's eyebrows shot up. "You are just always full of surprises. The *Queen* of Midnight. The hidden crown really is a bit much, though. I thought surely your mother wouldn't have done anything so stupid, surely you were mistaken when you stood up there, acting like you belonged, acting like you could *lead*," he said, his eyes lingering on my forehead, his head shaking in disbelief.

"I planned on turning you, planned on making you *my* queen. That's where you belong, next to me." He paused for a second. "But maybe I want you to drink from me anyways, even if it is useless. Just to feel your lips on me one more time, to be inside you *one more time*." He shoved his palm against my mouth, thick blood spilling down my throat. I choked on it, salt and iron coating my mouth. He quickly tore his hand away, and his soft mouth crushed itself against mine, his tongue prying my lips apart.

A sob ripped from my throat, hot tears rolling down my cheeks. His head backed away, something like regret flashing across his features, his blood smeared across his mouth from the kiss. I heard his blade unsheathe again, his arm cocking back, his shadows caressing me one last time. A phantom hand ran itself across my cheek, wiping away the tears.

"Shhhh, shhh, shhh. It will be over soon. Valhǫll awaits you." His blade slashed through the air, glinting in the fractured shards of rainbow light.

The world seemed to go blurry, time slowing, my eyes rolling back and my limbs going slack as his blade plunged itself into my chest, slicing through my breastbone with too much ease. The blades ancient magic reverberated off my bones. Pain seared through me and shock seized my body. My eyes fell to my chest, the dagger planted firmly in the middle, jutting out of me. I flicked my eyes back up to meet his, the world tipping. Anguish flashed in them for a brief second before his cold, bored stare returned.

He clutched me tighter then, pulling me closer against him, resting his cheek against mine, his hot breath embracing me. "If I was capable of love, it would have been you. It will always be you," he said, but his words felt far away, like I floated somewhere beneath the surface.

My breathing became labored, and I started choking, spitting up my own blood. I felt him twist the blade one last time; I heard my own gargled screams of pain. His shadows fell away from me, and I felt my body crumple to the ground, skull colliding with the rocky surface of The Gap.

Rhone's towering form standing over me, the onyx blade in his hand thrumming with magic, dripping with my blood was the last thing I saw before my eyes fluttered shut for the last time.

I thought of Niklas, bound next to me.

I thought of my friends, frozen in time behind me.

I thought of how I failed them, failed everyone, failed all the worlds as I took my last breath.

A deafening roar filled my ears as I felt my stardust seep into The Gap where it belonged, giving itself back to the worlds.

Rainbow-colored light flooded my vision behind my eyelids. Eyelids that would not open. Iron jaws clamped themselves harder around my heart, that golden thread pulling taut, before releasing me.

Pain exploded inside of me as the knot snapped, the thread that had anchored me to this world going slack.

I felt my heart jerk to a stop.

A coldness only meant for death seeped into me.

And then, there was nothing.

Made in the USA
Columbia, SC
27 October 2024

44803519R00205